Love in the
Time of Corona

Love in the Time of Corona

ELENA GRAF

PURPLE HAND PRESS

Purple Hand Press
www.purplehandpress.com
© 2020 by Elena Graf

Trade Paperback Edition
ISBN-13 978-1-7334492-6-7
Kindle Edition
ISBN-13 978-1-7334492-7-4
ePub Edition
ISBN-13 978-1-7334492-8-1

Editor: Laure Dherbécourt
Cover design: Castle Hill Media, LLC
Cover photo: ©georgeeb22 - Can Stock Photo Inc.

03.08.2025

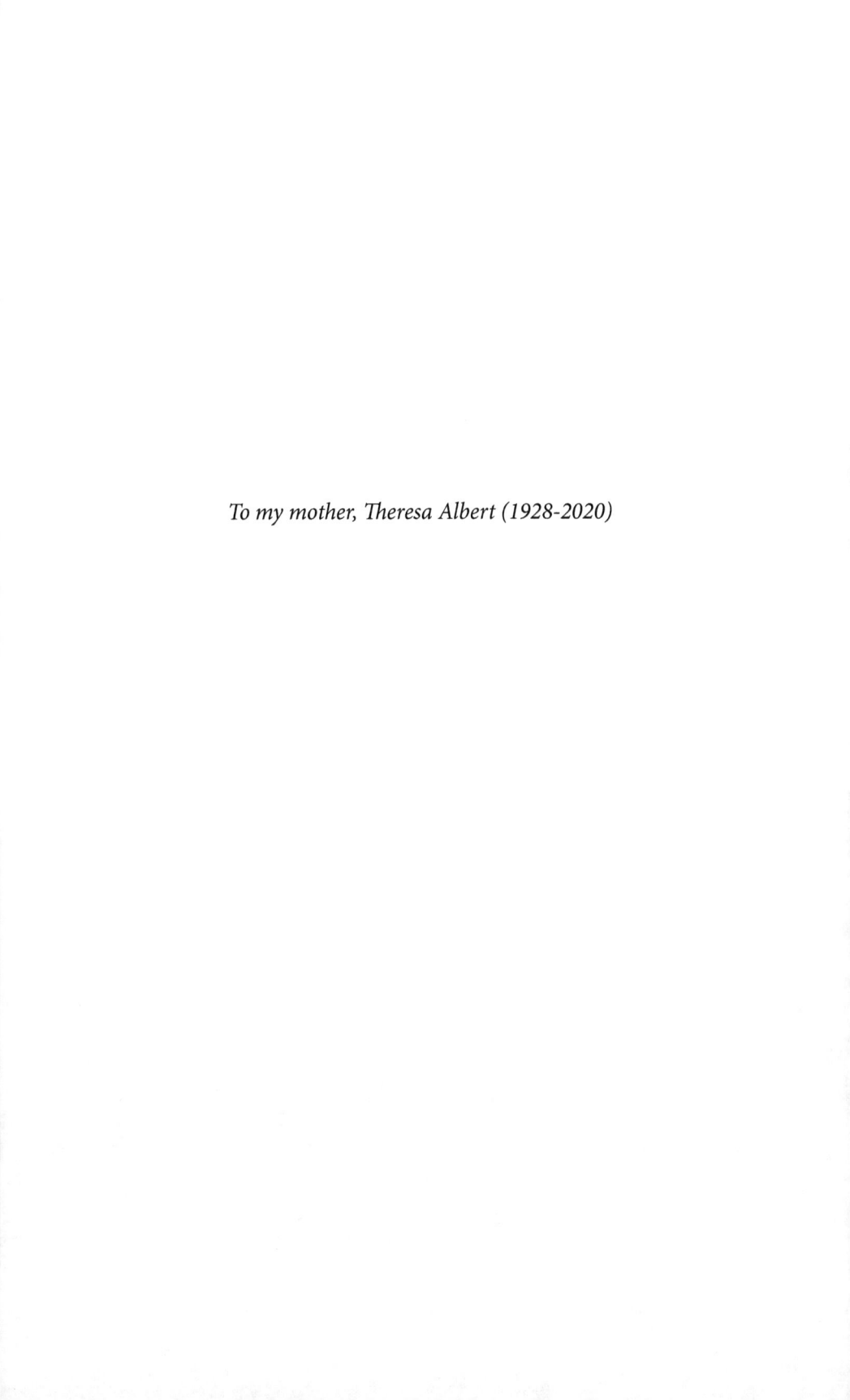

To my mother, Theresa Albert (1928-2020)

1

Liz Stolz felt a gentle hand on the back of her neck and looked up to see a steaming cup of coffee.

"Good morning," said Maggie, bending to offer a kiss. "I saw you left a full cup of coffee in the coffee maker. It was ice cold, so I made you a fresh cup." Maggie glanced at the screen of Liz's iPad and frowned. "Looking at the stock market again? You're just making yourself crazy."

"We've had two huge drops because of that virus in China. Now the futures are down over seven hundred points!"

Maggie gave Liz's shoulder a sympathetic pat and sat down with her coffee. "You're getting yourself all worked up before you go to work. Not a good idea."

Liz flipped closed her iPad and tasted her coffee. "Perfect. You always get it just right."

"After all this time, you'd think so."

"You always got it right." Liz smiled at Maggie, admiring her still sleepy face. The fine wrinkles around her eyes were a sure sign that she was no longer the college student Liz had fallen in love with forty-six years ago. As she gazed into Maggie's hazel eyes, Liz could still see that lively, young woman peering back.

Maggie had come down in her nightgown and bathrobe. Usually, she was dressed and wearing makeup before she appeared in the morning, but they were alone in the house. Vanity and a long career on the stage prevented her from showing her bare face to anyone but her wife.

At sixty-six, Maggie was pale without makeup. She'd let her long hair go completely gray because Liz had put the fear of God in her about hair dye causing cancer. Maggie had enough cancer risk from her BRCA2 without adding to it.

"What's spooking the markets?" she asked, surprising Liz with the question. Maggie hardly ever asked about finances, seemingly more than content to let Liz manage her portfolio. When Liz tried to explain how she was investing her money, her wife's interest was never more than casual and fleeting.

"This coronavirus is new. Nothing we've ever seen before. No one has natural immunity. It spreads quickly, and it's often deadly. If too many people get sick at once, it could shut down factories. China makes a lot of things we need, including parts for everything from cars to cell phones. An interruption in the supply chain would have a huge impact on the economy, and that's only the beginning."

Maggie, who'd been listening intently, studied her face. "You're really worried, aren't you?"

As a doctor, Liz tried to keep her facial expressions under control, so she wasn't happy to hear that her concern had been so obvious. "I'm not panicking yet, but I want to be prepared."

"What does that mean?" Maggie seemed more alert than when she had first come down, which meant she would be receptive to additional information.

"It means that we could be in for a pandemic. The medical system could be overwhelmed and there could be shortages of everything…like in a war."

"What should we do?" Maggie asked in an anxious voice.

"Well, for now, I'm going to order more PPE for the practice and advise Brenda and Duvaney to do the same."

"What's a PPE?"

"Personal protective equipment. You know, masks, gowns, gloves…"

Maggie put down her coffee cup. "You're serious."

"Yes."

Maggie patted her hand. "You'll do the right thing. You always do."

Liz glanced at her watch. Whenever she looked at the gold Cartier, she remembered the big party Yale-New Haven had thrown for her when she'd retired as chief of surgery. A gold watch! Could they have come up with something more clichéd? Fortunately, it was useful for counting pulse beats and timing medical processes, and it was accurate to the millisecond.

"I need to get moving soon," said Liz. "I have my breakfast with Brenda this morning, and I have to pick up Cherie first." Liz gazed out the window of the breakfast room. The lazy snowflakes had gotten larger and were coming down faster. "How much snow are we supposed to get today?"

Maggie checked her phone. "Channel Eight says eight to ten."

"Are the schools closed?"

"Yes, all the Hobbs schools are closed. No rehearsal this afternoon."

"Good. I'm glad you don't have to drive in this weather."

Maggie gave Liz a playful smack on the arm. "Stop. You know I'm a good driver."

"You hardly drove while you lived in New York. For twenty years, you didn't even own a car!"

"I'm still a good driver," said Maggie indignantly. "I don't get warnings all the time like you do. They'd give you tickets if you weren't a doctor."

"And I'm friends with the chief."

"I wouldn't play that card too often, if I were you." Maggie reached for *The New York Times.* Her preference for reading ink on paper still mystified Liz, but she paid for a subscription to the print edition without complaint. "I'm home all day, so I'll cook tonight," said Maggie. "I have my eye on those Cornish hens you defrosted."

"Thanks. I look forward to something amazing," said Liz, getting up.

Maggie gave her a critical look. "Put on some makeup. You don't want to scare the police chief and your new PA."

"Cherie's not new anymore. She's been with the practice for eight months," said Liz and headed toward the kitchen.

"Put on some makeup!" Maggie called after her.

Liz rolled her eyes, but after she showered and dressed, she put on some foundation, blush and a little mascara. After six years of marriage, Liz had learned it was easier to comply with Maggie's directions than to argue with her. Liz put on a polar fleece jacket over her top because it was always a little chilly in the old diner where she had breakfast once a week with the police chief.

The tradition had begun shortly after Liz bought the family practice on Beach Road. The head of the Hobbs chamber of commerce suggested the idea as a way to learn more about the town and its inner workings. Now that Liz and Brenda Harrison were close friends and fishing buddies, the reason for the weekly meetings was as much social as business.

Liz gave Maggie a quick kiss on the way out.

"Text me when you get there," Maggie ordered.

"Maggie..."

"Just do it, so I know you're safe."

Liz opened the garage door to the bay where her Audi was parked. The gray sky overhead promised more snow. It would be easier to brush off the top of an SUV than climb into the back of her pickup truck to sweep it out. Liz pulled the car out of the garage and sat for a minute to let the engine tick down. She engaged the gear shift and looked over her shoulder to back up. As much as Liz loved technology, she still didn't trust the backup monitor on the dash.

She sighed as she headed down the long drive to the street. Usually, she looked forward to her breakfasts with Brenda, but not this morning. Whenever Brenda and Cherie were in the same room, the tension was palpable. Liz guessed it wasn't personal. Brenda was affable and friendly. She was popular with the townspeople. The girl scouts brought her cookies and chocolate milk. The kindergarten students crayoned colorful portraits of the chief, which she proudly displayed on the walls of her office.

When Liz finally decided to talk to her PA about her problem with Brenda, Cherie admitted she hated cops. Probing the reason would have been inappropriate, but Liz urged Cherie to dial down the hostile looks. A town of nine thousand people was too small for petty animosities.

As Liz drove to the little cottage where Cherie lived with her father, she thought back to the day they'd first met. Liz was usually frugal with the practice's resources, but she had flown Cherie Bois up from Houston based on her strong résumé and compelling cover letter.

When Cherie had arrived for the interview, Liz couldn't help but stare. Cherie's beautifully proportioned figure was trim and toned for a woman nearing fifty. She had compelling blue-green eyes. Her flawless skin looked perpetually tan and provided a striking contrast to her blond hair. Her unique coloring, combined with perfect features, made her attractive enough to be a model, news anchor, or actress, but Cherie had started out as a psychiatric social worker before becoming a physician's assistant.

Hardly anyone in Hobbs knew Cherie was biracial. Her maternal grandmother had been black. In the first interview, Cherie had made sure to tell Liz that, despite being able to pass for white, she identified as African American. She also made a point of coming out. "In the interest of full transparency."

"That's fine, I'm gay too, but you do know Maine is one of the whitest states in the union. Ninety-five percent white. Will that bother you?"

"No, of course not."

"I see you've spent the majority of your career in the South. What brings you to Maine?"

"My father is a Mainer. He was born here and wanted to come home now that he's getting to the end of his life. He missed Maine. French Canadian."

"I noticed the French name."

"Yes, but I pronounce it Boyz."

"Got it," said Liz. To make her admiration of the woman less obvious, she pretended to peruse her résumé.

The interview had gone well, but that night Liz admitted to Maggie that she was reluctant to hire Cherie because she was so attractive.

"Liz Stolz! That's reverse discrimination. The woman can't help being attractive. Your eyes are on springs around Lucy Bartlett too, but you manage."

"Lucy is married to my best friend and she's a priest. I would never mess with her."

"And you're married to me. You can look, but don't you dare touch!" said Maggie, wagging her finger. "Dear God, give me patience." She raised her eyes toward heaven. "Sixty-three years old, and she still thinks with her crotch!"

Maggie's comments had shamed her into calling Cherie back for a second interview. This time, via Skype. After her partners had interviewed Cherie and given her glowing reviews, Liz couldn't find a reason not to extend an offer. That was back in July, at the height of the summer season. Cherie had hit the ground running and had since become Liz's right hand. Her diagnoses were always spot on. She knew when to make decisions on her own and when to ask questions. Not that she always took Liz's advice, but she asked.

Liz pulled into the short driveway to the cottage. Cherie was outside brushing off her car. She waved and opened the car door to put the brush inside. Every car in Maine carried a long-handled brush with a scraper on one end as standard equipment. In September, Reny's always had a bucketful by the front door. By the end of October, they were completely sold out.

Cherie's warm breath momentarily fogged the windshield on her side. "Good morning, Dr. Stolz," she said.

"Good morning, Cherie. How's your father today?"

Cherie shrugged. "The same. He's lonely since I made him give up his car. His COPD keeps him from taking walks like he used to. I encourage him to invite his friends to play cards, but he doesn't seem interested."

"Getting old is hard," said Liz. "Keep encouraging him. Isolation will only make him get old faster."

"Yes, it will." Cherie looked straight ahead. "Okay. Let's do this," she said in a determined voice.

Liz smiled. "It's not a colonoscopy, just breakfast with the chief. I think she likes you."

"I know. I wish she didn't."

"I know you don't like cops, but Brenda is not your average cop."

Cherie shook her head. "Let's just go and get it over with."

On the way to the diner, they passed the offices of Hobbs Family

Practice. "I see we have plenty of blood draws this morning," Liz said, mentally counting the cars in the parking lot. "Next week will be busy." She glanced at Cherie who was still bravely staring ahead. "How do you find the routine of family practice? It can be pretty monotonous at times."

"For you maybe. You were a surgeon. For me, every day is a new adventure."

"Surgery can be pretty boring too. I knew guys who did nothing but knee and hip replacements. I did so many mastectomies and lumpectomies, I almost got tired of seeing breasts." Liz turned to Cherie with a quick grin. "But I never did."

"You're so bad. But at least people can tell you're gay. Hardly anyone guesses about me. Looking feminine can be a liability."

"Not for the rest of us. We enjoy the view." Liz instantly realized she'd said the wrong thing. "I'm sorry. That was out of line."

"Apology accepted," said Cherie. "Just drive, Dr. Stolz. The roads are icy."

2

Brenda Harrison checked the time on her phone. She made sure the ringer was on because she'd turned down her radio to avoid disturbing the other diners. If there was an emergency, the dispatcher knew to call her phone.

"Hey, chief." Paula, the counter waitress, craned her neck to see over her breakfast customers. "Go ahead. Your table's free. You're the first one here."

Brenda took off her campaign hat and headed to the table in the back. She liked this spot because it was walled on one side by the coffee station and by a window on the other. The privacy allowed Brenda and the town doctor to discuss sensitive business without fear of being overheard.

Brenda looked for Liz's car in the parking lot, figuring she would take the Audi to avoid shoveling the snow out of the pickup. Liz was the practical sort. Brenda liked that about her. When it came to a police decision that required medical advice, she could always count on Liz to use common sense.

Brenda turned her camera app around to selfie position so she could check her appearance. As usual, she wore her blond hair in a thick French braid. Sometimes, she wore it in a ponytail or a bun, but a braid was more comfortable under her hat. She'd put on more makeup and a slightly darker shade of lipstick because she knew she'd be seeing Liz's PA.

Not bad, thought Brenda, scrutinizing her image. Her features were even and well proportioned. People told her she was attractive, but she was never quite sure they weren't just being kind.

Finally, the Audi raced into the lot. Liz always drove too fast. She was one of those risk-takers who love speed and danger. Brenda had her pegged as an A-type who always had to be top dog. Liz tried to show she'd mellowed, but, whether she liked it or not, she always ended up being the boss. Some people were just born that way.

The plow job in the parking lot wasn't great, so it took a few minutes for Liz to find a spot. Brenda caught a glimpse of her passenger, and her heart picked up a few extra beats. *Damn, that woman is beautiful.*

Brenda deliberately turned her attention to the waitress pouring her a cup of coffee. "Good morning, Lisa."

"Hey, chief."

"Snow hasn't kept away the customers, I see."

"You know Mainers," the waitress said. "We're not afraid of a little snow. Otherwise, we'd have to shut down the state for seven months."

"Yes, I guess we would. Hard to imagine." Brenda focused on Lisa to avoid watching Cherie approach the table. The cool, expressionless face didn't look in her direction either. *Why does this woman hate me?* Brenda wondered. *What have I ever done to her?*

The newcomers took their seats in the old-fashioned, tubular-metal chairs. The diner hadn't been updated since it had opened in the 1950s. The one exception was the vinyl on the padded seats, which had been replaced because the tape holding it together was sticking to people's pants. Otherwise, customers, especially the tourists, seemed to like the worn, slightly shabby look that suggested a place forgotten by time.

"Brenda," said Liz with a nod.

"Liz."

"Good morning, Chief Harrison," said Cherie. Her southern accent made her voice sound warm even though her glacial expression said otherwise. Then she smiled, and Brenda's heart skipped a few beats. *Maybe she doesn't hate me after all.*

"I brought Cherie along because I'm putting her in charge of the high school drug program," said Liz casually.

At the sound of her name, Cherie smiled again, a pleasant professional smile, but those gorgeous eyes stubbornly refused to meet Brenda's.

"I don't have time for it now that the Rotary has elected me president," Liz continued. "I have too many things on my plate."

"Well, that's an understatement," said Brenda. "President of the chamber of commerce, the Rotary…and the fish and game. Pretty soon you'll be in charge of the whole town."

"I don't think so," said Liz dismissively. "Cherie's background in social work makes her especially well-suited for the high school program. Plus, she's younger, so the kids won't feel like they're being lectured by their grandmother."

"How old are you, Cherie?" asked Brenda. "I hope you don't mind me asking."

"Forty-nine. Fifty in May."

Only a couple of years younger than I am, thought Brenda. *God, she would be so perfect, if only she didn't hate me.*

"Cherie has some ideas on how to do outreach to the kids. The problem is so many have access to the prescription opioids their parents use."

"Well, if you docs weren't so liberal with the scripts."

"You must be thinking of someone else, Brenda. You know it's not me or anyone in my practice."

Liz's phone vibrated in her pocket. She pulled it out and glanced at the screen. "Excuse me. I need to take this." She got up and headed to the anteroom at the entrance.

Brenda turned to Cherie and smiled. Cherie returned the smile, but it was strained. She glanced out the window.

Damn! Here I have a moment alone with her, and she won't even look at me. Brenda momentarily panicked as she tried to think of something to say.

"How do you like it in Maine?" she finally ventured.

Cherie turned and gave her a penetrating look. Then her eyes softened a little. "Except for the cold, it's like coming home. My father talked about it so much when I was growing up, I felt like I grew up here too."

That was the most Cherie had said to her since she'd known her. Encouraged by the response, Brenda asked, "Where did you grow up?"

"The Big Easy. New Orleans. We moved to Shreveport when I was eleven."

"You're a long way from home," observed Brenda.

"Yes. A long way," said Cherie. "How about you?"

"I'm a New Yorker. Born in Brooklyn, way out in Brooklyn, a forty-five-minute subway ride. I was a New York City cop before coming up here."

The open interest in Cherie's eyes suddenly shut down. "I'm not a big fan of cops."

Brenda blinked, startled by the remark. "Why?"

"It's a long story," said Cherie. "I don't like to talk about it."

"Okay," said Brenda drawing out the word. "Maybe you'll tell me another time."

"Maybe," said Cherie, but she sounded doubtful.

Heart pounding, Brenda decided to go for broke. "I'd like to get to know you better."

Cherie's eyes sought the tabletop. "I don't know if that's a good idea."

"Why not?"

Before Cherie could answer, Liz slid back into her seat. "Sorry about that. Mrs. Johnson was having heart palpitations again."

"She all right?" asked Cherie.

Liz nodded. "I'm starving. Where's Lisa?" She waved vigorously at the waitress.

In a moment, Lisa was standing at their table, pad in hand. She looked at Cherie. "What can I get for you, Miss? I already know what these two want." She smirked and nodded toward Brenda and Liz.

Liz shrugged. "What can I say? At least, I'm consistent."

When Cherie asked for eggs over easy with bacon and wheat toast, the others at the table started to laugh.

"So that makes three," said Lisa, busily writing on her pad. "I'll put it right in. Sorry for the wait. The plow guys are all in here at the same time."

"Just taking a break before the next run," Brenda said. "This is definitely a two-plow storm."

The waitress went off with their order. Liz looked from Cherie to Brenda and back again. "Everything good here?"

"Of course," said Brenda with false heartiness, but she could see Liz wasn't buying it. Fortunately, she chose not to share her thoughts. There was already enough tension. Instead, they talked about the storm.

Lisa brought their plates and refilled their coffee cups. They were all silent while they ate. Liz was a fast eater and polished away her breakfast before the others.

"Did you tell the chief your ideas for the drug program?"

"No," said Cherie, glancing at Brenda. "We got diverted to another topic, but I can send Chief Harrison my notes for her feedback."

"No need to be so formal. Just call me Brenda, please."

Cherie's only response was to glance in her direction.

"I want to talk about something else," said Liz, "something important."

Brenda finished chewing her toast and said, "Okay. Shoot."

Although it was just a figure of speech, Cherie flinched.

Liz, sitting next to her, asked, "You okay?"

"I don't like guns," she said, frowning in Brenda's direction.

Unconsciously, Brenda's hand touched the service weapon on her hip. *Maybe that's why she doesn't like me.*

Meanwhile, Liz went on about some Chinese virus she'd been reading about in the financial pages. Brenda listened, half-interested, while surreptitiously admiring the woman sitting across from her. Fortunately, Cherie's attention was focused on her boss, and she didn't seem to notice.

"That's scary," said Cherie. "Sounds like another SARS outbreak."

"Yes, it does," Liz agreed, "but it could be a whole lot worse than SARS. There's very little hard data coming out of China, but it sounds like the mortality rate is high. We should prepare now, just in case."

"I don't know," said Brenda skeptically. "We spent a lot of money getting ready for that SARS thing, and nothing ever happened."

Liz gave Brenda a direct look. "Just because nothing materialized in the past doesn't mean it couldn't happen in the future. Look. I'm no epidemiologist, but from what I've read, we're ripe for a pandemic."

Brenda sat back in her seat and studied her friend's face. She'd never known Liz to be anything but steady and thoughtful. That meant this could be serious. "So, what do you suggest?"

"I think we should plan ahead like we would for a natural disaster. Stock up on water, first-aid supplies, batteries, flares, whatever. But most important of all, we should order PPE. Gloves, masks, face shields, paper gowns."

Brenda threw her napkin on the table. "We had so much stuff left over from the SARS scare. The mice got in and pooped all over it. It smelled god awful!" Brenda made a disgusted face.

Liz glanced at Cherie's plate. "Thanks, Brenda. Don't you see Cherie's still eating?"

Cherie looked up. "It's all right. I have a strong stomach."

That's hopeful, thought Brenda. *She's forgiving me.*

"Next time put your supplies in airtight containers like I told you," scolded Liz.

"We did, but then we needed the containers for something else. Well, you know how it is."

"I don't," said Liz, scowling. "I'm sorry, Brenda. I know it's laid back up here, but we need to have discipline about our supplies."

Brenda glanced at Cherie for sympathy. "Still thinks she's the big boss down at Yale."

"Come on, Brenda. I'm not kidding. This could be serious. And we need to talk to Paul Duvaney about the fire department and ambulance corps. They need to do it too."

"You talk to Duvaney," said Brenda, folding her arms on her chest. "He never listens to me. He thinks I'm too bossy as it is."

"Well, you are bossy. And so am I. But I will talk to him if you want me to. I just need you to back me up."

"All right. If he gives you trouble, I'll chime in. But if this doesn't turn into anything, we'll both look like assholes. Not like we have the budget to throw away on PPE that the mice can shit on again. I thought the feds have a stockpile of this kind of thing."

"They're supposed to," Liz said, "but who knows? Remember all those RVs they bought for Katrina? They never got used by people who really needed them. They just sat out in a field, getting moldy."

"Do you want me to do some research?" asked Cherie. "Figure out what we might need and where to get it?"

"That would be great," Liz replied.

"I'll work with you on it," Brenda said in a hopeful voice.

The sharp look in Cherie's eyes was instant and definite. "I've got it."

Liz turned to Cherie. "That's actually a good idea. You should work with Brenda. She can help you figure it out."

Cherie audibly sighed, but she nodded in agreement.

3

Reverend Lucille Bartlett ended her vocal practice and flipped the switch of the enormous pipe organ at the rear of the church. As the bellows deflated, she headed downstairs to put on her vestments for the morning prayer service.

Erika had suggested that Lucy's singing was inspirational to others, so she'd been quietly spreading the word about her wife's secret morning practice. Now, it was no longer a secret. More and more parishioners slipped into the church by the side door to listen to their rector, once a star of the Metropolitan Opera, sing secular and sacred pieces. Since Tom Simmons had joined the parish as associate rector, Lucy had the time to revive morning prayer as a regular feature of the parish liturgy. As more people came early to listen to her impromptu recitals, the attendance grew.

On her way to the robing room to put on her vestments, Lucy surveyed the group who had come for morning prayer, pleased to see such a large crowd despite the bad weather. She was especially pleased to see some young people, not only the gray-haired ladies who formed the core of her congregation. Lucy's agnostic wife might be an ironic evangelist, but she was definitely effective.

Erika smiled as Lucy passed. She blew a kiss, then got up and quietly left. She was due in Waterville for her eleven o'clock class. As Lucy watched Erika leave the church, she silently prayed for her safety. It was a long drive to the Colby campus, and it would be even longer in the snow.

Lucy knew that Erika's professional life would have been easier if she'd kept her apartment on the Colby campus, but she wanted to be with her family. Since Erika's beach house had been renovated, they had plenty of room. As an opera star, Lucy had toured the world. Now, she couldn't imagine sleeping anywhere but the spacious bedroom overlooking the salt marsh, snug in the comfortable bed with her new wife.

Lucy buttoned up her cassock and pulled the white surplice over her head. She shook out her hair and tied it back again. She'd wear Susan's white stole this morning. Before putting it around her neck, Lucy kissed the embroidered cross. As she did, she blessed the woman who'd taught her how to love again and brought her back to God. She sent Susan a little prayer, wherever she was. Who knew when or if she would ever see her again? Strange how people disappeared from your life and then suddenly showed up. Like Emily. Lucy had given her up as an infant, and now her adolescent daughter was living with her. Life was full of weird twists, not all coincidental. As a woman of faith, Lucy didn't believe in complete coincidence. Some things did happen for a reason.

For morning prayer, Lucy liked to stand in the aisle rather than in the pulpit because she wanted people to feel her presence. She blessed herself and proclaimed: "Grace be unto you, and peace, from God our Father, and from the Lord Jesus Christ." She looked around at the sleepy faces. "Good morning!"

"Good morning, Mother Lucy," came the muted response.

"We're all so awake on this snowy morning."

There was a soft murmur of laughter.

"This morning's hymn is 'Oh, God, our Help in Ages Past.'" She glanced around to make sure she had everyone's attention. "Now, don't make me do all the work."

Again, there was a murmur of laughter. Lucy waited until it died out before launching into the hymn.

The liturgy followed the familiar pattern, which soothed Lucy as much as it comforted her parishioners. Mrs. Carlson, who was going through a difficult divorce, looked more relaxed. Mr. Bouchet, whose wife was dying, looked a little more peaceful. As they were singing the final hymn, Lucy noticed a newcomer slip quietly into the church from the side door. Cherie genuflected from the outer aisle and moved into a rear pew. Her face looked pinched. Lucy hoped there was nothing wrong.

When the service concluded, Lucy went down the aisle to shake hands with her congregants. Cherie hung back to be the last in line.

"Hello, Cherie," said Lucy, taking her hand in both of hers.

"Good morning, Mother Lucy." The worried look momentarily fled Cherie's face as she returned Lucy's handshake. "I wonder if you have a few minutes for me this morning."

Lucy mentally reviewed her schedule. Wednesday was the day she reserved for writing her Sunday sermon. She hated to give up the time, but she smiled warmly to make Cherie feel welcome. "Of course."

"Mother Lucy, has anyone ever told you, you have the most beautiful smile?"

People said that all the time, but it still made Lucy blush. She gave Cherie's hand another squeeze before letting it go. "Come with me while I take off my vestments. You can give me a preview of what you want to talk about."

Cherie followed Lucy into the robing room. She watched as Lucy took off the stole and carefully hung it on the coat tree along with the white surplice. When Lucy began to unbutton the cassock, she averted her eyes.

"It's okay. I'm decent under here," said Lucy, her fingers nimbly working the buttons of the cassock. Underneath, she was wearing black pants and a thermal shirt. She put on a long-sleeved black clerical blouse and added a black polar fleece jacket. "It's cold in the rectory," she explained. "Now that Father Tom is the only one living there, we've been keeping the heat down." Lucy carefully hung up the vestments with the others in the closet. "So? What's on your mind, Cherie?"

"I need someone to talk to. It's always embarrassing to admit that when you're a therapist yourself."

"We're all just human. We have problems like everyone else. Sometimes, we just need another perspective." Lucy reached out her hand. "Come with me to the rectory, and I'll get you some coffee."

At the door, Lucy stepped into some low duck boots. They looked ridiculous, but Lucy always smiled when she put them on because Erika had given them to her for Christmas. "You're a real Mainer now," she'd said. If that was all it took, Lucy would be grateful, but living there took real grit and stamina. Fortunately, the summers and natural beauty made it all worth it.

When they opened the door, a blast of snow came in. "Come on. Let's hurry," Lucy urged.

They walked across the quadrangle to the rectory. The pavement had recently been plowed, but the snow was piling up fast. It was dry and crunched under their feet.

"What a day!" said Lucy, looking down to avoid the windswept snow-flakes whipping into her eyes. "Do we have time to talk this morning? Don't you have to go to work?"

"Not until this afternoon. I have Wednesday mornings off."

They reached the rectory door. Inside, they stomped off the snow on an industrial grade mat from Marden's. Lucy changed her shoes.

"I'll take off my shoes," Cherie offered.

"No, don't. Your feet will get wet. We'll mop up the melt later." Lucy loosened the clip and shook the snowflakes out of her hair. She left it loose so it would dry. "Come on. Let's get you that coffee. I could use one too."

Once they were settled in Lucy's office, there was silence as they both sipped the hot coffee. Lucy set down her cup and smiled to signal she was ready to listen, but the silence continued until it was uncomfortable.

"Is it something hard to talk about?" asked Lucy gently.

Cherie nodded.

"Take your time. There's no meter running. You're on my pastoral counseling time."

"That's good. I'd rather not have Dr. Stolz know I'm coming to see you."

"How would she know unless you tell her? And why would she object?"

Cherie shook her head. "She wouldn't, of course. I'm just being paranoid."

"I understand," said Lucy. "There's a stigma attached to a medical professional who needs counseling. Of course, you know how common it is. If it makes you feel any better, you're not the first person from that practice to find your way here."

"Really?" Cherie's eyes looked curious. They were such a unique color. When Cherie had first moved to Hobbs, Lucy instantly realized she had competition for being the most attractive woman in town. Not having a vain bone in her body, Lucy welcomed it.

"You know I can't say more," said Lucy. "In fact, I shouldn't have said that."

"No, you should have. It reassured me. I needed reassurance."

Lucy settled back in her chair. "This is going to be fun. I always find having another therapist as a client a real challenge. We're so good at second guessing one another."

"One of the reasons I chose you is I hear you have an unconventional approach."

Lucy felt unaccountably flattered by the remark. "Not intentionally unconventional. I just follow my instincts. They're usually good."

"What makes you different is I feel the concern and warmth in everything you say, whether it's just talking like this or in church. It's like you just love everybody."

"That's my job. If God is love, as St. John says, and I am her priest, I need to reflect God's love to her people."

Cherie smiled. "You're one of those radical priests who believe God is female."

"Apart from Jesus, who was incarnated as a man, God has no body and no gender. Personally, I find the mother metaphor more evocative. When I use female pronouns, it wakes people up and makes them think."

Cherie nodded thoughtfully. "Hadn't thought of it that way."

"Were you raised in the Episcopal Church, Cherie?"

"No, Catholic. My father is French Canadian. Very Catholic, but he wanted to marry my mother, who was divorced. That doesn't fly in the Catholic Church. They were married by a judge. Eventually, my parents drifted toward the Episcopal Church because it was enough like Catholic to feel right. I was an adolescent by then, and questioning everything, but I came along for the ride. So here I am."

"I, for one, am glad you are." Lucy allowed a long pause to develop, hoping Cherie would say more. When she didn't, she finally asked, "How can I help you, Cherie?"

Cherie visibly squirmed at first, but then she said, "Dr. Stolz assigned me to work with Brenda Harrison on the school drug project. Tough love, I think. She's been encouraging me to get over my issues with the chief."

"Why don't you get along with Chief Harrison?"

"It's not personal. It's cops."

"I see," said Lucy, sitting forward in her chair. "Tell me more."

"Not many people know I'm biracial."

Lucy had to force herself not to show surprise. With her blond hair and stunning blue-green eyes, Cherie looked completely Caucasian. Yes, her skin was slightly darker than most white women, and she had beautifully shaped, full lips, but nothing else about her appearance even hinted at an Afro-American heritage.

"My grandmother was black," explained Cherie. "She was quite a woman, the principal of the black elementary school. My white grandfather absolutely adored her. She was gorgeous. So was my mother, who could also pass for white. I'm only one-quarter black. Of course, in the South, they have the one drop rule. If you have even one drop of black blood, you're black."

"I never would have guessed," Lucy honestly admitted.

"No one ever does. People ask if I'm Scandinavian because of my coloring. There are a lot of olive-complected Scandinavians. My blond hair and blue eyes make people think I must be white."

"Is that a problem for you?"

"Yes, because I identify as a black woman. My mother never tried to deny her heritage. She cooked traditional black food as well as Creole dishes. The church we attended was a black church. My father felt a little strange at first, but he fit right in. There's so much warmth in a black church. That's why I love St. Margaret's. It's not a black church, but I feel the warmth."

"That's wonderful to hear," said Lucy, smiling. "But back to police officers. What's your issue with them?"

"I witnessed some police violence."

"Obviously, it left a lasting impression."

"It certainly did. The victim was my sister. My half-sister really."

"Is she all right now?"

"She's dead."

Lucy sat back in her chair as if Cherie's words had physically pushed her. She hated to react so obviously, but in this case, she couldn't control it.

"Oh, Cherie, I'm so sorry."

Cherie nodded to acknowledge the sympathy.

"What happened? Can you tell me?"

Cherie took a deep breath. "We were riding along the highway, coming back from a party, being silly, having fun. A trooper pulled us over for a broken taillight. He was young and obviously very nervous. He took out his gun right away. He ordered us to get out of the car. When my sister didn't move fast enough, he shot her."

"My word!" Lucy exclaimed. "How horrible!"

"Yes."

"And you witnessed this?"

"I did. In fact, the bullet went right through her and hit me in the shoulder. I still have a little scar from it. Her blood spattered all over me. She died in the ambulance on the way to the hospital. I held her hand until she died."

"Oh, Cherie. I'm so, so sorry you had to witness that. What a tragedy!"

"In case you haven't guessed, I don't like guns either."

"I'm not too fond of them myself," Lucy admitted. "What happened to the trooper who shot your sister?"

Cherie shrugged, but she looked close to tears. "Nothing. There wasn't even a hearing." She shrugged again. "He just got away with it."

"You think it would have been different if she had been white?"

"Absolutely. The trooper kept apologizing to me. Of course, he thought I was white. Meanwhile, my sister was lying there, bleeding to death."

Lucy took a moment to dismiss her visualization of the scene. Finally, she said, "I can certainly understand why you have an issue with the police. But Brenda Harrison is different. When she was in the NYPD, she was in charge of sensitivity training for officers working in minority neighborhoods. She and Dr. Stolz do regular firearms training for the police to prevent unnecessary shootings. She's on your side."

"It doesn't matter," said Cherie, shaking her head. "I see the uniform and the gun and nothing else. Those are my triggers. As soon as I see them, I feel my heart race and my throat constrict."

"That's not good."

"No, it's not. I try to avoid her and other cops as much as I can. But now Liz has forced this assignment on me."

"So, you need to deal with it, or your job is in jeopardy."

"Pretty much."

Lucy took a deep breath as she considered the situation. "So, what would you recommend if the situation were reversed?"

"Cognitive therapy. Trying to desensitize the client gradually. But I've tried all that."

"Treating yourself usually doesn't work. You can't be objective enough," Lucy said, mostly to herself because she was still focused on Cherie's dilemma. "Wow! This is complicated."

"You bet it is. She likes me."

"Brenda is a friendly person."

Cherie gave her a hard look. "I mean, she *likes* me."

"Oh!" said Lucy, sitting up straight as if she'd been goosed. "Are you…?"

"A lesbian? Yes."

Lucy's eyes grew wide. "I would never have guessed."

"No one does," said Cherie with a sigh. "I just don't read."

"They don't read me either. And don't go by me. My gaydar is pretty weak."

Lucy took a moment to collect her thoughts.

"But that could work in your favor. Maybe you could meet in neutral territory…go out for dinner somewhere when she's not wearing her uniform."

"You're kidding, right?"

Lucy shook her head. "No, I'm not. It doesn't have to mean anything. Just a friendly dinner to get to know her."

Cherie gave her a skeptical look. "Mother Lucy, you certainly do have an unconventional approach."

4

The practice manager's voice blaring through the intercom made Cherie's patient jump. "Sorry to interrupt, Ms. Bois, but Chief Harrison is here for you."

"Thanks, Ginny, please tell her I'll be right with her."

Cherie smiled at her patient. "My apologies for that, Mr. Barnes."

The old man's broad smile revealed that two of his front teeth were missing. "Are you in trouble, Ms. Bois?"

"In trouble?" Cherie repeated, puzzled.

Mr. Barnes raised a bushy brow. "If the chief is looking for you, maybe you should escape out the back door like in the movies."

Cherie laughed. "No, it's nothing like that. We're working on a project together. I said I'd meet her about now, but I've been running late today."

"Never had a doctor see me on time," said Mr. Barnes with another gap-toothed grin. "Glad you didn't break my perfect record!"

Cherie released the lever to let down the lower part of the examination table so her patient could step down. "I think we're done here. You can get dressed now." She closed the door to give him privacy and headed to the office to finish her notes.

By the time she returned, Mr. Barnes was dressed and ready to be escorted down the hall.

"I've already sent your prescriptions to the pharmacy. They should be ready by this afternoon."

"I'll have my daughter pick them up," he said, heading to the door. "Thanks, Ms. Bois. And don't let the chief put you in jail. If she does, I'll speak up for you."

Cherie looked up to see Chief Harrison smiling. "You do something I don't know about?"

Cherie shook her head, not really paying attention to the question because she was so busy studying Brenda. She looked so different today, wearing an ordinary parka, not a police jacket. Her long, blond hair was down, and she was wearing more eye makeup than usual. For the first time, Cherie noticed her eyes were a deep shade of blue. Her cheeks were rosy, whether from the cold or makeup was hard to tell. The little blush made her look pink and healthy. She smiled fully, showing perfectly white teeth. Cherie wondered how she had missed the fact that this woman was really attractive.

Cherie took her parka down from the hook in the practice manager's room. "If Dr. Stolz is looking for me, tell her I'm off on my assignment with Chief Harrison." When she went out to the waiting room, she met another dazzling smile and couldn't help but return it.

"You know," said Brenda, "I think that's the first time you've really smiled at me."

"You're not wearing your uniform today."

"I'm off duty."

Cherie, who had set up the meeting, felt guilty for taking up Brenda's personal time. "You should have told me. We could have done it on a different day."

"It's fine. I didn't have anything special planned for today. I can think of worse ways to spend it." Brenda gave her another brilliant smile.

Cherie found herself studying Brenda's features, trying to place why she looked so familiar. Brenda had a very English look to her face, creamy, youthful skin, a square jaw, and a little cleft in her chin. Cherie, who was addicted to BBC series, finally remembered where she'd seen someone who had a face like that—the middle-aged policewoman in *Happy Valley*. Brenda even had the same expression of damaged vulnerability as the main character, Sergeant Cawood. Brenda was trimmer than the actress who played the role, but there was an uncanny resemblance.

"You remind me of Sarah Lancashire."

"Who?" Brenda asked, looking puzzled.

"She's a British actress who plays a police sergeant in a BBC series."

"Never heard of her."

"She's a very good actress. I bet you'd like that series, and I'd be interested to hear what you think of it."

"You would?" asked Brenda, beaming again. "Maybe we could watch it together."

"Maybe," Cherie found herself saying. She gazed into Brenda's blue eyes and saw her own image reflected back, a tiny, curious Cherie.

"You ready to go?"

Cherie realized Brenda was repeating the question because she hadn't answered it the first time. "Yes, let's go."

"I can drive and drop you off back here when we're done," said Brenda.

"Yes…okay." *Get a grip*, Cherie told herself. *You have a job to do.*

She followed Brenda out the door to the parking lot.

"Watch out here," said Brenda, reaching out her hand. "There's an icy patch."

Ordinarily, Cherie would wave off the offer of help to assert her independence, but for some reason, she took Brenda's hand. It was warm and held hers gently but firmly as it guided her down the stairs. They exchanged a warm smile when Cherie reached the bottom.

Brenda led her to a pickup truck, a bright red Tacoma. "Another truck fan," said Cherie.

After a confused look, Brenda said, "Oh, right. Liz drives one too. And for the same reasons probably—dump runs, hauling sheetrock and salt for the water conditioner."

"You Maine ladies are all so self-reliant and handy."

"Well, you're a Maine lady now, although you wouldn't know it from that Southern drawl."

"I do not drawl," countered Cherie indignantly.

"You sure do!"

"You should talk. I can hear a hint of Brooklyn now and then."

"Oh, don't tell me that. You don't know how hard I've tried to get rid of it. They hate New Yorkers up here."

"No."

"Oh, yes, they do. They think we're all wise guys and crooks. That we're only here to make a fast buck."

"How long have you been here?"

"Almost ten years. I put in my twenty in New York and headed straight up here."

"I guess you knew what you wanted."

"Sure did. Me and my lady had our retirement carefully planned."

Realizing Brenda had just come out to her, Cherie searched her face. "Your lady? Are you still together?"

A shadow passed in Brenda's face, and she shook her head. "Car accident. T-boned at an intersection."

"Oh, Brenda, I'm so sorry," said Cherie. "I didn't realize..."

Brenda compressed her lips and looked away. "Thank you." she said and cleared her throat. "We should get going. I told Duvaney we'd be there by four-thirty."

They rode in silence to the police station. When they went inside, Cherie noted that the interaction between the staff and their chief was relaxed and friendly. The staff nodded and greeted Brenda as they walked through the office on their way to the storage area.

It took Brenda a minute to find the right key from a ring holding a dozen. She unlocked the storage room door. "Let's see what we've got here." She took down the plastic storage bins from the shelves and spread them out on the floor. Cherie made a quick survey of the contents. There was everything from nitrile gloves to full HAZMAT suits.

"You're better prepared than I expected," Cherie said as she picked through the bins. She took out her iPad and began to write quantities on the list she'd prepared.

"Sometimes we get chemical spills on 95. Usually, the troopers and the state DOT handle that, but sometimes they call us in. We have to be ready for anything."

Cherie looked at Brenda with new respect.

"I bet you thought we just write speeding tickets. We write those too, so watch your speed, especially in front of the elementary school."

It took nearly an hour to write up the complete list of the supplies the Hobbs police had in stock. Some of the face masks were expired. "We should pitch those," said Brenda.

"No, let's keep them for now. They're better than nothing in a pinch."

They repacked everything carefully and replaced the bins on the shelves before heading to the fire department.

"Have you ever met Chief Duvaney?" asked Brenda as they walked to the adjacent building.

"Haven't had the pleasure."

Brenda made a little face. "He's old school, a little rough around the edges like a lot of Mainers, but a good guy. Try to look past appearances."

"Thanks for the warning," said Cherie.

They found Chief Duvaney in his office, wolfing down a sandwich. He was a middle-aged, stocky man, who made Cherie suddenly remember Liz's comment on her first day. "We grow 'em big up here. Always test their blood sugar."

"Hey, Paul," said Brenda knocking on the door. "Mind if we interrupt?"

"Nah, come on in," he said. He didn't get up for his visitors. He merely pointed to the two chairs in front of the desk. Brenda didn't take the offer. "Do you mind if I finish my sandwich?" he asked, taking a large bite.

"No, go ahead." Brenda beckoned to Cherie to come into the office. "Paul, I'd like you to meet Liz Stolz's physician's assistant, Cherie Bois."

Paul's eyes grew big as Cherie came in, and he unabashedly looked her up and down. As he took another mouthful of sandwich, Cherie felt like the piece of ham he was about to devour. Unfortunately, she was used to that reaction from men and ignored it.

"We're not going to take up your time," Brenda explained. "I just wanted to let you know we're here."

Duvaney gave her a little wave of acknowledgement and took another large bite of his sandwich.

When they were down the hall and well out of earshot, Brenda said, "Well, now you've met Paul Duvaney. He looks worse than he is. That man is fearless and absolutely dedicated to fire fighting. He's personally rescued more people than any other fire fighter in the state."

"So, he just looks like a stereotype."

Brenda frowned as she considered the statement. "Yes, I guess that's what I mean."

The fire department supplies were well organized, so taking inventory was easier. The ambulance corps storeroom next door was spotless, and each storage bin held a meticulously kept inventory sheet.

"That was quick," said Brenda, closing the door. "I guess we're done here. Time to get you back."

Cherie saw her reluctance mirrored in Brenda's face.

"Is your car in the lot at the practice?"

Cherie shook her head. "I live close enough to walk to the office, so I usually do."

"Okay. Then I'll drive you home. Where do you live?"

Cherie gave her the address.

As they passed St. Margaret's Episcopal Church, Cherie thought about Mother Lucy's suggestion. Socializing with Brenda while she wasn't wearing her uniform made sense. Today's experience had shown her another side of the woman, and she was beginning to like what she saw.

"I've enjoyed working with you today," Cherie said.

"Me too," agreed Brenda. "We should do it again sometime."

"We'll have to. After I make up the list for you and Chief Duvaney, I'll need to go over it with each of you. I'll let you know when I'm ready."

"Okay. Sounds good, but I wouldn't mind seeing you before that."

Cherie swallowed hard, knowing what was coming. She realized that if she took control of the conversation, it might be easier. "How about going out for dinner one night?"

Brenda glanced at her. "I'd really like that but at this time of year, most of the restaurants are closed."

Cherie debated inviting her for a meal at her house, but she couldn't decide if she was ready for that.

"I know where we can go!" said Brenda. "There's a country-western bar up in Lyman that's open all year. They have great Tex-Mex food and awesome music. How about that?"

Brenda's voice was so full of enthusiasm Cherie didn't know what to say. She didn't especially like country-western music, preferring jazz and classical. She finally said, "Sounds like a possibility."

"Oh, you're in for a treat! This place always has great bands, even in the winter, although sometimes, I think people just pack in there for the body heat. By this time of year, they're so desperate to see other people, they'll jam into any place that's open." Brenda gave her steering wheel a light punch. "Damn! I just remembered. I don't have a weekend night off for two weeks."

"It will keep," Cherie said softly. "I'm not going anywhere."

Brenda turned and gave her a little smile. "I hope not." She parked on the street in front of the cottage. "Nice working with you today," she said as Cherie opened the door to get out. "Looking forward to next time."

Cherie waved from the little porch of her cottage as Brenda drove away.

Before Cherie took off her coat, she went into the living room to look in on her father. His face was illuminated by the blue light of the television, but he was sleeping soundly. She checked the water level in the humidifier and topped it up before waking him. The winter's dry heat made it hard for COPD patients to breathe, but keeping the humidifier full and free of contamination was a real chore.

Her father stirred. "Welcome home, sweetie pie," he said with a big smile. For a moment, Cherie caught a glimpse of the handsome, virile man who had been the hero of her youth. Now, he was gray, faded, and frail. She constantly worried about the threat of pneumonia, especially during the winter. She made sure he was current on all his vaccines, but still.

"How are you doing, Daddy?"

"Oh, fine, I guess. I'm just sick of hearing all those complaints about our president."

Cherie glanced at the television. Of course, Fox News was on again. It always came back on, no matter how often she changed the channel. To rid herself of the sight of Laura Ingraham, Cherie turned off the TV.

"Come into the kitchen and keep me company while I cook dinner."

"Okay." Her father struggled to get up, but Cherie didn't try to help because that only made him angry. Finally, he got to his feet.

"I hope you had a good day," Jean-Paul said, taking a seat at the kitchen table.

As Cherie cut up vegetables to make her mother's favorite gumbo recipe, she wondered whether to tell her father about Brenda Harrison.

5

Erika Bultmann, lugging her laptop and two canvas bags of books, opened the door from the garage. A wonderful smell greeted her. Sniffing the air, she tried to identify the aromas—meat, recently browned, sautéed onion and garlic, oregano. *Lucy is cooking!* Erika realized with delight. She dropped her bags in her office chair and headed to the kitchen.

"Hello, love, what are you up to? It smells absolutely delicious." She bent to kiss Lucy, who was still wearing her clerical blouse. "Shouldn't you change before going full Julia Child?"

"I wanted to get dinner started right away. It needs to simmer for an hour."

"And what is in that pot that smells so good?"

"Lamb stew with eggplant. Liz gave me the recipe."

Erika reached for a wooden spoon and dipped it into the sauce for a taste. It was piquant with just the right balance of sweetness. "Very good, Mother Lucy. Nicely seasoned. You've become quite the chef. You're hired!"

Erika pulled her close to offer a second, less perfunctory kiss. She could feel Lucy clinging to her for balance, but Erika ended the kiss with a smile and a pat on her behind. "Now off with you and change your clothes. I'll watch your dinner while you're gone."

"But you have your work clothes on too."

"Yes, but unlike you, I know when to put on an apron."

Erika hung her suit coat on the back of a chair and took her apron from the hook in the pantry. As she tied the apron strings, she made a quick survey of the kitchen. Yes, Lucy had improved as a cook, but she still hadn't learned to clean up the cooking utensils during the process. The counters were littered with bowls, measuring cups and spoons. Erika shook her head and filled the sink with soapy water. As Erika washed the frying pan, she could hear Lucy talking to her daughter in the other room.

"Honey, I want you to finish your homework."

"Later."

"Now, please."

"I said, I'll do it later," replied the sullen voice.

Lucy's frustrated sigh was audible as she ascended the stairs.

Erika recognized a typical mother-daughter power struggle. She'd been teaching philosophy to college students for nearly forty years, and although this was her first time as a parent, she knew something about adolescent behavior.

The girl they had brought home from New York six months ago was still adjusting to life with her new family. Her strictly religious adoptive parents had trained her to be abnormally polite, almost obsequious, but lately, she was often rude beyond what could be excused by her high-functioning autism.

There were other signs that Emily's excitement at being reunited with her birth mother was beginning to wear off. Her ridiculously high IQ had allowed her to develop an enormous vocabulary and learn several languages, but now, her communication at home was often sullen grunts. Ironically, the more secure she felt with her new parents, the more she was becoming an ordinary teenager. The increased friction between mother and daughter was the predictable part. How it would manifest on a daily basis was anyone's guess.

After Erika finished washing the pans and cooking utensils, she went upstairs to change out of her suit and attempt to smooth Lucy's ruffled feathers. She found that Lucy had changed into a jogging suit and fuzzy slippers. She was sitting on the edge of the bed with a long face.

Erika sensed that Lucy needed a moment to herself, so she undressed without speaking. Taking off her dress shoes and suit after a day of classes and the long drive from Waterville gave her such pleasure.

"Sometimes, I don't think I can do this," Lucy suddenly said in a hopeless voice.

"Do what?"

"I missed my chance to be a real mother when I gave her up for adoption."

"Now, Lucy, that doesn't sound like you. You're the eternal optimist."

Lucy groaned. "But I never realized it would be this hard!"

"Of course, you did. Your specialty is family counseling. You know this is just garden variety acting out. Relationships between mothers and daughters are particularly strained at this stage of life."

"But it doesn't help when it's your own daughter. All the knowledge in the world doesn't help when you're in the middle of it!"

Erika sat down beside Lucy and put her arm around her. "It will be over soon. Yale was ready to take her. Remember, it was your idea to keep her at home so you could get to know one another."

"She'll be leaving home so soon, and she just got here!"

Erika nudged her with her arm. "Stop trying so hard and make the most of the opportunity." Erika kissed the pale, tender spot at Lucy's temple. Her hair, frizzy from standing over the stove, tickled Erika's nose.

"I like this view," Lucy murmured.

Erika looked down and realized that Lucy was admiring her cleavage. "You are absolutely shameless! You're miserable one minute, and the next, thinking about *sex*?"

"What do you expect? You're sitting there in your underwear with your boobs in my face!" Lucy gave Erika's nipple an appreciative caress. Because Erika wasn't expecting it, the touch of Lucy's fingertips tickled. Erika gave her a quick kiss to fend her off.

"Lucy, I absolutely adore you, but if you don't stir your stew, it will scorch on the bottom and spoil your lovely dinner."

Lucy pouted so Erika kissed her again.

"Give me a real kiss, and I'll go down and stir the stew."

Erika laughed. "You drive a hard bargain, woman. I had no idea what I was getting into with you. Perhaps I should have guessed from the red hair and the painted toenails."

"Stop complaining," said Lucy. "You love it!"

"I do. I will admit." Erika gave her a long, deep kiss. When they parted, Lucy's eyes were misty with desire.

"Now, go stir the stew!" ordered Erika.

With a sigh, Lucy got up and left. While Erika pulled on her jeans, her thoughts turned from sex to the long conversation she'd had with Liz on the way down from Waterville. Liz was still going on about that Chinese virus. No one at the college had said anything about it. When Liz had first mentioned it, Erika had asked the dean whether there were plans to expand online classes in the event of an outbreak. The puzzled look on Dean Clark's face made Erika think it was the first time she'd ever heard of it.

It was no longer Erika's job to worry about such things. She was glad to have given up being philosophy department chair and had sworn off administrative roles for good. As far as she was concerned, she was nearly out the door and would have happily retired had Morgan Collins not wooed her back with a generous offer and accommodations for working remotely. These days, she only went up to the Waterville campus once a week. She wouldn't miss the long drive now that they were on February break.

No, Erika needn't worry, but nevertheless, she did. She was a philosopher concerned with political communication and a serious person. Matters that didn't worry other people worried her. Liz was also a serious person who always paid careful attention to things she considered important. If she'd bent Erika's ear for an hour, her concern was undoubtedly warranted.

Erika searched for her slippers in the closet. It was harder to find things now that Lucy, with her dozens of pairs of shoes, had moved in. And yes, as Lucy had intimated before they'd become a couple, she kept a messy closet. Now, Erika almost wished she'd encouraged the architect's suggestion of separate closets.

Erika was relieved to come into the kitchen and find that the temperature between mother and daughter had gone down considerably. Emily was sitting at the kitchen table, doing her homework on her laptop. She waved to Erika to approach.

"Can you look at this? Does it make sense?"

Erika read the sentence Emily had written for her essay. "Yes, dear, perfect sense. But you need a comma." She tapped on the screen. "Right there."

Emily rolled her eyes.

"Never mind the eye roll. You asked," said Erika and began taking plates down from the cabinet to set the table. She gave Lucy's hip an appreciative caress on the way to the dining room.

"I saw that," said Emily, not looking up from her laptop.

"We are married, you know," said Erika. To her surprise, Emily gave her a radiant smile that rivaled her mother's.

"Yeah, I know. I was there."

"We'll be ready to eat soon," said Lucy. "Take your computer into the living room to finish your homework."

There was silence while they ate the succulent lamb stew. Erika sensed from Lucy's furtive glances at everyone's plate that she needed compliments. Lucy still wasn't as confident in the kitchen as she deserved to be. Since they'd moved back into Erika's house with its spacious, new kitchen, she'd diligently labored to improve her culinary skills. Maggie, who was a gourmet cook, was her mentor, but Lucy turned to Liz for down-to-earth recipes that she could manage on her own.

"It's delicious, my dear. You outdid yourself," said Erika with a warm smile.

"Really? It's good?"

"Excellent!" Erika turned to Emily. "What do you think of your mother's meal?" She nudged her gently with her elbow to encourage a response.

"Good, Mom. Really, really good," said Emily as if she'd just awakened from a day dream.

"Did your adoptive mother give you cooking lessons, Emily?" Erika asked, trying to strike up a conversation.

"Yes, but it was very plain stuff. We never had salad. They didn't like raw vegetables."

"Simple people," said Erika, trying to be kind.

"If Mom hadn't rescued me, I don't know what I would have done."

"You rescued yourself, Emily," said Lucy. "I just answered your call."

"Yes, I guess that's right," Emily replied doubtfully.

"What you did was very brave," Lucy continued. "I don't know if I could have done the same at your age."

Emily simply glowed under her mother's praise. "Thanks, Mom."

After dinner, Erika cleaned up the kitchen. The murmur of female voices from the other room was soothing. As a woman who'd been in open relationships all her adult life, she'd never imagined herself content to be with one woman or have a child. It was even more surprising to be married to a priest. Fortunately, Lucy respected her agnosticism and never tried to convert her. In return, Erika played the dutiful parson's wife and sat attentively during Lucy's Sunday sermons. Fortunately, they were always well reasoned and elegantly presented. Erika despised bad preaching almost as much as a shoddy argument.

When Erika turned off the kitchen light and went out to the living room, Emily was saying good night to her mother. "I have a history test tomorrow," she explained and planted a quick kiss on Erika's cheek. "Night."

Erika sat down beside Lucy and put her arm around her. Lucy leaned into her and Erika breathed in the fragrance of her wife's hair. Why did red hair seem to smell different?

"You have something on your mind, don't you?" Lucy asked, caressing Erika's thigh. It often surprised Erika that her wife could so easily sense her feelings. Sometimes, Lucy's perceptions bordered on being telepathic. Of course, being a psychotherapist helped. "What's bothering you?" asked Lucy with veiled concern in her green eyes.

"I had a long conversation with Liz on the way down. It was rather unnerving."

"Tell me," Lucy said, taking Erika's hand in hers.

"She's worried about this virus in China. She thinks there could be a pandemic, and if so, it could be quite devastating."

"Really?"

Erika nodded. "Yes, she says the virus is something new, and no one has natural immunity. As a consequence, many people could die."

Lucy's eyes widened. "You don't mean *here*?"

"Yes. *Here*. She explained how the infection rate could grow exponentially, overwhelming the medical system. The number of cases could rise so quickly, there wouldn't be enough hospital beds or personnel to treat them. We might be forced into dangerous ethical territory—triage to choose who will live and who will die."

Erika watched the expression on Lucy's face change as she processed this information.

"Why isn't anyone talking about it?" she asked.

"I don't know, but I suspect that it has something to do with the upcoming election. Besides, that madman in the White House is always doing something outrageous to divert attention, and most Americans are in a bubble, more worried about March Madness than an international crisis."

Lucy settled back into the safety of Erika's body. "What does Liz think we should do?'"

"She's still working it out, but she's been advising the services in town to bank critical supplies. She's made recommendations, but so far, no one seems to be taking her seriously."

"That's not good."

"No."

"Is there something I should be doing?" asked Lucy.

"Nothing I can think of…except pray."

"I thought you didn't believe in prayer."

"If this develops as Liz envisions, we'll all need to believe in prayer."

After that, they sat in moody silence until Lucy switched on the television to watch the ten o'clock news. There was brief mention of the virus in China. Clearly, it was still something "over there."

Erika nudged a sleepy Lucy awake after the weather report. "Come, love. Time for bed." They supported one another up the stairs. Lucy put on her nightgown, less fancy now that they were married, and seduction happened more naturally. Erika put on her lounge pants and Tee. They brushed their teeth side-by-side in the refurbished bathroom. The familiarity of the evening ritual was comforting.

Lucy was asleep before Erika switched off her bedside lamp. Or so it seemed. Erika leaned over to kiss her temple. "Good night, love," she said.

Lucy turned her face up for a kiss, which quickly became more than a good night gesture. She raised her nightgown and moved Erika's hand between her legs, where it was hot and wet.

"I thought you were asleep," Erika murmured into Lucy's ear.

"Almost. I always sleep better after we make love"

"Oh, my Lucy…" Erika moved closer. "I adore you," she whispered as she gently slipped her fingers inside her.

6

Maggie Fitzgerald awoke in the pitch dark and realized she was alone in bed. Even though the king-sized bed was enormous, and the super-firm memory foam never transmitted any movement, she always instantly knew when Liz wasn't there. It was the quality of the air in the room and the sound. It was different when Liz was gone.

Maggie glanced at the clock. The white digital letters read 3:35. That was the usual time when Liz's sleep was interrupted, and she got up to roam the house. It was so precise, almost as if she'd set an alarm. Sometimes, she went into Maggie's office to read, but tonight, the office was dark.

Maggie put up her long hair with a claw clip and grabbed her robe from the chair. As she pulled her arms into the sleeves, she called down the stairs, "Liz!"

No answer.

Maggie went downstairs to the second floor. Occasionally, Liz slept in one of the guestrooms if the snoring was really loud, but all the rooms were empty. There were two other possibilities. Liz could be watching a movie in the media room or working in her office. The media room was dark, so Maggie headed down the hall to the office. She could hear Liz's voice as she approached. She knocked on the office door and poked her head in. "Liz! What in God's name are you doing?"

"I'm talking to Erika's father." Liz turned the laptop in Maggie's direction. "Maggie just came in."

Maggie stared at the smiling, ancient face of Erika's father. "Good evening, Maggie," said Stefan Bultmann with a courtly nod. "That's a very nice nightgown."

Maggie modestly clutched her robe closer.

"Hey, watch it, Stefan. That's my wife you're talking to," Liz warned in a playful voice.

"Don't worry, Elizabeth, she's much too young for me."

"I don't know, Stefan. You're such a ladies' man. Is anyone off limits?"

The sound of a rich baritone laugh filled the room.

Maggie sat down in the chair next to Liz's desk. "What are you two doing? Do you have any idea what time it is?"

"Let's see," said Stefan, glancing up to see the time on the corner of his screen. "It is 3:47 to be exact."

"We are modeling potential Covid-19 infection rates in Hobbs," explained Liz, pointing to a spread sheet. "We're extrapolating from the Chinese and European data. Of course, it depends on the point of origin and the virulence of the strain. And projecting for a population of less than ten thousand people is highly speculative."

Maggie gave Liz a hard look. "And you're doing this in the middle of the night? How are you going to get up for work tomorrow?"

Liz shrugged. "I always do, don't I?"

"It's my fault, Maggie," said Stefan, his German accent still strong after years of living in America. "I saw Liz on Facebook, and I messaged her." Stefan's pale blue eyes looked contrite.

Liz came to his defense. "We were chatting about the data, and I figured I have a math professor at my disposal, so why not try to model it?"

Maggie glared at Liz, trying to look as disapproving as possible. Liz quickly turned the laptop around, so the camera lens was out of Stefan's view.

"I think my wife would like me to go back to bed," she explained to the screen.

"I think that's a good idea," Stefan's voice replied. "Good night, Elizabeth. Or should I say, Good morning?"

"Technically, yes."

"Then go to bed. I will talk to you later. Sleep well, my dear."

Liz closed her laptop and smiled at Maggie.

"Don't give me that innocent look, Liz Stolz. You're crazy. Messaging with a man in his nineties at four in the morning? That poor, old man needs his sleep."

"That poor, old man has insomnia just like I do. Better to chat with someone than stare at the ceiling for hours. He's lonely. He's a brilliant man. I don't think he gets enough stimulation in that senior residence. He misses his old friends from Yale."

"Then he should message with them in the middle of the night and let you sleep." Maggie got up and tugged at Liz's arm. "Come on, you. Back to bed. Now!"

Liz got up. "You're so bossy. Why did I ever think marrying you was a good idea?"

"Because you love me."

"Yes, unfortunately, I do."

They decided to take the elevator. Maggie continued to give Liz dirty looks as they rode up to the third floor. Liz conspicuously ignored her.

"Liz, you're obsessed with this virus thing. You need to stop thinking about it so much."

"I can't."

"You need sleep. Did I wake you? Was I snoring again? I'm so sorry. Why didn't you wake me?"

"I didn't have the heart. You've been so stressed waiting for your tumor markers to come back."

The elevator door opened, and they headed for bed. With a sigh, Liz got under the covers.

Maggie moved closer to Liz and stroked her thigh. "Remember when I was first diagnosed, and you held me every night? That helped us both get to sleep."

"That helped *you* get to sleep," Liz mumbled. "I don't like people touching me when I sleep."

"I guess we're old married people now."

Liz leaned up on her elbow. "Maggie, would you like me to hold you?" she asked impatiently.

"No, it's all right," said Maggie in her martyr's voice.

"All right. Come here." Liz put her arm around her. Maggie nestled against her breast. "Is that better?"

Maggie snuggled closer. "Yes. I can hear your heartbeat. It's very comforting."

"Yes, it means I'm still alive."

Maggie pinched her lightly. "That's not what I mean." Maggie reached under Liz's T-shirt and laid her hand in the flat between her breasts. "I can't feel it beating," she observed, "but I can hear it."

"Do you want me to explain why you can hear it but not feel it?"

"No, Dr. Stolz. Go to sleep."

Maggie's hand found Liz's breast. She wasn't especially aroused. It was meant as a friendly gesture, a way to claim her territory. She gently kneaded the nipple between her fingers, enjoying the familiar feel of it, the way it instantly rose to her touch.

"Keep doing that and you're going to have to make good on your tease," said Liz in a sleepy voice.

"You're not serious. You're half asleep." To make sure, Maggie slid her hand into Liz's pants. Between her legs, she found abundant, slick confirmation that Liz was serious. "We'll just have to take care of that," said Maggie, teasing gently. Liz liked strong, active lovemaking but she could be brought to her knees by the lightest touch.

"I never imagined anyone could drive me crazy with something so subtle," said Liz, opening her legs wider to get more of Maggie's touch.

"I've always known. You're sensitive to small gestures. It's one of the things I love most about you." Maggie repositioned herself so that she could reach her mouth to kiss her and found an enthusiastic response. A moment later, Liz had an orgasm. Maggie leaned her cheek against Liz's. "That was quick."

"Everything's quick when you know how," said Liz lifting Maggie's nightgown. There was no more talking after Liz began to stroke her and then enter her body with her fingers.

"Fuck me," said Maggie because it excited her to say the forbidden words. It excited Liz too. Maggie moved her pelvis in the same rhythm to Liz's fingers inside her. Maggie loved the strength of Liz's lovemaking, her powerful arm and shoulder flexing under the effort. It was all part of the pleasure, the feeling of abandoning herself to that strength, opening herself completely.

"Yes, like that." Maggie's breaths came faster. She was gripping Liz's fingers with all her might. During sex with a man, Maggie had seldom come on the inside, but with Liz the occasional surprise was wonderful. This was one of those times. Liz withdrew slowly and Maggie silently thanked her for the consideration.

Liz gave Maggie a sweet, deep kiss before rolling on to her back. "There. Now can you go to sleep?"

"As long as you stay close."

Liz sighed but she curled her body around Maggie's. "Sleep well."

A few moments later, Maggie heard the sound of Liz's breathing change and the very faint snore. It was sweet and comforting, a sound that could put Maggie to sleep rather than keep her awake. She wondered if Liz even knew she snored. She scoffed whenever Maggie told her.

❈❈❈

When Maggie awoke, Liz was gone, headed to Hobbs Family Practice for morning hours. Maggie was glad that Liz had mostly given up surgery except when called in to consult on a difficult breast cancer case or to help out at the urgent care. Maggie never complained when Liz chose to spend some of her new-found leisure time with her. They had been planning a month's long jaunt through Tuscany in the fall. Maggie looked forward to a time when she could have Liz all to herself.

Maggie had a quick cup of coffee before she showered and dressed. She hurried through her makeup because the kids would be arriving shortly. School was on winter break and closed for the week. When she was finished dressing, she surveyed herself in the full-length mirror. *Not bad for almost sixty-seven.* She always tried to give herself compliments. She'd found it a good way to keep up her self-esteem when she was going through the divorce from her husband.

Alina came in with the girls, bringing the fresh scent of February air in on their clothes.

"Chilly this morning," said Alina, stepping out of her boots before kissing her mother. The girls were bundled up from head to toe in parkas, snow pants, scarves and mittens. Their miniature galoshes were brightly colored and featured animal faces—smiling frogs for Nicki, cats and dogs for Katrina. Maggie helped Alina undress them.

"You could leave the girls here instead of driving all the way up and down from Scarborough," suggested Maggie as she poured hot chocolate into mugs for the children.

Alina glanced at the girls happily devouring blueberry muffins. "If you don't mind keeping them for a few days, I could use the break. I'm exhausted."

Maggie gave her daughter a critical look. Alina had been adopted by Maggie and her husband along with her older sister, so there was little resemblance between mother and daughter. Maggie wasn't exactly tall, but Alina was tiny. As fair as Maggie was, Alina was dark. Her hair was nearly black. When she was tired, obvious dark circles formed around her eyes.

"You look exhausted, sweetheart. I think you're working too hard."

"Maybe, but if I get this promotion, that will make a big difference. Money's still tight."

Maggie knew that Liz was secretly giving Alina money to help out, and she'd reduced the interest rate on the mortgage note she was holding from a ridiculously low percentage to zero. Only Liz thought her generosity was a secret. Of course, Maggie knew all about it since she'd mistakenly taken Liz's checkbook, thinking it was her own. She had never said anything. She'd allow her wife the illusion of privacy.

"Does it look like you'll get the job?" Maggie asked.

"My boss says my chances are good. They really liked the programming I've done about this Wuhan virus."

Maggie stared at her daughter. Now, she was talking about this virus too. "Liz is really worried. Should she be?"

Alina looked grave. "It's pretty scary. It could come here and be a big problem. With the way people travel nowadays, there's no containing it."

Maggie sighed. *Great. Another thing to worry about. As if my tumor markers weren't enough.*

"The coverage is so politicized," continued Alina. "Fox is saying it's a Democratic hoax. That's just irresponsible."

Maggie kissed her daughter. "Thank God, for ethical journalists like you. I'm proud of you for sticking to your guns."

Alina gave her mother a broad smile. "Can you keep them until Thursday night? I can really use the time to catch up on some work things and clean the house."

"Sure."

"And Liz won't mind?"

"You have to ask?"

Alina shook her head. "No. The world might be a crazy place right now, but fortunately, there are some things we can still count on."

7

Cherie looked through her closet to find something to wear to dinner with Brenda. She had a few western-style shirts from when she lived in Shreveport. Dallas was literally just down the road. All the bars had western nights when the patrons were expected to dress up. When Cherie was in school in Houston, she'd even bought a cowboy hat, but she'd left that with a friend when she'd moved. The western attire didn't mean she liked country music. In fact, she found it monotonous. To her ear, one song sounded just like another.

She had been tempted to suggest they choose another place for dinner, but Brenda had sounded so excited about this place, and Cherie didn't want to burst her bubble. It wasn't like Cherie to hold back her opinions, especially not from a potential girlfriend. Her counseling training had taught her that being clear and direct was the best policy, especially in a relationship. *Hold on there, Cherie. Isn't it too early to be thinking about the R-word?*

She pushed aside the western shirts she'd laid out on the bed and sat down. How had she gone from not being able to stand the woman to thinking about her romantically? *The uniform.* Mother Lucy was right about that. Without the uniform Brenda was funny, kind, and interesting. If she weren't a cop, Cherie would have been attracted to her from the start.

But being the Hobbs chief of police was an essential part of Brenda's life. And there was the gun. Most cops carried an off-duty weapon. Brenda would probably be wearing it during their dinner. The thought unnerved Cherie. She took some deep breaths and ordered herself to calm down. She decided that as long as she didn't have to see the gun, she'd be fine.

She chose a turquoise satin shirt with silver embroidery because it made her eyes seem even bluer. Her mother had always told her that her eyes were her best feature. The color of her mother's eyes had been amber, almost like those of a fox. As a child, Cherie thought the color was exotic and wished she could have fox eyes too.

Cherie went into the bathroom to refresh her makeup, then decided to start from scratch. It had been a long day and there wasn't much to salvage. Given the choice, she probably would have picked another night for this dinner, but this was the first weekend night Brenda had available.

When Cherie finished dressing, she went out to the living room where Jean-Paul was watching *The Five*. He looked up when she came in and whistled appreciatively.

"You look beautiful, honey. Just like your mama."

"Thank you, Daddy."

"Who's your lucky date?"

Cherie considered withholding information because she knew telling the truth would trigger a lot of questions. She finally decided in favor of honesty. "The police chief."

Jean-Paul's face took on an expression of exaggerated puzzlement. "I thought you hated cops."

"I do, but this one's different…at least, I think she is."

"Will you bring her in to say hello?"

"Maybe," replied Cherie with a sly smile.

"Of course, you will. You'll want Daddy to look her over, same as when you went out with the boys in high school."

"Nah, it's not the same. Not at all. Besides, how can you get a better reference than being the police chief?"

"What's her name?"

"Brenda…Brenda Harrison."

Jean-Paul looked thoughtful. "Yes, I think I knew that. I see the articles in the *Sentinel*. She's always doing a charity thing or giving some talk or other. I guess the police up here don't have much to do."

"Oh, I think you'd be surprised, Daddy. It just looks like a sleepy place." Cherie sighed at the thought of the mental health referrals she'd taken on to relieve pressure on Lucy and the one psychiatrist in town. The booming restaurants and motels on Route 1 were just a veneer. The real town below the surface had its share of drug addiction, depression, alcoholism, and domestic violence.

The doorbell rang. "That will be your lady cop, I guess," said Jean-Paul.

Cherie opened the door and found Brenda smiling like a fool. Cherie was relieved to see that she had dressed for a country night too. She was wearing a western-style leather vest over a buffalo-plaid, flannel shirt. Her blond hair was up, and she had that fresh-faced, rosy English look.

Cherie could see in Brenda's eyes that she approved of how she looked. She took her measure from head to toe. "Well, aren't you the perfect country date?"

"Would you like to come in and say hello to my father?" asked Cherie, tugging gently at her elbow.

Brenda glanced at her arm. "I guess I do."

"He wants to make sure you're good company for his little girl, so look sharp!"

Brenda laughed. "I'll try to make a good impression."

Cherie led her into the living room. Jean-Paul tried to get to his feet.

"Please don't get up, sir," said Brenda, reaching out her hand. "I'm Brenda Harrison."

"Hail to the chief." Jean-Paul grinned at his own cleverness. He took her hand. "Pleased to meet you, Chief Harrison. I'm Jean-Paul Bois. My friends call me JP."

"Pleased to meet you, JP."

"Where are you girls going to dinner?"

"There's a country bar and grill called The Eagle's Nest up in Lyman. Good Tex-Mex food. Great music."

When Jean-Paul glanced her way, Cherie could guess what he was thinking. He knew that country wasn't his daughter's favorite music, but he nodded pleasantly.

"I reserved a table for seven, so we probably should head out," said

Brenda. She raised her fingers to her forehead in a little salute. "Nice to meet you, Mr. Bois."

Cherie bent to kiss her father. "See you later, Daddy."

"Don't bring her home too late," he called after them.

After Cherie closed the door to the house, Brenda said, "Your father is adorable."

"He thinks he's still taking care of me when obviously, it's the other way around."

"It's sweet. Are you an only child?"

Cherie felt a flutter of anxiety. Did she want to go there?

"I had a half-sister from my mother's first marriage...but we lost her."

Brenda stopped walking, obviously waiting for Cherie to say more.

"I'll tell you another time," Cherie finally said.

"Okay," said Brenda in an uncertain tone. "Let's get in the truck. It's wicked cold out here."

Brenda yanked her seat belt around her. She arranged it to fall neatly between her breasts, which made Cherie give them an appreciative second look. *Stop looking at her chest,* Cherie ordered herself, but it had been a long time since she'd had sex and looking at Brenda's attractive breasts had given her a surprising jolt. She averted her eyes and deliberately faced forward.

"I hope you like this place," said Brenda, backing up the truck. "It can get a little rowdy at times, but it's mostly in good fun."

"Do they know you're a police chief?"

"Nah, I try to keep work life separate from my private life. Fortunately, Lyman is far enough from Hobbs that I never run into people I know." Brenda switched on the radio. It was preset to a country music station. "This is Luke Combs. He won best male vocalist last year." Brenda nodded her head to the beat.

"Is country your favorite music?" asked Cherie.

"I also like classic rock. You know, from when we were growing up. What kind of music do you like?"

"I lived in New Orleans, so jazz, of course. I love classical music."

"Actually, I do too."

It was so unexpected Cherie gasped a little. "You do?"

"Yes, but I didn't want to scare you off, so I was going to wait to tell you." Brenda pressed another preset and Maine Public Classical streamed through the speakers. "This will be a nice palate cleanser before we get to The Eagle's Nest."

"Thank you. This is nice."

"Sibelius is wonderful," said Brenda. "I really like the second symphony."

Cherie was intrigued. This was not what she'd expected. Not at all. But why shouldn't a cop like classical music? Cherie scolded herself for believing in stereotypes and assuming that Brenda couldn't have sophisticated tastes in music. She glanced at Brenda, smiling as she enjoyed the music, and suddenly found herself wondering where she carried her gun.

"Did you like living in New Orleans?" asked Brenda. "I always wanted to go there. It's on my bucket list."

"I loved it. I was happy to come back after we moved to Shreveport. I went to Tulane for college. How about you?"

"Oh, I went to John Jay. I'm blue through and through."

"Did you always want to be a cop?"

"Yep. Since I was a kid. My father was NYPD. He made sergeant before he died in the line of duty."

"I'm sorry," said Cherie.

Brenda shrugged. "It's always a possibility. And it's not just bad guys with guns. You can be writing a speeding ticket and some asshole might mow you down."

"Yes, I heard about that trooper who was killed on the interstate last year. A shame."

Brenda nodded. "Being a cop means putting yourself in danger so other people can be safe."

"How does that make you feel?" asked Cherie, genuinely curious.

Brenda turned to her with a frown. "You trying to shrink me?"

"No, of course not." Cherie realized her tone sounded unnecessarily defensive.

"But you are a shrink. Liz told me."

"That was my profession before I went back to school to become a physician's assistant. You get to a certain point in a career, and you just need a change."

"Really? Hasn't happened to me yet. I love police work."

Brenda turned into the parking lot of The Eagle's Nest. It was packed with vehicles, mostly trucks. "Busy night," she observed. "Like I said, sometimes I think they just come in to enjoy the animal warmth. Good thing we have reservations."

The line to get into the dining room clogged the entrance. Brenda led the way, threading through the crowd to the desk. "Two for seven...under Harrison."

The hostess grabbed two menus and led them to a table in the pub. Unfortunately, it was near the bar and the overflow of patrons waiting for drinks was uncomfortably close. "Sorry, it's the best I can do tonight," the hostess apologized. "As you can see it's packed. Can I put in a bar order for you? Corona is on special for a dollar a bottle."

"Can't beat that," said Brenda. "I'll have one."

Cherie chimed in, "Me too."

"Your waitress will bring it right over. Enjoy your dinner."

Cherie opened the menu curiously. Since coming north, she hadn't had much Mexican food because she was always disappointed. She would admit that she was spoiled. When she was doing her PA program at Baylor, she ate amazing Tex-Mex food.

Their beer arrived. Brenda popped her lime wedge into the bottle. Cherie carefully squeezed out the juice and set it aside.

"Concerned about the environment?" asked Brenda, watching. "I know it's hard to recycle the bottles with limes in them."

"Nope. I'm worried about germs. Citrus slices at bars are known to be riddled with bacteria and other filth."

"Now you tell me." Brenda picked up her bottle and eyed the pale lime wedge floating around in the beer. "Doesn't the alcohol kill everything?"

"No, but it's probably fine."

"My grandfather used to say, 'you have to eat a peck of dirt before you die.' He was a cop too."

"A peck is a lot of dirt. Does anyone even know what a peck is anymore?"

"Up here in Lyman, they do. Big apple orchard in this town." Brenda glanced at the people bringing in amplifiers and instrument cases. Every time the door opened cold air blasted into the room. "We're early. Music doesn't start until eight o'clock."

Cherie looked up from the menu. Brenda's eyes held a peculiar expression, and Cherie realized with some discomfort that it was pure attraction. Her first impulse was to glance away to break the spell, but she didn't. Instead, she found herself returning it.

"I don't mind. It's quiet now. We can talk."

The blue eyes across the table registered pleasure at that idea.

8

The loud music was making Brenda's ears feel like they were stuffed with cotton. The band was loud enough, but now everyone was singing along to "I Have Friends in Low Places." Cherie had to shout to be heard and even then, Brenda wasn't sure what she was saying. Why did she ever think The Eagle's Nest was a good place to bring a date? If she really wanted to get to know the woman, maybe they should get out of there and find a quieter place where they could talk.

But first Brenda had to pee. Beer went right through her, and that cheap Corona she'd been drinking desperately wanted a way out. She saw the line for the ladies' room snaking into the pub. She'd been watching out of the corner of her eye for a break. So far, it had only gotten worse. She'd just have to wait on the line.

"I have to powder my nose," Brenda shouted over the din.

Cherie shook her head. "I can't hear you," she mouthed and cocked her ear.

Brenda pointed to the line outside the ladies' room door. Finally, Cherie understood and nodded. Brenda threaded through the crowd, saying "excuse me" over and over again as she made her way through the crush of bodies near the stage. Fortunately, it looked like the line was moving quickly, but it was still a ten-minute wait. Brenda tried to be patient and think of something other than her bladder.

She still couldn't figure out the woman she'd left at the table. She seemed much more comfortable than the first few times they'd met, but she had such a calm, even demeanor that she was hard to read. Liz refused to tell her if she was gay, saying she'd have to ask her herself. Of course, that was the right thing to say, the professional thing. But they were good friends now. Couldn't she just wiggle her eyebrows or something to give her a hint? Brenda decided that until she was sure, she'd let Cherie take the lead.

Finally, she was in the bathroom. It was a mess after all those women had been through it. The floor and the vanity of the sink were littered with wet paper towels. She wished the women ahead of her would hurry up. All that beer was suddenly very impatient. Finally, the toilet flushed, and the stall door opened. Peeing had never felt so good.

There was a wait to use the sink too, but Brenda tried to be patient. She wanted to wash her hands after dealing with all that filth. Finally, she left the bathroom and retraced her steps, pushing through the crowd on the way back to their table.

As she approached, she saw something she didn't like. A man was sitting in her seat. Cherie was talking to him, except she didn't look happy. Brenda forced her way through the knot of people by the bar and hurried back to the table.

"Excuse me," Brenda said to the man. "That's my seat."

"Who are you?" he asked, looking up.

"I said, that's my seat."

"She said I could sit here."

"I did not!" Cherie protested in a righteous voice.

"Get up. The lady said she's not interested."

"Says who? Is she your date?"

"Get up," Brenda repeated in her most authoritative voice.

The man stood. He smelled strongly of whiskey. Brenda could see from his eyes that he was obviously drunk.

"Are you a dyke?" he asked Brenda.

"Look. I don't want trouble. Just leave us alone."

"You look like you could be a dyke. You lick pussy?" He stuck out his tongue and wiggled it suggestively.

Brenda adjusted her stance for a possible fight. She looked the drunk straight in the eye. "Jack, you've had too much. Now, move aside and give me my seat back."

"Or what?"

Brenda glanced at the bartender trying to get his attention. She preferred to have the management deal with the problem, but the bartender was clearly overwhelmed with customers.

Meanwhile, the man moved closer. He was rank with booze and body odor. Brenda resisted the urge to wrinkle her nose.

"Step back, dude. I mean it," said Brenda, refusing to give him an inch.

"Or what, dyke?"

Brenda could feel Cherie watching her carefully.

The man moved closer until he was nearly on top of her. Fortunately, he wasn't that tall, so he had no advantage in height. They eyed one another. His breath and his beard stank.

Brenda tried to get the bartender's attention again, but now the view of the bar was blocked. Brenda realized that she had no choice but to handle this herself. She reached into her pocket for her badge and waved it in the man's face. His mouth flew open like she'd slapped him, but instead of backing up, he shoved her away.

"Fucking cop!" he screamed. "Get the fuck away from me!"

Brenda pulled up her vest so she could reach her gun. Fortunately, the man's scream finally got the bartender's attention, and he raced over to their table. He stared at the badge and the gun on Brenda's hip. Brenda could feel Cherie was staring at it too.

"That's enough, Steve," said the bartender, grabbing him by the arm and yanking him in the direction of the entrance. "You had too much. Now get the hell out of here!"

The man gave Brenda a filthy look, but he headed toward the door. When Brenda sat down in her seat, she saw that Cherie looked queasy. Brenda felt pretty queasy herself. She hated off-duty confrontations. With all those people in there and the type who frequented the place, it could have gone bad really fast.

"I'm sorry you had to go through that," Brenda said. "I'd hoped I wouldn't have to pull out my badge."

"I want to go," said Cherie.

"Let's give him a few minutes to go on his way. I don't want another incident in the parking lot."

"I want to go," Cherie insisted.

"Okay." Brenda took some twenties out of her wallet. She handed the money to the puzzled waitress on the way out.

"Stay close to me," Brenda said, waving to Cherie to stand behind her as they headed outside. They hurried to the truck. Brenda clicked the doors locked as soon as they were inside.

"I'm sorry about that," said Brenda as she started the engine.

"I told him to leave," Cherie explained. "He just wouldn't."

"There are a lot of assholes up here."

"Why did you show him the gun?"

"I wasn't *showing* it to him. I just wanted access in case I needed it."

Cherie shook her head. "Take me home, please."

"Are you okay?" Brenda asked anxiously.

"No."

The silence was unnerving as they drove back to Hobbs. Finally, Brenda broke it by saying, "Well, my cover's blown at that place. I guess I won't be going back there any time soon."

"Why would you? It's loud. People are rude. That guy called you a dyke."

"Well, he's not wrong about that," said Brenda without thinking.

"It doesn't bother you?"

"Of course, it bothers me, but not enough to get into a fight or call the locals. I was just worried about protecting you."

"I don't need that kind of protection," Cherie said. Brenda realized from her tone that she was angry. Very angry. "I hate guns."

"You'd better get used to them. This is a constitutional carry state and a lot of people have them. Probably a lot of your patients carry concealed."

Cherie was staring out the window, even though it was dark, and there was little to see.

"I'm sorry," Brenda said again.

"I heard you the first time. And I understand why you did what you did. I just don't like it. Can you understand?"

"Were you frightened?"

"Yes, very frightened. Of him and of you."

"Of me?" Brenda asked incredulously. Then she realized why and was about to say, "I'm sorry" again but stopped herself. She focused on the road instead.

When she pulled into Cherie's driveway, Brenda intended to shut off the engine and walk her to the door, but Cherie jumped out as soon as she parked. "Thank you for dinner," she said. She closed the door harder than necessary and hurried toward the house. Brenda remained to watch until she was inside.

❈❈❈

Brenda awoke the next morning with a slight headache. She knew she shouldn't have had that glass of whiskey before bed, but she'd needed something to take the edge off. What an asinine idea to take a woman like Cherie to that kind of place! Of course, the men would hit on her. She was beautiful, and a lot of men assumed two women alone to be fair game.

While Brenda drank a cup of coffee, she gave herself a pep talk. *Don't be discouraged about Cherie. Figure out a way to make it up to her. You can do it.* She glanced at the clock. Seven o'clock. Liz would be up, but Maggie was probably still asleep. Brenda took her phone off the charger and called her friend.

"How did it go?" asked Liz. She never answered her calls with a simple hello, which could be unnerving. It was like she didn't have time for greetings and needed to get right down to business.

"It was a complete bust," said Brenda.

"Oh, no! What happened?"

"The place was packed. Some guy tried to hit on her. He was picking a fight. I had to pull out my badge, and she saw my gun."

"That sucks."

"I want to make it up to her somehow. Maybe I should invite her out to a nice place. What's open? Do you know?"

"Maybe you should leave it alone for a while. Let it blow over."

"Is that what you would do?"

"No," Liz replied with a chuckle in her voice.

Brenda laughed. "I didn't think so. What would you do?"

"I'd probably show up on her doorstep with flowers and a bottle of wine."

"Smooth, Dr. Stolz."

"The worst thing that happens is she doesn't open the door and you're back to square one. In that case, you can go home and drink the wine."

"Good point."

"But wait until later. You want to be close enough to evening, so you can sit down and drink the wine with her. Get a good Spanish wine. Nothing too expensive. You want it to be a friendly gesture, not like you're trying to impress her. Marques de Caceres is always reliable. Get the reserva."

"How do you spell that?"

"I'll text it to you."

"Later."

"Later."

In a moment, Brenda's phone pinged.

Liz was always good for her word.

❖❖❖

Brenda figured she'd head over to Cherie's around four. That was a civilized hour to begin drinking on a Saturday afternoon. It was also early enough to avoid the presumption of a dinner invitation. Brenda decided she'd stop at Hannaford first to pick up some flowers and the wine. The last time she'd shopped for groceries, she'd noticed they had some of those little daffodils.

She tried to pass the time getting her laundry done and catching up on her reports, but her eye always found the clock over the kitchen sink. Finally, it was getting on to three and she took a shower. She took extra time with her hair and makeup. As she was getting ready to go downstairs, she put her fingers over the sensor in the pistol safe by her bed. She was about to clip her off-duty gun to her belt when she stopped to think. Maybe this one time, it would be a good idea to leave the gun home.

Even bundled in a parka and wearing a polar fleece vest, Brenda felt strange without her pistol in the belt holster. She was more conscious of being without her gun than when she had it on her hip. That was one thing they trained into every cop. Always be conscious of your gun and know where it is at all times. Without it, she felt naked.

She found the little daffodils right away and spent a good five minutes trying to decide which one to buy, finally selecting the one that had two open blossoms and the most buds. She had to ask someone help her find the wine. Her Spanish accent was pretty good, but that didn't seem to make an impression on the boy she asked to help her find it.

As Brenda drove up to Cherie's house, she could feel herself tense. She screwed up her courage by reminding herself of what Liz had said: "The worst thing that happens is she doesn't open the door."

Cherie's car was in the driveway, so Brenda parked on the street. She took the wine out of the seat pocket behind her and snatched the plant out of the cup holder. "Here we go," she said aloud to herself as she headed to the door. She noticed the curtains in the front of the house were drawn. She rang the doorbell and stood back.

No answer.

After waiting a few minutes, Brenda was beginning to wonder if she'd have to accept the booby prize and go home and drink the wine. She waited another minute and rang again.

Finally, she heard the lock engage.

9

When Cherie opened the door, she realized she should have looked out first. There she was in an old Baylor sweatshirt, yoga pants and no makeup. She tried to smooth back her hair, but it was pointless. She'd run a quick brush through it that morning, but she had been running around since. She was sure it was a disaster.

The woman standing on the door stoop was carefully dressed and looking beautiful. Her pink cheeks just glowed. When she saw Cherie, she began to grin. The grin blossomed into a full smile that showed her perfectly white teeth. For some reason, she reminded Cherie of a yellow lab puppy. Brenda held out her arms. One held a little pot of blooming jonquils, the other, a bottle of wine.

"What's this?" asked Cherie.

"A peace offering."

"We're not at war."

"No, but I messed up big time last night, and I'm trying to make up for it."

Cherie looked uncertain, but she took the flowers and the wine. "Would you like to come in?"

Brenda smiled. "Thank you. I would." She stepped into the house, and Cherie closed the door behind her.

"I'm sorry it took me so long to get the door. My father's not having a good day with his breathing. I had to set up his oxygen."

"It's fine," said Brenda, still smiling. "I'm just glad to see you."

Cherie looked at the things in her hand. "Thanks for these. Let me just find a place to put them down." She nodded over her shoulder. "There are some hooks around the corner. You can hang your coat there," said Cherie pointing with the flowerpot. Brenda looked around the corner and took off her parka. "Come into the kitchen. I just put my stew on. I need to keep an eye on it until it comes to a simmer."

Brenda sniffed the air appreciatively, again reminding Cherie of a friendly puppy. As Cherie went in to stir the stew, she decided it was a perfect analogy. Brenda was affectionate and meant well, but she kept falling over herself by trying too hard.

"Come on. Daddy's in there too," Cherie called. "You can say hello to him."

Jean-Paul gave Brenda a smile when she came into the kitchen. "Back already?"

Brenda laughed. "It seems I can't stay away."

"Seems so," Jean-Paul agreed. "Please don't mind the get up," he said gesturing to the tank and tubing. "Can't breathe today."

"It's the dry air," explained Cherie, adjusting the tube to the nasal cannula. "It makes it hard for everyone to breathe, especially people with your kind of COPD."

"She kept nagging me to stop smoking," he said, thumbing in Cherie's direction. "But for the life of me, I couldn't quit. Not until I got this, and it landed me in the hospital with pneumonia."

"I told you so."

"Yes, you did. But it wasn't really the smoking that did in my lungs. It was the chemicals on the boats. We used all kinds of acids to etch metals. It would throw up green fumes like you wouldn't believe."

"My father was a mechanic in the Navy," Cherie explained. "They sent him down to New Orleans. That's how my parents met."

"You should have seen Cherie's Mama," said Jean-Paul, gazing into the air and smiling. "Goddamn! What a pretty girl she was, just like my Cherie. I took one look at her, and I knew I had to make her my wife."

Cherie loved the look that appeared on her father's face whenever he spoke of his wife. It was pure adoration. She wondered if she'd ever meet someone who'd look at her like that. She watched Brenda smiling and nodding as she listened to Jean-Paul go on about her mother.

"Cherie, I feel less dizzy now," Jean-Paul said. "I think I'll take my tank and go into the living room to catch the news."

"Okay, Daddy, but lay off the Fox News. It's pure propaganda."

He waved dismissively. "What do you know?" With effort, he got up from the kitchen chair. The wheels on his canister cart squealed a little as he rolled it into the living room.

Cherie stirred her stew and tasted it with the spoon.

"What smells so good?"

"Cajun beef stew. Mama's recipe."

"Really?" asked Brenda, taking a peek into the pot. "What makes it Cajun?"

"Sweet peppers. Some Jamaican jerk sauce."

"It smells delicious."

Cherie looked up. "Would you like to stay for dinner? We have plenty as you can see."

"I don't want to impose."

"You're not, or I wouldn't have asked. Sit down. Let me open the wine." She gestured to a chair and rummaged around in a drawer for the wine opener. "You even got the right color. How did you know?"

"I hope it's good. Liz recommended it."

"It's good. I've had it before." Cherie took down two wine glasses from the cabinet and poured a glass for each of them. "It probably should breathe a little, but this wine is usually good right out of the bottle."

She sat across from Brenda and reached with her glass to click Brenda's. "Cheers."

"Cheers," agreed Brenda.

"We have a couple of hours before dinner. I hope you don't mind."

"I don't mind. Not at all." Brenda's eyes looked dreamy, and Cherie could see a hint of that expression her father had when he spoke about his wife.

"Let me get you some snacks, so you don't faint waiting for the stew to be ready."

She felt Brenda's eyes on her back as she cut a block of pepper jack and arranged the slices on the cutting board. She took a box of rice crackers out of a cabinet.

"Don't make a fuss for me," said Brenda, lightly touching her arm, which felt good.

"It's no fuss," Cherie assured her with a warm smile. "Hold on a minute. Let me just give Daddy some of these." Cherie put crackers and cheese slices on a plate and brought them out to Jean-Paul. Of course, he had Fox News on again, but she wasn't about to argue with him with Brenda there.

"Thank you, honey," said Jean-Paul with a radiant smile. "You're an angel just like your mama."

"I don't know about that," said Cherie.

"I like your friend." He winked. "Not bad to look at either."

"Daddy!"

He grinned. "Go on. Don't leave her hanging there in the kitchen all alone."

Cherie found Brenda stirring the stew. "I hope you don't mind me interfering. It was boiling really hard. I turned it down a little."

"So, you can cook."

"Of course, I can cook. I always win the department chili contest."

Cherie shook her head. "It's probably rigged because you're chief."

"It is not!" protested Brenda indignantly. "It's a blind taste test."

Cherie laughed. "Only kidding. Oh, Brenda. You're so easy to tease."

"I'm very literal. Wit is not my thing."

Cherie looked her over carefully and wondered to herself, *what is your thing*? Her mind instantly started to roam, and then her eyes. Brenda glanced down, then up and smiled. Cherie realized she'd been caught admiring Brenda's breasts. Fortunately, with Cherie's coloring, blushing wasn't obvious.

"Sit down. I need to put the stew in the oven." She put the glass top on the old-fashioned chicken fryer and slid the pot in the oven. "Now, we don't have to worry about that anymore." She sat down and raised her glass.

Brenda put a piece of cheese on a cracker and handed it to Cherie, then she took a cracker for herself. She chewed thoughtfully and gazed out the window. "It's already staying light longer. That's nice."

"It is nice, but you didn't come over here to talk about that, did you?" She waited while Brenda took her time thinking it over.

"No, I wanted to talk about last night and what happened. That man was disgusting. I'm so sorry you had to put up with him."

"He called you a dyke."

Brenda nodded.

"So am I," said Cherie, "but I don't usually use that word to describe myself."

Brenda let out an exaggerated sigh of relief. "Thank God! My gaydar still works!"

Cherie laughed out of proportion to the humor in the statement.

"I like it when you laugh," said Brenda. "I like everything about you."

"I like you too, Brenda."

"I mean I *like* you."

"I knew what you meant. And I think I *like* you too, but there are some things we need to get straight."

Brenda sat back in her chair and eyed her cautiously. "Shoot."

"That's one of them."

"It's just an expression. You know that."

"I hate guns."

"You made that clear last night. It's okay. A lot of women are afraid of guns." Brenda lifted the hem of her polar fleece to show that she wasn't wearing her off-duty pistol. "I left mine home in your honor. It was a big deal for me. I feel naked without my gun."

Cherie was touched by the sensitivity of the gesture. "Thank you. That means a lot to me."

Brenda nodded. "I'm not saying I'll always do it, but it seemed important today."

Cherie searched Brenda's earnest blue eyes and decided she deserved an explanation. "I think I need to tell you why guns frighten me so much."

"Okay," said Brenda, a little frown puckering her brow.

Cherie took a sip of wine for fortification. It had been hard enough to tell the story to Mother Lucy.

Brenda picked up a cracker and began to nibble on it. "Go ahead. I'm listening." Cherie could clearly read the anxiety in her eyes. Usually so bright and sunny, they seemed to cloud over when she was worried.

"I'm black," Cherie said.

"What?" Brenda sat up straight, looking completely puzzled.

"I know I don't look black, but I am."

"You can't be!"

"I am. My mother was biracial. Her mother was black, probably biracial too. Her skin wasn't very dark. But as far as I know, I am one quarter black. In the old days, they would call such people 'quadroons.'"

"That's impossible," said Brenda. She looked mystified and slightly angry.

Cherie had been carefully watching for an angry response. That would be a bad sign, and a reason to limit what she shared. Then Cherie realized that Brenda was only confused and surprised, not angry.

"That's impossible," Brenda repeated. "You look as white as I am."

"I know, but I'm not. I can pass for white, but I'm not. I identify as a black woman."

"Why? Wouldn't it just be easier to let people think you're white? I mean especially up here. Everyone's white except for the Somalians up in Portland and the native Americans."

Cherie shook her head. "It's not easier for me to keep the facts from people I care about."

Cherie watched Brenda's eyes soften. "Who else knows?" she asked.

"You mean, besides my father? Liz Stolz and my coworkers at Hobbs Family Practice. Mother Lucy."

"Does it really matter? To me, you're white."

"Yes, it matters, and I'm going to tell you why. I could always pass for white. At some point I realized what a privilege it was to be white. I could go places my sister couldn't. Nobody ever followed me in a store thinking I might steal something, but they watched my obviously black sister like a hawk. It embarrassed me. It got to the point that I didn't even want to be seen with her…my own sister. The white part of me looked down on the black part." Brenda, whose eyes were focused directly on hers, shifted anxiously in her seat. "Then my sister died and everything changed. We were in college, riding back from a party, when we got pulled over for a broken taillight. A young, very nervous trooper approached with his gun drawn."

"Don't tell me that fucking cop shot her!"

"Yes. He did."

Brenda looked sickened. "What happened?"

"We'd been smoking some pot. I guess he could smell it on our clothes. He ordered my sister to get out of the car. When she hesitated, he shot her."

"Jesus Christ!" The horror spread across Brenda's face. "How could he do something like that?"

"No reason. She wasn't threatening him. We were just two women. No threat at all."

"I'm sure you weren't."

"When he shot her, the bullet went through her and hit me in the shoulder. Fortunately, I was just grazed by the bullet."

"What happened to the trooper?"

"Nothing. He got off. Not even a reprimand."

"That's wrong. It would never happen up here. Not even in New York in the worst neighborhoods."

"Things are different in the South. It's not easy to be a woman there. Black or white."

"I could never live in the South," said Brenda, shaking her head. "We have yahoos up here too, like you saw last night, but not like in the South. Even the women are backward."

Cherie gave her a hard look.

"Not you, of course."

"Don't lump everyone together."

"Why not? A little boy trooper, who was probably poorly trained and scared shitless, shot and killed your sister. Because of him, you hate cops. That's why you were always so strange around me. You paint us all with the same brush."

Cherie raised her chin defensively. What Brenda had said was uncomfortably close to the truth. "Most of the time, I can put it aside. I had to work with the police in my counseling practice from time to time. Professionally, I can be objective."

"Except with me."

"Except with you because I knew you had your eye on me."

"And that made the prejudice worse? Makes no sense."

"No, but phobias after trauma rarely make sense. Your uniform and your gun trigger me."

"Well, that's a problem," said Brenda, raising her brows.

"Yes, it is."

"Does that mean you don't want to see me?"

"No, it means I have to work on it."

"How?"

"I'm seeing Mother Lucy for therapy. She suggested the idea of seeing you socially…without the uniform and the gun."

Brenda nodded, evidently understanding. "But I blew it last night when that asshole confronted me."

"That whole scene was bad. The noise. The threats. His calling you a dyke. Seeing you ready to draw your gun was the icing on the cake."

Brenda, looking mortified, stared at the bowl of crackers. "I'm the asshole. I should never have brought you there. I knew it was rough. But there are so few places open this time of year."

"If you wanted to let me know you were interested, why not a romantic dinner at your place?"

Brenda glanced up shyly. "I didn't want to push too hard….just in case you weren't gay…or interested."

"Ah," said Cherie. "Your kitchen is too close to your bedroom." She let out her breath in a long stream as she thought about what to say next. "And here you are, and I look like shit in my old sweats, no makeup, hair a mess..."

Brenda smiled her adoring puppy smile. "I think you look beautiful." Brenda had said exactly the right thing, and she had that dreamy look in her eyes again.

Cherie forced herself back to earth. "We got off to a bad start," said Cherie, "but that doesn't mean we can't start over."

"Good. So, when can you come over for that romantic dinner?"

Cherie laughed softly. "Let's start with this dinner first."

10

Lucy had twenty minutes before her next counseling session. She decided to head over to the church to see how the choir practice was going. Not wanting to disturb the singers, she opened the side door of the church as quietly as she could. It was heavy and she had to lean into it a little. She genuflected as she passed the altar, a habit from her Catholic upbringing and the High-Church influence of her seminary mentors.

As she turned, she saw Liz Stolz sitting in one of the pews. She was a little surprised, although it was not unusual for Liz to stop in to listen while the a cappella group practiced. The group was Maggie's project, and Liz was her wife's most devoted fan.

Lucy slid into the pew beside Liz. "How are you?" she asked. She was concerned because Liz looked frazzled. She was never one to make a big fuss over her appearance. She'd given up trying to tame her unruly gray hair and had it cut to look naturally disheveled. She was wearing makeup but looked pale. "Are you all right?" Lucy asked, patting her thigh.

Liz let out a huge sigh. "I'm frustrated. That's why I came over to listen to the choir. I thought the music might calm me."

"What's going on?"

"I'm trying to help the town get ready for the coronavirus, and I'm getting nothing but pushback from the selectmen. They don't want to allocate money for something that might not happen. Same with the fire department. There are already shortages, and when they finally get around to ordering PPE, they might not be able to find it. I bought masks last month when I first heard about this thing, and even then, they were hard to get. I had to order OSHA masks from a woodworking supply house. They're actually better than medical grade, so that's good, I guess."

Lucy scrutinized Liz's face. Her blue eyes were always intense, but now even more so. "How worried about this virus are you?"

"Very worried. Except, I seem to be the only one."

Lucy took Liz's hand and squeezed it. "I believe you. What can I do to help?"

That question brought an instant smile to Liz's lips. Her whole face brightened. "Thank you, Lucy. I'm going to need your help."

Lucy felt herself tense as she listened to Liz's suggestion to close the Sunday school and after-service fellowship. She held her breath when she heard her name several platforms for hosting services over the internet.

"You don't really think it could come to that?"

Liz nodded solemnly. "It's surging in Italy. That's what we could see here if we don't take precautions now."

"Would you be willing to join a meeting with me, Tom, and the warden?"

"Sure," said Liz. "I wish everyone in town would take it seriously. Thank you."

"No need to thank me." She smiled and saw her smile mirrored in Liz's face. "How's the practice going?" she asked, gesturing toward the choir loft.

"They've been talking more than singing. It doesn't matter. I'm so frustrated, I'm just sitting here, zoning out."

Lucy laughed and patted Liz's hand. "A church is a good place to zone out. You never know. You might even hear voices." She wiggled her eyebrows.

Liz groaned. "Don't try that with me, Lucy. You know you'll never convert me."

"Never say never." Lucy realized she needed to pay attention to the time. She slipped her hand into her pocket for her phone, but remembered she'd left it in her office. "Liz, what time is it?"

Liz pulled back her blazer sleeve and showed Lucy the time on her watch.

"Gotta go," said Lucy, getting to her feet. "Give Maggie my love."

"Say hi to Erika. Tell her I'm coming over with scotch this Saturday. Otherwise, I never see her."

"I'm sure she'll be glad to see you." Lucy gave Liz a quick kiss.

"I'm going to remember that one, Lucy. If this virus comes to town, we may not be able to do that for a while. Not even shake hands."

"Oh, I'm going to miss that," said Lucy.

"You especially. You're the most affectionate person I know."

Lucy headed toward the door. "Keep up the good work!" she called to the singers in the choir loft before she left.

***

Cherie was waiting in the anteroom to Lucy's office. She looked especially attractive today in a heather-blue sweater that complemented her unique coloring.

"Come in, Cherie," said Lucy, opening the door to her office.

Cherie closed the book she was reading and followed her.

"I'm glad I'm not the only one who still reads paper books," said Lucy as she took her seat behind the desk.

"Yes, there are a few of us. This is an old book from college. *The Plague* by Albert Camus. Dr. Stolz suggested I read it again."

Lucy nodded thoughtfully. "Yes, my wife suggested I read it too. Is it good?"

"It's a philosopher's look at a pandemic. Very interesting. I'll lend it to you when I'm done."

"Yes, please, if you don't mind."

Lucy closed her laptop so it wouldn't be a distraction during the session. "This is our fifth session. That's all I'm allowed for pastoral counseling. We have two options going forward. I can take you on as a client in my practice, or we can continue talking as friends."

"I don't want to take advantage of you or the parish. My insurance will pay."

Lucy liked that answer because it spoke to Cherie's character. She did things by the book, unlike her boss, who never met a rule she liked.

"You're not still worried about Dr. Stolz finding out?"

Cherie shook her head. "It's fine."

"Okay. Remind me to get your information when we're done today."

Lucy sat back in her chair to make a quick evaluation of the physical state of her client. As always, Cherie was dressed attractively and carefully made up. She looked perfectly professional.

"How was your week?" asked Lucy.

Cherie flashed a quick grin and rolled her eyes. "Very interesting."

"Tell me."

"Well, I followed your advice. I asked to see Brenda when she was off-duty."

"You mean you asked her out on a date? Good for you!"

"Well, it wasn't meant to be a date. Just an experiment, you know. But she took it as an invitation to a date."

Lucy chuckled. "Saved you the trouble of explaining your intentions. So, good. You went from zero to sixty like that." Lucy snapped her fingers. "And how did it go?"

"It was a disaster."

"Oh, no!" Lucy exclaimed. "What went wrong?"

Cherie sighed. "She took me to a country-western bar called The Eagle's Nest. Not a good scene."

"I've been there. Very loud. Full of sweaty, smelly men with beards."

Cherie gave her a curious look. Yes, it probably didn't seem like a place a former opera singer would frequent. "I like country music," explained Lucy. "So does Maggie Fitzgerald. We go up there sometimes when there's a band we like."

"Two gorgeous women alone? Do they hit on you?"

"Of course!" said Lucy with faux indignation.

"Aren't you intimidated?"

"Honey, I have a brown belt. I'm not afraid."

Cherie laughed. "You never cease to amaze me, Mother Lucy."

Lucy took it as a compliment. "I amaze myself sometimes," she admitted candidly.

"A very drunk man sat down at our table when Brenda went to the ladies' room. He was really obnoxious. When she came back, it almost came to blows. She had to flash her badge and reach for her gun. She didn't draw it, of course, but I saw it."

"And that triggered you."

"Yes. I broke out in a cold sweat. I had trouble breathing."

Lucy let out a big sigh. "We'll have to figure out how to help you get over the gun thing, especially if you're dating a police chief." She pursed her lips and gazed out the window while she thought. "I'm going to tell you something personal because I think my solution could help you." She paused to make sure she had Cherie's attention. "I was date raped."

"No! That's terrible!"

"Yes, it is, but I ended up with Emily, and that's just some of the good that came out of it. I was also called to be a priest."

"But how did you overcome the trauma?"

"Years of therapy. The love of a very dear woman who helped me find my way back to God. One thing she suggested made a big difference in my recovery. " She paused for effect. "I began martial arts training. That helped me feel strong. It helped me feel I had some control. Suddenly, I felt less like a victim. Instead, I was a big, powerful Amazon." Lucy pumped herself up in imitation of a bodybuilder.

Cherie laughed. "Mother Lucy, you're so tiny, but you're right. You are powerful. How does this apply to me?"

"Master the thing that frightens you."

Cherie took a moment to consider the idea. "How?"

"Well, if you're afraid of guns, you could take Liz Stolz's firearms class. She teaches one just for women. Or, more romantically, you could ask Brenda to teach you how to shoot."

Cherie looked stricken at the suggestion. "I don't know…"

"Okay, maybe that's too much. Start with Liz's class. I took it. It helped me get over my fear of guns. And believe me, they terrified me. Now, I have a healthy respect for them, but they don't scare me half to death."

Cherie shook her head. "I don't know if I could do that. I'm not saying it's a bad idea…."

"Just think about it."

"Okay. I will. But there's also the problem of the uniform. When Brenda's not in uniform, I feel perfectly comfortable with her. I see her as just another woman. That's not true," said Cherie with a shy look. "I see her as a very attractive, sexy woman."

"And that's great. She is...attractive and sexy."

"But I don't know how I'll react when I see her wearing that damn uniform."

Lucy thought for a moment. "Some women find uniforms a turn on."

Cherie looked impatient. "That's never been one of my fetishes."

"Yes, but think about what certain uniforms suggest: authority, strength, power, discipline. Used for good, those are all good qualities. If you hadn't been traumatized by a policeman, Brenda's uniform could be sexy."

Cherie's frown relaxed. She looked thoughtful. "It was a turn-on when she came to my defense and flashed her badge. I felt protected and cared for. Not in the moment, of course. I was too scared, but later when I was remembering it."

"What if Brenda wore another kind of uniform? A military or pilot's uniform. Would you still hate it?

"No, it's only the police uniform."

"That's because you have bad memories of the night your sister was killed. What if you made new memories?"

"How?"

"Cherie, let's get creative here. What else can you do when you see Brenda in her uniform?"

"You mean, besides run and hide?"

Lucy nodded enthusiastically and waved her hands toward herself as if they were playing charades. "Come on. What would you like to do with Brenda if you could?"

"Kiss her?"

"Good way to start. What comes next?"

"Undress her…"

"Yes!" said Lucy, throwing up her arms triumphantly. "Another way of taking control of the thing that scares you."

"Mother Lucy, you are full of surprises!"

Lucy let out an enormous sigh. "Unfortunately, people say that all the time."

"People don't usually expect priests to talk about sex."

Lucy wagged her finger. "See? Now that's a big misconception. Priests have to talk about sex more than you might think. I counsel couples who are going to marry. Women come in here with marital problems. You know. You're a therapist. And sex is really important to intimacy. It should be talked about openly."

Cherie shook her head. "Undress a cop. Now, why didn't I think of that?"

11

Liz tried not let her disapproval show while Cherie gave her report on the stock of personal protective equipment at the town agencies. The police department's request was on backorder. The fire department hadn't done a thing, still waiting for budget approval. Only the ambulance corps had full stock.

"That's the best I could do, Dr. Stolz. I'm sorry."

"It's not your fault, Cherie. I know you're doing your best. How's it going with Chief Harrison? Is she being helpful?"

Cherie glanced away. "Yes."

Liz tried to read what that meant. She hadn't heard anything since she'd recommended the wine as a peace offering. For all she knew, things between them could be worse.

"Brenda has a good head on her shoulders," said Liz. "She made it to lieutenant in one of New York's toughest precincts."

"Yes, she told me." That statement spoke volumes. At least, they were speaking.

"Okay," said Liz to wind down the meeting. "Let's keep after these people. They won't do what we need them to do unless we push them. You got this?"

Cherie closed her iPad. "Yes, Doctor, you can count on me."

"Good. If you need me to step in here, let me know. Now, is there anything I can do to help you?"

Cherie's eyes focused intently on hers. "Tell me how to sign up for your gun class."

Liz was so startled she couldn't modulate her reaction fast enough. "Well, that's certainly not what I expected," Liz admitted candidly. "Why? Are you thinking of getting a gun?"

"No. I want to get over my fear of guns."

Liz exhaled a long breath. In every class there were a few people, mostly women, who were taking it solely to get over their fear. They were usually difficult students, who required a lot of personal attention and literally, handholding.

"The schedule is on the fish and game website, but I won't be teaching any classes until July. The indoor range is closed for renovations." Liz glanced out the window. It was a nice day, warm for March. "We still have a couple of hours of daylight. I'm done for today. Would you like to go to the range?"

"You mean *now*?" "

"Why not? Classes are great, but it's easier to learn to shoot one-on-one, especially if you're anxious. There's no peer pressure."

"Well…okay," Cherie said uncertainly.

Liz scrutinized her. "I don't want to force you if you're not ready. Maybe you should take some time to think about it."

Cherie's face registered determination. "No, the sooner the better."

Liz unlocked the cabinet where she kept her gun in a special purse with a holster in the side pocket. "We need to swing by the house first and pick up a few things. Let's go."

Cherie was silent while they rode to the house. Liz could practically feel her anxiety as Cherie stared straight ahead, limbs rigid, her hands gripping her knees so tightly the knuckles were white.

"What made you decide to do this?" Liz finally asked to break the silence.

"It was Mother Lucy's suggestion."

Liz barked a little laugh. "I should have known! Lucy always comes up with the most unorthodox solutions."

"She thinks if I can learn to handle a gun, I will be less anxious around them."

Liz nodded thoughtfully. "There's something to that idea, and it does work. In fact, I've made my whole life about getting over my anxiety."

"What do you mean?"

"When I was about seven, I had an accident. I was playing with my brothers and put my arm through a glass door. That was in the days before they used tempered or safety glass. When I pulled my arm back, the glass sliced open my arm from the wrist to the elbow right down to the bone. The cut came within millimeters of the radial artery. I could have bled out on the spot."

"I've seen that long scar on your arm and wondered where it came from," said Cherie.

"My mother became paralyzed by the sight of me lying on the kitchen floor, blood everywhere. All she could do was stare in horror. Fortunately, we had a housekeeper who had some nursing experience. She knew to put pressure on the wound. She was able to calm my mother enough to drive me to the doctor. He closed the wound in his office with only novocaine for anesthesia. I remember every suture…all twenty-two of them."

"Wow. That must have been painful," Cherie said, grimacing.

"Believe me, it was, but that was just the beginning. As I was growing up, I witnessed other instances when I couldn't count on adults to deal with health emergencies. I became a world-class hypochondriac. Every small symptom became the reason for a panic attack. I think that's the reason I studied medicine…to have some control over my health."

"That's quite a story."

"But it proves Lucy's suggestion is smart. She knows that mastering your fears goes a long way."

"She told me why she became a brown belt."

Liz smiled at the memory of Lucy defeating men twice her size in a martial arts demonstration at the parish fair. "Never get into a fight with that woman. She may be small, but she could easily kill someone."

Cherie looked skeptical. "She could never kill anyone. I've never met anyone so full of love."

"Even so, I'd never want to test that assumption."

When they arrived at the house, Liz parked in front of the garage. "Let me run in and get what we need. I'll just be a minute," she said, hopping out of the truck.

Maggie came downstairs from her office. "You're home so early. Is everything all right?" she asked with a worried look as she reached for Liz to give her a kiss.

"Yes, fine. I'm taking Cherie to the range to teach her to shoot. I just came home to get my equipment. I hope I have enough ammo."

At that, Maggie looked even more worried. "Are you sure it's a good idea?"

"No, but Lucy suggested it, and she knows what she's doing. At least, I hope she does."

Liz hurried to the basement and unlocked the gun safe to remove two .22 pistols and a box of ammunition. She took earmuff hearing protectors, safety glasses and targets from a nearby cabinet and threw everything into the canvas tool bag she used to carry her equipment to the range.

"What did you need to get?" asked Cherie curiously as Liz stowed the tool bag behind the driver's seat.

"Hearing and eye protection. As a certified safety instructor, I'd be setting bad example if I took you to the range without PPE."

"Seems like PPE is the thing of the hour."

Liz pulled on her seat belt. "That it is."

The long dirt road to the fish and game club was full of potholes. The truck bounced up and down until Liz was almost seasick. She slowed to a snail's pace. When they approached the gate, she reached over Cherie's lap to take her magnetic pass out of the glove box. "We keep it locked," she explained. "We don't want people coming in and getting hurt." Liz could tell Cherie was only half-listening. She was rigid and pale. "Don't worry. You can do this. I'll make sure everything we do is absolutely safe. Okay?"

"Okay," said Cherie, but she didn't sound convinced.

They parked at the end of one of the shooting bays and got out. Liz carried the canvas tool bag to a graying picnic table. There was nothing fancy about the outdoor range. Earthworks were piled high to stop overshot bullets from landing in the wrong place. Behind the gun club were acres of open land. Separating the bays were twenty-foot high concrete barriers.

Liz walked down the bay to put up some targets on the plywood backboards. The boards were shot up from last season and it was hard to find purchase for the push pins. She'd deliberately chosen traditional bullseye targets because the type with a human figure always seemed to alarm new shooters.

She walked back to the truck, where Cherie stood, hugging herself even though it wasn't cold.

"Are you ready?" Liz asked.

"As ready as I'll ever be."

Liz handed her a pair of safety glasses and switched on one of the hearing protectors. "They're electronic and designed to block the sound only when it reaches a certain decibel level. That means we can hear one another, and you can hear me giving you instructions." Liz handed one to Cherie, who put it on.

"Can you hear me?"

"Yes."

Liz opened one of the pistol cases and Cherie instantly recoiled.

"Take it easy," said Liz. "They're not loaded. Let me show you." She took out the pistol, dropped the magazine into her waiting hand. After she racked the slide, she sighted down the barrel. "This is how we make sure the gun is empty. This pistol also has a little window so you can see if there's a round in the chamber, but I never trust it. I always check twice."

Liz put a box of ammunition in her pocket and gestured to Cherie to follow. They walked down the bay to a little wooden table about ten feet from the targets. Liz demonstrated how to load the magazine. "This is called a magazine, not a clip. If you call it a clip that just says you don't know what you're talking about. Real shooters like to make fun of people who don't use the right vocabulary. Do yourself a favor and learn to talk the talk."

She finished loading the magazine but left the slide open. "When we're on the range, we keep the slide open and pointed down range, so other shooters know there's no round in the chamber. When it's your turn to shoot, you rack the slide back like this." Liz demonstrated. "Are you ready?"

Cherie shook her head.

"You want me to show you first?"

"Not really…but go ahead."

"First, here's how to stand." Liz put one foot in front of the other and crouched a little. "You want to have a good, solid stance. In a real shooting situation, you don't want someone to be able to push you over." Liz gave Cherie a shove from her shoulder to emphasize her point. "These .22 rounds won't give you much recoil, but you want everything about your stance to be rigid and solid for accuracy and safety." Liz showed how to extend her arms and curl one hand over the other under the trigger. "When you shoot, you're going to align the marks and aim at the center of the target. I'll show you that later. Now stand behind me about six feet. I don't want the ejected casings to hit you."

Liz emptied the magazine. She put the gun down and turned around. Cherie was back at the old picnic table, hugging herself. Liz sighed, wondering if they should try again another day. She walked back and sat down beside Cherie. "You okay?" she asked, rubbing her back.

"No," murmured Cherie.

"Want to leave?"

"Yes, but give me a moment."

"Okay," Liz agreed and sat back to enjoy the cold air and silence while Cherie pulled herself together. It was too early for bird song, but a few crows complained as they flew overhead.

Finally, Cherie sat up and turned to Liz. "I came this far. Let's try again."

Liz nodded. She opened the other pistol case. Once again, she went through the drill to make sure the gun was empty and replaced the empty magazine. She sat down beside Cherie. "Always keep your finger off the trigger until you're ready to shoot. Just lay your finger along the slide like this." Liz showed her how, then reached for Cherie's hand. She felt the instant tension. "Don't look at it. Just feel it in your hand."

Cherie snatched her hand away.

"It's just a thing," said Liz in a calm voice. "Without human intervention, it has no power. It's just a tool like a screwdriver or a scalpel."

"Screwdrivers or scalpels don't kill people."

"No, but they could."

When Liz reached for Cherie's hand again, this time she took the gun.

"It's heavier than I expected."

"It will be even heavier when it's loaded. Wait til you hold my 9mm. How does it feel?"

"Strange."

"I know. It always feels strange to hold a real gun for the first time."

"Let's do this," said Cherie impatiently. "I just want to get it over with."

Liz looked at her carefully. The poor woman was plainly terrified.

"You're sure?"

Cherie nodded and Liz escorted her back to the little table. She loaded her own magazine to reinforce the earlier lesson, then watched while Cherie loaded hers. Liz repeated the stance demonstration and showed how to line up the sights. "Remember to aim and then squeeze the trigger. Don't jerk it. And keep your eyes open. Loud noises make people want to close their eyes. Don't." She patted Cherie's shoulder. "Okay. Give it a try." She stepped back to avoid the ejected shells.

The first time Cherie positioned herself to shoot, she was shaking uncontrollably. She carefully set the gun down on the little table. Liz waited, gazing at the brilliantly blue sky overhead. Finally, Cherie raised her arms and fired a shot, then another. She wasn't hitting the target, shooting low because she was too tense and still shaking, but then she started to get the hang of it. She began hitting the paper around the bullseye and finally placed a few shots on the target. Liz could hear the slide rack open when the magazine emptied. She approached and gave Cherie an encouraging pat on the shoulder.

"Congratulations. You did it." Still trembling, Cherie turned into Liz's arms and began to cry. "That was a big step you took," Liz whispered into

Cherie's ear as she stroked her back soothingly. "You should be proud. I know I'm proud."

Cherie clung to her for a long moment, then finally let go.

"Would you like to try it again?" Liz asked.

Wiping away her tears, Cherie nodded.

They continued the target practice until they'd used up all the ammunition. Liz encouraged Cherie to shoot her 9mm to get the feel of it. The recoil startled her, but she continued until she emptied the magazine. Finally, they collected their targets.

"You have a good eye, Cherie. Well done."

"Thanks," murmured Cherie.

Liz handed her a rusty rake, explaining, "We always clean up after ourselves when we shoot. We used to recycle the brass, but it's too expensive now." Liz took another rake and the old snow shovel standing next to it and showed how to collect the spent shell casings. "Good range etiquette is important," said Liz, pouring the casings into an old oil drum.

"You say that like you expect me to come back here."

"Now that you know what to do, maybe you can ask Brenda to take you shooting."

"We'll see," replied Cherie vaguely. "But I would appreciate it if we could do this again."

"Sure. Next nice afternoon when we're both free."

12

"What does Liz think?" asked Alina.

"She's worried, especially because no one seems to be taking it seriously."

"Well? What should we expect? The man in the White House is saying it will be gone by the warm weather…that it's a Democratic hoax!"

"Calm down, Alina. We share your views. Don't preach to the choir."

"So, can I talk to her?"

"You know Liz won't give you any statements about the virus. She doesn't want to be on the record with her opinions about politics."

"Of course, not…and especially not in that fucking Republican town of yours."

"Alina!" Maggie had tried so hard to teach her children to avoid bad language, but Alina had always been a rebel. Of Maggie's two adopted daughters, she had been the more difficult. After the horror of their early childhood in a Romanian orphanage, both girls had a difficult adolescence that challenged their adoptive parents. Sofia, the elder, had been a brilliant student. She dealt with her anxieties by retreating into her studies. She was now an oncology resident at Dana-Farber. Her sister, Alina, was constantly getting into mischief with her friends and talking back to her mother. It was her stubbornness that made her such a good journalist. She never took "no" for an answer.

"Mom, I want to talk to Liz. I need to ask her something."

Maggie frowned despite the fact that Alina couldn't see her. "She's in a pretty foul mood. She's been analyzing our portfolio. As you know, the stock market has been a roller coaster. We've had big losses."

"Makes me almost glad I don't have any money."

Although it was said lightly, the remark saddened Maggie. Alina had once been doing very well as a regional news producer for a network affiliate. That was before her ex-husband spent everything, even her retirement account. They'd lost their house to foreclosure. Now, her daughter was starting over again with no money and a wrecked credit rating, which was why Liz was holding her mortgage. Fortunately, Alina was still young and had time to build up her savings again.

"All right," said Maggie. "Hold on. Let me see if Liz can talk to you now."

"Thanks, Mom."

Maggie knocked on the door of Liz's office. Liz motioned to her to come in. Maggie muted the call.

"Sweetheart, Alina wants to talk to you."

Liz sighed. "I'm downloading data." She glanced at her screen. "Okay, put her on speaker."

Maggie put the phone on speaker and set it down on Liz's desk. Liz pointed to a chair and Maggie sat down.

"Hey, girlie, what are you up to?" asked Liz in a cheerful voice.

"Hey, Mom." Liz smiled broadly at that. She might not admit it, but she really liked being called "mom" by Alina. "I wanted to ask you some questions."

"Okay, but I have you on speaker because I'm downloading some data, and I need to keep an eye on it. Your mom's in the room, so don't say anything bad about her."

Liz shot Maggie an off-centered grin. Maggie momentarily saw the young Liz of seventeen she had known forty-six years ago. The eyes were the same, still full of mischief.

"First, I want to ask if this virus turns into something, can the kids stay with you?"

Liz glanced away from the screen to engage Maggie. "Of course. Why are you asking me?"

"I know Mom would always say, 'yes,' but it's your house."

"It's *our* house. Your mother is my wife."

"You know what I mean."

Liz leaned a little closer to the phone. "I want you to listen carefully. You and the kids are always welcome here. So is your sister. We are a *family*."

There was a long pause. On the other end, Alina loudly cleared her throat.

Liz frowned. "What's behind this question, Alina? What do you know?"

"I hear there are some sick kids in the Scarborough schools. People are wondering if it's the virus."

With a plainly worried look, Liz held Maggie's gaze. "Alina, I want you to pack up your stuff and come down here right away. If there's a quarantine, we have more space."

"But Mom, I have to work. I have to drive up to Portland."

"I know it's a long drive. I'm sorry about that. Just put the gas on my card."

"You gave her your gas card?" asked Maggie with surprise.

Liz nodded but raised her hand to keep her from saying more.

"Do you hear me, Alina?" asked Liz. "It will be safer here for the kids and for you."

"Honey, I made a nice stew," said Maggie in an encouraging tone. "I can heat up some for you and the girls."

"Oh, Mom, that sounds so good," said Alina in a voice that sounded surprisingly young. "We'll be there in about an hour."

"Can't wait," said Maggie and tapped off the call. She tried to read Liz's response to the conversation. In difficult situations, Liz always carefully masked her feelings, but Maggie could tell from the pinch around Liz's mouth that she was concerned.

"What are you thinking, Dr. Stolz?" asked Maggie. "Come on. Out with it."

"The coronavirus has come to Maine, and it's probably been here for a while." Liz emitted a long sigh. "I wish we had reliable tests. It takes ten days for them to process them. People could be walking around infecting people and we don't even know it!"

"But wouldn't those people be really sick?"

"Not necessarily. Plus, we're in the middle of flu season. The flu can have many of the same symptoms and can be really nasty too. Remember last year when the vaccine was only thirty percent effective and you got it? You thought you were dying!"

Maggie smiled. "That was mostly an act to get your attention. When you're married to a doctor that's not always easy."

"Hah. Very funny. You were really sick. Remember I can hear it when your lungs are congested."

Maggie got up and rubbed Liz's back. "Oh sweetie, I was only teasing. You always take care of me when I'm sick. The best."

"I'm not in the mood for humor tonight."

"So, I see. What can I do to cheer you up?"

Instantly, Liz grinned and wiggled her eyebrows suggestively.

"Not that! The kids will be here in less than an hour."

"So? We can be quick."

"I don't like it when it's quick. Later. I promise."

Liz growled.

"Stop it," Maggie said, gently squeezing Liz's cheeks. "You're not a bear, although sometimes, you act like one. Everyone knows it's all for show."

Liz growled again.

Maggie laughed and gave her a kiss. "I'll let you sulk over our finances. I'm going to heat up the stew."

Maggie headed to the kitchen. She took out the pot of beef stew they'd had for dinner and set it on the stove to heat. As she waited for it to come to a simmer, she looked around the well-appointed kitchen. The stove, the refrigerator, the farm sink, everything had been planned to cook for a large crowd. Sometimes it seemed that they were cooking for an army, especially in the summertime when the five guestrooms and the apartment over the garage were full. Liz said she knew when she'd moved to Maine, she'd get plenty of visitors, so she'd designed the house with guests in mind.

Liz came into the kitchen and hugged Maggie from behind.

"You're gazing into that stew as if animal entrails will rise and reveal your fortune."

"I see you found your sense of humor…weird as it is."

"Can't be glum around the kiddies. You know they count on Grandma Liz to help them find mischief."

Maggie turned and put her arms around Liz's waist. "I think you've got that backwards. Grandma Liz counts on them to help her find mischief."

"That's probably more accurate."

"Come watch the news," said Maggie, giving her a squeeze. "When the girls get here, we won't have time for anything."

"Let me get a beer. I'll be right there."

Maggie headed to the media room and switched on the enormous TV. She landed right in a news story about the spread of the virus in Italy. The masked and gowned reporter took them inside a Roman hospital where Covid-19 victims on gurneys lined the halls. A disembodied voice explained that doctors were forced to choose who would live and who would die based on the prognosis and available equipment.

Liz sat down beside her. "I'm not surprised they're down to doing triage. It's like an accident scene."

Maggie reached for Liz's hand. "Could that happen here?"

"Yes," said Liz, "if we don't take a lesson from this and figure out how to slow the spread."

"I'm scared."

"It's very scary," Liz agreed. "But don't worry. We'll figure out how to stay safe."

Maggie leaned forward to look at Liz's face. "You always sound so confident, but I know you. You're frightened too."

Liz nodded solemnly. "People have been predicting a pandemic for years, but we haven't had one for generations. Seventeen million people died from the Spanish flu, and many people think that's a low estimate."

Maggie put her head on Liz's shoulder. "I don't want anything to happen to you."

"I don't want anything to happen to you either. We're both in the high-risk group because we're over sixty." Liz chuckled softly. "You read that seniors are more at risk and then realize you're a senior!" Liz reached for the remote and clicked off the television. "This isn't helping. Let's listen to some music." She put her arm around Maggie.

After a glass of wine, Maggie felt calmer. As she listened to the easy jazz and the faint clatter of Liz setting the table in the dining room, she felt safe and content. By the time the ship's bell on the porch rang, she felt ready to deal with her active grandchildren.

13

Brenda put on extra makeup because she would appear on the livestream of the selectmen's meeting that evening. The lights they used made everyone pale, so a little extra makeup accentuated her features and kept her from looking like a corpse.

Maggie Fitzgerald had passed along her makeup tips for TV, and Brenda had religiously followed them for every broadcast. Of all of Liz's girlfriends, Maggie was Brenda's favorite. Jenny and Alyson, both doctors, had always intimidated Brenda, but Maggie, once you got to know her was warm and friendly. She respected Liz's friendship with Brenda and never tried to horn in on it. "There are things Liz likes to do that I don't really enjoy," Maggie had explained. "I'm glad she has friends who enjoy doing them with her." One of those things was fishing. Liz had confided that, early in their relationship, Maggie had asked to come along on a fishing trip. That had been the one and only time.

As Brenda used the sculpting powder to define her cheekbones, she recalled Maggie's first makeup lesson. Maggie gave her a complete makeover, but Brenda would never go out in public wearing all that makeup. With a little frown, Liz watched from the doorway. "She tries to do this to me, but I never let her."

Brenda tried to explain as diplomatically as possible that she preferred a more natural look. Maggie looked disappointed, but her face brightened when Brenda asked how to avoid looking like a ghost during the town-meeting broadcasts.

Brenda slicked on some lipstick and threw the tube into the belt pouch where she kept her wallet and keys. As she inspected herself in the mirror, she wondered what Cherie would think of her TV-star look. She'd told Cherie about being on local TV, and she'd said she would definitely tune in.

Brenda clipped the paraphernalia on her duty belt. She still carried the full complement despite sitting at her desk most of the day. She'd thought about lightening up, but it was a small force, and Brenda never knew when she might be called out for backup.

On the way to the diner, Brenda's stomach growled. She was looking forward to her breakfast with Liz. Paula waved from the counter when Brenda came into the diner. "Doc is over there already." She pointed to the usual alcove table in the back.

Liz glanced up from her phone. "Hey, Brenda. How the hell are you?"

"Eh. Okay. You?"

"Same. Can't wait for winter to be over. Hold on I just need to respond to this message from Maggie."

"Okay." Brenda looked around for a waitress. Lisa waved and brought over an old-fashioned white mug that looked like it went back to the diner's founding. The present owners had bought it in 1983. Brenda wondered what would happen to the place when they retired.

Lisa poured the coffee. She reached into her apron pocket and put a handful of creamers on the table. "The usual for you two?" she asked.

They both nodded.

Liz finished her text and put down the phone. "One of these times, we should order something different. Just to keep them guessing."

Brenda chuckled. "Good idea." She peeled back the foil on two of the creamers and dumped the contents into her coffee. "What's happening over at the Stolz household?"

"Alina moved in with her kids. There are rumors about the virus in the Scarborough school system."

"You're kidding."

Liz shook her head. "Nope. Alina has an inside line being the news producer."

"But there are no cases in Maine."

"No *confirmed* cases. But who knows? We don't have reliable tests, and they are hard to come by."

Brenda frowned as she considered what Liz had said. "Does that mean people could be walking around spreading the virus and we don't know it?"

"That's exactly what it means. The incubation period is supposedly one to two weeks. We're not sure about that either."

"Shit," said Brenda and gave Liz a worried look.

"Ayuh. Not a happy thought."

The waitress delivered their breakfast. "More coffee, Doc?"

"Please." The waitress grabbed the coffee pot. She refilled Liz's cup and topped off Brenda's. "I have two boxes of N95 masks for your officers," said Liz. "Good thing that woodworking supply company appreciates all the business I give them, but they sent a text saying they were only supplying them because I have an M.D. after my name."

"Always good to have connections."

"I talked to the dry-wall contractor who worked on Erika's house. He coughed up another two hundred masks." Liz finally realized what she'd said was a pun. "Hah. Not trying to be funny."

Brenda wasn't laughing. "It's incredible that here, in the richest country in the world, we don't have enough masks to go around."

"I read an article about that in the financial pages. You wouldn't think so, but masks and paper gowns are commodities like paper towels and napkins. We closed our own mills and factories and sent all that manufacturing business to China," said Liz, adding more cream to her coffee.

"Can I stop by later and pick up the masks?"

"Be my guest. Cherie will be there all afternoon." Liz grinned.

"Are you trying to set me up, Liz?"

"Nope. You can set yourself up. I'm just your wingman."

❊❊❊

As Brenda rode down Route 1 on her way to Beach Road, she remembered the awkward goodbye on the night she'd shown up with the wine.

Cherie's Cajun stew turned out to be delicious. After the big revelation, the conversation became more relaxed. JP told stories about growing up in Calais. Brenda had a wonderful time. When she was ready to leave, she leaned forward for a goodnight kiss, but Cherie backed up.

"I'm sorry, Brenda, but I'm just not ready for that."

Brenda swallowed her hurt. "I was only going to give you a kiss on the cheek to thank you for the wonderful dinner." It wasn't completely a lie. She was going to start with a kiss on the cheek and work her way around.

"Let's wait until we get to know one another a little better."

The memory of that little scene stung. It had kept Brenda awake that night. Maybe she'd lost her touch with women. She'd been with Marcia for fifteen years before she passed. Her dates since had been disasters. Once and done. She just hadn't been ready for a new love. Now, things were different.

She certainly didn't want to blow it with Cherie. Since that night, they'd exchanged a few friendly emails on innocuous topics like the health of Cherie's father and the sudden snowstorm that had dumped nearly ten inches and closed the schools again.

Brenda pulled into the Hobbs Family Practice parking lot and turned off her engine. This was a professional call, so she decided she should put on her hat.

The eyes of all the patients in the waiting room followed her as she walked through on her way to the counter.

"Hey, Chief, how are you today?" asked Ginny cheerfully.

"Well enough, thank you. And you?"

"Never better."

"That's what I like to hear. Is Ms. Bois available? I'm here to pick up something."

"She's with a patient, but she should be done soon. Should I page her to let her know you're here?"

Brenda waved her hand. "No, please don't disturb her. I'll wait."

"Do you want me to hang your hat back here?" asked Ginny, reaching for it.

"That's very kind. Thank you." She handed over her hat and took a seat in the waiting room. The patients gave her another curious look, then went back to their magazines or cell phones. Brenda dialed down her scanner so the noise wouldn't disturb them. She gazed out the window at the salt marsh and noticed the tide had come in.

Cherie finally came out with her stethoscope around her neck. "Chief Harrison? Are you looking for me?"

Brenda stood and Cherie gave her a look of apprehension. *The uniform.* Brenda had forgotten that Cherie didn't like it. Cherie's expression instantly changed from dismay to a professional mask.

"Follow me, please," said Cherie in a chilly, formal voice.

As they headed down the corridor, Brenda said, "I hope I'm not interrupting anything."

"One of my patients canceled, so I have a few minutes."

Brenda lightly touched Cherie's shoulder to slow her pace. "I'm sorry. I know my uniform frightens you."

Cherie turned around. "It does, but I'm trying to get used to it." She pointed to an open door. "Dr. Stolz said you'd be by this afternoon. I have everything ready for you in here."

They went into the storage room, and Cherie closed the door behind them. "How are you?" she asked, her eyes searching Brenda's face. The look felt unnervingly intimate.

"Fine," Brenda stammered.

"I want to say I'm sorry for pushing you away the other night."

"You don't have to apologize. I understand. You want to take it slow. That's okay with me."

Cherie reached for Brenda's hand. "I like you. In fact, I like you a lot, but I really want to get to know you before…anything happens." She nodded toward Brenda's uniform. "This outfit scares the shit out of me."

"Still?"

"Yes, still. Please…give me time."

Brenda smiled. "For you, I have all the time in the world."

Cherie returned the smile. "I was hoping you'd say that."

"Can I give you a hug?" Brenda asked hopefully.

"That might be a little too much. And we are in the office." Cherie raised a suggestive brow. "I don't think Dr. Stolz would approve of hanky-panky in the storage room."

Brenda snorted a laugh. "Are you kidding me? Liz has been in more mischief than you and me put together!"

"I bet she has." When Cherie smiled, her whole face lit up.

"When can I see you again?"

"Tonight?" asked Cherie in a hopeful voice. "Maybe we can go to dinner at a nice place. I'd have to go home and get dinner for my father, but after that I'm free."

Brenda sighed. "I can't tonight. I have the town council meeting."

"Oh, that's right. I almost forgot."

"Liz will be there too. We're discussing how the town should respond to the virus. She's speaking both as the town doctor and the president of the chamber of commerce."

"Well, if that's not a conflict of interest, I don't know what is," replied Cherie with a thoughtful frown.

"I'm sorry about tonight. How about tomorrow night? I can make you that romantic dinner we talked about."

Cherie looked momentarily shy. Then she smiled. "All right," she said. "That's even better. I can plan for Daddy's dinner, and he can heat it up in the microwave."

"Are you sure?"

"Yes, I'm sure. Daddy is pretty self-sufficient. And he won't mind. He likes you."

"He does?" asked Brenda.

"Yes, he said you look kind."

Brenda found that oddly touching. "Despite the uniform…and the gun, I am kind." Brenda found herself moving closer to Cherie, holding her gaze.

"I know," said Cherie, looking deeply into Brenda's eyes. "Can I have that hug you offered?"

"Sure," said Brenda. She glanced down. "Sorry about all the crap on my service belt."

"It's okay. We can hug like society ladies. No body contact."

As Cherie touched her cheek to hers, Brenda could smell the sweet scent of freshly washed hair. The warmth of her soft skin was delicious. Brenda wanted to linger, but Cherie told her that she had a patient on the way.

14

Cherie hadn't worn a dress since fall had brought its first frost. She remembered staring with fascination at the glittering ice crystals on the grass. When they'd had their first snowfall, a few days after Halloween, she couldn't take her eyes off the snowflakes. As a Southerner, she still found the cold shocking. Her friends had questioned her sanity when she'd said she was moving and warned her about the northern winters.

Although Cherie longed for the long winter to end, she was glad for an opportunity to wear the green sweater dress she'd bought in an L.L. Bean winter clearance sale. The dress was warm and clung just enough to accentuate her curves. Cherie worked hard in the gym to maintain her figure, and she wasn't shy about showing it off. She slipped on high-heeled pumps and inspected herself in the mirror. After a winter in jeans, hoodies and boots, it felt good to look feminine for a change. She suspected that Brenda would agree.

When Cherie came into the living room to tell her father she was ready to go, he whistled through his teeth and exclaimed, "*Ooh la la! Très jolie!*"

"Thank you, Daddy." She kissed him on the forehead. "Have everything you need? Your oxygen is right here if you're short of breath."

He waved her away. "Stop babying me. I'm fine, honey. I raised you, didn't I? How do you suppose I did that?"

Cherie smiled. "You were a wonderful father and still are."

He tried to look around her so he could see the TV. "Get out of here," he said in a slightly cranky voice. "Have a good time," he added, apparently to make amends for the crankiness. He turned up his face for another kiss. His cheek was rough with a day's growth of beard.

"You need a shave, Daddy."

"Tomorrow," he replied in a dismissive voice. "No one sees me except you."

"Well, then shave for me. I'm the only woman in your life now."

"Yes, you are, my beautiful baby girl." He reached for her hand and gave it a kiss. "I promise I'll shave later. Just for you."

Cherie slipped her arms into her dress coat and called goodnight to her father as she headed out the door.

She needed the GPS to find Brenda's house. When she'd said it was in the woods, she wasn't exaggerating. To keep down the light pollution, there were no streetlights except at major intersections. The same with street signs. The locals all knew where they were going, so it didn't matter to them. The summer people kept to the shoreline and had no idea that anything existed on the other side of I95.

Finally, Cherie found the entrance to a development in the middle of nowhere. She drove around twice before she found the mailbox with the correct number and pulled into the driveway. The light on the porch went on as soon as her headlights hit the house. A moment later, the front door opened, and she saw Brenda's familiar figure silhouetted against the light from inside.

Heavy rain and warm weather had melted most of the snow in the last few days. The walkway to the house was dry. The scuff of her heels on the pavement echoed against the house.

The storm door opened. "Welcome," said Brenda, holding it open for her. "I see you found your way in the dark."

"You were right. You do live in the woods."

"Yes, and I love it. Come on in."

Brenda took Cherie's coat. "What a pretty dress. So dressed up! Now, I feel like a slob."

Cherie took in Brenda in a glance. She was wearing corduroy pants and a knit top, but no shoes.

"Would you like me to take off my shoes?" asked Cherie. "Most people up here don't seem to wear shoes in the house."

Brenda's eyes were welded to Cherie's feet. "Most people up here don't wear sexy shoes like yours. Please leave them on." Brenda gestured toward a door. "Come into the living room. I have a fire going in the wood stove, and it's nice and toasty." Brenda led her into a casually furnished room with leather furniture, gleaming wood floors, and colorful woven wall hangings. "Some people think it's strange that I have rugs on the wall instead of on the floor."

"Those aren't rugs," said Cherie. "That's wall art."

Brenda smiled, evidently pleased with the response. "My wife was a fiber artist. She used to exhibit at all the juried shows."

Cherie studied each wall hanging carefully. The work was exquisite, and the color schemes, imaginative. "Beautiful," she said. "Your wife was very talented."

Brenda nodded sadly and gestured to an open bottle of wine and two glasses.

"Wine?"

"Yes, thank you." Cherie sat down on the sofa while Brenda poured the wine. She noticed the pile of hardcover books on the coffee table, a biography of Ruth Ginsburg, a book of photographs of Acadia National Park, and the latest James Patterson novel.

"You like real books," observed Cherie with pleasure.

Brenda glanced at the pile. "Yes, I do. I get most of them second hand, but I like the feel of a real book." She handed Cherie a glass of wine and clicked her glass to Cherie's. "Welcome to my little house in the woods."

Cherie gazed around, taking in that the house was anything but little. From the outside, she could see that it was a full-size, center-hall colonial from an earlier era.

"It's a lot of house for one person."

Brenda shrugged. "I don't mind. When I make one room messy, I move on to the next one."

Cherie gave her a skeptical look. "I don't believe that. This place is neat as a pin."

"That's because you were coming. I wanted to make a good impression."

"How'd you find this place?" Cherie asked.

"The usual way…a real estate agent. Marcia had been following the listings on Zillow and Realtor.com for years before we moved out of Brooklyn. After living in our tiny house, she wanted a bigger place with a real yard. She liked to garden. She grew veggies too because she liked to cook." Although Brenda looked a bit sad, she didn't seem overly emotional talking about her wife. Sometime, when they knew each other better, Cherie would encourage more conversation about her.

Cherie sipped her wine and looked around. She could see other touches that she doubted were Brenda's taste—fanciful lamps with bases like old-fashioned ship's lanterns. A collection of Maine-inspired carved figurines. Brenda didn't strike her as a collector, but who knows? Liz Stolz collected minerals. There were even colorful rocks in her office.

"It's nice and quiet out here in the woods," said Brenda. "It's an interesting neighborhood. Couples in their sixties, who have raised their families here but stayed on. Young couples, who see these older houses as good starter homes. And people like me, who upsize but get more house after selling expensive real estate elsewhere. A lot of retirees 'from away'— as they say up here."

"Most of my practice is older people," said Cherie.

"You like being here?"

"I love it! When my father said he wanted to come home to die, I wasn't so sure about the idea."

"The coming to Maine or the other part?"

Cherie managed a defective smile. "Both, but especially the dying. The COPD has really slowed him down. He used to walk miles every day, now he can barely make it from his TV chair to the bathroom without huffing and puffing."

Brenda gave her a sympathetic look. "That's hard."

"Yes, it is." Cherie sighed and for the first time noticed a delicious smell. "What are you cooking for dinner?"

"That's the rouille for the bouillabaisse. I made it from scratch. Sorry about the fishy smell."

"Don't apologize. I love bouillabaisse," said Cherie. "By the way, it's roo-ee," she said sounding out the word, rouille.

"Your name is French," said Brenda. "Did you take it in school? I did, but I don't remember a word."

"Then you'll have to practice French with me. I often speak it with my father. Up here, the French influence was so strong, there used to be French-language public schools. My father was always better at reading and writing French than English. Sometimes, I have to translate official things like government documents for him."

"Rouille," Brenda tried but failed to get the accent right. "How do you say it again?"

Cherie said it for her slowly, sounding it out. Then she repeated it. Brenda looked charmed. "I like it when you speak French. It sounds like you."

Cherie gave her a puzzled look. "Sounds like me?"

"Yes, you know. Elegant…exotic."

"Exotic? Now, that's something I've never thought about myself."

"How can you get more exotic than a blonde who's secretly part black? That's not your everyday background."

Cherie drew on her counselor training to offer a neutral response. "Does it bother you that I have black blood?"

Brenda made a face that said, are you kidding me? "Hell, no. I know a lot of people think cops are racist, but I'm not one of them."

"I find that we're all a little racist when we scratch the surface. The white part of me is racist about the black part sometimes, and vice versa."

Cherie watched as Brenda tried to process that idea. When it had first occurred to Cherie, she'd had trouble with it too.

"I have to think about that," Brenda admitted.

"Why don't we go to the kitchen while you think about it? Those good smells are making me hungry."

Brenda grabbed the wine bottle. Cherie followed her through the dining room, where the table had been elegantly set with china, cloth napkins and what looked like real silver. There were tall tapers in crystal candle holders in the shape of six-pointed stars.

"Your table looks beautiful," Cherie said as they passed.

"I'm just following your instructions. Romantic dinner for two coming right up! What the doctor ordered," Brenda said with a sly smile.

"I'm not a doctor."

"Technically, not, but can't you do almost everything a doctor does?"

"Yes, but I'm not a doctor. When I got the idea to switch professions, it was too late to go to medical school."

"Too bad. You would have made a good doctor."

This was a sore subject for Cherie. "Let's talk about something else, if you don't mind."

"Okay," said Brenda, pulling out a chair from the kitchen table. "Have a seat while I finish dinner." She took a platter of cut-up fish and lobster from the refrigerator and a bowl of clams and mussels. She turned on the oven to preheat.

"Is there anything I can do to help?" asked Cherie, watching Brenda toss the salad. She was pleased to see how competent Brenda looked in the kitchen. Then she wondered why she would have thought otherwise. Stereotypes again. They always seemed to pop up.

"I have everything under control at the moment," said Brenda. She gave Cherie a sheepish look. "Would it spoil the romance if I asked you to light the candles?"

Cherie smiled warmly. "No, of course not."

Brenda handed her a box of stick matches. "Thank you."

Cherie returned to find Brenda adding a bowlful of diced potatoes to the stock pot. She slid the bread into the oven.

"Just a few minutes now," Brenda assured her. "I can give you some cheese and crackers if you're really fainting with hunger."

"Do I look like I'm fainting?" Cherie grinned.

"No, you don't look like the fainting type."

"I'm not. In my profession, fainting is not a good thing."

"I bet not," said Brenda, adding the fish to the pot.

Cherie leaned on her hand. "I like watching you in the kitchen. It's nice to have someone cook for me. Usually, I'm the one doing the cooking."

"Well," said Brenda with a definitive nod. "We'll just have to change that, won't we?"

"If you say so." Cherie smiled. Brenda was saying all the right things. Cherie admired Brenda's strong profile as she stood working at the stove. She allowed her eyes to travel down Brenda's body, pausing at her breasts. In the knit top that clung slightly, they looked abundantly round and soft. Cherie felt a definite response below. It had been such a long time since she'd been with a woman. What she missed most of all was feeling the softness of a woman's body. Sometimes, she thought she missed that more than sex.

"I really hope this is good," said Brenda, interrupting Cherie's thoughts. "I've only made it once before."

"I'm sure it will be delicious," said Cherie with a reassuring smile. For a long moment, they were silent, holding one another's gaze. The oven timer pinged and brought them back to reality.

"Time for the shellfish and lobster to go in," Brenda explained.

After a few minutes, the timer pinged again. Brenda ladled out the bouillabaisse. Cherie brought the bowls to the table while Brenda cut the bread. Finally, they sat with steaming bowls of fish stew before them.

"*Bon appétit*," said Brenda.

"*Merci*," replied Cherie. "Your accent is improving already."

"Hah, anyone who's watched Julia Child can say that right."

Cherie tasted the bouillabaisse and found it incredibly delicious. She was a little embarrassed when she took a piece of bread and crumbs fell on the brilliantly polished dining table. She tried to collect the crumbs into her cupped hand.

Brenda said, "Forget that. Food is meant to be enjoyed. We can clean up later."

"You notice everything, don't you?"

"Cops are trained to notice every detail."

"So are medical personnel."

"Something we have in common," observed Brenda, dipping a piece of bread into her stew.

"Oh, I think we probably have a lot more in common."

Brenda looked thoughtful as she chewed the bread. Finally, she swallowed and said. "It wouldn't seem like it on the surface, but I think we do."

After they finished eating, Brenda tried to shoo her out of the kitchen, but Cherie insisted on helping her clean up. She held the door open while Brenda carried the pot of stew out to the screen porch to cool.

"It's cold enough for that to stay out there overnight," she said, locking the door. "Would you like to sit in the living room and listen to music? I found this jazz station I thought you might like."

"Sure," Cherie agreed. When Brenda offered her hand, she took it.

They sat side by side on the sofa, listening to the music, not talking for a few minutes. Then Brenda said, "Do you mind if I sit closer?"

Cherie smiled in her direction. "I'd like that." Brenda slid closer until their thighs were touching. "Can I put my arm around you?"

Cherie nodded. Tentatively, Brenda put her arm around Cherie's shoulders. "It feels really good to sit with you like this."

Cherie gently stroked Brenda's thigh to indicate her agreement.

"Do you think we can be friends?" asked Brenda hopefully.

"Yes, I think so." Cherie leaned against her. Her cheek found Brenda's breast. Yes, it was as deliciously soft as she had imagined. Cherie could smell Brenda's cologne rising from her warm body.

"It's so nice just relaxing with someone, listening to music," Brenda murmured.

Cherie sighed and snuggled against Brenda's breast and put her hand on her waist. She could feel the instant response in return and a little puppy moan of appreciation. Her hand on Brenda's waist told her she could stand to lose a few pounds, but the softness felt so good to her touch.

"I want to kiss you," said Brenda.

Cherie sat up. She searched the blue eyes that now looked so anxious, then she closed her own, hoping to make her permission obvious. After a long moment, she felt soft lips on hers. The pressure was so gentle, like the brush of a butterfly wing. She opened her eyes.

"I don't want to push," Brenda explained.

"You're fine." Cherie put her hands on Brenda's cheeks to draw her face closer. She pressed her lips to hers and opened her mouth to invite her in. She felt the tension and hesitation through her fingertips, but then a warm tongue came into her mouth, gently finding its way around. Cherie felt the arousal below begin to purr like a large, friendly cat. Brenda's kisses became more assertive. Then she relaxed and let Cherie take the lead. Cherie liked the taste of Brenda's mouth. Sweet, despite the wine, and the tasty meal. She loved exploring its warmth.

They stopped there and parted to evaluate.

"More?" asked Brenda in a whisper.

Cherie shook her head. "Not right now. Just hold me while we listen to music."

Brenda looked anxious. Cherie trailed her fingertips down Brenda's cheek. "I like the way you kiss. Don't worry."

Brenda smiled broadly and put her arm around Cherie.

15

Lucy reread the bishop's email twice. She'd listened in on the monthly clergy meeting earlier in the week. The email confirmed the recommendations they'd discussed. Celebrants should wash their hands thoroughly with soap and water before celebrating the Eucharist. Lucy always did that anyway, but Liz had made a point of showing her how surgeons scrubbed. She'd given Lucy a box of fine-bristled surgical brushes. Lucy kept one in the lavatory off the robing room.

"Fingernails are especially important," said Liz, inspecting Lucy's. "You keep yours short. That's good."

Doesn't every woman who loves women? Lucy had wondered at the time. Then she thought of the lesbian porn videos she occasionally watched with Erika. Mostly they giggled through them, although a few had been inspirational. The actresses with long French nails always made Lucy shudder. How painful that must be.

Lucy shook off the thought of porn by focusing on the other points in the bishop's email. It recommended alcohol-based hand sanitizer for anyone distributing communion. Lucy would discuss this at the vestry meeting. She'd make sure the warden bought small bottles of sanitizer that could be left in strategic places.

She carefully read the next part of the message. Obviously, drinking from the common communion cup was a sure way to spread disease. Instead, communicants should be encouraged to bow to the consecrated wine to acknowledge the Divine presence. The bishop reminded them that, in Episcopal theology, communion is complete when received in either of the elements.

The email went on to make recommendations about offering the sign of peace. Kissing and hugging made no sense during flu season, and she often mentioned that, but now even a handshake would be discouraged.

Lucy sighed. She was glad that her bishop was ahead of the curve on addressing these issues, but she was sad to see the parts of the Eucharist lopped off in this way. She knew that her associate rector, Tom Simmons, would be on the mailing list, but she forwarded the email to him, just in case.

She had a few minutes before her counseling session, so she reluctantly dug into the text of her Sunday sermon. Lenten sermons could be so dreary. She always tried to find a cheerful note or some humor to brighten them. She was in the middle of figuring out how to shorten a bad joke about giving up swearing for Lent when there was a knock at her door.

"Mother Lucy, Cherie Bois is here for you."

Cherie came in. She was smartly dressed today in a wool pants suit. Lucy wondered if the outfit was for a special occasion.

"Nice suit," said Lucy.

"I had to give a talk at the senior center about special measures if the virus comes to Hobbs."

Lucy opened her arms for a hug, but Cherie kept her distance and shook her head. "That's part of it. No more hugging."

Lucy sighed. "I just read that in the bishop's memo to active clergy. The kiss of peace should be a nod or a wave. Maybe bumping elbows will be allowed." Lucy grinned at her own humor, but Cherie didn't break a smile.

"Maybe, but I probably wouldn't get close enough even for that."

Chastened, Lucy nodded and pointed to one of the visitors' chairs. Cherie sat down. As usual, Lucy allowed her client a moment to settle down and get her bearings before opening the session.

"So how have things been since the last time we met?"

"Pretty well. I told you that Dr. Stolz took me to the shooting range."

"Yes, and that seemed to help with your fear of guns."

"We went again the other day. The more I shoot, the more confident I feel and the less frightened. I don't think I'll ever want to own a gun, but I understand them better."

"Good. Good," said Lucy, mentally patting herself for the good idea. "And so, is it easier to be around Brenda?"

Cherie gave her a shy smile. "We had another date."

"Really? And how did that go?"

"Nice. In fact, very nice."

Lucy nodded to encourage her to say more.

"I think this friendship may have some potential."

"Just friends?"

"Maybe more. We'll see."

Lucy waited with that patient, open look that seemed to compel clients to reveal more. "That's a good start," she said in an encouraging tone.

"It is. But I have some things to figure out first. I don't have lots of experience with women. I had one female partner. We broke up when I moved from Shreveport to Houston to do my PA program." Cherie let out a big sigh. "I was ready for it to end. It wasn't a forever thing, if you know what I mean."

Lucy nodded.

"I don't really know how fast or slow to go with Brenda because I have so little experience with women. I guess I'm what they call a 'late bloomer.'"

"That's pretty common with women. We're raised to do the socially acceptable thing and date men. That works for some women…at least, for a while."

Cherie raised a blond brow and gave Lucy a canny look. "Sounds like you know something about that."

Lucy shrugged. "Maybe I do."

Cherie waited, turning the patient, open look back on Lucy.

Lucy laughed softly. "You want me to tell you my story."

"You don't have to," said Cherie casually.

"Oh, you're good, Cherie."

Cherie gave her a direct look. "One of the hazards of shrinking a shrink."

"Damned right," replied Lucy. She laughed at Cherie's slightly shocked look. "All right. I'll tell you my story if you tell me yours."

"It's a deal."

"I was going through a really rough time in my life," began Lucy. "It was so bad, I had to give up my operatic career. Everything was going wrong. I was really depressed and thought things couldn't get any worse. A friend of mine, another professional singer, was singing for an Episcopal ordination at St. John the Divine in New York. They needed a soprano soloist and after working me over and plying me with wine, my friend talked me into taking the part. I was really a mess and hadn't sung in months. I had to work hard to get my voice back into shape, but I did. Since then, I've never let my voice go like that. I practice every day."

Lucy gazed out the window as she thought back to the day of the ordination.

"At the reception after the ordination, an attractive woman came up to me and introduced herself. Her name was Susan. She said she'd recognized me and that she'd been a big fan of mine while I was singing at the Met. She was studying theology and hoped to be ordained to the diaconate. Before she was called to the priesthood, she'd been a Roman Catholic nun for almost twenty years."

"Another late bloomer," Cherie conjectured.

"You'd be surprised how many people are called to the priesthood later in life. Obviously, I was. After the reception, Susan and I struck up a friendship and then it became…well, more. I'm sure you can figure it out from there."

"So where is Susan now?"

Lucy shrugged. "I really don't know. Her Catholic sensibilities ran deep. She felt that once she was ordained to the priesthood, she should be celibate. In fairness to her, that's what the Church was teaching at the time."

"So, you split up?"

"Yes. She wanted our goodbye to be final."

"That's a shame," said Cherie in a sympathetic voice. Lucy noticed how kind her eyes were when she was showing sympathy. *She's probably a great therapist*, thought Lucy. Liz had raved about her PA's patient management skills, and Liz was pretty picky about her staff.

"Your turn," said Lucy.

Cherie touched her steepled fingers to her chin as she considered where to begin. Finally, she said, "I dated men until I was in my late thirties. Then I just gave up dating for years. Obviously, there wasn't Mr. Right out there. I dated mostly white men. When I told them that I was part black, it was a turn off to some of them. The black men thought I wasn't black enough. Race can get in the way of a lot of things."

Lucy nodded. "I'm sure it can."

"The sex with men wasn't bad. I enjoyed it. Some lesbians find it weird when I say that."

"I don't," said Lucy. "I know exactly what you mean."

Cherie smiled. Obviously, she liked the idea that someone understood.

"I finally decided to be single. I'd hang out with my friends, not looking for anyone in particular. Then I met a woman I really liked. We started going out. We both liked classical jazz, so we went to all the best clubs in Shreveport. I really enjoyed her company. Then one night…it just happened. I thought I'd died and gone to heaven. Even the best sex with men was nothing like the way this woman made love to me. So, we kept seeing each other, going out to the clubs, to dinner, coming back to my place. She never stayed the whole night. At first, I didn't question it, but after a while, it became really important to know why she couldn't stay. Turns out she was married…to a man. He was a high-profile corporate lawyer. She was a lawyer too. They had an agreement that they could sleep with other people as long as every night they slept together in their own bed. I was faintly disgusted, but not enough to give her up. When I got accepted into the Baylor PA program, that made the decision for me."

Lucy had been listening intently and without judgement, but she felt sad that Cherie had deprived herself of a full relationship while wasting her time with the duplicitous lawyer.

"Have you ever heard from her?"

"She sends me a Christmas card."

"That's nice of her," said Lucy in a rare, sarcastic tone.

Cherie looked surprised. Lucy realized she was surprising Cherie too much in this session. She'd better rein it in a little.

"But now you have the possibility of a real relationship with a woman. What are you going to do about it?"

"See how it goes?" said Cherie tentatively.

"Sounds like a plan."

"She's a widow, you know."

"No, I didn't."

"Her wife was killed in a car accident."

"That's terrible. Sudden death is so hard on the survivors."

"It worries me a little that she was married before. I don't want to try to fill someone else's shoes."

"You're making assumptions."

Cherie looked guilty and nodded. "Yes, I am. Just my fear talking, I guess."

"What are you afraid of? I mean, apart from the things we've talked about…the uniform and the gun. Sounds like you've been handling them pretty well."

Cherie frowned as she thought. "I've never had a successful relationship. I'm almost fifty years old. Maybe I just can't have one."

"Okay, Cherie. Now, if the situation were reversed, how would you respond to that remark?"

Cherie looked surprised again. "Everyone loves you, Mother Lucy. When you smile, your face just beams love."

"That's a dodge. Try again."

Cherie anxiously adjusted her position in her chair, literally squirming under Lucy's firm look. Finally, she said, "It's a pessimistic attitude, probably the result of poor self-esteem."

Lucy waved her hand dismissively. "Poor self-esteem is an overrated excuse. I only believe in lack of success. You won't believe you're lovable until you let yourself be loved. Sounds like Brenda is willing. The question is, are you?"

Cherie chuckled and stared at Lucy incredulously. "You are one tough lady, Mother Lucy."

"Let's get rid of the 'Mother Lucy.' I think we know one another well enough. Just Lucy will do, all right?"

"You are tough."

"Good. That's what some people need."

16

Erika watched Lucy walk around the front of the house on her way from the garage. She could instantly tell when it had been a trying day because Lucy had already taken off her collar. Sometimes, Erika found them in the pockets of Lucy's suit jackets when she was readying clothes for the dry cleaner. Other times she needed to take them out of the light laundry before she threw it into the washing machine. The linen collars really needed to be washed by hand. Those that went through the washing machine puckered and never looked right.

In the beginning, Lucy's casual disregard for this obvious sign of her vocation made Erika wonder if it was a subconscious message. Then she realized it was a false assumption. Lucy was completely devoted to the priesthood and the Church. Although her personal appearance was always flawless, she was just untidy about certain things.

They hadn't even been married for six months, and they were still feeling their way with one another. Erika tried to turn a blind eye to her beautiful, red-haired wife's shortcomings, but untidiness was one thing Erika couldn't abide. She was kind but firm about it. So far, Lucy was resistant to correction. All she had to do was smile one of her incandescent smiles, and Erika completely forgot her complaints.

Lucy dragged as she came through the front door, but her face brightened as it always did when she saw Erika.

"Hello, Sweetie," she said, sloughing off her black coat and hanging it on the coat tree. She threaded her hands through Erika's arms and gave her a hug. Then she raised her face for a kiss.

Erika kissed Lucy and gave her a little hug. "My dear, you look so absolutely exhausted."

"I am. The accountant was there this afternoon. Good thing Tom has all that experience running a big parish. I have no patience for it. My eyes were beginning to swim."

Erika kissed Lucy's forehead and patted her cheek. "I'm afraid we have company. If I'd known you'd had a hard day, I wouldn't have asked her to stay."

"Who?" said Lucy, looking around.

"Liz is in the family room, having a beer."

Through her fatigue, Lucy managed one of her radiant smiles. "I don't mind. I love Liz." She gave Erika another squeeze. "Let me go in and say hello."

Erika had always admired Liz's charming, old-fashioned manners. She got up when Lucy came in. "I'm sorry to still be parked here when you came home. That wasn't my intention." She kissed Lucy on the cheek.

"To what do we owe the pleasure?"

"Erika and I are trying to figure out what to do with her money during the market crash."

"Thank God, I have my money managed by a financial advisor," said Lucy. "I don't have to think about it."

Liz raised her brows. "It doesn't really work that way. You might want to check in with them."

Lucy shook her head "No, let them worry about it." She patted Liz's shoulder. "Sit down and enjoy your beer. I'm going up to change."

"Liz, are you ready for another beer?" asked Erika, getting up to head to the kitchen.

"Sure. If you'll have another."

As Erika opened the refrigerator, she noticed a strong smell, not like anything had spoiled, more like the smell when they had an extended power outage. They'd stored broccoli leftovers from the night before, so Erika ascribed the odor to that source. Cruciferous vegetables could be pungent.

She flipped the caps off the two beers. Before she left the kitchen, she opened a bottle of Chardonnay and set a wine glass beside it for Lucy.

Liz, who was something of an aficionado, carefully poured her beer down the side of her glass. "I am really in a quandary about the markets," she said. "I was in London when Lehman Brothers collapsed. I could watch the news on British TV, but I couldn't do anything about it. Not that I would have. Never sell in a downslide, they say. Otherwise, you enshrine your losses. I'm trying to follow that advice myself, but I admit I've lost some sleep over this one."

Erika sat beside Liz and tapped glasses with her. "I trust you. If you tell me to sell, I shall."

"We should have a few dead cat bounces before that. Then you can sell."

Erika laughed. "I love that expression. What does it mean?"

"It's a temporary recovery after a big fall, mostly speculators buying to cover themselves. The idea is when the fall is hard and fast enough, even a dead cat will bounce."

"You Americans come up with the most colorful language."

Lucy came into the room with her glass of wine. She was wearing a workout suit and her fuzzy slippers. Her figure was still perfect, although she'd put on a few pounds since the wedding thanks to Erika's cooking. She'd looked like a model in her wedding gown. Erika didn't mind her new softness, especially because it had gone to all the right places.

Lucy insinuated herself between Liz and Erika. "Are you two still talking about money?"

"Yes," they said in unison.

"You can stop now. I've had enough business for one day."

"Yes, Mother Lucy," said Erika in a crisp voice. "Your wish is my command."

"Playing dead and ignoring the volatility is one strategy," said Liz, still focused on the previous conversation. "Don't look at it. The problem is, we're at an age when we don't have the luxury of time. The market may not come back until we're dead and buried."

"Oh, Liz. You're always so optimistic," said Lucy with a sigh. "Can't you look at the bright side?"

"You're a priest. That's your job. I'm a realist. I call them as I see them."

"Liz, keep me informed," said Erika. "But now, let's leave off the discussion of the stock market, or Lucy will find other entertainment."

Lucy sat up and looked around. She cocked an ear in the direction of the family room. "The TV is off? My daughter is actually doing her homework?"

"I think the novelty of the TV has finally worn off," Erika said. "She's in her room. Like most girls she prefers texting her friends and surfing the internet to TV."

"More likely playing video games." Lucy sighed. "Lucky me. I can barely add, and I have a geeky genius for a daughter."

Erika patted Lucy's thigh. "Now, now. Don't disparage yourself, Lucy. You have many talents, including a spectacular soprano voice. Not everyone is gifted in maths."

"My wife is a mathematician, my father-in-law, my daughter, the associate rector of my church...wouldn't you feel stupid too?"

Erika laughed. "No. Should I feel lacking because I can't sing opera? We all have our gifts."

"Speaking of kids," said Liz. "I'd better go home and see what's going on. Maggie is probably ripping her hair out after being with the girls all day." Liz swallowed the beer left in her glass and got up. Lucy caught her wrist.

"Liz, do you have time to come to our vestry meeting tomorrow afternoon?"

"Me?" asked Liz, looking surprised.

"Yes, you," said Lucy, holding Liz's hand and giving her one of her brilliant Lucy smiles. "I want you to speak from a medical point of view...and as a tech head. There's talk of going to online worship. We have a lot of conservative people at St. Margaret's. People respect you. You have influence. When you speak, people listen."

"No pressure or anything," Liz quipped, glancing at Erika.

"You know what I mean," said Lucy firmly.

Liz sat down again. "Where is this coming from?"

"The bishop mentioned it in a telephone meeting this morning. Just a few days ago, we were talking about staying home if you didn't feel well. Now, we're talking about staying home period!"

Liz nodded approvingly. "Your bishop is pretty damn smart."

"He is, and he genuinely cares about people."

"I'm sure Tom will support you," said Erika. Her old friend from graduate school and one-time boyfriend, now the associate rector of St. Margaret's, was an ardent Lucy fan.

Liz had that look of intense concentration that told Erika she was deep in thought. "You should have heard them the other night at the chamber of commerce meeting. The idea that we might have to close businesses right before tourist season opens terrifies them."

"As well it should," said Erika. "This town would die without the summer visitors."

"Liz, please come to the meeting," Lucy said looking directly into Liz's eyes. "I really need you there. Your opinion carries so much weight in this town."

Erika knew Liz would never refuse Lucy. She also knew that her friend had a hopeless crush on her wife, totally innocent, but not as secret as Liz would like to think. All Lucy had to do was to turn her green eyes on her, and Liz would do anything she asked.

"What time?" asked Liz, still looking skeptical.

"Four thirty."

Liz threw back her head and sighed dramatically. "All right. I'll be there." She kissed Lucy on the cheek. "See you tomorrow."

Erika followed Liz into the kitchen and watched her as she rinsed out the beer bottles and put them in the recycling bin. Liz knew exactly where everything was and always seemed perfectly at home there, which was as it should be after over forty years of friendship. Erika felt equally at home in Liz's house.

"Thanks for the beers," she said.

"Say hi, to Maggie."

Liz waved on her way out the door.

Erika switched on the oven light to check on the lamb shanks braising in a cast-iron pot. Lucy came in to refill her wine glass. She opened the door to the refrigerator to get the bottle. "Have you noticed a funky smell in here?"

"Yes. Maybe the box of baking soda needs to be replaced. I think I have another in the cabinet."

Lucy opened the door to the freezer. "The ice is melting together. Everything in here is frosty. Is that normal?"

Erika frowned. "Do you suppose one of us accidently left the door open?"

"Maybe. If I did, I'm sorry." Lucy corked the wine bottle and returned it to the refrigerator door.

Erika took the glass of wine out of Lucy's hand and set it on the island. She took Lucy in her arms. "If you did, you are forgiven."

"It is Lent. I don't mind doing a little penance for my sins."

"Hmmm. I'll have to think of something."

"There they are again." Emily came into the kitchen and opened the refrigerator to get a bottle of seltzer. "What would you two do if you couldn't glom on to one another all the time?"

Lucy gave Erika another gentle squeeze before releasing her. "I wouldn't like that," she said. "And I wouldn't like it if I couldn't glom onto you."

"Don't you know about social distancing, Mom?"

Lucy sighed. "Yes, I've been hearing a lot about it."

"It's coming. Soon," said Emily conclusively. She sat down at the kitchen table and flipped open the tab of the can of seltzer.

"Take a glass, please, sweetheart," said Lucy.

Emily gave her mother a dirty look but got up to get a glass. "I thought I'd escaped the nagging when I moved out of the Cummings' place."

"You wish," said Lucy. She gave Emily's shoulder an affectionate squeeze.

"Love you, Mom," said Emily, "but sometimes, it's not easy."

"Love you too, but sometimes, it's not easy."

17

Liz waited until everyone was settled before beginning the meeting. One of the new medical assistants was still in the back. Cathy Pelletier, Liz's partner, had sent someone to get her. Meanwhile, people stepped up to help themselves to free pizza. Everyone was quiet while they ate. The usual banter during their lunch meetings was conspicuously absent. As Liz wolfed down a slice of meatlover's pizza, knowing she wouldn't have time to eat once the meeting began, she could sense the anxiety in the room.

The medical assistants returned. Each took a slice of pizza and quickly found a seat.

"Okay, people, get your food and settle down," said Liz. "We have a lot to discuss today."

People hurried to grab another slice of pizza. While she waited, Liz gulped down some water. Finally, everyone was seated, and all eyes were on her.

Liz looked around the room. "Thanks for giving up your lunch time to be here. Before we get into the agenda items, I'd like to hear from you how you think things are going."

Jim Bowden, one of the partners raised his hand. "People are asking a lot of questions about the virus. Now that they see what's going on in Italy, they're scared."

"What are we telling them?" asked Liz, glancing around for a volunteer.

Cathy raised her hand. "I'm telling them to go to the CDC website for information. I tell them how important it is to wash their hands and not touch their faces. I emphasize that it's the same advice we give during flu season."

"Good," said Liz. "That's about all we can say at this point. We should also ask them to call ahead if they think they have the coronavirus and not come straight to the office. I'm going to post that on the website too. Everyone good with that?"

Heads nodded. *What a great group*, thought Liz.

"I want to thank everyone for following the hygiene protocols. We may get to using exam gloves, but I'd rather wait until we know for certain it's needed. I hate to examine a patient through gloves. The CDC isn't recommending masks yet."

"Isn't that because there's a shortage?" asked Cherie.

"It could be," said Liz, trying to sound neutral, although the shortages made her furious. Everything was so politically fraught at the moment, and she knew she shouldn't add fuel to the fire. "It's hard to sort the hard facts from speculation. But out of an abundance of caution, starting tomorrow, I want everyone to wear masks. Don't go hog wild, please. One mask per day. We have a limited supply. We need to make what we have last."

There was a chorus of groans.

"I know. I hate it too, but this is for the patients as well as for us. Any of us could be carrying it."

"Won't that scare people even more?" asked one of the medical assistants.

"It might," said Liz, "but it also says that we're serious about preventing the spread of the virus."

"Some of the older people don't even believe there is a virus," Ginny, the practice manager said. "They say it's a hoax or a political conspiracy."

"I guess we know what news station they watch," said one of the medical assistants with a snicker.

Liz shot her a disapproving look. "I don't want to get into the politics of it, and we shouldn't engage patients in that discussion either. I know it's frustrating, but we need to be calm and professional."

"Some people won't even listen to me when I say we need to practice careful hygiene to prevent spreading the virus," Cathy said. "They think it's all a joke. Meanwhile, we can't even get test kits."

"Well, that's the one bright spot. We finally got some kits."

"How many?"

"Fifteen. I ordered fifty."

Jim rolled his eyes. "Fifteen? You've got to be kidding!"

"I'm afraid not," said Liz. "I think we should use them to test ourselves first. We're going to be on the front lines. There are nine of us. That leaves six kits for patients. Let's use them wisely. I'm putting Cherie in charge of testing. She's also in charge of PPE, which is going to be tight, so don't give her any grief."

Liz gazed around the room.

"Any questions?"

The billing clerk raised her hand. "Can we get pineapple and ham pizza next time?"

Everyone laughed, and that seemed a good place to end the meeting.

While Liz bolted down another slice of pizza, Cherie approached. "It's not good for your digestion to eat that fast."

Liz swallowed a mouthful. "You think you need to tell me that?"

"No. And I'm not being a smart ass."

"I know you're not, Cherie, but you know how doctors are. They never follow their own advice."

"I wish you would follow mine."

Liz studied Cherie's face and realized her advice was kindly intended. "Maybe I will. Thanks." She bit into the pizza but chewed more carefully this time.

"Thank you for giving me so much responsibility. I appreciate the experience."

"You have a good head on your shoulders. You think things through. I trust you."

Cherie's eyes widened momentarily with surprise. "Thank you, Dr. Stolz."

"Liz," growled Liz. "No one here calls me Dr. Stolz."

"Just being respectful." Cherie smiled, which disarmed Liz. "I'll start swabbing this afternoon."

Another smile from Cherie made it hard for Liz to avoid smiling back. "Okay. Get the tests rolling and thanks for the advice."

Cherie walked away and Liz went back to her pizza. As she watched Cherie talking to the support staff, she thought, *she's so good with people. Great hire.*

***

Liz squirmed a little, sitting with the members of the vestry at the big conference table. She felt completely out of her element with all those devout church members. Well, maybe some of them weren't that devout, and this was just a social connection for them, like the Rotary or the chamber of commerce. By comparing it to her civic clubs, Liz felt more comfortable. Community service she completely understood. The religious part, forget about it! Liz always said that phrase like the New Yorker she was, even when she only said it in her mind.

Tom Simmons, the associate rector, opened the meeting with a prayer. Liz had known Tom since he and Erika were graduate students at Yale, and Liz was a resident in surgery. Oh, the stories Liz could tell about Tom, but while he prayed, she tried to look respectful. She felt Lucy studying her out of the corner of her eye. Liz winked at her. Lucy's lips curved into a little smile, and she raised an auburn brow.

Liz took a mental vacation while parish business was being discussed. Lucy, sitting beside her, had to nudge her when it was her turn to join the discussion.

"So far, the bishop has left it up to the local clergy, but I hear a rumor that a change may be coming. Dr. Stolz, do you think we should continue holding public worship services?" Lucy asked.

Damn it, Lucy, you're going to stick it on me! But Liz was never one to dodge a hard call. She took a deep breath and said, "No, I think you should suspend public services."

There was a murmur of surprise along the table. Someone said, "But the president says there's nothing to worry about. The virus will go away soon. As soon as the weather gets warm. Like the flu."

Liz laughed. "I'm sorry to laugh. But that's ridiculous. The president is not a scientist. He knows nothing about the behavior of this virus. It's not a cold. It's not the flu. It's something we haven't seen before. No one has natural immunity. That means anyone can get sick. Some people will get very sick and die. I think out of an abundance of caution, you should suspend public services."

An older man started to speak in an angry voice, but Lucy raised her hand to silence him.

"We asked for Dr. Stolz's opinion, and she gave it."

"Thank you, Mother Lucy," said Liz, sliding into her authoritative persona. She'd thought she'd happily left her leadership role behind when she'd retired from Yale, but people kept asking her to step up. No matter how much she tried to take a back seat, she kept being shoved to the front of the bus to drive.

"First of all, most of the congregation is elderly," Liz said. "That's just a simple fact of demographics. Maine is a gray state and frankly, most mainline churches have a larger percentage of seniors than younger people. This virus is much harder on older people. Almost everyone sitting at this table is in the high-risk group. Most viruses, like the flu or a cold, have an incubation period where the host is asymptomatic. That means any of us could be harboring the virus and yet seem perfectly healthy. It's fine to tell people to stay home if you don't feel well, but by that time, it's often too late."

"Are you saying that right now, we could be endangering one another?" asked Tom.

Liz realized Tom was lending support by asking a leading question and nodded in his direction.

"Yes, although I think at this point, the risk is relatively low. There are no confirmed cases in the state."

"So why close down the church?" asked the man who had quoted the president.

"I'm not an epidemiologist, but I do know one thing. Contagious diseases can spread rapidly. It only takes a few infected people exposing a few more people for diseases to spread like wildfire. Look at it this way. Let's say

I have it. I give it to all of you. You go home to your families and businesses and give it to them. They give it to other people, at work, at school. In a large group, like a church service, the exposure is magnified. I don't care how many precautions you take." Liz glanced at Lucy. "Sorry to be so blunt, but this is potentially a dangerous situation. It's real. This is not a drill."

"But this is exactly the time that people need reassurance and comfort," a woman said anxiously. "You already suspended the home and hospital visits. How will people receive communion?"

Tom said, "If someone is dying or ill, then I or Mother Lucy will do our best."

Lucy nodded in agreement. "In the interim, I am looking into ways to have prayer services on the internet. My wife, Professor Bultmann, has shown me an interactive app that her college is using for classes. I think it can work to help us keep our community together."

"But some people don't have the internet," a man protested.

"I know, and I'm sorry," said Lucy, "but I'd rather keep my congregation alive. These are difficult times. We'll all have to make accommodations." She looked at each person around the table. "I'm going to take a vote on this matter, but I want you to know I will take final responsibility for the decision. All in favor of suspending services, please raise your hands."

Liz breathed a sigh of relief when the raised hands showed a clear majority.

They discussed how to let parishioners know that services were being suspended. Obviously, they could post a notice on the church sign. Everyone who passed on Route 1 would see it. Someone suggested a postcard mailing to people without internet access. The parish admin said she would send out an email blast and post the notice on Facebook.

The meeting concluded with a prayer for safety and good health in the crisis. The vestry members filed out, but Tom remained behind. He offered Liz an elbow bump. "You were great, as always," he said. "Simple to follow information. Perfect."

"Maggie says I'm too direct."

"This isn't the time to mince words," said Tom. He nodded to Lucy. "Good decision, Lucy," he said, heading out.

"I'm sorry I put you on the spot like that," said Lucy with a contrite expression that made Liz instantly forgive her.

Liz shrugged. "I'm used to it. When I ran the surgical department, I had to make a lot of tough calls. Some made me very unpopular."

"I know this is really bad to ask," said Lucy, "but I could really use a hug."

"It's not the best idea, but I showered and changed clothes before I left the office. I don't want to drag bugs home to Maggie or the kids." Liz pulled Lucy into a hug and held on tight.

"Thank you for being so supportive and strong," Lucy said, hugging back fiercely. "We're going to need it in the coming days."

"Thank you for being smart and kind. We're going to need that even more."

18

Maggie, who'd been reading *The New York Times* while the kids watched cartoons, tried to hang on to them when the door from the garage opened. Liz would be tired after a full day of office hours and a church meeting. The last thing she needed was to be tackled when she walked in the door.

Maggie found Katrina and Nicki hugging Liz's legs. "Hello, girlies! I missed you too," Liz said in a cheerful voice. Maggie loved her for making the effort.

"Let me say hello to Grandma." She leaned over Nicki to give Maggie a kiss.

"I'm sorry, sweetheart. I didn't mean for them to accost you at the door." She gave the girls a little tug. "Okay, you two. Back to your cartoons. Let Grandma Liz take off her coat."

The girls ran back to the media room. Maggie held Liz's bag while she took off her coat.

"You look beat," said Maggie.

"Too many meetings. Not used to them anymore. Seems like that's all I did when I was at Yale. Always hated them. Such a waste of time."

Maggie nodded, although she knew the value of meetings to consolidate support for an idea. Liz was a "get it done" kind of person who despised politics. Sometimes, she wished Liz would use more people-sense to make her life easier.

"Come into the kitchen, I'll get you a drink."

Liz glanced in the direction of the media room.

"Don't worry. The kids will be all right for a few minutes. I never get any private time with you anymore." Maggie put her arms around Liz's waist. "I miss you."

Liz kissed the top of her head. "Miss you too."

In the kitchen, Maggie dispensed some ice into Liz's favorite crystal glass and poured in some whiskey. "A double, please," said Liz, watching her.

"That bad?"

"I ordered fifty test kits and got fifteen. That's enough to test the staff and just six patients. At that rate, how are we supposed to know what we're dealing with?"

Maggie put the glass into Liz's hand. "Have a drink, sweetheart. There's nothing you can do about it." Maggie bent to check her dinner baking in the oven. "Kid comfort food again," she said, sliding the racks back into the oven. "Chicken wings and mac and cheese. I hope you don't mind."

"Keep making all that comfort food, and I'll need to buy new pants." Liz patted her belly.

"You're not the only one. Although the kids keep me hopping. I hardly ever sit down."

"Brenda told me they're going to close the Hobbs schools tomorrow. It was decided in the selectmen's meeting last night."

"I know. The head of the English department at Hobbs High asked if I would teach some online classes. I also got a call from the community college."

"They could do worse than a Yale Ph.D. for that." Liz frowned. "But can you manage it with teaching the kids?"

"Yes, I think so. I give Katrina assignments to work on. There's plenty of Kindle content to keep Nicki occupied for hours."

"You're lucky you know how to access and use digital resources. What will other people do?"

Maggie shook her head. She had no idea what they'd do. She feared both for the parents and the children. Now that she was a stay-at-home grandmother, she realized how much work it was to care for young children full time.

"Where's Alina?" asked Liz, glancing at her watch. "It's late for her."

"She said she needed to pick up some equipment at the studio. Starting tomorrow, they're letting her work from home."

"They must like her up there. Good for her. She's very talented."

"They're letting all employees not essential to the live studio work from home."

"Really?" asked Liz, looking up from sorting the day's mail. "That's smart. I think there's going to be more of that soon."

"Probably a good idea."

Liz threw the pile of junk mail into the recycling bin under the sink. "If Alina is going to be working here, she'll need a place to work."

"How about one of the guest bedrooms?"

"I think she'll need more privacy." Liz looked thoughtful. "I'd lend her my office, but I might need it soon myself."

"She can use my office upstairs."

"Are you sure? That's your private space, and where are you going to teach your classes? There's the room behind the media room. It's sound-proof. It would make a great studio for video editing. It's full of junk now, but we can clean it out."

"I'll help you," said Maggie, taking Liz by the arm. "Now, go out and sit down while I finish dinner."

"You just want me to check on the kids."

Maggie put up her hands. "Guilty!"

As Maggie was setting the table for dinner, she heard her daughter's voice along with the excited sound of children's voices. Liz was there too. Maggie couldn't hear the conversation but from the sound of heavy bags rolling across the floor, she could guess Liz was helping her daughter move in her equipment.

Maggie poured ranch dressing into a bowl for the children and tossed the salad she'd made for the adults. She heard more equipment coming in and thought how lucky she was to be married to such a welcoming person. Of course, when the house was full in the summer, Maggie sometimes thought differently, especially when she was off for the summer, and the task of entertaining the guests fell to her.

Maggie watched the children enjoy her meal. She tried to ignore all the food that fell under the table or got smeared across the surface. Liz said it didn't matter because when she'd built the table, she'd sealed the top with polyurethane. Maggie knew that Liz would give Ellie, the cleaner, something extra in her pay to compensate for the mess the kids made.

Liz tidied the kitchen while Maggie and Alina got the children ready for bed. The girls wanted Maggie to tell them a bedtime story. She had been with them the whole day, and she was eager for some adult time, so she told a short one.

She found Liz and Alina in the small room off the media room. "I'll put all these cables and speakers down in the basement," Liz was saying as she carried out a box.

When Maggie looked in, she was impressed with their quick progress. The space was finally free of boxes and spare electronics. Liz had brought up a folding table from the basement and set up some power strips.

"Hey, Mom," said Alina, noticing Maggie standing in the doorway. "My new office. What do you think?"

"A little small," answered Maggie honestly.

"My office at the station isn't much bigger." Alina plugged in her laptop and adjusted the desk lamp.

"I'm sorry there's no window," said Liz, "but the light is pretty good in here." She scanned the ceiling with a frown.

"Come on, you two," ordered Maggie. "You can finish tomorrow. I'm desperate for adult company."

Alina and Liz looked at one another.

"Never refuse an order from your mother," Liz advised in a playful voice. "I'll bring this box to the basement. Then I'll open some more wine."

They settled in the living room with glasses of wine and oatmeal cookies that Maggie had baked with the girls. "I've become such a traditional grandmother," Maggie observed, taking a bite. "But the cookies are good."

"I appreciate all you're doing, Mom. You're such a good teacher. The girls are probably learning more from you than in school."

"I never taught little ones, except you and Sophia when you were very small, but I'm doing my best."

"I'm sure you're great," said Liz and finished her cookie in a bite.

"Liz, when you're home on Monday, you can take over the science lessons. I'll look up the lesson plans for you."

"I don't need lesson plans," Liz said, reaching for another cookie.

"Yes, you do, Dr. Genius. There's a curriculum you have to follow."

"I'm sure I can figure it out."

Sometimes, Liz was so arrogant, but after a draining day with the children, Maggie didn't have the energy for an argument, even a minor one, so she changed the subject. "That is so nice of your boss to let you work from home."

Alina made a little face. "Nice has nothing to do with it. The governor is weighing a stay-at-home order. She can't go there yet because there haven't been any confirmed cases in Maine."

"There haven't been any confirmed cases because we can't get our hands on test kits!" said Liz impatiently.

"And there's that piece," Alina agreed. "It's all so political. What a mess!"

"Ali, you look so tired," said Maggie. "You should think about making an early night of it."

"I thought you needed adult company, Mom."

"Despite rumors to the contrary, Liz is an adult."

While Liz glared at her, Maggie laughed hilariously at her own joke. "I'm sorry. I'm so tired I'm giddy."

They all decided to go upstairs. Maggie let Liz get ready for bed first because she was quicker. Maggie's bedtime preparation involved makeup removal and facial creams.

As soon as Maggie came to bed, Liz switched off the light and slid down under the covers. She raised her arm so Maggie could snuggle against her.

"It's a lot with the kids," Maggie admitted. "Thank you for letting Alina stay with us."

"We have the room," said Liz. "If she was shut up in her little condo with the kids, trying to homeschool and work, she'd lose her mind."

"I'm surprised she hasn't had any panic attacks yet."

"Shhh. Don't tempt the gods."

"If the governor issues a stay-at-home order, a lot of people will be losing their minds. I'm sure Lucy and Cherie are going to have their hands full." Maggie snuggled closer. She slid her hand under Liz's T-shirt because she liked the feel of Liz's breasts even when she wasn't interested in making love. Liz stopped the movement with a soft press of her hand.

"Honey. I'm too tired, even for a tease."

"I'm sorry." Maggie slid her hand back out. "You want me to leave you alone so you can sleep?"

"Please."

Maggie slipped out of Liz's arms and rolled on her side. She was almost asleep when she felt movement on the mattress. She instantly identified it as small hands and knees making their way toward her pillow.

"Grandma!" Katrina whispered in a loud whisper directly into her ear. "Grandma!"

"What is it, Katie?"

Katrina sat cross-legged on the bed between Maggie and Liz. "Mommy is shaking like this." Katrina mimed exaggerated shivering.

"Okay, sweetie. You stay here with Grandma Liz, and I'll go see."

Liz sat up. "I'll go," she said, getting out of bed. "Maybe she's running a fever, but she didn't feel warm earlier."

"Can I stay here tonight, Grandma?" asked Katrina in a mournful voice.

Maggie flipped the covers over so Katrina could get under them. The girl cuddled against her.

"Will you tell me a story?"

"I already told you a story."

"I know. *Please.*"

Maggie knew it would be a few minutes before Liz came back, so she began to recite a fairy tale. By the time Liz returned, Katrina was asleep. Liz crept into bed carefully to avoid waking her.

"Is Alina all right?" Maggie whispered.

"Panic attack. I gave her a sedative. She's asleep now and so is Nicki. That kid snores like a buzz saw. I should take a look at her adenoids."

"I'm so sorry you had to get up."

"All good now. Next time, don't tempt the gods." Liz rolled over and pulled up the covers.

19

"**A**nother Guinness, chief?"

Brenda looked up into the woman's face. Sinead had been waiting tables at Sláinte since Brenda had first come to Hobbs. She'd arrived from Ireland as a young teenager but still had a charming brogue. Now, she was in her thirties, a teacher by day, but a pub waitress at night. Although Hobbs paid better than most towns, teachers' pay wasn't high enough to afford the rent.

Not that Brenda was paid that well, even as a police chief. Compared to what she'd made in New York, it was laughable. Her pension from New York, combined with her salary, made it possible to afford the mortgage. Marcia's death and the loss of her income had put a big dent in Brenda's finances. Good thing the taxes in Hobbs were so much lower than in Brooklyn.

Sinead leaned on the table. "Don't worry. I'm sure your friend will be here soon. Would you like me to get you something to eat while you wait?"

"Yes, and another Guinness, please."

"What would you like? We have Irish poutine on special tonight." Brenda knew what poutine was because she and Marcia had traveled through Quebec. French fries with cheese curds slathered with gravy had never really appealed to her, so she made a little face.

"Try it," Sinead urged. "It's wonderful. Maine cheddar, our own homemade corned beef, and curry sauce instead of gravy."

Brenda wrinkled up her nose. "Sounds fattening."

"It is, but delicious. Trust me." Sinead winked.

"You never steer me wrong. Okay, I'll try some."

"You won't regret it. I promise."

Brenda gazed around the pub. It was nearly empty, only a few patrons at the bar and two tables with couples. Brenda had taken the table closest to the propane stove for warmth. The dance floor separated it from the restaurant. There was always a little draft from the back door, so Brenda got up and moved the table and chairs closer to the fire. She'd done it before, and no one had complained. Cherie was from the South and always cold. Hopefully, she'd appreciate the gesture.

When Sinead returned with the beer and poutine, she brought something else. "I found your friend. Why didn't you tell me you were waiting for Ms. Bois?"

"You know each other?" Brenda raised her brows in surprise.

"The Hobbs Family Practice people come in here for drinks after work sometimes," Sinead explained. She glanced at the stove and her eyes measured the new distance to the table. "I see you moved closer to the fire. Smart." Sinead smiled at Cherie. "Wine, right? Merlot?"

"Yes, good memory."

Sinead smiled and headed off with their order. Cherie reached over and took Brenda's hands. "I'm so sorry I'm late." Cherie's eyes looked deeply into hers. "Dr. Stolz put me in charge of testing the staff, and it's like herding cats."

Brenda had to rouse herself from gazing into Cherie's eyes. "That means Liz trusts you. Take it as a compliment."

"Oh, I do."

"Why do you call her, Dr. Stolz? No one else does. Even the kids in town call her Dr. Liz."

"I was taught that it's important to use titles to show respect."

"Don't tell Liz that."

"Hah! I'm stubborn, not stupid." Cherie released an exasperated breath. "Only trouble is, I was so busy testing everyone else, I forgot to test myself! Then I got all wrapped up in getting the application right. Everything with this virus is such a mess. There's such a shortage of tests. CDC refused the WHO's design because it had to make its own test. You know, we're so exceptional. Of course, we had to come up with our own test."

"If Liz thinks everyone should be tested, you should be too." Brenda narrowed her eyes to make her point. "You will, won't you?"

"If I have time tomorrow."

Sinead returned and placed a glass of wine in front of Cherie. "Would you like some time with the menu, or do you know what you want?"

"I'll have the stuffed haddock special," said Brenda.

"I haven't even looked at the menu, but that sounds good," Cherie said. "I'll have it too."

"Wonderful," said Sinead, "you won't regret it." She collected the menus and headed back to the hostess desk.

"What's this?" asked Cherie, looking at the basket of fries covered with brown sauce. "Poutine? How fun!"

"It's Irish poutine," Brenda explained. "I haven't even tasted it yet. Let's see. I never really liked the Canadian kind."

Brenda carefully watched Cherie's face, pleased to see it brighten at the taste. "It's good. Try it." She took Brenda's plate and spooned on some of the gooey mixture. Brenda tasted a few fries, found it was good and helped herself to more.

Cherie glanced around the pub. "This place is dead tonight."

"Usually is this time of year. They'll have a big crowd this week for St. Patrick's Day. Then the place dies until about the end of April."

"I heard they closed the Hobbs schools today," said Cherie.

Brenda nodded. "A lot of people are worried, and I don't blame them. I'm worried too. All those people dying in Italy. Scary."

"It is scary…very scary."

"Did you watch the emergency selectmen's meeting on Wednesday?" asked Brenda.

Cherie swallowed before answering. "I did. I never miss watching you on TV."

"Did I look okay?" asked Brenda anxiously.

Cherie's eyes smiled in amusement. "You always look okay. More than okay."

Brenda audibly sighed in relief. "There's a new selectman…I should say selectwoman…who annoys the shit out of me." She glanced up at Cherie. "Pardon the language."

"I've heard that word before," Cherie said, "but thanks for the apology."

Brenda nodded an acknowledgement. "The woman moved up here three years ago. Now she thinks she should run the whole town. She has one of those big houses on Gull Island. Thinks she knows everything." Brenda rubbed her fingers together. "Money."

Cherie frowned. "I think I know who you mean. She sure had a lot to say at last night's meeting."

"Republican. Town is full of them." Brenda lowered her voice. "I think she's gay."

"There are some gay Republicans, you know," said Cherie.

"So, I hear. I just don't understand it. How can any woman vote for them?"

Brenda looked up from her plate to see Cherie regarding her curiously. "I guess you're not Republican," she said.

"God no! Are you?"

"No," said Cherie with a little laugh.

Brenda mimed wiping imaginary sweat from her brow. "Thank God. That's a relief."

"What would you have done if I were? Drop me?"

"No," said Brenda, drawing out the word. She shifted uncomfortably in her chair. "But it would have taken some adjusting."

"I'm surprised you're not a Republican. A lot of cops are."

"A lot of blues went to the dark side after Reagan started playing the race card. I wasn't one of them. I went to school with black kids. I worked with officers of all ethnicities. My father had a black partner while he was still on patrol. I grew up calling him Uncle Dave. He really went out of his way to look after our family after Dad was shot."

She watched Cherie's calm eyes evaluating her words but couldn't read her judgment. Cherie turned her attention back to her meal.

"If you don't mind, let's not talk about politics. I'm fried tonight and could use a break."

Brenda instantly worried that she had burdened Cherie. "I'm sorry."

Cherie shook her head. "I think we could all use a break from politics. I have outrage overload. Let's talk about something else."

Sinead came with their dinner plates. "Anything else I can get you ladies?" she asked as she collected their appetizer plates and picked up the empty basket that had held the poutine. "Guess you liked it."

"Delicious," said Brenda.

"Told you so. You need to trust me."

Cherie's eyes followed Sinead as she walked away. "She seems to know you pretty well."

"Oh, I come in here a lot when I'm lonely, and I want to see other humans."

Cherie made a sad face. "I'm sorry you're lonely."

"Thank you, but things are looking up since I met you," Brenda replied with a smile. She hungrily dug into her meal. "So, what would you like to talk about instead of politics?"

Cherie raised a forkful of fish to her mouth. After she tasted it, she smiled. "Food is good here." She took another bite and chewed appreciatively. "What shows do you watch on TV?"

"Cop shows."

"How did I know you would say that?"

"They make me laugh. Everything is always so dramatic. The perps are always big shots. Real police work isn't like that. A lot of it is really boring. What do you watch?"

"I'm not a big TV fan. My father is usually hogging the big screen in the living room. I watch a lot of BBC series on my laptop." She gave Brenda a long critical look. "Speaking of which, I still can't get over how much you look like Sarah Lancashire in *Happy Valley*."

"Never saw it."

"Would you like to? It's on Amazon Prime."

"Maybe. When?"

"After we eat. I might be able to convince Daddy to watch TV in his bedroom. Then we could stream it to the big screen."

"Tonight?" It was a Friday night. Brenda had no duty the next day and could stand to get home a little later. "That sounds like fun." She began to eat faster at the thought.

When Sinead brought the bill to the table, Brenda snatched away the plastic folder. "My treat," she said, "and I'm not taking any argument from you."

"Well, thanks," said Cherie, "but can I, at least, leave the tip?"

"Okay, but I always give Sinead a good tip. She works hard for the money. She's a teacher and this is her side gig to pay the rent."

"Ten dollars enough?"

Brenda glanced at the bill and did a quick mental calculation. "Fifteen."

Cherie opened her purse, fished in her wallet and took out a twenty. "Okay?"

"Generous, but thank you. Sinead will appreciate it."

The cold was biting when they opened the door. Apparently, March still had some chilly blasts to offer before it went out like a lamb.

"I'll meet you there," said Cherie as she climbed into her Subaru. "Think you can find it?"

It took Brenda a moment to realize that Cherie was messing with her. "I'll try," she said.

Cherie waved before closing the car door. As Brenda followed her to the cottage, she noted that Cherie was a careful driver. She scrupulously observed the speed zone past the school. Maybe she was just on good behavior because she knew the police chief was following her, but somehow Brenda knew that wasn't the case. Cherie was what they used to call a "good girl." She willingly followed the rules. Then Brenda thought back to what Cherie had told her about her sister being shot and realized there was a very good reason to toe the line. Getting stopped by the police for a traffic violation would absolutely trigger her.

Brenda pulled in behind Cherie and watched her head inside the house. She'd give Cherie a head start to let her negotiate the TV arrangements with her father. Meanwhile, she scanned her phone messages to see if there had been any incidents. She was relieved to see it was completely clear. At this time of year, when Hobbs was down to its smallest population, things were pretty quiet.

Cherie came to the door and waved to encourage Brenda to come in. By the time she went inside, Jean-Paul was already in his room and the door was closed.

"I hope I haven't disturbed his routine," Brenda whispered.

Cherie shook her head. "No, he's usually in bed by this time of night. He falls asleep with the TV on, although I don't know how. He always has it so loud. I think his hearing's starting to go." Cherie pointed to her ear. Brenda noticed that it was small and delicate. She liked the way Cherie's curly, blond hair curved around it. She was momentarily tempted to touch it, but Cherie turned and headed to the kitchen. "I'll get some wine. Or would you like a beer since you've been drinking Guinness?"

The thought of another beer appealed to Brenda, but she didn't want to belch or fart in Cherie's presence. It was a little early in the relationship for that. "Thanks. I've had enough for now," said Brenda.

Cherie returned with a glass of red wine and gestured toward the sofa in front of the big TV. Brenda sat down and she was surprised when Cherie sat close enough for their thighs to touch. Unsure about the invitation, Brenda laid her arm across the back of the sofa instead of around Cherie's shoulders. Cherie played with the remote, switching screens until she found *Happy Valley* on Amazon Prime.

"Ready?"

Brenda nodded. She watched, fascinated. She hadn't seen many British cop shows. One thing she noticed right away was that none of the British cops carried a gun, just a baton. She frowned until she realized that gun control was so strict in Britain, few perps would have guns, so the cops wouldn't need them either. What an amazing thought. Perps without guns.

Brenda scrutinized Sarah Lancashire, the lead actress, to see the resemblance. Yes, they looked a little alike. The blue eyes and blond hair certainly. Also, the pink complexion and the slight cleft in the chin.

"You really think she looks like me?" asked Brenda, tilting her head from side to side as she studied the actress. "She's kind of fat."

Cherie laughed. "TV makes everyone look fat." She gave Brenda a conspicuous once over. "In fact, you could stand to lose a few pounds."

Brenda opened her mouth wide in faux shock. "Are you telling me this as a PA or as the woman I'm dating?"

Cherie raised a blond brow. "We're dating?" she asked innocently.

"You know we are!" Brenda sounded more indignant than she'd intended. She stared at Cherie, who was holding her hand over her mouth in a desperate attempt to stop laughing. Finally, the laughter sputtered out.

"I'm sorry," said Cherie. "You're such an easy mark."

Then the amusement left her eyes, and she put her hands on Brenda's cheeks. She drew her down into a sensual kiss. Cherie's lips were soft and velvety. Her tongue gently explored Brenda's mouth until her head began to spin. She gave Brenda a final, soft kiss, then let her go.

"I guess we are dating," said Brenda still dizzy from the kiss. She noted the response in her crotch.

"I guess we are." Cherie had a misty look of affection and indulgence in her eyes, but when Brenda reached for her, she turned and leaned into her body. "Let's watch one episode. Then maybe we can continue." Cherie reached for the remote and ran the video back to the point where they'd stopped paying attention.

Brenda was uncertain about what to do next. Should she push harder to continue what they had started or follow Cherie's lead? She had her answer when she put her arm around Cherie, who sighed and snuggled closer. She put her hand on Brenda's thigh and rested her cheek against her breast. That felt right, so Brenda held her close.

20

Cherie finished cleaning up the kitchen and left her father happily enjoying the pork tenderloin she had prepared for his dinner. She bent to kiss him on the cheek.

"Good night, Daddy."

"Good night, Hon. Say hi to Brenda for me."

Cherie stood back and gave him a worried look. "You okay by yourself with your CPAP?"

"Of course," he said in a confident voice. "I did it before I moved in with you. Now, stop waiting on me hand and foot. I can manage!"

"Okay. Call me if you need me."

"Never happen. Now, get out of here. Have a good time." Jean-Paul went back to his meal.

Reluctantly, Cherie headed to the door. She felt guilty leaving her father alone. He seemed frailer every day, but so far, he was healthy. Despite his compromised breathing, his heartbeat was strong. Even so, Cherie knocked on the wooden door for good luck as she went through.

She turned on her GPS because she still didn't trust herself to find her way in the dark woods. It was so dark at night in Maine, the darkest place she had ever lived, but on a clear night, she loved to see all the stars overhead.

Once Cherie left the main road, she tried to focus on the mechanical voice barking directions, but she was distracted by the memories of her evening with Brenda. She'd patiently honored her request to watch the entire episode of *Happy Valley*. As soon as it had ended, she'd reached for the remote and switched it off.

"You're pretty bossy in my house," Cherie had teased.

"I am not. Just following your orders." Silly Brenda had given her a crisp salute. Cherie smiled to herself at the memory. What followed made her smile even more. Brenda had taken her in her arms and kissed her.

Cherie had felt every ounce of feeling in that kiss. Brenda wasn't aggressive, but Cherie could feel her strength in the way she held her, a quiet strength magnified by the profound gentleness of her touch, as if Cherie were delicate crystal that would be crushed by anything more. It wasn't at all what she'd expected when she'd first met the tall, blond woman and was repulsed by the police uniform and the gun.

After that smoldering kiss, Brenda had eased her down on the sofa and stroked her cheek and her hair. Her eyes were full, and Cherie realized she was nearly weeping as she touched her.

"What's the matter?" Cherie whispered anxiously.

"You're so beautiful it breaks my heart. I have this sweet pain right here." Brenda pressed a spot near her solar plexus. "I've only felt it one other time…the first time I kissed my wife."

That brought tears to Cherie's eyes. She pulled Brenda's face to her shoulder. Tears ran down Cherie's cheeks into Brenda's hair. What a crazy thing. In the moment when she was so excited, she'd ended up crying like a baby. It made no sense.

When Brenda kissed her again, she didn't protest. When Brenda's hand wandered under her top and cupped her breast, Cherie could barely breathe.

"Is this okay?" Brenda asked.

"Yes," whispered Cherie. "More than okay."

The adamant female voice of the GPS suddenly demanded Cherie's attention. "Turn here!" Cherie knew she was close. She recognized the entrance to the development, but that was all. The loops and circles inside were a maze. She squinted to make out the road signs in the dark. Her heart pounded for a few moments when she realized she'd made a wrong turn and had no idea where she was. She felt so stupid for getting lost with a GPS shouting orders. "Go North! Go North!"

She lowered the volume and sat for a minute to take a few deep breaths and calm herself before she proceeded further. Finally, she regained her confidence and headed back in the right direction.

The driveway and porch lights burned brightly when she arrived at Brenda's driveway. She caught Brenda peeking out from behind the drapes when the headlights hit the house.

She opened the door. "Come in, stranger," she said, standing back.

Cherie put the bottle of wine in Brenda's hands, which seemed to befuddle her for a moment. She smiled and set the bottle down on the floor while she helped Cherie out of her coat. She carefully hung it in the closet.

She gave Cherie a quick kiss, snatched up the wine bottle and headed to the kitchen. Baffled at first, Cherie finally realized after the previous night's emotional kiss, Brenda was shy. *The police chief is shy. Imagine that!*

Cherie followed her into the kitchen. "What are you cooking that smells so good?" she asked, trying for a light, casual tone to put Brenda more at ease.

"Chili."

Cherie couldn't stop the apprehension from showing on her face. This was the night they might make love and Brenda was making *chili*?

Brenda stared at her. "What's the matter?" Then she realized the implications and laughed. "Don't worry. I don't put beans in my chili. I spent some time doing sensitivity training with the Cincinnati PD. They make chili differently there. And I serve it with mac and cheese, not rice."

She lifted the lid of the pot so Cherie could look in. To Cherie's relief, there were no beans. "Smells delicious."

"Hot. I mean, spicy hot."

"I have Cajun blood. I don't mind hot. The spicier the better."

Brenda gave her a positively seductive look. "I'm glad to hear that." Brenda dipped a spoon into the pot and offered it to Cherie. "Taste?"

After a quick, puzzled glance, Cherie took the spoon and tasted the steaming chili. "Hot!" she mumbled with food in her mouth. "Physically *and* chemically. Wow!"

"Too hot?"

Cherie tasted it again. "No, it's spiced just right." She realized Brenda was studying her mouth. She wiped it in case there was some stray chili.

"You have the most beautiful mouth," said Brenda. "Your lips are so full and soft."

Cherie put down the spoon because she knew what was coming next.

Brenda took a step forward. "I want to kiss you."

Cherie nodded. Brenda put her arms around her. The kiss was deep and so intense that Cherie felt faint. She allowed herself to be supported by Brenda's arms. When it finally ended, Brenda held her against her shoulder.

Cherie could smell the laundry soap Brenda used to wash her shirt, straightforward and clean. That was part of Brenda's appeal. What you saw was what you got. No games. No agenda. Cherie felt the press of Brenda's soft breasts against her. She never wanted to leave those strong arms, but Brenda let her go. Once the warm breasts went away, Cherie felt chilled. *Come back. Please come back*, she begged in her mind.

"We should eat," Brenda said, taking two bowls down from the cabinet. She spooned some macaroni and cheese into each. Then she ladled in some chili. "Do you want to eat in the kitchen or out by the wood stove?"

After that intense kiss, Cherie could hardly make sense of the question. Fortunately, Brenda answered it for her.

"Let's eat by the stove." She took out two trays and added silverware and napkins. She put the bowls on them. "If you take them out and put them on the coffee table, I'll open the wine."

Cherie had been raised to be helpful in the kitchen, so she followed orders without question. Brenda followed with the wine and two glasses.

"Here's to no-gas chili," Brenda said, tapping glasses.

"You'll have to give me your recipe."

"Remind me." Brenda dug into her chili. It was obvious she enjoyed her own cooking and had a good appetite. Cherie looked at her with a clinician's eye. Apart from the few extra pounds around the middle, which many women acquired at her age, she was fit. Her eyes were clear, and she had a healthy glow. Brenda became aware that she was being watched. She frowned. "Go on. Eat up if you want to watch your show."

Cherie put her spoon into the bowl. The chili, combined with the macaroni and cheese, had lost some of its punch. It now had just the right balance of savory richness and spice. As she ate, Cherie realized she was hungry.

"How was your day?" asked Brenda between spoonsful.

"Busy. And I forgot to test myself again. I only realized when I was coming home from the office."

"You better do it, or you'll catch hell from Liz." Brenda suddenly jumped up. "I almost forgot! I made jalapeno corn bread to go with it."

"Sit down, Brenda. We can have it later…for a snack."

"Are you sure?"

"This is so rich I'm getting full already."

They finished the chili. Brenda offered more, but Cherie didn't have room for another bite.

"Let me put the food away, then we can watch your show." Brenda put the pot of chili out on her screen porch to cool while Cherie rinsed the dishes and put them in the dishwasher.

"We make a good team," said Brenda, obviously pleased to see everything scrubbed and put in its place.

"We do," Cherie agreed.

They went into the living room. Brenda fiddled with the remote until she found the right app and navigated to *Happy Valley*.

"I hope you're enjoying this show," said Cherie.

Brenda shrugged. "It's entertaining."

Cherie took the remote from her. "You don't really like it."

"I didn't say that."

Oh no! We're going to have our first fight. Cherie felt her chest constrict at the thought. She hated unnecessary quarrels. Then Brenda gave her a long, earnest look.

"I'd rather be doing something else," she said. "If you know what I mean."

Cherie sat up and studied her face. "Are you sure we're ready for that?"

"I don't know," said Brenda with an earnest look. "I guess there's only one way to find out." Brenda's face turned in the direction of the stairs.

Cherie laughed. "How romantic. You make it sound like a science experiment. You should see your face!"

Brenda reached for her and gave her a soft kiss. "Better?"

"Do it again, and I'll let you know."

"Hmmm. You don't need to ask twice. I love your lips and how you kiss."

Something about Brenda reminded Cherie of herself as a young woman. Her kisses were curious rather than aggressive. Meanwhile, Cherie had been keeping track of where Brenda's hands were to avoid getting too far too fast. Despite each being a half century in age, they sat on the sofa, making out like two adolescents. The thought made Cherie giggle.

Brenda drew back to look at her. "Am I doing something wrong?" she asked with charming innocence.

Cherie caressed Brenda's flushed face with her fingertips. "No, Brenda, you're doing everything right."

Brenda glanced at her hand in Cherie's blouse. She gave her breast a quick caress and withdrew it. "I don't know about you, but I'm too old to make love on the carpet."

"Brenda Harrison, are you inviting me to your bedroom?" asked Cherie, batting her eyelashes.

"Yes, I think I am."

"We might be more comfortable there."

"I think so." Brenda looked momentarily anxious. "Are you sure about this?"

Cherie placed a soft kiss on her lips. "Let's go before I change my mind."

Brenda took her hand and led her up the carpeted steps to a large airy room with a king size bed. "I made the bed in your honor," said Brenda with a quick grin. "I put on clean sheets."

"You expected we'd end up here?"

"No, but I hoped we would."

Brenda unbuckled her belt and let her jeans fall off. She tossed them on a nearby chair and began to work the buttons of her shirt. She picked up a scrunchie from the night stand and tied back her hair. With a little smile, Cherie watched the perfunctory way her would-be lover undressed. Realizing she was being watched, Brenda looked up.

"I'm sorry. Not very romantic, I guess. I should have waited for you."

Cherie shook her head. "I'm getting an interesting preview."

Brenda grinned. "I looked through my drawer to find my nicest panties. Marcia used to throw out the ones with holes." Then she realized what she'd said and glanced away. "I don't know why I said that."

"It's okay," said Cherie, coming closer. "You're nervous. So am I." She took Brenda's hands and placed them on her blouse. "Since you're so good with buttons, try mine." Cherie smiled at the instant, frank desire in Brenda's eyes. She held her gaze while Brenda unbuttoned her blouse and slipped it off her shoulders. She let Brenda unzip her pants, but she wiggled out of them. She sat down on the bed and extended her hand. Obediently, Brenda came to her side.

The kissing resumed. While Cherie was distracted by what Brenda was doing to her mouth, she felt her bra being unhooked. She enjoyed the feel of soft fingers kneading her breast, gently pinching the nipple. Warm lips replaced the fingers. Cherie let a soft moan escape. She loved having her breasts sucked. Wordlessly, Brenda urged her to lie down. Before she did, Cherie made sure to relieve Brenda of her bra.

They lay side by side, gazing into one another's eyes. "How long has it been for you?" Cherie asked in a whisper. She caressed Brenda's cheek with the back of her hand.

"Three years. I just couldn't be with someone else after she died."

"I understand."

"How about you?"

"About the same. Since I left Shreveport."

Brenda grinned. "Do you think we'll remember how?"

"Oh, I think so." Cherie took Brenda's hand and placed it between her legs. Soft fingers began to stroke her gently.

"Your underwear is very sexy," said Brenda, smiling against Cherie's cheek,

"I'm glad you like it."

Brenda kissed her, filling her mouth with her tongue. Her hand slipped under the waist band of her panties. Fingers stroked gently, finding their way around. Cherie could hear how wet she was. The sound of her slickness aroused her even more. Brenda pulled Cherie's panties off and flung them over her shoulder. She pulled off her own and dropped them on the floor.

Cherie found it exciting to be skin to skin with a woman after such a drought. She rolled Brenda on her back and climbed on top of her. Brenda's little sigh of approval encouraged her. Cherie gently nudged her legs apart and pressed against her. Brenda moaned softly.

"You like that?" whispered Cherie into her ear.

"Oh, yes. Don't stop."

Cherie gently rocked her body, pressing closer. "Can you come like this?"

"Probably not, but it feels really good."

Cherie paused to give Brenda's breasts some attention. They were large and soft. The nipples instantly stood at attention when Cherie's tongue teased them.

She rolled off. "I like it to be mutual," said Cherie, taking Brenda's hand.

"I find it hard to concentrate, but all right." She mirrored what Cherie was doing, then surprised her by going inside. Cherie opened her eyes and saw she was grinning like a guilty child. "I couldn't wait any longer," Brenda explained.

Cherie closed her eyes again to enjoy the drag of Brenda's fingers inside her. Brenda expanded her presence with another finger, enhancing the feeling of being filled. Cherie knew she was close now. When Brenda's fingers emerged to stroke her clitoris, Cherie was right on the edge. Then it surged through her. She felt her face and breasts flush as the climax rushed to completion.

She saw Brenda looking at her intently even as Cherie tried to remain focused enough to return the favor, but Brenda reached down and stopped the motion of Cherie's hand.

"Don't you like what I'm doing?" Cherie asked anxiously.

"I'm just sensitive right now." She brought Cherie's hand to her lips and kissed it. "It's hard for me to trust someone enough to come the first time. Sometimes for a while. Is that all right?"

"Of course!" said Cherie, squeezing Brenda's cheeks. She kissed her too for reassurance. "Everything is all right as long as it feels good and no one gets hurt. Take as long as you need."

"I like the way you make love. I'm sure it won't be long. Lucky you. You came so quick."

"I was very excited…and you have good hands."

"Can I make you come again?"

"No, that's enough for now."

Brenda nodded and pulled Cherie closer. "Can you spend the night?"

Even though Brenda couldn't see her, Cherie shook her head. "I can't leave my father alone."

"I was afraid you'd say that."

"Do you understand?"

"Of course, I do. Can you stay a little longer? Please?"

"Yes." Cherie snuggled deeper into the curve of Brenda's body.

21

Erika opened the refrigerator to get cream for her coffee and felt something wet seeping into her socks. *No, it's too damn early for this.* She looked down and saw a puddle under the refrigerator. There was water dripping from the freezer compartment. "Fuck!" she said aloud.

She opened the freezer. It was packed. The day before, they'd gone shopping and stocked up to comply with the governor's stay-at-home order. Erika had noticed when they rearranged the meat to make better use of the space that everything in the freezer was covered with ice crystals. She'd thought the frosty appearance was because they'd left the door open too long. She touched a pack of chicken parts. Usually, it was rock hard. Now, it gave to the touch. "Fuck!" she repeated.

Lucy, wrapped in her flannel robe and wearing fuzzy slippers, came into the kitchen, looking for her first cup of coffee. She went straight to the coffee maker to fill a pod. Usually, Erika would have heated a cup for her by now, but the refrigerator situation had distracted her.

"I think we have a problem," Erika muttered.

Still groggy from sleep, Lucy turned around and looked quizzical. "What's the matter?" Erika pointed down to the puddle on the floor. Lucy blinked. "Where did that come from?"

"The freezer I think."

"Oh, no!"

"Oh, yes, and everything in there is defrosting."

"We just went shopping!"

"I know." Erika nodded in the direction of the coffee maker. "Have a cup of coffee while I call Liz."

"It's a little early, isn't it?"

"She has those kids over there," said Erika, taking out the carton of half-and-half to hand to Lucy. "She'll be awake." She picked up her foot and stared at it. "My socks are soaked."

"Go change your socks and then call Liz," advised Lucy. She threw some towels in front of the refrigerator to absorb the water. "I'm praying this isn't as bad as it looks."

Erika went to change her socks. She despised wet feet with a passion. To make sure it didn't happen again, she put on clogs.

She met Emily on her way to the stairs.

"Morning, Erika."

"Good morning. Put something on your feet. We have a leak from the freezer."

Emily made a face, but she went back to her room.

Erika tried to calm herself enough to think clearly. Being without a refrigerator in the middle of a lockdown was a disaster not even to be contemplated, but she forced her mind not to jump to conclusions. She was confident that Liz would figure out what was wrong and know exactly what to do.

Erika brewed a fresh cup of coffee and went into the dining room to call Liz. A moment later, Lucy came out and sat across from her, presumably to offer moral support. Her red hair was wild from sleep, and she was pale without makeup, but the mere sight of her could make Erika sigh.

"I love you," said Erika.

Lucy offered a brilliant smile. "I love you too, sweetheart."

Erika tapped Liz's number in her favorites. She put the call on speaker so she could drink her coffee. "What would we do without her?" she wondered aloud as the phone began to ring on the other end.

"Good question," said Lucy.

"What the fuck?" asked Liz when she answered. "It's not even six-fucking-thirty!"

Lucy almost spit her coffee and began to laugh.

"Erika, do you have me on speaker?"

"Yes," admitted Erika. "Do you mind?"

"Well, yes. I don't want Lucy to hear me swearing."

"Oh, Liz, we all know you love to use expletives. Your mouth could curdle milk. Right now, the cream in my coffee is rather lumpy." Erika looked up and saw Lucy trying to keep from spitting her coffee again. Maybe she should take the phone off the speaker.

"Oh, for God's sake!" said Liz.

"Eh, eh. Lucy will tolerate the F-bomb but not taking the Lord's name in vain."

"Oh, for fuck's sake, then. What do you want at this ridiculous hour?"

Erika put on her serious persona. "We have a little problem over here. Our freezer is defrosting."

"Did you bump a switch when you put things in?"

"Not that I know of. There are no switches."

"I need the make and model number."

Lucy went into the kitchen. A few minutes later she slid a pad with the information in front of Erika, who recited it to Liz.

"I'll do some research and be over soon," said Liz. "I need to get dressed first. Give me half an hour."

The call ended without a goodbye, which was usual for Liz.

Lucy kissed Erika's cheek on the way to the kitchen. "You're lucky to have such a good friend."

"Don't I know it!"

❁❁❁

Liz arrived, as promised, within thirty minutes. She brought her flashlight and a tool bag that looked like it could weigh fifty pounds. Erika watched with her arms folded on her chest as Liz rolled the refrigerator away from the wall and unscrewed a panel on the back. With the flashlight, she carefully inspected the hardware inside.

"You're the only doctor I know who still makes house calls," said Erika.

"Only for refrigerators, not people."

"You mean if I were sick and called you, you wouldn't come?"

"For you, I would come. For Lucy. Or Emily. Hell! Of course, I would come!"

Liz frowned as she looked at the circuits behind the refrigerator. "It looks like the defrost switch got stuck. It's an auto, not a manual switch. It probably got damaged during that power outage after the ice storm. All that cycling on and off will do it. Eventually, the circuits fry and your compressor goes. Then you're fucked." Liz glanced at Lucy with a wordless apology.

"But it's only six months old!" groaned Erika. "It cost over two thousand dollars, and it was on special order for months!"

"I told you not to get fancy appliances," said Liz, switching off her flashlight.

"Says the woman with the Aga stove in her kitchen."

"That's different."

"Of course, it is. Everything's different for Liz Stolz."

Liz gave her a filthy look. "Thanks, I like you too."

As much as Erika enjoyed their sparring, she realized she was being unnecessarily mean to a woman who'd just dropped everything to come to her rescue. She noticed Lucy giving her a very disapproving look. Fortunately, Liz never seemed to care about the insults they exchanged, nor did Erika.

"I brought some coolers," Liz said. "We have room in our refrigerator in the basement. I turned on the refrigerator in the apartment over the garage. You and Lucy can stay there. Emily can stay in the house."

"What are you talking about?" asked Erika.

Liz gave her a look that said, "don't be dense." "Obviously, you can't stay here with no refrigerator. You're coming to stay with us."

Lucy, who'd been anxiously watching this exchange, said, "We could stay in the studios at the rectory. There's probably space in the refrigerator in the common room."

"Forget about it," said Liz in her New York accent. "You'd kill each other in those little rooms. This stay-at-home order is not going to end any time soon. The apartment is very nice." She counted off its benefits on her fingers as she enumerated them. "It has a sitting room, a little alcove study, a large bedroom, its own kitchen, a great view of the garden."

"Why do you have an apartment when you have so much room in the house?" asked Lucy.

"I built it for my mother. You know, my mother who never wants to come to Maine? It would be nice if someone used it. Maggie and Alina are doing a quick clean and changing the linens."

"You assumed that we would accept your invitation?" asked Erika, giving her a fish-eyed stare.

"Of course, I did. You never turn down my invitations."

Erika glanced at Lucy to get her opinion.

"I think it's very generous of Liz. She's right. We can't stay here without a refrigerator. Even if we order a new one today, it will take weeks to arrive," said Lucy in a sensible voice. "We can't ask Tom to move out of the rector's apartment, and we'd go crazy in the curates' studios. I vote we accept Liz's kind invitation."

Emily came into the kitchen. "What's going on?"

"The refrigerator is no longer functional," explained Erika, "and your mother says we're moving in with Liz."

"Oh, okay," said Emily. "I'll take a shower and pack."

Lucy's brows rose in surprise. She glanced at her wife. "You have the magic touch today. If I'd said that, I'd get an argument."

Erika raised her palms. "What is she going to do? Stay here alone?"

Liz started taking soggy food boxes out of the freezer and tossing them on the island. "All this stuff will have to go to the dump. Can I have a big trash bag?"

"I can do that, Liz," said Erika.

"Go pack. This is a team effort, and your stuff is defrosting fast. Now, let's go!"

Erika remained to hand Liz the food as she arranged it in the coolers. Everything was packed and ready to go within twenty minutes. Liz carried the coolers out to her truck and strapped them to keep them secure in transit. She threw the black bag of frozen food that couldn't be saved into the back. "I'll bring it to the dump on the way home."

Erika went up to pack. She watched Lucy laying out her black suits and clerical blouses.

"We can come back later for our clothes," said Erika. "We only need things for a few days."

Lucy gave Erika a firm look. "We're not coming back for a while. Why not move as much as we can today?"

Usually, Erika was the practical one, but the refrigerator problem had put her off balance. It was a relief to see Lucy taking charge.

"You're right, as usual," said Erika and began arranging her clothes to pack.

❋❋❋

To Liz's frowns of disapproval, Maggie welcomed them all with hugs. "I keep trying to explain social distancing," complained Liz. "It falls on deaf ears."

"They're our friends, Liz," said Maggie, enfolding Emily in her arms. "They're not going to give us anything."

Liz opened her mouth to say something, then obviously thought better of it. Instead, she asked for Erika's keys. "I'm going to move your car."

Maggie gave Erika a hug. "Ignore Liz. She's making such a big thing of this."

Erika dropped her voice. "It is a big thing. She's not exaggerating. We could be carrying the virus."

"We're all going to get it eventually. Liz said so."

"The idea is that we don't all get it at the same time and overwhelm the system," Erika tried to explain.

"I understand," said Maggie, "but we're all going to be living together and eating together, so what's the point?" She led them into the kitchen. "When Liz gets back, we can have some breakfast. I took some quiches out of the freezer." She turned to Lucy. "I've planned some meals with your defrosted meat, but there's way too much for us to eat. Maybe you know some elderly people or shut-ins who would like a home cooked meal?"

Lucy put her arm around Maggie. "That's a great idea! I do know some people. What are we offering?"

"We have all this sauce we made last summer," Maggie said, gesturing to the sweating plastic containers on the counter. "You had lots of chopped meat. We have pasta. Baked ziti? Between your lettuce and ours, we can make an enormous salad. And we can turn your loaves of Italian bread into garlic bread."

Lucy hugged Maggie. "How many extra people can we feed?"

Maggie shrugged. "Six? Maybe eight?"

"I'll call around and see who's interested," said Lucy.

Liz came back into the kitchen. "Emily and I have all of your bags up in the apartment."

"Oh, Liz," said Erika, feeling genuinely guilty. "I would have helped you!"

"I know, Professor, but you were soooo busy," said Liz with obvious sarcasm. "So, has my wife told you her plan to multiply the loaves and fishes?"

Lucy turned to Liz. "I had no idea you knew about that."

"Hah! I know a lot of things you don't think I know."

"I bet you do."

"Come on. Let me show you to your new digs." Liz led them upstairs. "The bridge to the apartment is on the second floor." She pointed in the opposite direction. "Emily will be in the seashore room. The girls have already commandeered her for a game of Chinese checkers. Nicki hasn't a clue, so Emily helps her cheat."

"How very nice of her," said Erika in a droll voice.

Liz unlocked the door at the house end of the enclosed bridge. "I turned on the heat pump, so it should be comfortable by now. I put your perishables away. If you need anything, I'm sure we have it."

Liz unlocked the door on the other side of the bridge. "You can access it from the garage through that door." She handed Erika the keys.

"I can't believe you added this beautiful apartment for your mother, and she never stays here," said Erika looking around.

"She hates Maine."

"A shame. It's such a beautiful place."

"New Yorker's chauvinism," said Liz, as if that explained it. "I'll let you get settled. Then Maggie expects you for breakfast."

Erika was surprised to find the place much larger than she'd expected. There was a spacious living room with a gas fireplace, an efficiency kitchen, an alcove with a dining table for two, a nook with a desk, and a large bedroom. The bed was covered with a warm quilt and a colorful afghan crocheted by Liz's grandmother. Erika remembered the pale-eyed, old woman, whose drop-dead look was terrifying, despite her obvious kindness.

"This is such a nice place," said Lucy. "Why don't you rent it?"

"I don't want strangers walking around my property. Besides, I might need it for summer guests."

"Not this year," said Erika. "I doubt you'll see anyone up here this summer."

Liz nodded thoughtfully. "I'm afraid you're right."

They went back to the main dining room to have quiche and grilled sausage for breakfast. Erika felt like she'd come home again. When Liz had first moved to Maine, she'd often invited Erika and her partner to spend time with her during the summer. The house was always full of people. Liz's niece and her children came every summer. Liz's ex, Jenny, brought her nieces and nephews. Liz's old friends from Yale came for long weekends. As much as Erika liked her privacy, she found the communal living stimulating and comforting. Like a summer camp for adults.

Over the babble of conversation at the table, Liz tapped Erika's hand to get her attention. "We need to get your father out of that senior residence."

"Why?"

"If this thing spreads, those senior communities will be a hotbed of contagion. Nursing homes, especially."

"I hadn't thought of that."

"Stefan can stay in the downstairs guestroom. He'll have everything he needs there."

"Except his library," said Erika.

"He's already read all those books."

"I know, but he likes to have them near."

"So put some of them in boxes and bring them over. I'll clear off the bookshelves."

"Are you sure, Liz? You already have all of us here. That's a lot of people."

"I'd rather have you all here where I can keep an eye on you." She tapped her temple and pointed to Erika. "*Verstehst du?*"

Erika nodded. "After we finish eating, I'll go down to Ocean Terrace to pick up my father."

"Good."

22

When Lucy opened her eyes, she had to remind herself of where she was. She glanced at the pine branches outside the enormous window and imagined she was in a tree house. The queen-sized bed was as comfortable as any in the Grand Lux European hotels where she'd slept while on tour as an opera singer. Sometimes, it seemed she slept in a different city every night. She vividly remembered those days, learning new blocking and stage gestures for the same role in each production, a new tempo for each conductor. She always told herself she didn't miss singing, but if she were completely honest with herself, she did. She still missed pouring out sound into the darkened theater while the lights blazed overhead.

She'd wondered how she would get in her daily morning practice, but Maggie had explained that the media room was sound-proof, and Lucy could exercise her voice to its capacity. The only thing that could escape from that sound trap was the bass vibrations when Liz was watching a superhero movie on full volume.

Lucy turned and gazed at Erika sleeping. Her blond hair was now nearly white. Her lashes were so pale they were almost transparent. Her eyelids fluttered delicately as she dreamed.

Lucy wanted a playmate, so she kissed Erika's shoulder and teased her nipple with fingertips. "Good morning, Professor," she whispered into Erika's ear.

"Good morning, Mother Lucy," Erika replied. The sound of her English accent with that little hint of German still made Lucy smile. It was the same voice that whispered sexy suggestions when they made love and explained complex philosophical concepts whether Lucy wanted to hear them or not.

Erika raised herself on her elbows to look at the bedside clock. "It's still early!"

"Yes, but it's Sunday, and Liz is going to help me set up for a virtual morning prayer service."

Erika flopped down on her pillow. "Then you and Liz go play, and I'll come watch when you're all done." She rolled over and took all the covers with her.

"Please get up and have a cup of coffee with me? Please...." Grinning wickedly, Lucy gently reached between Erika's legs.

Erika jumped. "Lucy!"

Lucy, overcome with laughter, hugged her sides.

"You are a beast! An absolute and utter beast!" declared Erika.

Lucy stopped laughing long enough to say, "But you love me."

"Yes, I do, although sometimes, I wonder why."

Erika flung off the covers and headed to the bathroom. Lucy lay back on the pillow and admired the pine trees outside. How lucky Maggie and Liz were to live deep in the woods, away from all this virus madness.

When Erika returned, they sat in the little kitchen alcove to drink their coffee. Erika was grouchy after being awakened, but the caffeine eventually made her friendlier.

"Will this be a full service with communion?" she asked. Since the first time Erika had wandered into a worship service, she had come a long way in understanding the rituals of the Episcopal Church. She now had an appreciation for the rhythms of the liturgy and Lucy's role as a priest. Lucy loved her for making the effort. She still despaired about converting Liz, but Erika had potential. Lucy wasn't ready to give up on her. Not yet.

"I think the morning prayer is enough until we have more of these under our belt. Did you know that morning prayer was the usual Sunday service and the Eucharist was celebrated only once a month?"

"No, I did not know that, but really, it's too early for a lesson in church history." Erika got up to prepare another cup of coffee.

"I'm going to shower and dress so I can get in some practice before everyone gets up."

"You wake me up to keep you company, and then you abandon me?" Erika complained in a dramatic voice.

Lucy kissed her. "You'll be fine."

After showering, Lucy took time with her hair because something in the water at Liz's house made it softer, and it wasn't as cooperative. A few more grays seemed to have appeared, but she told herself it was the lighting in the bathroom. It was excellent for makeup, however, and Lucy made quick work of that. She decided that she looked presentable. The video camera slightly distorted color, and she didn't want to frighten her congregation.

Lucy began her vocal practice, as she did every day, with the exercises her mother had taught her. Her mother had briefly been a principal soprano at the Boston Lyric Opera. After Patricia Bartlett died, the memories had brought on terrible grief. Now, Lucy saw the ritual as a daily tribute to a woman who had given up her own dreams so her daughter could become a success. Lucy was glad her mother hadn't lived to see her quit the stage.

Lucy was just finishing up when she saw she had company. Liz was the first to stumble in with a cup of coffee. Lucy wondered if it was her imagination or was Liz looking a bit more put together than she would usually be on a Sunday morning. She had attempted to give some order to her iron-gray curls. She was wearing a very nice polar fleece zip-up and knit pants.

Liz bent to give Lucy a kiss on the cheek. "Good morning, Lucy."

"You've given up on the social distancing?" Lucy asked reaching up to give Liz a hug.

"We're all breathing the same air, cheek to jowl, as they say. For better or worse, we're all in this together now."

"How long does it take to get this virus?"

Liz shrugged. "We suppose it's a week to fourteen days."

Lucy studied Liz's handsome face. It was becoming more sculptural as she aged. The character lines were becoming firmly etched. Scars from childhood cuts were emerging like hidden items on a photographic plate exposed to light. There was a permanent furrow between her brows.

"You're very worried about this, Liz. Aren't you?"

Liz flopped into one of the home theater seats and nodded solemnly. Lucy sat down beside her and reached for her hand. "Liz, you are a superb doctor, brilliant and caring. You are so good with your patients. I can say that because I'm one of them. I trust you."

Liz squeezed her hand, then let it go to pick up her coffee cup. "Thank you, Lucy, but this is something we've never seen before. I'm flying blind. I have no fucking idea what I'm doing."

"You'll do the best you can. That's all God asks of you."

"Then maybe he has lower standards than I do."

"Liz, be good to yourself. God loves you and you should too."

"Are you preaching to me, Lucy? I'm immune to that, you know." Liz gave her a look that indicated she was trying very hard to be patient.

"Not as immune as you think." Lucy bent her head a little and mimed giving Liz's face a careful inspection. She tapped Liz's forehead. "Right there…I can see it…just a little inkling of faith."

Liz sat back in her chair. "I do believe in something…a higher power or whatever you call it. Sometimes when I was in a difficult surgery, and everything was going wrong, I prayed for help."

"And did it come?"

"Yes, it usually did."

Lucy nodded. Maybe Liz had potential too. One step at a time.

The door opened and Maggie came in with a cup of coffee. She sat down next to Liz. "I thought we could use a rehearsal."

Liz threw her head back and groaned. "Of course, you do!"

"Emily volunteered to watch the kids during the service," said Maggie. "She's very good with them."

Lucy was disappointed that Emily had found an excuse to avoid the prayer service. "I understand. The poor girl had an overdose of religion from her adoptive parents."

"She'll come around," said Maggie. "Right now, the kids are a novelty, and they worship the ground she walks on."

Alina came in with a cup of coffee. "I knew I'd find you all in here."

"I thought we could use a brief rehearsal, so we know everything is working right," said Maggie.

"I'm used to setting up for video on the fly," Alina said, sounding slightly defensive. "Of course, it works right."

"Alina, don't argue with your mother," said Liz. "She's a very directive director."

Lucy was used to their affectionate banter and knew it was in good fun. She was more worried about Alina's response. From counseling sessions, she knew the young woman's difficult history. Her young childhood in a Romanian orphanage was bad enough, but as an adult she'd had to flee an abusive husband. Medication controlled her PTSD, but she still had panic attacks.

"Let's all just relax and get in the right spirit for worship," Lucy suggested.

Lucy turned to Liz. "Liz, would you mind giving a brief update on the medical aspects of the virus before the homily?"

"Wait a minute," protested Liz. "I'm the audio technician. I didn't sign up for this."

"Please…" said Lucy.

"Well, all right. Dammit, Lucy! You can make anyone do anything!"

"Yes, it's my superpower."

"All right, people," said Maggie, clapping her hands. "Let's get to it."

Lucy got up to stand behind the table Liz had moved onto the stage to use as an altar. Liz had built it for the sitting room on the second floor. She often made period furniture, but this piece was Shaker-inspired and made of book-matched, quarter-sawn, white oak. It was simple and perfect for this purpose.

"Do you mind standing for the service?" Maggie asked. "We could bring in a smaller table and a chair and go for a tight focus."

"Listen to her," said Liz. "Like she knows something about shooting video."

"I do know something about it!" Maggie protested.

"Maggie, I think we should let Alina direct," suggested Liz. "She does this for a living."

Alina looked pleased. Maggie opened her mouth to speak but Liz shot her a warning look.

"Okay. This is not for transmission," said Alina. "We're going to record an introduction you can post on Facebook. We can record it as many times as you like until you're satisfied. Then you can watch it and make improvements."

"I'm used to doing live performances," said Lucy. "I don't need a rehearsal."

"Ready?" asked Alina and began to count. While she did, Lucy prayed. She begged God to comfort her people, ease their fears, and envelope them in her grace. She opened her eyes just in time to see Alina's signal.

Lucy beamed her warmest smile. "Welcome, everyone. I'm Lucille Bartlett, rector of St. Margaret's Church. I invite you to join a livestream prayer service that we'll be having here at nine o'clock. The information on how to download the app to join an interactive meeting is on your screen. We'll be able to see one another and interact, including during our fellowship. I have a few friends with me to join us. Of course, it would be better to meet in person, but in this dangerous situation, it's wonderful to be able to get together this way. Please call the number below if you have any trouble connecting. Dr. Stolz is standing by to help you with any technical questions."

Alina gave her the cut sign. "It's a take, I think."

Maggie, who'd been watching on the monitor, nodded in agreement.

"You want to watch it to see if you need to make changes?" asked Alina. "You have ten minutes before going live."

Lucy shook her head. "No, I'm ready."

23

From the door of the screen porch, Maggie watched Liz's science class with her granddaughters. They sat at the mahogany table Liz had originally built for al fresco meals on the deck. She later decided to bring it inside to avoid the bugs. In the summer, it was their favorite place to eat. Now, it was the foundation of a makeshift classroom.

Maggie was surprised to see how patiently Liz worked with the girls. When she was doing a project she enjoyed, like building model rockets, she could sit with them for hours. Maggie suspected the children were Liz's excuse to revisit her childhood. What she was witnessing today looked different. Liz seemed to be taking her role as a teacher seriously. She had drawn pictures of the coronavirus to explain what it looked like and how it worked. Then she encouraged the girls to draw their own pictures. They were completely absorbed in the lesson.

Instruction was going on in other parts of the house. Erika was teaching her Colby philosophy class, and Emily was working on a complicated math theorem with Erika's father, the famous mathematician who had once been short listed for the Fields Medal. Maggie was also back to teaching online. She reflected that there were enough advanced degrees in that house to open a college.

She thought of all the poor parents with no teaching experience who were now forced to homeschool their children. Many of those parents were also trying to work remotely. How did they do it?

"What are you thinking about?" asked Lucy's voice behind her. Maggie turned to see Lucy dressed casually in yoga pants and a sweatshirt. Maggie could instantly tell she wasn't wearing a bra. Of course, hers weren't the only unsupported boobs in that house. Maggie focused her eyes on Lucy's smiling face.

"How nice to see you! Getting bored over there in your little garret?"

"Not bored exactly, just disconnected. I'm used to being very social and busy. I can't do hospital visits or my grief counseling group. Suddenly, I have so much time on my hands. I finished my Sunday sermon early, believe it or not. I even miss my counseling clients. I can only call them, not see them. It's not the same."

"You could use Facetime or Skype."

Lucy shook her head. "There are privacy issues with that, and many of my clients are poor or elderly. They don't have the wonderful technology we have here."

"Tea before you go back to work?" asked Maggie.

Lucy smiled with delight. "Oh, Maggie, that sounds wonderful! I need a break. Listening to Erika teach her philosophy class makes my head hurt."

"Listening to Liz and Erika talk always makes my head hurt," said Maggie, commiserating.

Lucy leaned against the countertop while Maggie heated the water in the electric kettle and put loose tea into the infuser of an elegant china teapot. When the water was hot, she filled the pot and put it on a silver tray with matching china teacups, sugar bowl, and cream pitcher.

"How civilized," observed Lucy.

"At least we can pretend, virus or no." Maggie gestured toward the breakfast room.

As Lucy sat down, she threw her hair over her shoulders and out of the way. "Everything seems so off with this 'stay-at-home' order. I feel strange and disconnected. Like I'm in the twilight zone."

"Everyone does. Americans aren't used to following orders, and they're certainly not used to being told when to come and go." Maggie poured a little tea into her cup to make sure it had reached the proper strength. She filled Lucy's cup. "You're not even in your own home. That must feel really strange."

Lucy reached for the sugar bowl. "I'm used to being a vagabond and living wherever I land. I think it's harder on Erika. She misses her beach."

"I can't tell you how many times, I've thought, 'What a nice day. I think I'll drive to the beach for a walk.' Then I remember I can't because the beaches are closed. I miss the outdoors." Maggie gazed out the window, noticing that the snow pile off the deck was finally beginning to melt.

"What were you thinking about so hard before?" Lucy blew on her tea before she took a sip.

"Alina tells me my fairy tale readings on the station's website are a big success. There must be other things we can do to entertain kids during the lockdown. You're a priest. Maybe you could tell Bible stories."

Lucy's auburn brows tipped toward the bridge of her nose. "Why does it have to be so religious? Why not sing together? Or skits? Puppet shows with sock puppets? There are a lot of opportunities, especially with all the technology Liz and Alina have in this house."

"But I want it to be educational to support all the parents suddenly homeschooling their kids. And I want it to be meaningful. Everyone's giving away free content. People are overloaded with it."

"Oh, but some of it is wonderful! Erika and I are watching the livestream from the Met every night."

"I hope that's not interfering with your love life," said Maggie with a sly smile.

"Not a chance."

"Well, you're newlyweds. You wouldn't know about that."

Lucy gave her an innocent look. "You mean it changes?"

Maggie was about to say something when she realized she was talking to a trained marriage counselor, and she'd been had.

"Lucy, sometimes you're so wicked!"

Lucy laughed. "It's been said. But back to your suggestion. I think we should focus on having an impact right here in Hobbs. Let's start with St. Margaret's. Alina has some very good ideas for creating a mixed liturgy. She knows how to split the feed and integrate transmissions from various sources. Holy Week and Easter are coming up. We could do so much more with multimedia. You could sing. We could have a virtual choir!"

Maggie hadn't heard Lucy sound so enthusiastic since they'd worked together on the Labor Day Benefit for the Webhanet Playhouse.

"I was thinking education," said Maggie. "We have all these big brains in this house. We should be able to do something special."

"Erika is already teaching. You've agreed to teach remote classes. And you've said yourself, there's the curriculum to consider."

Maggie tapped her fingers on the table. She was hurt that her friend had shot down her idea so quickly. "I thought I could count on you."

Lucy leaned forward so she was in Maggie's face. "You *can* count on me. But we shouldn't try to compete with the resources already flooding the internet. Free movies. Free online access to libraries, museums, concerts. It's all wonderful, but it's overwhelming. I'm sure if we put our heads together, we can come up with unique ideas that will make a difference right here in Hobbs."

"In Italy, opera singers are singing to their neighbors."

"In Italy, people live right on top of their neighbors. That's why they're all getting sick. Here, we can't even see the next house."

"So, what can we do?"

"We can use the church Facebook group to livestream entertainment. That would cheer up parishioners. Maybe we can start a separate Facebook group. Let's call Tony Roselli and see if we can reach out to our friends at the Webhanet Playhouse."

"But no Bible stories?" asked Maggie, disappointed.

"Maybe for the Sunday school we had to cancel."

Maggie looked up as Liz came into the breakfast room wearing a little frown. She bent to speak confidently, and Maggie reached up to touch her cheek. "What's the matter, sweetheart? You look worried."

Liz's frown deepened as she glanced at Lucy.

"Oh stop," said Maggie. "You know you can talk in front of Lucy. She's a priest. She's sworn to secrecy."

"Maggie, can you take over the science lesson? I need to get to the office."

"Is there an emergency?"

"Could be. Cherie Bois's father is really short of breath, and she had to leave. I'm going over there to see her afternoon patients."

Maggie sat up straight, instantly concerned. She was very fond of Cherie, who sang with her in the choir. "Is it serious?"

"I don't know. She told him to put himself on his CPAP. That might help." Liz kissed Maggie. "I've got to go. The kids are occupied for now."

"I'll bring them in here. They can finish their project, and we can keep an eye on them."

"I hope that JP is all right," said Lucy. "Cherie is devoted to him. The only reason Cherie moved up here was because he wanted to die at home."

"Hopefully, he doesn't get his wish sooner than later."

Lucy gave her a sharp look. "Oh, Maggie, don't even say such a thing!"

Maggie shook her head. "I shouldn't, I know. I should be praying for him instead."

24

Liz scrolled through the screens. Negative. Negative. Negative. All of the SARS-CoV-2 tests for the office staff had come back negative. Liz was about to shut down the test portal when she realized she hadn't seen a report for Cherie Bois. Liz scrolled through the screens again, scrutinizing them more carefully. She still didn't find Cherie's name. Liz pulled up Cherie's complete lab records to double check. The file showed everything from her TSH for thyroid, which was normal, to a hormone test confirming that yes, she was in menopause. There was nothing for SARS-CoV-2.

Liz called the practice manager's desk. "Ginny, has Cherie come in yet?"

"No, Liz, she called out this morning. Her father is still having respiratory problems."

"What's on her schedule?"

"Nothing until this afternoon."

"What's on my schedule?"

"Mrs. Peterson is coming at 8:00 to review blood work. And you have three lab reviews after that. Mr. Lafferty, Mrs. McGee, and Mrs. Duval."

"I have an important errand to run. Could you call them and push everyone back an hour?"

"Sure thing."

Liz hadn't opened the box that had arrived yesterday. She was fairly certain it contained test kits, but she had delayed opening it because the box was smaller than she had expected. She could guess that meant they'd again received fewer tests than she'd ordered.

She took a razor knife out of her desk drawer and sliced open the tape. She counted the kits. There were twenty-five, marginally better than last time. She pulled out two kits and put them in the pocket of her vest along with a stethoscope. She headed to the supply room to pick up a mask and gloves.

"I'm going down to Cherie's," Liz told Ginny as she passed the registration desk. The practice manager looked concerned but nodded in reply.

The sun was shining brightly overhead. So far, March had been warmer than usual. Liz glanced at her watch. 7:45. She had time to walk if she set a brisk pace and didn't dawdle once she got there.

When Liz arrived at Cherie's cottage, the drapes were still drawn in the picture window. The old-fashioned cape was from another era. Despite its vintage and size, the value of the tiny house was ridiculous because it was within walking distance to the beach. Liz knew the owner of the property from the chamber of commerce, which was why Cherie could afford the rent. Liz was not above pulling strings for a good cause.

Liz made her way up the gravel walk to the front door. She tried to look through a small gap in the drapes to see inside. Maybe Cherie had had a bad night with her father and was sleeping in. No, there were lights on inside. Liz rang the bell and listened carefully. Finally, she heard the sound of footsteps. Liz slipped on her mask.

The door opened a crack. "Dr. Stolz?" asked a surprised voice. The door opened wide. In a workout suit, her blond hair tied back, and no makeup, Cherie still looked heartbreakingly beautiful. Liz put her weakness for her beauty aside and assumed a professional expression.

"I've never had my boss show up at my house," said Cherie, sounding slightly annoyed.

"That's because you've never worked for me."

"I've always heard you do things differently."

"Believe what you hear," said Liz. "May I come in?"

Cherie stood back, and Liz stepped into the house. "How is your father?"

"He's resting comfortably. It was a bad night."

"Coughing?"

"Hacking away."

"Fever?"

"Elevated two and a half degrees."

Liz frowned. "Do you suspect the virus?"

"I suspect a virus. Could be the flu."

"What about you? Are you feeling all right?"

"I feel fine. If I could find someone to sit with him, I'd be at work."

"Maybe that's not a good idea," said Liz. "I was reviewing test results this morning. Everyone in the office was negative as of the test date."

"That's a relief," said Cherie.

"It is. Except I didn't get a test result for you."

Cherie stared at her worn, fleece-lined moccasins. "I kept meaning to get to it."

"When I give an order, I mean it," said Liz. The even tone of her voice belied her anger. "I'm glad we started wearing masks in the office."

"So am I," said Cherie, sounding contrite. "I wouldn't want to infect anyone."

Making a concerted effort to sound more gentle, Liz said, "Since I'm here, would you like me to take a look at your father?"

Cherie finally looked up. "That's so kind. Yes. I'd appreciate it."

"First things first." Liz tore the cellophane off the test kit and opened the box. Cherie made a face. "Yes, I know. I don't like having a swab stuck up my nose either. Head back." Liz gently routed the swab up Cherie's nostril and deposited it in the test tube. She corked it carefully. "I brought one for your father too."

"Can we spare it?"

Liz looked at her incredulously. "He's your father, Cherie. He's seventy-two and he has COPD. Who are we saving them for?" Cherie looked properly chastened, so Liz stopped scowling. "Show me where."

Cherie led Liz into a large bedroom. It was obvious that she had given her father the master bedroom. The small, gray-haired man was lying on an adjustable bed, not hospital-issue, but a commercial bed that looked expensive and comfortable. He was scrupulously clean, and, although a bit thin, he wasn't significantly underweight. Cherie was taking good care of him.

His eyes opened when Liz stood over the bed. "Hello, Mr. Bois. I'm Liz Stolz, remember me?"

"Hello, Dr. Stolz," he said in a charming voice. "How nice of you to make a house call."

"Your daughter is my favorite PA, so of course, I'd make a house call. How do you feel?"

"The coughing is nasty. Cough. Cough. Cough. Nothing comes up. Just hacking away."

"So, it's a dry cough? What else? Do you have body aches?"

He smiled weakly. "I was a mechanic in the navy. I used my body hard. I have bad arthritis in my knees, my hands, my wrists. I'm achy all the time. I wouldn't know the difference."

"Believe me. You'd know the difference. Does it hurt more than usual?"

He nodded. "It hurts pretty bad."

"I'm going to listen to your lungs, but first I'm going to stick a swab up your nose to test for the new virus. Okay?"

When Liz turned to open the test kit, she noticed that Cherie was watching her intently and wondered if she was evaluating her bedside manner. If she didn't approve of it now, she should have seen her when she was still a surgeon.

Liz swore at the cellophane wrapper, wondering why everything had to be packed so tightly that you needed a knife to break into it. It was even harder with gloves on. She handed the box to Cherie. "Can you open this, please?"

"Let me wash my hands."

Liz tried to be patient while she waited. Cherie returned and opened the kit. "Do you want me to do it?"

"You're the test maven," said Liz. "Have at it." She stood back. Cherie gently removed the nasal cannula and swabbed her father's nose. Deprived of oxygen for a few minutes, he began to gasp. Cherie replaced the cannula.

As Liz listened to Jean-Paul's chest sounds, she became concerned. He was Jim Bowden's patient, so she didn't have an actual memory of how his lungs sounded when he was healthy, but she certainly didn't like the sound of them now. The characteristic crackling of lung disease was fierce. Liz felt his forehead with the back of her hand. She didn't care if Cherie thought it was old-fashioned. Liz had been trained in another era, when physical examination still meant something to doctors. Now, it was test, test, test.

"Thanks, Mr. Bois," said Liz, stepping back. "I'll let you rest now."

Jean-Paul managed a smile. "I appreciate you're coming to see me, Doc."

Liz put away her stethoscope and gestured toward the door. When they stepped into the hallway, Cherie closed the door to her father's room. "What do you think?" she asked anxiously.

"Without the test, we can't say conclusively, but I think he might have the coronavirus. His lungs sound really bad."

Cherie's eyes widened with alarm. "Should I call an ambulance?"

Liz frowned as she thought through the options. If he had the virus, taking him to the hospital was a risk to him and other patients. On the other hand, his pulmonary function was already compromised, so the hospital was the best place for him if things went bad quickly, and he'd be at the front of the line for care because there were still so few cases in Maine.

"I see you have him on a CPAP. You could give him excellent care here, but if he needs to be on a vent, which, given the state of his lungs, is a real possibility, he should be in a hospital. Better safe than sorry."

"Okay. I'll call 911."

Liz put her hand on her arm. "Make sure this is what you want to do. As you know, there are risks in the hospital too."

"I know, but I agree with you. The hospital is the best place for him. Once he's settled there, I'll come into the office."

"No, you won't. You're on self-quarantine."

"Why?"

"Cherie, think. Your father never goes anywhere without you. Where do you think he got this?"

"From me? I feel fine."

Liz looked at her intently, hoping to make her point without the need to elaborate.

"But I wear a mask in the office, just like everyone else," Cherie protested.

"Do you wear a mask everywhere else? To the supermarket?"

"The CDC doesn't recommend it. Only social distancing. I always use those disinfectant wipes they have at the door to clean my cart."

"You're the one who reminded us that the CDC is hedging its bets because of shortages. You can't trust anything they say."

"Then who can we trust?"

"Our own good judgement and verifiable scientific data." Liz extended her arm so she could see her watch without touching her sleeve. "I've got to get back to the office. Make the arrangements for your father and call me later. If you need anything, we'll make sure you get it."

Cherie's eyes started to fill. "Thank you."

Liz began to realize how frightened the woman was. "We're here for you," said Liz in her most reassuring voice. "Remember that. Now, get yourself together. I can find my own way out."

Liz walked back to the office at a brisk clip. She dropped off the test kits with Ginny. "Wear gloves."

"Has she been exposed?"

Liz shrugged, but she said, "Wash your hands afterwards." She headed back to her consulting room. On the way, she stopped into an exam room and carefully washed her own hands. She used an antiseptic wipe to clean her stethoscope. *For fuck's sake, she thought, how are we ever going to keep everything clean?* For good measure, she washed her hands again.

She'd changed her routine from taking a shower in the morning to showering before she left the office to avoid bringing any bugs home with her. She decided to shower now to avoid passing the virus on to her elderly patients. She rooted around in the drawer in her consulting room where she kept clean underwear and a clean top. After she showered, she'd wear a clinical coat to keep herself as free from contamination as possible. Clinical coats reminded her too much of the old days, but she'd wear one if it kept her patients and family safe.

Liz was reviewing the blood work for the patients on her schedule, when her cell phone lit up. She leaned over to take a look and saw a text from Brenda Harrison coming in.

In a meeting. Ambulance dispatch to Cherie's house. Know anything?

Liz texted back: *Suspected C-virus case. Cherie's Dad. Hospital transport.*

That bad?

Just a precaution. Call me later. DON'T GO OVER THERE!

Liz put down the phone and went back to studying her patients' labs. Then she thought about it. If she were Brenda, she would be heading to Cherie's house by now. Liz picked up her phone and called Brenda. It rang and rang before going into voice mail.

25

The salesman demonstrating the new radar equipment looked startled when Brenda jumped up in the middle of the meeting and said, "Excuse me. I need to go." Everyone turned around to look at her as she climbed over people's legs to get to the door.

As Brenda passed the dispatcher's window, she told her that she was responding to the 911 call.

"But, Chief, we already dispatched a car."

"Doesn't matter," Brenda muttered as she opened the door to the parking lot.

After she jumped into her cruiser, Brenda was tempted to turn on the sirens but resisted the impulse. After all, she was the chief of police, not some young rookie playing cop. There was hardly any traffic on a weekday in March, so she didn't need to force cars off the road to get to her destination. Then she decided to turn on the bumper lights to let the cars ahead know she was on a mission.

In a matter of minutes, Brenda was turning into Cherie's street. One of the white Hobbs PD SUVs was already parked in front of the house. Brenda pulled in front of it.

Officer Cote was standing on the walk, talking to Cherie from a distance. Either the ambulance hadn't arrived or had already left. Brenda saw that Cote was wearing a mask and gloves, per regulations. Grumbling, Brenda rummaged around in her console for the plastic bags holding masks and gloves. As chief, it was her job to model correct behavior.

She looked up to see flashing lights in her rear-view mirror. The Hobbs volunteer ambulance had just arrived. Brenda got out of the squad car to wave it down.

"You can go, Cote," she called to the officer, standing in front of the house. "I've got this."

"It's fine, Chief. I can handle it."

"I know you can. Go back and take notes for me in that meeting on the new radar. I'd appreciate it."

The young woman hesitated, but she knew better than to disobey an order. She nodded and headed to her car.

When Brenda turned around, she saw Cherie regarding her with a frown from the doorway. She was wearing a mask, so she couldn't see the set of her mouth, but she could guess it wasn't smiling.

Brenda approached gingerly. "Come in," said Cherie in a flat voice. "I'm sure you want to make sure they do everything right."

"It's not that," Brenda tried to explain. "I wanted to make sure you're all right." Cherie's eyes narrowed, making it obvious she wasn't buying her explanation.

"You came with your lights flashing. Could you draw any more attention?"

"You saw that? I'm sorry. I just wanted to get down here as fast as possible."

Cherie opened the storm door and gestured toward the interior of the house. "They're going to have their hands full transferring the equipment. He'll probably need to stay on the CPAP until they get there. It's big. One of the old ones from the VA."

"That will make a tight squeeze if you're riding with him down to the hospital."

Cherie shook her head. "I can't. Dr. Stolz put me on medical self-quarantine. I'm not allowed to leave the house."

"I'm sure there can be an exception—"

"No, there can't," said Cherie in a surprisingly adamant tone. "This is serious, Brenda." She motioned for her to follow her into the back of the house. "But keep your distance! I'm glad you had the good sense to wear a mask."

"I had to. I couldn't let my officer see I wasn't following my own orders."

Cherie turned and gave her a sharp look. Brenda felt like a freshman being stared down by the principal.

Cherie led her down the hall to Jean-Paul's room. They watched from the doorway as the EMTs tried to make sense of the tubes and wires. They finally decided to put Jean-Paul on portable oxygen while they loaded the CPAP on the rig.

"I'll make sure the equipment comes back," said Brenda.

"That's not the most important thing." From the flat tone of Cherie's voice, Brenda realized the seriousness of the situation.

She watched as the EMTs, two older women, deftly lifted Jean-Paul onto the stretcher. Hobbs was lucky to have so many retired nurses on the volunteer ambulance corps. These two ladies obviously knew exactly what they were doing.

Brenda saw they were going to have some challenges getting the stretcher through the door. She stepped into the room to help.

"We've got it, Chief," said one of the EMTs, blocking her with a raised hand. "The bed's on rollers. Now, if you could just give us some room."

Feeling put in her place, Brenda went back into the hall.

"We should probably get out of their way," said Cherie. She motioned to Brenda to follow her. When Brenda hurried to catch up to her, Cherie turned and said, "You need to stand back. I'm not joking."

Startled, Brenda stopped. "But just yesterday, we were…"

Cherie pointed in the direction of the bedroom. She waved Brenda into the kitchen and spoke in a hushed tone. "Yes, we were tongue kissing and breathing each other's breath. That puts you at big risk."

"It does?"

Cherie shook her head. "Don't you get it?"

"No," Brenda answered honestly.

"My father hasn't gone anywhere except for a ride in the car when I go to the supermarket. Then he just sits there while I shop. He hasn't been exposed to other people for weeks. The only way he could have gotten sick is because I brought it home. I must be a carrier."

Brenda stared at Cherie. "But you're not sick."

"I've had a headache that won't quit for a few days. I don't have any other symptoms. I may be an asymptomatic carrier." Cherie's eyes searched

Brenda's. "I may have infected my father. And he's in real danger because of the COPD. I may have infected you. You look healthy as a horse, but who knows? If something happens to either one of you, I'll never forgive myself."

Brenda moved forward to take Cherie in her arms, but Cherie backed away.

"I'm wearing a mask and gloves!" Brenda protested.

"It could be on my clothes, my hair. You need to stay away."

"No...please," Brenda begged. "Oh, baby, please let me hold you. You look so scared."

Cherie took another step back. "No, you can't. You just can't."

One of the EMTs came to the kitchen door. "We're ready to go now," she said. "I'll give you a call once he's in the ED and settled." She glanced at Brenda. "Thanks for coming down, Chief."

"I wasn't much help."

"Moral support is always appreciated," said the woman on her way out.

"You should leave now," Cherie said. Brenda heard the words, but she could also hear the reluctance in Cherie's voice.

"I know you're scared," said Brenda, "but it will be all right."

"You can't know that."

"No, I can't, but I believe in the power of positive thinking. Otherwise, I couldn't do my job."

"You need to go," Cherie repeated.

"I'll call you later." She reached out and patted Cherie's arm. Cherie stared at Brenda's hand on her arm and gave her a disapproving look, so Brenda withdrew it. "I'll see you later."

"Brenda, I don't want anything to happen to you. Please don't come back."

"I'm coming back," Brenda insisted, "even if I have to leave your groceries outside the door and wave to you through the window. Okay?" Brenda raised her fingers to where her lips were under the mask to throw a kiss. "I'll be back."

In the car, Brenda ripped off the gloves. She pulled the canister of disinfectant wipes out of the door pocket and wiped down the steering wheel as Cherie had demonstrated during a virus response training session. She took out her phone and wiped that down too. Then she called Liz. It went into voice mail, so Brenda headed to Hobbs Family Practice around the corner and pulled into the parking lot. She called again from her car. This time Liz answered.

"So, did you go after I told you not to?"

"You told me not to?" Brenda tapped open her message app and saw Liz's message. "Oh, I see it now."

"You went there, didn't you?"

"Yeah," Brenda admitted sheepishly. "I jumped in my car and drove down."

"A woman of action," said Liz with a sigh.

"That's me."

"Where are you?"

"In your parking lot."

"Are you wearing a mask?"

"Yes."

"You can come in. Tell Ginny to send you straight through."

Brenda tapped off the call. She looked at the door handle before she touched it and realized everything needed to be wiped down, even the outside handle. *What a fucking pain in the ass!* she thought, but she ripped another wipe out of the canister and cleaned the inside handle. She got out and cleaned the handle on the exterior.

She took the wipe along so she could clean the door knob when she went into Liz's waiting room. She held it up when she approached the registration desk. Ginny picked up the trash can for her to throw it in.

"Go on," said Ginny with a wag of her head. "She's waiting for you."

As she passed through the hall, she saw all of the staff wearing masks and gloves. They were taking this very seriously. A medical assistant was wiping down the railing for handicapped patients with disinfectant from a spray bottle. Brenda realized that at work, Cherie would have observed all these careful measures. Outside of the office she had probably relaxed her practices and that's how her father could get the virus.

Liz was on the phone when Brenda came in. Liz gestured for her to take a chair.

"Yes, I'll make sure she understands," said Liz, glancing at Brenda. "Talk to you later." She tapped off the call and put down the phone.

"Cherie?" Brenda guessed.

Liz nodded. She crossed her arms on her chest. "I have a good mind to put you on medical quarantine too."

"You can't do that. I'm the chief of police."

"I can, and I will, if I have to. It's likely you've been exposed. Are you and Cherie having sex?"

Liz's direct question shocked Brenda. She glanced away and nodded.

"I won't ground you yet because I don't have proof that Cherie has the virus, or that you've been exposed. I will test you today. We just got more test kits, and you definitely qualify. It will take ten days to get the results. Do you have any symptoms? Cough? Feel feverish?"

"No."

"Well, that's good," said Liz. She took a razor knife out of her desk drawer and slit open the test kit wrapper. "You're going to have to wear a mask all the time when you're in public, including at the office. You don't want to risk spreading this to the officers and staff over there. Do you understand?"

"Yes."

Liz put on gloves. The probe looked like an oversized Q-tip. It was at least six inches long. Brenda didn't like the looks of it.

"Okay. Take off your mask," ordered Liz, "and tilt your head way back."

Brenda was startled when that nasty probe was shoved up her nose.

26

Cherie woke from her nap and set the alarm to snooze. She still had an hour before her call with Lucy. It would be so good to hear her priest's voice and see her face, but it wasn't the same as sitting in her office and basking in her radiant smile.

Cherie considered Lucy one of the few truly Christian women she'd ever known. The other was Isabelle Bois, her mother. Like Lucy, Isabelle was a stunning beauty, a little darker than Cherie, but not much. From old photos, anyone could see why Jean-Paul had fallen so hard for her, but her beauty was more than skin deep.

Isabelle wore her Christianity on her sleeve and truly walked the path of Christ. She belonged to every service group in their church and volunteered for the Red Cross. There was nothing she wouldn't do for a person in need. One time, Isabelle sat up all night with the neighbor's crying baby because the mother was sick, and the father, a sailor, was out at sea. Cherie was young at the time and kept calling for her mother. Jean-Paul sat Cherie on his lap in the old rocking chair in the living room and rocked her to sleep.

Cherie imagined her father in his room at Southern Med. She'd talked to the hospitalist there twice that day. She'd reported that Jean-Paul was stable. They'd kept him on the CPAP, and so far, that was helping him breathe. Maybe he didn't have the virus and was just going through a bad time with his COPD. It would be at least a week before the test results came back.

The hospitalist looking after Cherie's father was excellent—smart and a great communicator who always answered questions directly. Liz Stolz liked to disparage hospitalists, but she was trained in an era when doctors made their own rounds. In a time like this, when people were being asked to avoid hospitals and emergency rooms, the hospitalists would certainly earn their keep.

The alarm went off again, and Cherie forced herself to get up. She'd been sleeping too much since she'd been quarantined. She decided to take a shower and wash her hair. She had the option of a voice telephone session or Facetime. Cherie had chosen Facetime so she could see Lucy's smiling face. That meant Lucy could see hers too.

Today, made day five of her quarantine. For the first two days, Cherie hadn't showered. No one could see her, so why bother? Then she realized that wasn't completely true. Brenda came by the first day, just as she'd said she would. She'd brought flowers, wine and a personal pizza. She'd kept her distance while Cherie brought the things inside. Then they'd stood at the picture window, gazing in one another's eyes while they talked by phone. It was all silly stuff, nonsensical lover talk. The closest they could get was their hands or lips pressed against the glass. Cherie never wanted it to end.

Brenda had come by every day since and left little gifts outside her door. She reminded Cherie of a large, blond puppy bringing home trophies. At first, she'd imagined Brenda as a yellow lab. Now that she'd seen her with her hair down, she'd decided a golden retriever was more apt.

Cherie put on some makeup. Lucy always looked terrific, and Cherie didn't want her to think that she was letting herself go while on quarantine. Being a therapist herself, Cherie knew Lucy would make assumptions about her mental state based on her appearance, and she didn't want to give her any ideas.

Cherie decided to do the session on her laptop instead of her phone. She went back into her room and turned it on. She had five minutes before calling in, so she checked her email. There was one from Liz through the secure portal. Cherie put in her code and opened it.

> How are you doing? We all miss you, especially me because it means I've got all your patients. Stay well. We need you back soon.—L.

She needed to use the secure portal for *that? Habit, I suppose.* Out of the corner of her eye, Cherie noticed the clock ticking down to four-thirty. She opened Facetime and rang Lucy's number. In a moment, her priest's beautiful face came into view. Cherie adjusted her screen to center her own image.

"Hello, Cherie. It's so good to see you," said Lucy. "How are you feeling?"

"I feel fine. The first few days, I had some chills and felt achy, but if I hadn't been paying attention, I probably wouldn't have noticed."

"I'm glad you feel so well. Do you think you have the virus?"

"Who knows? It takes so long for the tests to process I could have infected most of Hobbs by now."

Lucy laughed. "I doubt that."

"Oh, I don't know. They might soon be calling me 'Typhoid Cherie.'"

"If you did infect anyone, it wasn't intentional. You know that."

"I do know, but guilt isn't rational."

"No, it's not."

Lucy was wearing a clerical collar, but Cherie noticed she wasn't in her office. There was a large pine bough behind her on the screen. "Where are you? That's not the rectory or your house."

"No, I'm in Dr. Stolz's garage apartment. We've been here since our refrigerator failed. It could take two months to get a replacement, and that's a maybe. Most appliances are built from components made in China. If we can't get a refrigerator, we might be here for the duration."

"Oh, I'm sorry. I hope it's a nice place where you're staying. A garage apartment?" Cherie wrinkled up her nose.

"Oh, it's very nice. It has a wonderful view of the woods. Kind of like being in a tree house. But how about you? Are you comfortable where you are? Do you have everything you need?"

"Oh, yes. Dr. Stolz drops off groceries. Chief Harrison comes by every night."

Cherie admired how well Lucy controlled her face in therapy sessions. "That's very nice of her." She continued to smile pleasantly, waiting for Cherie to say more.

"We slept together," Cherie blurted out. It had actually happened two weeks ago, but for some reason, Cherie hadn't felt ready to share that in therapy.

Lucy looked thoughtful as she formulated her response. Finally, she said, "That's a big step." Her tone was completely neutral. She was a great counselor. No judgement, not even a little frown.

"It is. But it felt right. We were ready."

"That's a lot of progress in a very short period of time. How did you get to that point?"

"You think it's too soon?"

"I didn't say that."

"No, you didn't. Sorry. I didn't mean to put words in your mouth."

Lucy shook her head which indicated she wasn't offended. "The timing felt right for you. That's what really matters. So how did you get past your issues?"

"I followed all of your suggestions to the letter. I went out with her when she wasn't wearing her uniform. I learned how to shoot. The only thing I haven't done is undress her while she's wearing her uniform." Cherie grinned. "No offense, but I thought that was a little kinky for the first time."

Lucy laughed. "Yes, I guess it might be. But it sounds like you might have the opportunity to try it another time."

"I'm beginning to see why some women might find it sexy."

"Something to explore," Lucy suggested. "As long as it feels right to both of you. It's good to experiment to keep your love life interesting."

"I wouldn't know. I've never been in a relationship long enough for it to be anything but interesting."

"Well, you're just starting out here, so don't let your past short circuit your future."

"I'll try, but it's hard to escape gravity."

Lucy gave her a long penetrating look that exuded compassion. "You can. I know you can. And if you need me, I'm here for you. Otherwise, it sounds like the problem you came to me for is solved."

"The immediate problem, yes. Once I got past seeing Brenda as a cop, I found we are very compatible...emotionally and physically."

"That's good." Lucy's voice was full of encouragement.

"But I don't want to let go of our sessions yet. I have other things I want to explore."

"We can, if that's what you think you need."

"Of course, like everyone studying for a counseling credential, I went through therapy. But I felt like I was putting on an act to make the right impression. I'm past that now. I have issues to work through. I've never met anyone like you, Lucy. I really feel I can talk to you."

"Cherie, I can continue in a therapeutic role if you wish, or we could talk as friends. Your choice."

"You offered that before. I don't know if you'd hold my feet to the fire as my friend instead of my therapist."

Lucy laughed. "You really don't know me very well, do you?"

Cherie smiled in return. "No, but I'm getting the idea."

"I promise to hold your feet to the fire until your toes curl, but if you want the formality of sessions, we can do that too."

"Yes, I think I need the discipline."

"Okay. We'll do it your way."

"But I don't want to be a burden. I know you have a lot of clients and other people, who have needs greater than mine."

Lucy gave her a direct moment. "At this moment, and whenever we are working together, you are the most important person in my life. No one has needs greater than yours. Is that understood?"

"Yes. And thank you."

Through the camera lens, Lucy adjusted her position in her chair. "So, give me a little preview of what we'll be discussing in our sessions."

"Well, there's the guilt for one thing. I'm full of it. I just can't get rid of it. I absolutely believe I am the cause of my father's illness. What if something happens to him?"

Lucy sighed. "Someday, something will happen to him. No matter how well you care for him and protect him, someday, he will die, and that's how it is. It's part of life."

"I know, but I can't help but feel responsible. I followed all the protocols in the office. I was so careful in the supermarket. I've been wiping down everything in the house like crazy."

"You're trying your best, but there are things you can't control. You know that."

Cherie nodded.

"So, guilt. What else?"

"My own racism. Sometimes, I hate white people. Not you, of course, but those angry white men you see at political rallies. Of course, if I hate white people, I hate myself too. I'm mostly white."

"Yes, you are. And race is a myth. It's so superficial. We are more alike than we are different. But you already know that too. Okay, racism is another topic. Anything else?"

"Sex."

"Sex," Lucy repeated. "Is that something you want to talk to me about? Is it something medical? If it is, you should talk to Dr. Stolz. She's great on that topic."

Cherie thought but didn't say that Liz was the last person she'd ask about sex. "No, not medical. And why not talk to you? You're married to another woman…It doesn't make you uncomfortable to talk to me about sex, does it?"

"No, not at all. I often talk about sex in marriage counseling before and after the wedding. Is there a specific issue you want to address?"

Cherie took a moment as she wondered if talking about sex with Brenda would be a betrayal.

"In my present relationship, I can't bring my partner to climax."

Lucy nodded. "We're all so vulnerable in that moment. Do you think it's a trust issue?"

"It could be." Cherie sighed in frustration. "I've tried everything."

"Maybe you just need to give it time," suggested Lucy. "You've just begun your physical relationship. Keep trying. Maybe you need to get used to each other."

"That would be nice, but I can't even touch her. Right now, I can't even be in the same room with her."

"I know, Cherie. That must be so hard for both of you. When Erika and

I first got together, I couldn't keep my hands off of her. I can't even imagine what you and Brenda are going through."

Cherie sighed deeply. "You must think this concern is so trivial and selfish. My father is in the hospital and may die, and I'm worrying about orgasms."

"It's not selfish. Sex is an affirmation of life. It's probably more important now than ever. Have you asked Brenda to show you how she makes herself come?"

Cherie felt her face flame. "That sounds almost as kinky as undressing her while she's in uniform."

Lucy smiled. "Then ask her to tell you. Talk to one another." Lucy looked like she just had an idea. "You can still talk to one another even if you can't touch." Lucy cocked her head to one side, and her red hair fell over her shoulder. "Maybe this strange situation will present some interesting opportunities."

"Phone sex?"

Lucy shrugged.

27

Lucy looked down the table where nine people sat—four generations, including lively children and a man in his nineties. As an only child, who'd come from a small family, Lucy had never experienced raucous multigenerational holiday gatherings. Someone else might be put off by the noise, which sometimes made it hard to focus on any one conversation, but Lucy savored the energy of this extended family.

Maggie and Liz, who entertained a houseful during the summer, were in their element. Mealtimes were organized and efficient. They rotated responsibilities. Erika had been the cook tonight. She'd had no classes that day, so she'd volunteered to prepare dinner. Erika had made Liz's recipe for chicken cacciatore. Lucy had special memories of that dish because it was the first dinner Erika had cooked for her in the beach house.

"We're lucky Erika and Lucy brought us so much food, and we have a big freezer," said Liz. "There are shortages in the supermarket. No chicken. Very little meat except expensive cuts no one can afford. You can't find toilet paper anywhere. I can't figure that one out. The virus doesn't usually cause intestinal problems."

"People are never rational in a crisis," pronounced Erika in her crisp English accent. "Shortages bring out the worst in human beings."

"But really? Toilet paper?" said Maggie in a disapproving voice. "Good thing Liz was already stocking up for our summer guests every time BJ's had a sale. We'll need it with all the women in this house."

Stefan made a little face. "It's like a convent here. I have taken to Facetiming Tom Simmons just to see someone who can grow a beard."

Everyone laughed.

Lucy was glad to hear that Stefan had maintained his friendship with his former student. Stefan had been Tom's dissertation advisor when Tom and Erika were pursuing doctorates in mathematics. Like Lucy, Tom had come to his vocation later in life.

Although they chatted everyday by Facetime, Lucy wondered how

Tom was faring in the rectory. When she'd moved in with Erika after the renovation of the beach house, she had vacated the comfortable rector's apartment and had encouraged Tom to move into it. She was glad he had agreed to move into the larger quarters. In this lockdown, being shut up in one of the tiny curate's studios, each with only one window, would have been like solitary confinement.

"Do you talk about math with Tom?" Lucy asked, leaning forward so she could see Stefan at the other end of the table.

"No, I have enough mathematics with your Emily. Tom and I play chess."

"How long has this been going on?" asked Erika, looking surprised.

"Since you forced me to move to Maine."

"I did not force you, Papi," Erika protested in a mild voice. "Don't spread rumors. You came willingly."

"Yes, I did, but my version has more drama."

"And who is winning this virtual chess game?" asked his daughter.

"I am, of course."

"Tom's probably throwing it to make you feel good," Erika said and reached for the salad bowl.

"How dare you say that!" Stefan protested. "He is a priest. He would never cheat!"

Lucy chuckled. She was used to the sparring between father and daughter, but she would not put it past Tom to throw the game to make his old mentor feel good.

"We could have a chess tournament," suggested Emily. "Aunt Liz, do you have a chess board?"

"I do. Several, in fact. Some of my summer guests are avid chess players. What did you have in mind, Emily?"

"We could set up pairs, the winners play winners, until someone wins. I could play Stefan. Erika could play you. Mom could play Tom."

"What about me?" asked Maggie. "I know I'm not a big brain like the rest of you, but I like to play too."

"You can play me, Mom," said Alina.

"That sounds like fun," said Maggie, "but I also vote for a movie night. Any suggestions?"

"That new Tom Hanks movie, the one where he plays Mr. Rogers," Lucy said.

"I'll put the kids to bed first," Alina said. "I hear it's not a kids' movie."

"I don't know if it's available for streaming yet. I'll check after dinner," said Liz.

"And I vote for planning a talent night," Maggie said, gesturing to Erika to pass the salad bowl.

***

Maggie and Liz cleaned up the kitchen while their guests relaxed in the living room. Lucy scanned her phone for messages. The virus might be on everyone's mind, but Lucy knew from past disasters that a mental health crisis would follow. Her parishioners were as stressed as everyone in this strange situation, and she wanted to be available to them.

Nicki, Alina's youngest, leaned her elbows on Lucy's thigh. "Mother Lucy, can I sit on your lap?" At three, Nicki's speech still wasn't completely clear, but Lucy could usually understand what she was trying to say.

Lucy put her phone away and lifted the girl into her lap. Out of the corner of her eye, Lucy saw Emily watching the scene with a little envy.

"Are you Emily's mommy?" asked Nicki. The girl's dark eyes were curious.

"Yes, I am Emily's mommy." Lucy glanced at her daughter and gave her a warm smile.

"I can tell," said Nicki.

"You can?" asked Lucy with exaggerated surprise. "How can you tell?"

Nicki picked up a handful of Lucy's hair. "This. She has orange hair too."

Lucy laughed. "People usually say it's red, but Emily's hair is still orange. It will probably get darker as she gets older."

Katrina insinuated herself between Erika and Lucy and leaned heavily against her.

"You're very popular tonight," Erika observed, moving over to make room for Katrina.

"Everyone loves Mother Lucy," Alina said.

Nicki made herself small by curling into a ball. Lucy gave her a little hug. "I love you, Mother Lucy," Nicki murmured. Her sister repeated it like a chorus.

"Can I sleep with you tonight?" asked Nicki, snuggling closer.

"You can have them, Mom," said Emily. "They've moved in with me, and now I can't get rid of them."

"Are they bothering you?" Alina asked anxiously. "I'll take them back. I was happy they were giving Mom and Liz a break."

"No, they're not bothering me," Emily admitted. "It's kind of nice. They keep me warm at night. Like living stuffed animals."

Katrina evidently liked that. She sprinted across the room and leaned against Emily. "I love you, Emily."

Erika looked up from her iPad. "Now, aren't you sorry you said that, Emily, dear?"

But Emily didn't look sorry or seem to mind. A moment later, Nicki followed her sister and climbed into Emily's lap.

"All right, you two, you can have some ice cream and then bedtime," said Alina. "Say goodnight to everyone." The girls made their rounds of the room, wishing everyone goodnight and turning their faces up for a kiss.

Alina turned to Emily. "Thank you for putting up with the kids. I'll put them to bed in my room. Maybe they'll leave you alone tonight. They're so spoiled having all this adult company."

"Their stuffed toys are on my bed," said Emily.

Alina nodded and herded her brood into the breakfast room for ice cream.

"You're very good with the children," Lucy said to her daughter. "Very kind. Do you mind them taking up space in your bed?"

Emily shook her head. "When I dreamed of finding you, I always hoped I might have brothers and sisters too."

"It's not easy being an only child," said Erika. "Yes, you have all of your parents' attention, but it's a bit lonely at times."

Emily looked at Erika with cool, blue eyes for a long moment before saying, "It was especially lonely because I couldn't invite any of my classmates home. My parents thought they were a bad influence and didn't want them playing with me."

Whenever Emily spoke about life with her adoptive parents, Lucy felt a twinge of guilt. Not only had she missed her daughter's young childhood, she'd unwittingly left her to be raised by religious fanatics. It was a miracle, and a testament to Emily's resilience and resourcefulness that her daughter had turned out as intact as she was, especially given her autism.

Alina shepherded the girls upstairs while Katrina talked non-stop. Her poor sister could hardly get in a word. No wonder she was having trouble with her speech.

Erika said in a voice intended for Lucy's ears only. "I dearly hope they don't find their way across the bridge to our place. For selfish reasons, of course."

Maggie came into the living room to offer dessert.

"Thank you, dear, but I think I shall decline," said Erika, "I'm growing rather fat sitting around here with little exercise. I understand why they closed the beaches, but was it really necessary?"

"They closed the beaches to keep the summer people from coming up on the first warm day," said Maggie. "We have so few cases here. They want to keep it that way."

Erika sighed. "I know, but I so miss my walks along the ocean. I walk on even the coldest days. I can't tell you how much I miss it."

"You could park in our driveway and walk along Ocean Road," Lucy suggested.

"The last time I tried that, the police drove by giving me dirty looks. Good grief! I was on my own street, parked in front of my own house!"

Liz came into the room. "Anyone for an after-dinner drink?"

"What are you offering, Elizabeth?" asked Stefan. "I may have something tonight. Everyone is so bloody glum." Stefan seldom used the British expletives he'd acquired when he was a tutor at Cambridge, but when he did, his German accent made them sound almost laughable. No one laughed this time.

"I've opened a bottle of German brandy. Unfortunately, my stash of alcohol is running low. I'm leery of going to the New Hampshire liquor store, although I have no idea how they intend to enforce the fourteen-day self-quarantine if I cross the state line."

"How can they know?" asked Erika. "Are they stopping cars at the border?"

"I don't think so," Liz said, "but they have cameras all along 95. Who knows?"

Lucy felt a vibration in her pocket and took out her phone. The screen showed that Cherie Bois was calling. Lucy looked at the time. 7:55. Late for a call, but not overly so. She went into the kitchen for privacy.

"Hello, Cherie," said Lucy. "How are you?"

"Oh, Lucy, I need you to pray for my father. I just got a call. They had to intubate him and put him on a vent. Just yesterday they were talking about sending him home!"

"Oh, dear. That's not good news, but at least he's there where they can help him. Certainly, I will pray for him, but you should too. Your prayers are just as powerful as mine."

"I know, but I just wanted to hear your voice."

"I'm glad it's a comfort to you. Would you like me to pray with you?"

"Yes, please."

Lucy took a seat in the breakfast room and recited the Lord's prayer with Cherie. She added her own benediction. "Dear God, please bless Jean-Paul and hold him safely in your arms. Comfort him in his distress. Breathe hope into him in this, his hour of need."

"Thank you, Lucy," said Cherie. Lucy could hear that she was close to tears.

"You're welcome. Is there something else I can do for you? Do you want to talk?"

"Is Dr. Stolz there?"

"Yes, she is. Would you like to talk to her?"

"Please."

Lucy went into the living room and signaled to Liz with her phone. She mouthed Cherie's name. Liz instantly jumped up. Lucy handed her the phone and reclaimed her seat beside Erika.

When Liz returned to the room, her grave expression told Lucy all she needed to know.

28

Maggie saw Liz's face and instantly knew something was wrong. She got up and went to her. "What's wrong, honey?"

Liz shook her head, but that wasn't good enough for Maggie. She knew Liz avoided sharing the burdens placed on her by her medical practice. Maggie was grateful she didn't tell her everything. Maggie had no context to understand all the horrible things Liz experienced as a doctor or the terrible secrets she had to keep. But she recognized when the sorrows Liz kept bottled up inside needed a release. This was one of those times.

She took Liz by the arm and led her into the kitchen. "What's wrong? You look like you lost your last friend."

"I'm sorry. I thought I was covering it up well." Liz grinned the off-centered grin that Maggie found so endearing.

"Your face is so expressive when you don't think anyone is watching. Besides, you could never fool me." Maggie encircled Liz's waist and gave her a squeeze. "Honey, what is it? Please tell me." Liz made a sad face. Maggie didn't push. She knew that sometimes it took Liz a long time to find words to express her feelings, so she'd learned to be patient. "Let's go to your office for privacy."

Maggie kept her arm at Liz's back as they walked down the hall. She waited while Liz opened her credenza, took out a bottle of cognac and poured them each a glass. Liz flopped down on the sofa next to her.

"Cherie Bois's father was moved to ICU. He was intubated and put on a vent."

"Oh, no."

"Oh, no is right. In his condition, this is a last resort. He was doing so well, then BAM!" Liz hit her hand smartly with her closed fist. "That seems to be how this virus works. A patient is doing well. It looks like he's recovering, then he suddenly crashes for no apparent reason and becomes critical. Jean-Paul was going into this with compromised lungs. I don't think he's coming home again."

206

Maggie stroked Liz's arm gently. "I'm sorry, honey. I know this is always hard for you."

"It's different in family practice. It's hard to avoid becoming emotionally involved. I like Jean-Paul, and I'm very fond of Cherie."

"How is she?"

"She's a mess. We talked candidly about her father's chances of survival. Many vent cases don't make it, and if they do, they're impaired and have a real struggle to come back. Of course, she knows all this, but that doesn't make it easier. She started to cry, I mean, really sob. I asked if she wanted me to put Lucy back on, but she said no."

"Maybe Lucy should call her."

Liz shook her head. "Let her have a good cry first. She knows where to find Lucy when she's ready to talk about it." A frown wrinkled Liz's forehead. "If we weren't in this crazy situation, I'd take a ride over there and see if there's anything I could do. Maybe she'll call Brenda to talk."

"Brenda? They're together?"

"I shouldn't be spreading it around, but yes, they're together."

"I'm happy for them, but that's a tough start to their relationship." Maggie remembered her own tough start with Liz. They'd come home from their camping trip in Acadia. After a blissful reunion—the first time they'd made love in forty years—Liz told her she'd found a lump in Maggie's breast. Real life had intruded on Lucy and Erika's first time too. Erika's mother had just died. The superstitious part of Maggie's nature, nurtured by her upbringing in a traditional Irish Catholic family, always resurfaced at times like that. She wondered if there was a price to pay for happiness… whether the sublime pleasure of a new relationship had to be balanced with pain and grief. *That's crazy*, she told herself. *It's no one's fault. It's not punishment. It's just life.*

"I'm thinking of closing the office," said Liz, bringing Maggie back to the present. The expression on Liz's face told Maggie she'd been wrestling with the decision and still wasn't sure about it.

"I think that's a smart idea," said Maggie.

"We don't want people who have the virus to come in and infect others. There's nothing we can do for them anyway. There's no effective treatment, despite what that gas bag says in his nightly press briefings. We've used up all our tests, and, until Abbott releases theirs, we're not getting any more. And frankly, people are afraid to come in."

"Liz, I'm so glad you're closing the office. I don't want anything to happen to you."

"I don't either," said Liz. "I was reluctant to close down, especially after the urgent care closed. Scared people need to know there's someplace to go."

"They do," Maggie agreed, "but you don't always have to be the hero, rushing in to save the day!"

"That's left over from my days as a surgeon. It's a huge high when you can save a life under extreme circumstances." Liz finished her cognac in a swallow. Maggie knew it was expensive and was surprised to see Liz belt it down. "I thought about keeping the office open for a few hours a day and holding down the fort myself," Liz continued. "I hate all the paperwork, but I can do it if I have to."

Maggie sat back and gave Liz a long hard look. "Why do you always have to be the one?"

Liz got up to pour herself another glass of brandy. "I'm the managing partner. The others are younger. They have children and families."

"You don't believe those idiots who say seniors should sacrifice for future generations? You have children and a family," Maggie countered. "Aren't we important too?"

"Yes, of course, but I'm really good at keeping hygiene protocols because I was a surgeon."

"Liz Stolz, sometimes you are so damned arrogant!"

Liz looked startled, then smiled. "Oh, you're just yanking my chain."

"And it should be yanked. You're not expendable. The people in this town need you. Everyone in this house needs you. *I* need you."

Liz put her arm around Maggie. "I need you too. And don't worry. On

Friday, we're shutting down the office except for Telehealth calls. I'm about to discover what it is to be a virtual doc. I'll be like the medical hologram on the Starship Voyager. Someone will press a button and I will appear saying, 'Please state the nature of the medical emergency.'"

Maggie rolled her eyes. "You'll never grow up."

"God, I hope not." Liz threw down the rest of her brandy.

Out of the corner of her eye, Maggie noticed Lucy hovering in the doorway.

"I'm sorry if I'm intruding. I can come back later."

Maggie reached out her arm to Lucy. "Lucy, dear, you're never intruding. Come in."

Lucy approached cautiously.

"Drink?" Liz asked, gesturing with her empty glass.

"What are you offering?" asked Lucy.

"Cognac. It's between that or single-malt scotch."

"Thanks, I'll pass." Lucy mocked a shudder. "I hate brown liquor."

Liz laughed. "I can get you some wine."

"No, thanks. I want to talk to you."

Liz got up and sat in her desk chair. Maggie gestured to the space beside her on the sofa, and Lucy sat down. "I've never been in here before," she said gazing around the room. "Wow, Liz. Is all this stuff yours?" she asked, gesturing to the plaques and photos hanging on the wall. "Mind if I take a look?"

"Knock yourself out," said Liz, pouring herself another glass of cognac.

Maggie gave her a hard look. "You're getting loaded, Liz. Take it easy. And be nice to Lucy."

"I am being nice to Lucy," Liz protested.

Lucy, busy studying the photos and citations on the walls, wasn't paying attention to their little sidebar argument. "This is really impressive. Erika always said you were famous. I never realized."

"You sang at the Met. You're famous too."

"But in your world, you were just as famous."

Liz saluted her with her brandy glass. "And like you, I deny it whenever I can."

Maggie shot Liz a look of annoyance. "Stop. Lucy's paying you a compliment."

Liz slid down in her seat. "I know. That's the problem."

Lucy sat down beside Maggie. "I'm not easily offended, Maggie. You don't need to defend me. Besides, I know Liz is crazy about me. Right, Liz?"

"Absolutely," said Liz. From the odd cadence of her speech, Maggie knew that Liz was well on her way to inebriation. Usually, Liz could hold her liquor very well, but when she was upset and pounding down the glasses of alcohol, it went right to her head.

"You should go to bed," Maggie advised.

"It's still early," protested Liz.

"I mean…really," said Maggie in a firm voice. "Otherwise, you'll be sorry in the morning."

"Okay," said Liz and pulled herself to her feet. She made a deep, formal bow in Lucy's direction. "Good night, Mother Lucy."

"Good night, Liz."

Maggie's eyes followed Liz to the door to make sure she was steady enough to make it upstairs.

"I'm sorry," said Maggie once Liz had left. She got up and closed the door.

"You don't need to apologize for her. She's under a lot of stress right now. Not like the emergency department people in New York, but she's responsible for the health of the people of this community…her staff, all the people who can't get tests, all of us in this house." Lucy patted Maggie's hand. "Be patient with her."

"Oh, you have no idea how patient I am."

"Oh, I think I do. I'm married to Liz's best friend, another icy German who's too smart for her own good. But I've discovered a common language."

Maggie raised a brow. "Sex?"

"Much more than sex. The emotional texture of a relationship is very complex, like a symphony. There are many notes, but some are more important than others."

Maggie allowed herself the luxury of a long sigh, and Lucy gave her a critical look.

"You seem very stressed too. Is it too much to have all of us here? We could go to a motel."

Maggie dismissed the suggestion with a wave. "Don't be crazy. First of all, you'll never find an open motel. Second, we love having you here. Liz and Erika are like sisters. She would never turn her away."

"But it's a lot having us parked here with Alina and the kids. You're teaching online and trying to help out with the kids. Alina is trying to work…"

"And we're all succeeding. Emily is a big help with the kids. Who knew?"

"Not me. I was so worried when we came over here. Erika accepted without a second thought. But I thought, oh wow! That's asking a lot of you and Liz."

Maggie patted Lucy's thigh. "No, it isn't. Actually, it's better that we're all together. We can help one another. We can entertain one other. Think of all those people who are alone with no one to talk to. Here we have our own little village."

"Funny you say that. That's exactly what I thought the other day."

Maggie took Lucy's hand and threaded her fingers through hers. "Don't even think about leaving. I'm glad you are here. Yes, Liz and Erika get into mischief together, but they would with or without us. They go back such a long time, nothing can get in between them. I'm just glad to have my best friend here."

"Me too." They leaned toward one another until their foreheads touched.

"Liz is so solitary sometimes. I'm glad to have someone to talk to."

"Believe me, I know what you mean. I live with someone who thinks for a living, but Erika can be quite chatty when she wants to be." Lucy sat back a little and studied Maggie's face. "Liz looked really upset after she talked to Cherie."

Maggie knew she was fishing, but it was for the right reasons. "Cherie is upset. She thinks she caused her father's illness."

"I know," said Lucy with a sigh. "Unfortunately, a lot of people will realize that, and it won't be easy to take."

"Is there anything we can do to help?"

"I'm trying to figure that out. Cherie can't go see her father, but as clergy, I can. They haven't banned us from the hospitals yet."

"Oh, Lucy, that's a very big risk!"

"Yes, I know. But I could also see other parishioners."

"You'd better talk to Liz first. I keep telling her not to be a hero. You shouldn't be one either."

Lucy looked injured by that remark. "It's not about that."

"I know, but think! I'll say the same thing to you I said to Liz. You have a child. You have a family. You have friends who love you. Me, for example! Please don't take unnecessary risks. *Please.*"

Lucy patted Maggie's arm. "I won't, but thanks for the reminder." She got up. "Let me see what my family is up to."

Maggie sat for a moment to finish her drink. All these years since she'd faced down cancer, feared it like a wild animal poised to spring out and devour her, she'd begged and pleaded for peace. Just one moment of peace when the fear receded, and she could be normal again. Now, a virus, a tiny, invisible enemy, threatened her and the people she loved most.

She took the brandy glasses into the kitchen to wash them. She wished she could go straight to bed, but they had guests and she was the hostess. She went into the living room to wish them goodnight. Everyone looked so relaxed and at home. As much as she loved all of these people, she longed for a moment to have her house to herself. Yes, it was selfish, but she wished for it anyway.

She was too tired to climb the stairs, so she took the elevator to the third floor. Liz was a lump under the covers, so Maggie quietly crept into the bathroom to get ready for bed. As she wiped off her makeup, she saw the age lines around her eyes and mouth. It seemed they'd grown deeper in only a few, short weeks. She wondered how many other women had looked at their reflections in the mirror and felt exactly the same.

Maggie got into bed and pulled the covers over her. A moment later, an arm came around her waist.

"I love you," murmured Liz.

"I love you too, but sometimes it's hard."

"Sometimes, it's hard for me too." Liz slid closer, spooning her with her body. "But it's so worth it."

Maggie reached back to pat Liz on the thigh.

"You're naked!"

"Ayuh," said Liz, reaching under Maggie's nightgown.

29

As chief, Brenda didn't usually respond to 911 calls, but three of her officers were out sick, so she needed to provide backup. The nature of their illness couldn't be confirmed. They had high fevers and a dry cough, but Liz had run out of tests, so there was no way of knowing the cause.

Brenda's headache had lasted the entire day. She blamed it on stress and gobbled some ibuprofen, but it hadn't helped. She couldn't wait to get home and get some sleep.

The station was eerily quiet. The office staff was working from home. The dispatchers were still coming in because they were considered essential workers. The town offices were closed, the schools, and most businesses. Hobbs was as tight as a drum. Hardly anyone was on the road, so the officers weren't writing tickets for traffic violations. Petty crime had fallen to an all-time low.

Two types of 911 calls hadn't stopped. In fact, they were increasing. Brenda had expected the drug overdoses, but she hadn't anticipated an increase in domestic cases. Of course, being shut up day after day with an angry person made abuse more likely.

Responding to those calls was Brenda's least favorite duty. Despite being a cop and having a 9mm on her hip, she felt frustrated and sometimes helpless. She knew all the ways to talk down an antagonistic male. The abusers were almost always men. The few female offenders were usually women at the end of their rope because of abuse, or sometimes, hardship.

Brenda knew that even if she could calm a desperate situation and prevent it from escalating, it would happen again. Maybe next time it wouldn't end as well. Maybe next time, the call would never come.

Brenda always tried to block the memories whenever she walked up to the door to investigate one of those cases. Everyone had always said her father was a good man, but as a girl, she'd seen another side of him. When her brother had been caught in some minor mischief in the eighth grade, her father had cut a piece of garden hose and beaten him until he was black and blue. The team doctor was so appalled by the damage to his body, he wanted to report it, but Brenda's father was a cop, a respected member of the community, so it never went anywhere.

Brenda remembered Jimmy as a tall, strong fourteen-year old, sobbing in his room as he tried to hide the red welts. She knew his tears were as much from anger and humiliation as from the pain. When they'd spoken about it, years later, Jimmy confessed he'd never forgiven his father and never would.

There had been times before that fateful beating, when her father drank too much and there were loud, angry arguments. Everything in sight was a potential missile. Fortunately, Kevin Harrison never hit his wife in Brenda's presence. He reserved the beatings for his children. Brenda, the youngest, was mostly spared, but the boys had been hit and kicked on a regular basis. Mike had once coughed up blood.

Her brothers were all cops too. She wondered if they were carrying on the cycle of abuse. That was common, and it was all too common among cops. Everyone knew it, but no one did anything about it. That's why, when given the choice of equally qualified candidates, Brenda tended to hire female officers. That wasn't any guarantee that they weren't full of anger too, but the odds were against it.

Brenda had already decided that when things were more normal, she would talk to Cherie about her feelings about domestic violence. Maybe Cherie could give her some tips about how to handle the bad memories. Right now, Cherie had enough on her plate with her father in the hospital.

When Brenda arrived at the scene, she realized she knew this family. The husband was the night shift manager at the bottling plant. The wife was the teacher at the elementary school, who organized the annual cookie-bake for the police department. They were quiet, decent people. The only time the police had been called to the house was when Mr. Gavin's father had collapsed from a heart attack.

Brenda put on her mask and got out of her cruiser. Twenty feet away, Officer Davis got out too. She exhaled before she put on her mask. In the twilight, Brenda could see her breath emerge as vapor.

"Ready?" asked Brenda into her radio.

"Copy that, Chief."

They approached together, but Brenda said, "I'll go in first. Cover me."

They rang the bell, but no one came to the door. Brenda tried the knob. The door was open. Cautiously, she stepped into the house. She saw the place was tidy and clean. Mrs. Gavin was a good housekeeper.

Brenda walked down a short hallway to the living room. There were fragments of broken figurines scattered on the rug. A shattered lamp lay on the floor, the shade torn in half. Next to it was a pizza box. Crusts and part of an uneaten pizza lay nearby, along with empty beer bottles. In front of the wood stove, a man sat cross-legged, weeping.

As she approached, Brenda's foot found a .45 pistol on the floor, half hidden by the skirt of an upholstered chair. She picked up the gun, dropped the magazine and ejected the round, which she caught in her hand and put in her pocket. She glanced around and saw a woman hovering in the doorway.

"Mrs. Gavin?"

The trembling woman nodded.

"Are there any other firearms in the house?"

"Hunting rifles in the gun safe in the basement."

"Do you know the combination?"

"No. Only Steve has it."

"Is this Steve?" Brenda asked, gesturing to the weeping man. "He's your husband?"

Mrs. Gavin nodded.

Brenda called out to Officer Davis. "You can come in now!" Davis came into the house and gave the room a quick scan. Satisfied everything was under control, she holstered her gun.

"What happened here?" Brenda asked.

"Steve lost his job. We're behind on our mortgage as it is. We were eating pizza, and everything was fine. Then all of sudden, he whipped out his gun and said he was going to kill himself."

"Was he drinking?"

"Just a few beers. Well, maybe more than a few."

Brenda knelt beside Mr. Gavin. "Why don't you come sit on the sofa?"

Mr. Gavin took his face out of his hands and stared at her.

"Okay? Come on," urged Brenda. "I'll help you get up." Her bad knee gave a twinge as she got to her feet and offered her hand. She guided Mr. Gavin toward the sofa and sat down beside him. "You okay?"

Mr. Gavin nodded mournfully. "I thought if I killed myself, the insurance would pay."

"Well, that's a bad plan. There's probably an exclusion for suicide. That's how it is for most policies. Besides, you know that's not the answer."

Mrs. Gavin stepped forward. "Steve, how could you even think of this? You know it would kill me!"

Brenda put up her hand to silence her. "It's all right now. Save that for another time." She reached out for the man's hand. "Mr. Gavin, I'd like to take your pistol back to the station with me. If you surrender it voluntarily, you can have it back anytime you want. Okay?"

Mr. Gavin nodded.

Brenda took a notebook out of her utility pouch. "Will you give me the combination to your gun safe? If it's all right, I'll take your long guns too. Don't worry. I'll keep them safe for when you're ready to take them back."

Mr. Gavin recited the combination numbers, and Brenda wrote them down. She tore off the paper and handed it to Davis. "Leave the ammo, of course, we don't need that."

After Davis left, Brenda turned her attention back to Mr. Gavin. "Ordinarily, I'd take you down to Southern Med for mandatory observation, but the ED doesn't want anyone there except life-or-death cases. Who's your doctor?"

"Dr. Stolz is Steve's doctor," said Mrs. Gavin.

"When I leave, I'm going to call her and ask her to give you a call. I'll ask Reverend Bartlett to call in the morning. Meanwhile, you have to be strong for your wife and yourself. Can you do that?"

Mr. Gavin nodded.

"If Dr. Stolz prescribes any meds, I'll pick them up at Walmart and bring them over. Do you think you need medicine to calm down?"

"No, no drugs! I'm a recovering opioid addict. I've been clean for two years."

"Okay, then maybe drugs aren't the answer. I'll have Dr. Stolz call you anyway."

Davis returned to say all the firearms were in her cruiser. Brenda patted Mr. Gavin's arm.

"Are you gonna be okay until Dr. Stolz calls?"

"Yes," said Mr. Gavin. "I'm embarrassed that you had to come." He tore at his forehead with his fingertips.

"That's what we're here for. Now, hang in there. Call us again if you need us." She pulled out her pad. "I'll give you the number of the suicide hotline too, but I'm hoping you won't need it. If you do, call them right away. They can help you better than we can."

"I'm all right now," said Mr. Gavin. "What a dumbass thing to do."

"Take it easy, Mr. Gavin," said Brenda, getting up. "Mrs. Gavin can you take it from here?"

Mrs. Gavin still looked anxious, but she nodded.

Brenda sighed as she headed down the hall to the front door. Her head was really aching now. It had been all she could do to keep herself together to get through the call. In her car, she took off her mask and washed her hands with hand sanitizer. They were getting chapped from so much washing and alcohol. All the hygiene was getting old fast.

She called Liz before she set off. After she told her what had happened, Liz said, "Nope. No drugs for Mr. Gavin, but I'll give him a call. He shouldn't have been drinking either, but I get it. A lot of people are suddenly out of work. Thanks, Brenda."

Brenda glanced at the clock. Her shift was over. She was close to home, so she'd go straight there and pick up her truck in the morning. She started the engine and called Cherie through the Bluetooth.

"Hey, sweetie, how are you feeling?" she asked when Cherie answered.

"I never felt that bad. In fact, I feel fine. I want to go back to work but now, Liz is closing the office."

"She is?"

"Yes, starting tomorrow, we're using Telehealth."

"I suppose that's good. How's your dad?"

"Same. He's stable on the ventilator."

"That's good news, right?"

"Sort of good news. There's no improvement either," said Cherie in a steady, professional-sounding voice. Brenda could sense that Cherie's medical training was all that was keeping her together.

Brenda suddenly felt the overwhelming impulse to cough. She stifled it as long as she could. Then it erupted and she couldn't stop. "Sorry about that," she murmured when the jag finally ended.

"How long have you had that cough?" Cherie asked in a concerned voice.

"Oh, it's nothing. Spring allergies."

"I don't like the sound of that, Brenda. Do you have a thermometer?"

"Yes," said Brenda, but she didn't like where this conversation was going.

"I want you to take your temperature when you get home and call me."

"Yes, Doctor," said Brenda, knowing it would annoy Cherie. At least, she'd given up trying to correct her. "I miss you soooo much."

"I miss you too like you can't even imagine!"

"So, I'll come over," said Brenda. She grinned even though Cherie couldn't see her.

"No! We don't know if I'm still contagious."

"Oh, come on! You've been home for what? A week now?"

"But we don't know anything about this virus…how long the incubation period is…whether the antibodies you develop provide immunity."

Brenda pulled into her driveway and yanked up her parking brake. "I'm home," she announced.

"Okay. Get settled and call me later," said Cherie. "And take your temperature!"

Brenda was about to say something fresh again but decided against it. "Okay, sweetheart, I'll call you right back. First I have to find the damn thing." She made a loud kissing sound and ended the call.

Brenda got undressed before looking for the thermometer. She put on lounge pants and an old Yankees hoodie that she'd never dare wear outside in Red Sox country for fear of being stoned. Well, that was an exaggeration. But Sox fans were almost as bad as Patriots fans.

She ransacked the medicine cabinets in both of the upstairs bathrooms. Nothing. She went through the drawers in both vanities. Finally, she found the thermometer in the downstairs bathroom. She pulled off the protective cap and pressed the button. The screen remained blank. Brenda tried to remember the last time she'd used a thermometer and realized it was probably the year she'd moved to Maine and had the flu. Brenda shook the thermometer, hoping it would wake up, but it was pointless. The battery was dead.

"Fuck," said Brenda. She wondered if she still had an old-fashioned glass thermometer somewhere. She redoubled her search but came up empty handed. Cherie was expecting her call. Sooner or later, she'd have to fess up.

Brenda took a bottle of beer off the refrigerator door, reasoning that a little alcohol would kill anything. She wearily flopped on the cushion of the living room sofa and tapped Cherie's number in her favorites. While it rang on the other end, she took a slug of beer.

"Well?" asked Cherie. "What's your temperature?"

"Haven't a clue. The battery died."

Cherie groaned. "How can you be without a thermometer!"

"Don't know, but I seem to be."

"Do you have a replacement battery?" asked Cherie in a patient voice.

"Are you fucking kidding me? It's some little weird hearing aid battery. No."

"I'm coming over," said Cherie.

"What?" Brenda sat up straight. This was serious. "You just said ten minutes ago it was too risky."

"It is risky, but I'm coming over."

"Then pack a bag and stay a while."

There was an extended silence on the line. "Actually, that's a good idea."

30

At the last minute, Cherie realized that she should probably bring along some of the food from the refrigerator, at least the milk and fresh vegetables. Liz came by every few days to deliver groceries, so the refrigerator was well stocked. Liz had dropped off food the night before, so it would be a few days until she returned. Eventually, Cherie would have to tell her boss that she had disobeyed her orders and left the house.

Technically, breaking quarantine imposed by a medical officer was illegal. Cherie, stuck at home and bored out of her mind, had researched the penalty. According to the U.S. Code, someone who broke quarantine was subject to a fine of up to a thousand dollars or a year in jail or both! Of course, Liz would never report her. And who would arrest her? Brenda?

After packing up the groceries in a thermal bag, Cherie checked her medical kit to make sure she had everything she might need. These days, hardly any doctors bothered with a medical bag. They had everything they needed at their workplace and bringing their own specialized tools was unnecessary. Everyone had their favorite stethoscope, of course, but that was about it.

Liz Stolz was the exception, which showed her vintage even more than her gray hair. Like most doctors, she almost never made house calls anymore, but she still kept an old-fashioned bag at home in case of an emergency. Every few months, Liz brought her bag into the office to replenish the stock of expired medications and check that everything was in working order. When she'd laid out the contents on her desk to make a visual inventory, Cherie had perceived the value of the critical instruments and medications. It inspired her to put together her own medical kit. Fortunately, it included a working thermometer and surgical masks.

The bag of refrigerator items was heavy. Cherie slung her duffle bag over her shoulder to see if she could make it to the car in one trip and decided to try.

As she drove, she wondered how she could deal being in the same house with Brenda and maintain isolation. By the time she arrived in Brenda's development, Cherie had convinced herself it was possible.

Brenda had the door open before Cherie even got out of her car. "You're wearing a mask?" Brenda asked incredulously.

"I may still be contagious. You may be too," said Cherie, handing her the bag of groceries. "Supplies. I don't want these things to spoil in my refrigerator and come home to a stench."

"So, you're staying a while." Brenda smiled broadly.

"Looks like it," said Cherie stepping inside. "How are you?"

"I have a headache, but otherwise I don't feel too bad."

Brenda closed the door. "Since I can't kiss you, can I have a hug?"

"That's probably not a good idea either."

Brenda made a sad puppy face, reminding Cherie once again of a golden retriever. "Stop. You'll survive," said Cherie, taking off her coat. "Put away the groceries and then I want to examine you."

"Oooh, I like that idea!"

Cherie rolled her eyes. "You are incorrigible."

"I don't know what that means, but it sounds like a compliment."

Cherie laughed. "Believe me. It's not."

"What does it mean? I was never good at vocabulary."

"It means no one can reform you," said Cherie with a firm look.

Brenda grinned broadly. *What a thing she is! She's proud of it*, thought Cherie as she followed Brenda into the kitchen.

"Where can I put my stuff?" asked Cherie.

"You know where my room is," Brenda said into the refrigerator as she put the groceries away.

"Um, I can't sleep with you."

"Why not?" Brenda stood up. The open refrigerator began to chime annoyingly.

"I may have the virus!"

Brenda shrugged in resignation. "Take the room next to mine. Or if that's too close, any bedroom upstairs. The linens are clean on all the beds."

Cherie carried her bag upstairs. The guilt over breaking quarantine nagged her, so she virtuously chose the room farthest away from Brenda's bedroom. When she came downstairs, she found Brenda staring into the refrigerator. "I'm looking for something to eat."

"How about a cheese omelette?" asked Cherie. "Sit down, and I'll make you one. I brought over all the ingredients."

"Hmm," said Brenda with a smile. "I haven't had that for a long time. Sounds yummy."

"First, let me take your temperature."

Brenda's smile instantly inverted. "Can't it wait?"

"It's the reason I came over here, so no."

Cherie took her temporal thermometer out her medical kit and put it against Brenda's forehead. It beeped momentarily, and Cherie checked the reading, relieved to see the temperature was only elevated by a degree. There were normal fluctuations at different times of the day, so that didn't truly indicate a fever, but it was worth watching. Cherie checked Brenda's forehead with the back of her hand. It felt a bit warm.

"My mother used to check for fever by kissing my forehead," said Brenda.

"Sweet idea, but not accurate, and certainly not healthy in a pandemic."

"How can love be unhealthy?" asked Brenda.

"Ever hear of venereal disease?"

"You're so romantic."

Cherie started opening cabinets. "I need a frying pan and a bowl to beat the eggs." Brenda got up to find them for her. She set the frying pan on the range and handed Cherie a beater.

"You look very domestic," said Brenda. "It suits you."

"Don't get any ideas."

"I'm not. I just like how you look in my kitchen, like you belong here."

"It's a nice kitchen," said Cherie gazing around, as she beat the eggs.

"Bigger than mine." She poured the eggs into the frying pan, tilting the pan to spread them evenly. She cut up some cheddar cheese into thin slices. "I like your stove better too."

"Maybe you'll get more opportunities to use it."

"Maybe I will," said Cherie, turning around to give Brenda a knowing look. She saw that Brenda's gaze was focused on her backside and widened her eyes to show disapproval. "Brenda, I'm trying to cook now. Behave." She arranged the cheese slices in the pan.

"Have you ever lived with someone?" asked Brenda. Her chair creaked a little as she sat back.

"I never had the opportunity." Cherie flipped over one side of the omelette, so the cheese would melt.

"Would you like to?"

"Don't you think it's a little early for that question?"

"I didn't mean me in particular," Brenda said impatiently. "I meant in general."

"I don't know. I have a big responsibility right now with my father. Would I like to share my life with someone? Yes, of course. Doesn't everyone?"

Cherie turned around and saw that Brenda looked thoughtful. "I don't know about everyone. Liz was fine on her own before Maggie showed up. I don't really like being alone. I like having someone around to share meals, watch movies, compare notes on things. You know?"

"Well, it looks like you'll have an opportunity to road test that idea. I'll be here for a few days…at least." Cherie shoveled the omelette onto a plate and put it in front of Brenda. "Do you want a salad too? I'll make it for you."

"No, sit down and keep me company while I eat." She dug into the omelette and ate hungrily. "It's delicious. Thank you." She looked up and studied Cherie's face. "Do you really have to wear that mask?"

"Yes, I do."

"Shit," said Brenda.

"I agree. I don't like it either," said Cherie in a flat voice. "Eat."

There was silence while Brenda ate. Afterwards, Cherie rinsed the dishes and cleaned the frying pan. "Where do you want to do this examination?" she asked, drying her hands on a dish towel.

"My bedroom. It's a mess, though. I wasn't expecting company."

"How about the living room? We can close the drapes."

Brenda sat on the sofa while Cherie took out her instruments. She took Brenda's temperature again. It was still slightly elevated but not much. Cherie gave her a quick visual evaluation. Brenda looked tired but otherwise healthy. "Maybe you don't have it, or you might get a mild case."

Cherie tried to assess whether she could hear properly through the bulky Yankee's sweatshirt. "Do you mind taking off your shirt?"

"I don't have a bra on," said Brenda, reaching for the hem of the shirt. "It's the first thing I do when I get home."

"I've seen your breasts before." Behind the mask, Cherie managed a little smile. "But I'll try to ignore them while I listen to your chest." She placed the diaphragm of the stethoscope on Brenda's back. She noticed for the first time that it was sprayed with faint freckles. The sight touched her, and she realized how dear to her this woman had become.

Cherie pushed the thought aside as she listened to Brenda's lungs. They were slightly congested, but not so much that Brenda's self-diagnosis of seasonal allergies didn't apply. Cherie closed her eyes to concentrate on the sound of the blood rushing through her heart and the steady rhythm of the valves opening and closing. No strange sounds. No murmurs, just a strong, steady beat.

Cherie hung the stethoscope around her neck while she felt the nodes and glands in Brenda's neck.

"You have a very gentle touch," said Brenda.

"Thank you, but I can finish faster if you don't talk."

"Sorry," said Brenda, looking contrite.

"You're a little congested," said Cherie using hand sanitizer. She wiped down her instruments with an antiseptic towelette. "But otherwise, you look pretty healthy. So far, so good."

Brenda wiggled into her sweatshirt. "If I was going to get it, wouldn't I have caught it by now?"

Cherie shrugged. "Who knows? We know so little about this virus. It would depend on the viral load during exposure, the strain of the virus. Your immune response. It's like any virus, some people get mild symptoms, some get none at all. Other people get hammered."

"But if one of us has it, it's likely the other has it too."

"Yes."

Brenda looked pensive. "Then why can't you take off that mask?"

"Better safe than sorry," said Cherie.

Brenda pouted, which made Cherie laugh. She bent down and, through her mask, gave her a kiss on the top of her head.

"Be patient."

"But I want to kiss you so much."

"I know. So, do I, but let's not right now."

Cherie put away her medical bag. When she returned, she found Brenda waiting with the TV paused at the start of the next episode of *Happy Valley*.

"I thought we could watch me playing a heroic British cop."

"Now, you think she looks like you."

"I'm better looking," said Brenda with a quick smile.

"I agree."

Sitting at opposite ends of the sofa, they watched three episodes, pausing only for a tea break, during which they sat on opposite ends of the room. Cherie was so happy to have company after a week of isolation that she would have done anything, even stared at the walls with Brenda. Finally, in the middle of the fourth episode, Brenda's eyes began to close and her head nodded forward. Cherie turned off the TV and nudged her with her foot. She woke with a start.

"Time for bed."

"Okay." Brenda sat up and tried to focus.

They trudged up the stairs and reluctantly headed to separate bedrooms.

"Can I have a hug?" asked Brenda with a forlorn look.

"No," said Cherie. She blew a kiss. "Good night, sweetheart."

31

Brenda stepped out of the shower and wrapped her hair in a towel. After she dried her body, she put on a terry cloth robe that went to her ankles. Ordinarily, she'd head down to get coffee, but with Cherie in the house, she decided to make a good impression and dress first. She ran the dryer on her hair for a few minutes and tied back her damp hair with an elastic band.

She found Cherie in the kitchen making coffee while she listened to a phone call on speaker. Brenda instantly identified Liz's voice.

"Cherie, you need to know, three strikes and you're out. This is number two. I can't have my PA disobeying my orders. I need to be able to trust you."

"You can trust me, Dr. Stolz. You know you can."

There was a long silence.

"Yes, Cherie, I know your heart is in the right place. But I have more experience than you. You need to listen to me."

"Yes, Dr. Stolz."

"All right. Let's start over. How's Brenda?"

Cherie looked up and noticed Brenda. She nodded to her.

"She's a little congested, but so far seems okay. Would you like to talk to her? She just came in.

"Good morning, Liz," said Brenda crossing the room to get two cups down from a cabinet.

"Brenda! I see you found a way to get a house call."

"Yes, I have connections."

"You'd better take good care of her, or you'll have me to answer to. I need her."

Brenda glanced at Cherie. "I think she's the one taking care of me."

"I have another question for you, Doctor," said Cherie. "If I've already exposed Brenda to the virus, why can't I take off my mask while I'm with her?"

"Cherie, you know the answer to that. Until the test results come back, no, you shouldn't. We have no idea whether antibodies to the virus confer immunity. If you both have it, or one of you had it and recovered, you could still infect one another. Oh, hell. What do I know? None of us knows. Cherie, do what you think is best, but I would wait a few days for the test results. And if you relax social distancing, I'm going to ground Brenda too."

Brenda silently mimed clapping.

"Now that we're on Telehealth," Liz continued, "you can go back to work. Make sure you bill for the time, Cherie. Even Brenda."

Cherie laughed silently and pointed to the phone.

"Can't I extend professional courtesy?"

"It's on your time, but the department pays for her insurance, and the practice can use the revenue."

"Okay. Thanks. Talk to you later." She tapped the call off.

"Good morning, you sexy woman," said Brenda, approaching. "So, what are you going to do?"

"You want to stay home with me for fourteen days?"

"Are you kidding me?" asked Brenda.

Cherie pulled the elastic straps from her ears and took off the mask. Brenda's eyes instantly went to her full lips. What a luscious mouth she had! All Brenda wanted to do was kiss it. She leaned over and fell on her like a woman dying of thirst. The soft lips parted, but she hardly needed an invitation. She probed with her tongue until she became short of breath. "Oh God! I missed that!"

Cherie's eyes were smiling along with her mouth.

"Let's go to bed," said Brenda.

Laughing, Cherie gently pushed her away. "Let's have coffee first and then we can go to bed." She began pouring coffee into a cup. Brenda, meanwhile, kissed the back of Cherie's long, graceful neck, thinking of the exotic water birds she'd seen in the marsh.

"I can't wait," murmured Brenda, her lips nibbling the soft skin.

"Yes, you can. Come on. It will help me wake up. Then I'll be more responsive. I promise." Cherie handed her a cup of coffee. She let out a groan of protest, but she took the cup and sat down at the table. Cherie sat across from her, smiling over her coffee cup.

"Did you sleep all right?" asked Brenda.

"I would have slept better if I wasn't thinking of you when I was falling asleep, but I dreamed of you."

"What did you dream about?" asked Brenda, leaning forward.

"What do you think?" Cherie wiggled her brows suggestively and gave Brenda an intense sidelong look.

"I want you to tell me. You know, like how you'd talk to me when we were apart."

"You want to have phone sex before we have real sex?" asked Cherie with a little chuckle.

"Something like that. It turns me on to hear what you want to do to me."

"Want to hear what I dreamed last night?"

Brenda nodded.

"I dreamed you finally let me go down on you."

Brenda's eyes grew wide. The last time Cherie had brought this up, Brenda had fended her off because she hadn't taken a shower since morning and had had a busy, sweaty day.

"I dreamed you opened your legs really wide, so I could get really close and kiss you. I used my tongue gently at first, and you jumped a little because it felt so good. Then I licked you wide and soft, making you so wet. You kept saying you wanted more. So, I licked your clit and put my fingers deep inside you…first one, then two, then three! And in no time at all, you came." Cherie snapped her fingers. "Just like that!" Cherie wiggled on the seat of her chair. "Oh, I'm getting wet thinking about it."

"Sure you want to finish your coffee?" asked Brenda.

"No, let's go to bed."

They left their coffee to get cold and ran upstairs. Trailing clothes on the way, they catapulted themselves onto the bed. Brenda nudged Cherie onto her back and slipped her hand between her legs. Cherie had been right about being wet, amazingly wet and open. Brenda's fingers quickly found their way inside.

"Everything about you is always so soft and open," Brenda whispered, gazing into Cherie's eyes. "I love that about you, and the way you come so fast and so many times."

"You make me so hot," Cherie whispered back. "Go deep. Fill me up, woman!" Her eyes closed and her hips began to dance to the rhythm of Brenda's hand. She raised her legs to get more. Brenda watched her face change. Her lips parted and her whole body began to move to the pace of Brenda's strokes. She came out to tease her clitoris. Cherie made a little moan of protest, but then her back arched and she held her breath. Her eyes flew open and she gasped. She moaned, then let out a little cry. After panting for a moment, she reached down to grasp Brenda's hand. "Enough now. I'm too sensitive," she said between breaths. "Let me calm down."

"Okay," said Brenda, reaching up to caress Cherie's cheek. She kissed her. "You are the sexiest woman I've ever been with."

Cherie opened her eyes. "That's because you make me feel sexy."

"I do?" Brenda liked that idea.

"But now, I want to make you feel good. Will you let me go down on you? Maybe I can make you come."

Brenda felt herself tense. She hated that her body wouldn't let Cherie give her a climax. A few times, she'd gotten so close and strained to push herself over, but then she would hang there, and it wouldn't happen, no matter what Cherie did. It had taken months for Marcia to figure out how to make her come. After the first time, she was fine. She worried that Cherie might not be patient enough to wait.

"I don't know..." Brenda began.

"Let's try it. If it doesn't work, we'll try something else." Her blue-green eyes gazed intently into hers. "Okay?"

"Okay," said Brenda in a doubtful voice.

Tugging on Brenda's shoulder, Cherie rolled her on her back. As Cherie leisurely explored Brenda's mouth with her tongue, she allowed her weight to rest on Brenda's body. She was slight so it wasn't oppressive. Cherie's knees nudged her thighs open. Brenda opened them wide as Cherie had described in her dream.

"Good girl," said Cherie with a grin. "You're getting the idea."

Cherie bathed her gently with her tongue, beginning with her ear, working down her neck, her collar bones. Her sensual lips found one nipple while her fingers worked the other. Brenda felt her clit pulsing with anticipation. It actually twitched. Brenda tightened her muscles to increase the pleasure. She hadn't even been touched yet, but she felt nearly ready to come. Maybe it would happen this time!

Cherie gave the other breast attention, circling the nipple with her tongue until it was hard as a pebble. She rubbed her cheek against Brenda's breast. "I love your breasts," said Cherie. "They're beautiful. Did you know that?"

"Thank you," Brenda murmured because she felt it was expected, but Cherie gently pinched her nipple, and it was so distracting.

Cherie made a little sound, a laugh of pleasure. "I could suck them all day." The tongue bath continued. Cherie kissed her belly, explored her navel. Her lips followed the downy trail of blond hair leading to the springy pubic hair. It was torture to have all that pleasure and no focus for it.

"You're driving me crazy," said Brenda.

"That's the idea." Cherie sat up between Brenda's legs. She parted her lips with her thumbs. "What a sweet, pink pussy you have, and it's all nice and wet for me. All sweet and wet, like a little flower covered with dew." Cherie parted the inner lips.

"I feel like you're giving me an examination."

"I am," said Cherie, sounding amused. "But not the medical kind. This is the first time you've let me see you. I'm surveying the geography, so I know where I'm going." She stroked with two fingers on both sides of her clitoris. *Please. Touch me!* thought Brenda, but Cherie continued the leisurely stroking. With her other hand, she penetrated her deeply with her fingers.

"How's that?" she asked. "Feel good?"

"Good," agreed Brenda, almost unable to make her mouth form the word.

Finally, Cherie withdrew and lay down between her legs. She kissed her inner thighs and trailed her tongue along the sensitive skin there. Then she blew gently on her clitoris, and Brenda thought she would jump out of her skin. Cherie's breath came again, warm and soft. Finally, she felt her tongue touch her gently, barely a suggestion of what might come next. Then she felt the flat of Cherie's tongue trail fully from below to above. It settled delicately on her clitoris and began to work it cleverly, creating a slightly off rhythm that was driving her insane. Cherie's tongue let off for a moment, and her fingers went inside. Brenda longed to feel that soft tongue on her again. *Please!* She begged in her mind, hoping to convey the urgency of her need through telepathy. She opened her legs wider. That was the signal! Cherie's tongue came back and found a rhythm that worked with the pace of her fingers.

Brenda felt the tension building, the sensation unfocused, both inside and outside at the same time. She was confused about which one to follow, and then her body made the decision for her. It was both! She'd never had an orgasm like this before. She stopped thinking about it and let the pleasure wash over her like undulating waves. Her face burned, and her skin, up and down her chest. She was still throbbing after it was over, and the warm tongue let her go.

Cherie climbed back up Brenda's body and rested her weight. "Did that feel good?" Brenda could hear the smile in Cherie's voice.

"Oh, my God! What did you do to me?"

"What I dreamed about. Did you like it?"

"Did I like it? I thought my head would explode or my clit or both!"

"You came on the inside too. I could feel it with my fingers. You squeezed them so hard!"

"That was amazing," said Brenda.

"I'm glad." Cherie sighed. "I could go right back to sleep now. I feel so calm and relaxed."

"So let's. I don't have to report until noon. I'll call in later and tell them I'm grounded."

"Okay. Can you sleep with me on you like this?"

"Probably not," Brenda said honestly. "Come here and lie in my arms."

Cherie adjusted her position. Brenda kissed her forehead.

She was dozing lightly when she became aware of a sound, a phone ringing in the distance. The ringtone was unfamiliar.

"I think your phone is ringing."

"Let it ring," said Cherie. "I'm off duty."

The ringing stopped. After a minute, the ringing began again. Brenda nudged Cherie awake. "Your phone again. It might be important."

With a sigh, Cherie got up. She pulled on her nightgown. Brenda heard her footsteps on the stairs. She tried to listen, but the urge to sleep was overwhelming.

The footsteps returning were rapid. Cherie was running up the stairs.

"That was the hospitalist at Southern Med. My father is in bad shape."

32

"Cherie, can you hold on a minute? I have to get off another call." Lucy tapped on the call on hold. "Tom, can I call you back later? I have a situation I need to handle."

"Sure, Lucy. Call me when you can." Lucy ended Tom's call. He made such a wonderful partner in ministering to the parish. He'd already been the rector in a high-profile church in New Haven, Connecticut, so there was no need to prove himself or push for advancement. They were collaborative in everything. As a result, there was no competitive tension, and neither was burdened or overworked.

Lucy tapped back to Cherie's call. "Now, please tell me again. I'm sorry. I was distracted because I was on two calls at once."

Erika, who was reading on her iPad beside her, looked up. "Is everything okay?"

Lucy shook her head and mouthed, "I'll tell you later."

Erika nodded and went back to her reading.

"How bad is it?" Lucy asked, heading into the bedroom. She closed the door for more privacy. Because Cherie was a counseling client as well as a parishioner, this call counted as double duty. Either case would require confidentiality, even from Lucy's wife.

"His kidneys are suddenly failing. They think it could be blood clots. Everyone knew about the pulmonary symptoms. No one knew it could affect other organs."

"What can they do for him?" asked Lucy. She slipped off her shoes and pulled herself up on the bed.

"He may need dialysis to keep him going. But even if he recovers from the virus, his lung function will be even more compromised than it was before. He may never get off the ventilator."

"Oh, no," said Lucy, realizing the implications.

"I'm his healthcare proxy. I'll have to make a choice soon."

"Is he conscious? Can you speak to him about his wishes?"

"No, he's sedated because of the ventilator, but he's told me before he doesn't want to be kept alive by extraordinary means. We've talked about it many times."

"What can I do to help?" asked Lucy. "I mean, apart from praying for your father?"

"I can't go see him. Even though I'm a physician's assistant, I have no more standing than any other family member to get into the hospital."

Lucy realized where this was going and felt uneasy. "It's terrible that people can't visit their loved ones."

"But you can, as a hospital chaplain."

Lucy tried to think of something to say. The bishop had issued orders to reduce hospital visits to a bare minimum during the pandemic. Home visits to the sick were prohibited, even for the last rites. A beautiful message delivered by a priest-physician, who was a canon of the cathedral, explained why these strict measures were necessary, but that was small comfort to a grieving family member like Cherie.

Lucy tapped the icon to open a video chat. It was obvious that Cherie had been crying. Her eyes were red, and her cheeks, tear streaked. "Oh, Cherie. I'm so sorry," said Lucy. "If your father is sedated, will he even know I'm there?"

"He'll know you're there. Please, Lucy. My father adores you. He thinks you look like an angel. He said if he saw you at the pearly gates, he'd know he was in the right place."

Lucy frowned as she digested this message. So often she disregarded her own physical beauty, knowing it to be an accident of genetics, like having red hair or green eyes, yet so many people told her how it inspired them in good, positive ways to turn their thoughts to spiritual matters. They often said the same about her singing voice. She tried so hard to be a good priest, to write sermons that moved people to think and to turn their hearts to God, and yet it sometimes seemed her natural gifts were all she needed.

"I can't be there," said Cherie, "but he'll know you're there. If yours is the voice he hears, he'll know it's all right to go home and be with Mama." Her voice broke on the last words, which brought tears to Lucy's eyes. "Honestly, Mother Lucy, if yours was the last voice I ever heard, I would think I had already gone to heaven."

"That's very kind of you to say, Cherie, but I need to think about this. Yes, I am allowed to visit the hospital as a chaplain. Obviously, I risk bringing the virus into the hospital or bringing it back here to my family and friends. Fortunately, we have few parishioners from St. Margaret's in the hospital, so yours is the first request to visit."

"Please, Lucy, you're my father's priest and he needs you now. You're my priest, and I need you now."

Cherie's pleas were pulling on her heartstrings, and yet there were many people who couldn't visit a family member because of the virus. Cherie was one of thousands of grieving people who couldn't hold a dying loved one's hand in their last hours.

"Let me talk to Dr. Stolz and get her advice on this," said Lucy. "I'll call you back in a little while."

"All right," said Cherie, "And thank you."

When Lucy returned to the sitting room, Erika glanced up from her reading. "You look perplexed. What's the matter?"

Lucy sighed deeply. "Cherie Bois's father isn't doing well. She's asked me to pray with him at his bedside. He's in Southern Med."

The expression in Erika's pale eyes suddenly changed from curiosity to frank concern.

"I don't know if I like this idea. Will you go?"

"I think I should. I want to talk to Liz about it."

"That's wise," said Erika. "Let me know what she says."

Lucy crossed the bridge from the apartment to the main house. She never took the elevator, although she always glanced at it because it seemed so out of place in a private home. She knew the rationale. Liz had designed the house with all the amenities so that she could age in place. Her bedroom was on the third floor. If she became infirmed, she needed a means to get there.

The door to Liz's office was open when Lucy got there. She could hear Liz saying, "Is CVS still your pharmacy?" Lucy realized Liz was on a Telehealth call, so she retreated to the hall to give her privacy.

After a moment, Liz came out to look for her. "Hey, Lucy. What's up?"

"I'm sorry. I didn't realize you had office hours."

"Neither did I, but Cathy needed to talk to her daughter's teacher, so she asked me to cover for her for an hour. Fortunately, that call was an easy one. Any woman who's had a UTI can diagnose it herself." Liz gave her a brief, questioning look. "Is something wrong?"

"I need to talk to you."

"Come in," said Liz and closed the door behind them. "Sit down." She gestured toward the chair by her desk.

"I hope you were able to help that woman," said Lucy, taking a seat. "Remember when I had that awful bladder infection after my honeymoon? I was so uncomfortable, and the blood scared me half to death."

"Unfortunately, UTIs are common when women are having lots of sex," said Liz with a slightly lewd tilt of her brow.

"You were so kind to bring me antibiotics even though it was the middle of the night."

"You know I'd do anything for you, Lucy." Liz's blue eyes were almost as compelling as Erika's. She was a natural mesmerist. "I love you."

"I love you too."

Liz's gaze became so intense, Lucy had to look away.

"Lucy, I have a confession to make."

Oh, no, thought Lucy, *what is she going to say?* "Are you confessing to me as your friend or as a priest?"

Liz chuckled softly. "I'm not asking for absolution, but what I'm going to tell you is considered a sin." She took a deep breath. "Sometimes, I lust for you in my heart."

Using those words, once used to pillory a president, was obviously an attempt at humor, but Lucy could see Liz wasn't joking. She was completely serious. Lucy's mind raced, trying to think of something to say. She could admit to the same thing, because it was true. She found Liz's strength and boyish charm very attractive. Her body reacted when Liz gave her one of her long, soulful hugs. Lucy knew it was sexual arousal but admitting her feelings would only mislead Liz.

"I love you too, Liz, but I know you would never betray your wife or your best friend, and neither would I."

Liz patted Lucy's hand. "I knew you'd say that, but thanks for reminding me to keep my head screwed on straight. Around you that's hard sometimes."

"I understand," Lucy admitted.

Liz gazed at her with a thoughtful look. Finally, she said, "Glad I got that off my chest."

"Do you want absolution? I can give it to you."

"Hell, no." Liz's sardonic grin indicated the serious moment had passed. "Sorry for the detour. You came to talk about something. What was it?"

Lucy was relieved that Liz could so easily make the transition from one conversation to another. The heavy feeling was instantly dispelled. Unfortunately, it would now be replaced by something equally weighty.

"Cherie's father isn't doing well. His kidneys are failing."

Liz nodded gravely and took a deep breath. "I've been reading in the medical bulletins about how other organs can be affected. Fucking hell! There's so much about this damn virus we don't know." She looked instantly sheepish. "Sorry about the profanity."

Lucy ignored both the profanity and the apology. "Cherie wants me to go to the hospital to give her father the last rites."

"Well, that's a dumbass idea," said Liz bluntly.

Lucy made a concerted effort to sound patient. "Liz, you are a great doctor, but sometimes, you forget about the people side of things. Cherie is distraught because she can't see her father. He may die, and she will never see him again."

"So, she wants to send you and expose you to danger instead," said Liz in an irritated voice. "Brilliant!"

"Aren't they careful in the hospital? Won't they give me protective clothing?"

"Yes, but they don't have enough for themselves. Going there is not only stupid, it's selfish!"

"Okay, thanks for your opinion, but I think it's insensitive and unkind." Lucy got up to leave.

"Will you go to the hospital?"

"Yes, I will."

Scowling, Liz got up. "Fucking stubborn woman! Why do I live in a house full of fucking stubborn women?" Liz was making such faces Lucy wanted to laugh, but she knew that would only insult her. She patted Liz's arm in an attempt to calm her. Liz stared at her with pursed lips and a frown. Finally, she said, "All right, Lucy. I'll go with you to make sure you suit up right."

Lucy's mouth opened in surprise. "You will?"

"Yes. Give me a few minutes to see if any more calls come through before Cathy comes back online. Then we'll go together. I'll stop in the office and grab some PPE for both of us. I want to make sure you're safe. I don't want anything to happen to you."

Lucy was moved. "Thank you," she murmured. "You're my Lohengrin. My very own swan knight. How can I thank you?"

"Well, you just said it. You can sing Elsa's aria on our next talent night. Promise?"

"Promise," said Lucy and stood on tiptoes to plant a kiss on Liz's cheek. "And your little secret is safe with me."

Liz studied her face for a long moment. "I expected as much, or I wouldn't have told you." Liz sat down and turned her eyes to her screen. "Bring clothes and some towels so you can shower in the office on the way back. You don't want to bring the virus home with you."

33

While they headed to the office of Hobbs Family Practice, Liz took in the sights along the way. The town was pretty much dead at this time of year, but there was abnormally little traffic on Route 1. The parking lots of the hotels and restaurants were completely empty. Only the supermarket and pharmacy had cars parked outside.

"It's like one of those bad 1950s apocalypse movies," Liz said, speaking her thoughts aloud. "You know, how the world looks after an atomic war.... minus the destruction, of course."

"Are you always so pessimistic?"

"I'm not pessimistic, just observant."

"It's a good thing I know you, Liz. I know your grumpiness is all for show. Underneath, you're one of the kindest, gentlest, most loving women I've ever met." Lucy glanced at the big diamond ring on her finger. It had once belonged to Liz's grandmother, but Liz had given it to Erika so that she could propose to Lucy. "Do you ever regret giving away your grandmother's ring for me?"

"No. Never," said Liz. "And don't spread it around that I'm not mean and grumpy."

"I don't have to." Lucy gazed out the window. "Everyone already knows."

As Liz flew into the parking area of Hobbs Family Practice, she could see Lucy gripping the grab bar over the passenger side window. Evidently, Lucy didn't like the way Liz drove any more than Maggie did.

"Wait here," said Liz, yanking up the parking brake.

Once inside, she headed straight to the supply closet and found gowns, masks, gloves and goggles. She was about to head out when she thought about their stash of PPE. It wouldn't be needed for the period the office was closed. They could afford to share with the ICU personnel at Southern Med. She found a nearly empty box and started filling it with masks. She grabbed a few bottles of hand sanitizer and stuffed them into her jacket pocket.

"That was fast," said Lucy when Liz opened the back door of the car to put the box on the seat. "What's in the box?"

"Our PPE and extras for our friends at Southern Med."

Lucy looked at her. "See what I mean?"

"See what you mean what?" asked Liz, climbing into the driver's seat.

"It's all a façade. Underneath, you're a marshmallow."

"I tell you, Lucy, if you try to blackmail me with this, I'll..."

Lucy laughed. "Don't worry. I'll save the blackmail for a very special favor."

"Lucy, you're shameless."

Lucy just smiled.

When they arrived at Southern Med, the doctors' parking lot was nearly empty. "Wow, I've never seen it like this," said Liz, swinging into a spot. "I heard they had to furlough people because all elective procedures are cancelled. That's a hell of a lot of lost revenue. This place must be really hurting financially."

Lucy stared at the building. "I would never have thought of that."

"This place can survive, but a lot of the rural hospitals will go under." Liz took off her jacket and threw it into the back seat. "You should do the same. The less clothing exposed to the virus, the better. Good thing it's not too cold today.

Lucy got out of the car and took off her coat. Clad in only her clerical blouse and a black pants suit, she hugged herself against the brisk wind coming off the ocean.

"Heads up." Liz tossed her a small bottle of hand sanitizer. Lucy fumbled but caught it, which for some reason pleased Liz. "You'll need that. Keep it close." Lucy slipped the bottle into her suit pocket.

Liz took out the box of PPE and carried it under her arm as they headed to the entrance of the hospital. They hurried to get out of the wind. Lucy's cheeks were pink. Even Liz, who usually didn't mind the cold, was trembling by the time they got inside. She pulled out her hand sanitizer in the lobby. "Assume that everything you touch, including door handles, could harbor the virus."

"This is crazy," said Lucy.

"I know, but you're the one who wanted to come down here."

She led Lucy to the elevator and pressed the button for the ICU. Once they arrived at the floor, Liz whipped out her hand sanitizer and nodded to Lucy to do the same.

In the visitor's lounge, Liz helped Lucy dress, carefully bending the metal strip around her nose to seal the air flow. She tied the strings of the sterile gown and showed her how to get her long hair into the cap. She handed her safety goggles and held the gloves while Lucy put her hands into them.

"So, this is how you look as a surgeon," said Lucy after Liz finished dressing.

"More or less. Usually, I'd be wearing scrubs and washable clogs."

On the way to Jean-Paul's room, Liz dropped off the box of supplies at the nurses' station. The duty nurse approached.

"Hello? Can I help you?"

"Liz Stolz. Hobbs Family Practice. I thought you might be able to use these."

The nurse looked in the box, and her eyes lit up. "These are the good ones! Yes, we certainly can use them. Thank you, Dr. Stolz!"

"Is Jean-Paul Bois still in bay fourteen?"

"Yes."

"How's he doing?"

The woman shook her head. "Are you his primary?"

"No, one of my partners, but we're all covering for each other. I have surgical privileges here."

The nurse handed Liz a tablet so she could read the notes.

"Thanks," said Liz after giving it a quick scan. "This is Reverend Bartlett from St. Margaret's." She gestured with her thumb over her shoulder toward Lucy. "She's here as Mr. Bois's priest."

"You'll see I'm a registered chaplain," Lucy quickly added.

"You're with Dr. Stolz. You're fine," said the nurse, wagging her head in the direction of Jean-Paul's bay.

"See?" said Liz as they headed down the hall, "You needed me."

"I *do* need you."

Liz didn't quite know how to interpret that remark, so she let it go.

"Our bishop will only allow us to give last rites to patients in the hospital under controlled conditions," said Lucy. "If Mr. Bois were at home, this wouldn't be possible."

"It's still a risk," said Liz, unable to resist the urge to underscore the point. "He's sedated. He won't be able to respond. He won't even know you're there. Can you still give him the last rites?"

"I won't be able to give him communion, but studies suggest that people can hear, even in a coma."

"Whatever," said Liz in a disparaging voice.

Lucy stopped and turned to her. "Whatever you or I believe, it's a comfort to the family to know the soul has been prepared to meet God. That's why we're here."

Liz had never heard Lucy scold her so adamantly.

"I'm sorry."

"You're forgiven."

They found the correct bay. Liz approached Jean-Paul's bed and gave him a quick assessment. *It won't be long*, she decided and stepped aside to let Lucy do her priest thing. She was tempted to zone out and ignore all the religious mumbo jumbo when she realized that Cherie would probably like to see this. After all, she was putting Lucy's health in jeopardy for it. Liz pulled out her phone and pulled off her gloves so she could tap Cherie's number. "Hold on, Lucy," said Liz. "Let's Facetime this with Cherie. Okay?"

Lucy turned. Liz could tell she was smiling from her eyes. "Good idea. Why didn't I think of that?"

Cherie answered and Liz put the call on video. "Lucy's going to start. Would you like to watch?"

"Oh, yes! Please."

As Liz held the phone to video the ceremony, she remembered some of the tricks Maggie and Alina had taught her for positioning the lens and using the zoom to emphasize things. Wrapped up in the process, Liz tried to ignore the religious part of the service, but her mind couldn't help but hear the words Lucy was reciting. "Almighty God, look on this your servant, lying in great weakness, and comfort him with the promise of life everlasting, given in the resurrection of your Son, Jesus Christ, our Lord. Amen."

Lucy looked up at Liz. "Would you do Jean-Paul the honor of reciting the antiphons?" Lucy beckoned her closer. "Here, follow along with me in the text. You read the italics. God, the Father."

"Have mercy on your servant," read Liz. Lucy looked up and gave her a warm smile.

The ceremony proceeded. Liz took her role seriously, but she was glad when it was over.

"Cherie? Would you like to say something to your father?" asked Lucy. "Liz can hold the phone closer." Lucy nodded in her direction, and Liz put her phone near Jean-Paul's ear. "Go ahead, Cherie."

"I love you, Daddy. I love you so much," said Cherie's mournful voice. "I miss you already." She began to sob. "I don't know what to say."

"You're doing fine, Cherie," Lucy said. "Say what's in your heart."

Tears started to form in Liz's eyes. She could see that Lucy's eyes were already full. The sobs coming through the phone speaker grew louder, punctuated by the words, "I love you, Daddy. I love you."

Finally, Liz couldn't stand it anymore. She turned the camera on the phone around and said, "We should let him rest, Cherie. I'm sure he was glad to hear your voice. We'll call you later."

"Thanks so much, Liz. Thank you, Lucy. You don't know how much this means to me."

"You're welcome, Cherie," said Lucy. "We love you."

"Talk to you later," said Liz and tapped off the call.

As they were depositing their protective clothing in the bin at the end of the hall, Lucy asked, "Did you believe what you told Cherie? About her father being glad to hear her voice?"

Liz shrugged. "I don't know," she said. "I don't know what I believe anymore."

Before they got in the car, Liz took out her bottle of hand sanitizer and gestured to Lucy, who did the same. They rode to Liz's office in silence.

"You can take the first shower," Liz said, throwing her keys on the desk. "Don't hog all the hot water."

Liz sat in her consulting room while Lucy showered. She could hear the beat of the water against the wall and smiled when Lucy began to sing in the shower. She didn't take long, evidently taking Liz's warning about using up the hot water seriously. She came out dressed in a workout suit and her hair in a turban. "There's a hair dryer on the wall," said Liz. "Dry your hair. It's cold outside."

"I can wait until you're done," said Lucy.

Liz showered quickly, dried her own hair and came out. "Go ahead," she said. She could hear the drone of the hair dryer while she checked the messages on her phone.

Finally, they headed home. "Do you often pray at the bedside of dying people?" Liz asked as she navigated the back roads to the house.

"It's part of my job," said Lucy.

"When I was a surgeon, I had to tell the families of people who died on my table. I hated it. I'd go out and deliver the bad news. Then I'd leave it to the social workers and the chaplains to mop up the mess. I was never good at that part."

"You did very well today," said Lucy. "I admire you. It must be hard to do what you do without faith."

"Thanks, but your iron age fairy tales don't impress me."

"Who hurt you, Liz? Why do you hate religion so much?"

"It's not about hurt. It's anger over the double standard, the hatred of women and gay people. The money grabbing. The pedophilia. It's disgusting."

Out of the corner of her eye, Liz saw Lucy nod. "I understand. I feel the same way myself."

"You do? So how do you keep doing this?"

"Because I know that God loves us, and I want to help people know it too." Lucy reached over and patted Liz on the shoulder. "She loves you too. Even you, grumpy Liz Stolz."

"That's nice," said Liz cynically.

"It's okay," said Lucy with a nod. "God has infinite patience."

34

They were ready to begin their talent night, but Liz was nowhere to be found. Maggie knew exactly where to look for her. As Maggie had expected, Liz was in her office, staring at her computer screen.

"Aren't you coming to our show?" asked Maggie. Then she saw the stock market charts on the screen and the pad scribbled with figures on Liz's desk. She hugged Liz around the shoulders. "Honey, you have to stop worrying. There's nothing you can do about it."

Liz twisted out of her embrace. "You don't understand." She tapped the pad. "THIS is how much we've lost so far."

Maggie glanced at the figure and her stomach lurched. It was hard to wrap her mind around a sum that large. "It's a lot, but you always say it will come back." She rubbed Liz's shoulder sympathetically. "You're obsessing about this. Now, close the laptop and come to the show. We rehearsed all afternoon for this. Lucy is singing her special aria, the one you requested."

"Tell her I'll take a rain check."

Maggie stood straight. "Liz, you can't do that!" She narrowed her eyes and scrutinized Liz's face. "Have you two had a fight?"

"No," said Liz, but she had that guilty look Maggie knew very well.

"I hope not, because with all of us living together, we can't afford petty arguments."

"She keeps trying to convert me. It's fucking annoying."

Maggie laughed. "Then she has way more patience than I do. I know you're a lost cause." Maggie stroked the back of Liz's head. "Honey, you need a haircut. You're starting to look like a sheepdog."

Liz raised her shoulder to avoid Maggie's hand. "I don't know if I trust you to cut my hair."

"With the salons closed, I'm your best option." Maggie mussed the wild, gray waves on the top. "Besides, with your grunge hairstyle, no one will ever notice if I screw up." Maggie patted Liz's shoulder. "Come on. Everyone's waiting."

Maggie watched Liz log out of the brokerage site and close her laptop. She stood at the office door, waiting to make sure Liz accompanied her.

When they came into the media room, Tony, the director of the Webhanet Playhouse, could be seen on the giant TV screen above the small stage. "Hello, Liz!" he said, his baritone booming in the room. "About time you got here."

"Sorry, Tony," Liz called back. "Counting my money."

"Speaking of money, we could use your help. I think we're going to have to cancel the season."

"That's a shame, but I've taken some heavy losses in the market. I'll do what I can," said Liz, finding a seat. "Did the Bush family come through?"

"Yes, they doubled their usual contribution."

"Well, I won't be outdone by some Republicans, so I guess I'll have to double mine too."

Tony looked genuinely touched. "Thanks, Liz. We appreciate it."

Maggie went up to the stage and clapped her hands. "All right, let's settle down everyone. Welcome to our second stay-at-home talent night." She gestured to the big screen overhead. "As you can see, Tony Roselli is joining us by Zoom." She stood back and waved to the screen. "Hi, Tony!"

"Hi Maggie and friends," Tony called back.

Erika went to the laptop on a nearby table to adjust the volume coming from the big screen.

Alina stepped to the front and stood beside her mother. "Okay, everyone. We're going to begin. We're livestreaming this performance on the Hobbs Facebook page and recording it for my station. I need everyone in the audience to be as quiet as possible, so the audio isn't full of coughing and shuffling. Does everyone understand?"

Maggie glanced around the tiny audience and saw the nods of agreement.

"Mom? Will you be ready to switch so Emily can come down for her piano numbers? I have to go up and watch the kids."

"Yes, dear. Don't worry." Maggie tried to sound confident, but she realized her palms were sweating and blotted them on a tissue. Despite decades in the theater, she was still nervous before a live performance.

Lucy came up to the stage to join her. She smiled one of her brilliant smiles, and Maggie instantly felt better. Tony began to play the introduction to "For Good," from *Wicked*.

Maggie counted the beats to her entrance. She always felt humbled singing with a world-famous opera star, but Lucy was so warm and encouraging that Maggie never felt diminished sharing the stage with her. As they sang the meaningful lyrics celebrating friendship, the staging called for them to join hands. Maggie gave her friend's a little squeeze.

They reprised many of the numbers from the Webhanet Playhouse's Labor Day Gala, minimally choreographed and costumed for the tiny stage. They had planned for Lucy to do a solo number, her aria from the *Merry Widow* so that Maggie would have time to get ready for the camera switch. Maggie anxiously scanned the control panel, trying to remember all the instructions Alina had given her. They'd gone over it several times in the last few days and tested it for the livestream of Lucy's Palm Sunday service.

Lucy was winding down her aria, and Maggie saw Emily coming down to the front. This was the tricky part. She needed to swing the position of the camera to focus on the grand piano, but she waited, as they'd agreed, for Erika to redirect on the lighting. Right on cue, the spotlight over the piano came on. What an amazing crew they made.

Maggie allowed herself to relax while Emily brilliantly played Liszt and Chopin. The girl had such native talent as a musician. Of course, Lucy, her mother, was a brilliant singer and musical talent seemed to run in families.

After Emily took her bows, Maggie trained the camera on the stage. Lucy was coming out to sing "Elsa's Dream," the aria she had promised to sing for Liz. Maggie had been an actress and director for decades, but she always marveled at the discipline it took to sing such sophisticated music and act at the same time.

Maggie finally allowed herself to relax. The little concert was almost over. This number was the finale. Afterwards, they would switch to the live feed from the Webhanet Playhouse, where Tony would make an appeal for donations. The Playhouse couldn't survive without philanthropy, and the losses from a canceled season would be crushing. So many theaters, opera houses, and museums would be devastated by the loss of ticket sales, never mind the actors, musicians and stage crew thrown out of work. Most arts institutions were streaming archival material in a gesture of good will during the shutdown, but how long could they survive?

Maggie turned around to rest her eyes from the bright lights on the stage. She saw Liz, sitting at the edge of her seat, gazing with pure adoration at Lucy singing on the stage. If Liz thought she was hiding her crush on Lucy, she was kidding herself.

Sometimes, Maggie felt a little twinge of jealousy when she saw her wife fawning over Lucy like a fool, but everyone fell in love with Lucy. Even Maggie, who never felt drawn to very feminine women, felt the attraction. What did Lucy have that was so compelling? She was beautiful, yes, no one could deny it, but there was something else…

As the aria came to a close, Maggie reviewed the steps for switching the feed to the Playhouse. Tony would wind down the show and thank the participants. There would be no curtain calls. Instead, they would play a video clip of the curtain calls from last year's Labor Day show with Tony's voice over pleading for money. Maggie switched over to the Playhouse and turned off the camera.

Maggie made sure the local audio was off and announced, "We did it!" The tiny audience clapped and cheered.

She watched Liz go up to the stage, offer a courtly bow to Lucy, and kiss her hand.

"Hey, Liz, what about me?" Maggie called to her.

Liz hopped down from the stage and offered Maggie a hug of congratulations and a kiss.

"Hey, everyone! Time for the cast party," announced Liz. "We have champagne and brownies in the kitchen!"

Liz uncorked bottles of champagne and filled the waiting flutes. Erika put out the platter of brownies. Maggie put two on a plate for Stefan, who had found refuge at the table in the breakfast nook. His hearing aid bothered him when there was too much ambient noise.

"You were delightful, my dear," he said as Maggie put the plate in front of him and handed him a glass of champagne. "It is wonderful to have not only your hospitality, but such wonderful entertainment."

Maggie slid next to him on the bench. "We're glad you could join us."

He trained his pale eyes on her. "You are lucky to have so much space for guests, and we are lucky to be invited."

"Are you comfortable in the downstairs guestroom? I stayed there for a while when I broke my leg."

"Yes, I am very comfortable. I miss my books…and my friends at Ocean Terrace, but the company here is much more stimulating. It's quite a lively household."

"Not too lively I hope," said Maggie, patting his hand. The skin was crepey and soft. She could feel the bones below prominently. He might be ninety-two, but the twinkle in his eye showed the spirit of a much younger man, and a shameless flirt at that!

He laughed softly. "Not at all. I will miss all the activity when I go home again."

"That doesn't look like it will be anytime soon."

He sighed. "No, it doesn't, I'm afraid."

Maggie looked up and saw Liz staring at her phone. With a frown, Liz headed to where Lucy stood, and now the two of them were looking grim. Maggie patted Stefan's hand.

"Excuse me," she said. "I see my wife needs me. I'll be back."

"Take your time, Maggie. Meanwhile, I will sample your lovely brownies. I'm sure they will be delicious."

Liz and Lucy were speaking in hushed tones when Maggie approached.

"Is something wrong?" asked Maggie.

"Cherie just texted," said Liz. "Her father died."

"Oh, no!" said Maggie.

"I'm going upstairs to call her," said Lucy. "You'll have to hold down the fort for me."

Before Lucy left, she headed to where Erika stood. Maggie guessed she was telling her the sad news.

35

As Cherie moved the diaphragm of her stethoscope around Brenda's chest, she thought she heard the doorbell ring. Finally, she pulled out one earpiece to listen.

"I should see who's at the door," she said, smoothing back Brenda's hair. "Your lungs sound a little clearer." She kissed Brenda's forehead. "Be right back."

Brenda smiled weakly. "If you don't mind, I'll sleep now so I can be with you for the funeral."

"That's not necessary," Cherie said.

"Yes, it is," insisted Brenda before launching into a coughing jag. "And I want to take a shower, so I don't look like a homeless person."

"No one cares how you look."

"I care." Brenda rolled over. She was almost instantly asleep. The constant coughing had been keeping her awake at night and preventing Cherie from sleeping too. Finally, Cherie had moved back into the bedroom farthest from Brenda's so that she could get some much-needed rest. She'd need all her strength. Between Brenda's health deteriorating and the funeral, there was plenty to handle.

The doorbell rang again. Fortunately, whoever it was had the decency not to lean on the bell. Cherie put on a knit jacket and ran down the stairs. She opened the door and looked out.

Standing a healthy distance away was Liz Stolz, but she looked so different from the boss Cherie was used to seeing. Liz was wearing a smart, black skirted suit and high heels. When Cherie opened the storm door, Liz looked up from her phone and stuffed it in her pocket.

"Good morning," said Liz. "I know it's a little early, but I wanted to get back so I can drive Maggie, Lucy and Emily to the church. They want to do a quick rehearsal before the service. I brought you a few things." She gestured to the bench on the little porch.

Cherie glanced over and saw the oxygen canister she'd requested and three shopping bags. There was also a small stock pot.

"I'd help you bring the stuff in but I'm trying to stay out of range because I don't want my clothes and hair contaminated. No offense, of course. The cannulas and tubing are in one of the bags. That's chicken soup I made yesterday. Maggie sent you a blueberry bread."

"Thank you," Cherie murmured, still admiring Liz in her dress-up clothes. Her hair and makeup were perfect. "You look so different. Is this how you used to dress when you were chief of surgery at Yale?"

"Yes, unfortunately," said Liz, "but after all those years of playing grown up, I try to avoid it if possible."

"I understand," said Cherie, "but you look fantastic."

"Thanks. Can't go to your father's funeral looking like a slob." She gestured to the bags on the bench. "I'm sorry the groceries are so limited. The shelves are still bare. The only chicken I could get is defrosted wings and boneless thighs. There were plenty of fresh fruits and vegetables. What does that tell you? Still no toilet paper though, but I threw in a few rolls from our stash."

Cherie brought her clasped hands over her heart to show her appreciation. "That's so kind of you!"

Liz nodded. "Lucy wants you to know that she won't be going to the cemetery. This church funeral is a special favor to you. She doesn't want someone in town to see her at the grave with the hearse parked there and think the church is open for business. She said she'll say the graveside prayers later, hopefully when you can attend."

"I understand, and I appreciate the favor."

"I'll call five minutes before we're actually ready to start so you can get set up." Liz glanced at her watch. "I'll see you later...in a manner of speaking."

Cherie took a shower and styled her hair. Because she would be witnessing her father's funeral, she put on makeup and dressed in a fairly nice outfit, but her choices were limited by what she'd brought to Brenda's.

She went to wake Brenda, whose eyes were glassy and unfocused when she opened them.

"Honey, you don't need to get up for this," said Cherie, kissing her forehead. "I'll understand if you want to rest."

"No," said Brenda swinging her feet to the floor. "I want to be with you. I'll feel better once I take a shower and wake up a little."

Cherie read on her iPad outside Brenda's bathroom while she showered, alert to any indication that she might be weak or in distress. She was relieved to see that, when Brenda came out and began to dress, she looked almost like her old self.

"You look better."

"I feel better."

"Probably the steam in the shower helped you breathe more easily. Maybe we should do that when you're really bad, fill up the shower with steam and you can sit in there for a while."

"It does seem to help."

"I can ask Liz to bring over the humidifier from my house. I don't know why I didn't ask her to bring it along with my father's oxygen tank."

"She'll bring it. Just ask," said Brenda, putting her foot into her jeans. She swayed a little and flopped onto the bed. "A little dizzy this morning."

"You should be careful. You don't want to add a bump on the head to your other troubles."

Cherie held up a jar of Vicks VapoRub. "Look what Liz included in her bag of goodies. I wanted to laugh."

"Don't laugh. My grandmother used to rub that on my chest when I was a kid. It works."

"Sometimes Liz is so old fashioned, but that's what I like about her."

"Where do you want to do this?" Brenda asked, slipping her arms into an oversized corduroy shirt.

Cherie realized she meant where did they want to watch the virtual funeral. "On the sofa in the living room?"

They went downstairs and settled on the sofa. Cherie wrapped a crocheted afghan around them. "Did someone make this for you?"

"My grandmother. She used to make them like a human loom. She'd donate them to be raffled at church bazaars. She made this one for me when I went away to college."

"That's nice to have something she made especially for you."

The phone rang. Cherie picked up right away because she knew it would be Liz's five-minute warning.

"Ready?" asked Liz. "The funeral people just arrived. I'll call when they're ready to begin the service."

"We're ready," replied Cherie. She wondered if Liz knew the call was still open when she heard: "Look guys, wear masks in the church or I'll ground you both. I can. I'm a medical officer."

Brenda snickered. "That's Liz all right."

There was a muffled response from whomever Liz was addressing, followed by a crunching sound. Obviously, Liz had the phone in her pocket. "Jack, if you don't put on a fucking mask, you're not going into this church and exposing my friends. Do you get that?"

Brenda laughed out loud. "Yep, that's Liz."

Although this was the saddest occasion that she could imagine, Cherie laughed.

"I hope she doesn't threaten to break their legs," Brenda said. "Or pull out her gun."

Cherie stared at her.

"Just kidding," said Brenda. "She follows the rules to the letter. Besides, she knows if she tries anything, I'd yank her permit like that." Brenda snapped her fingers. "Hang up on her. I don't think she'd want us to hear what comes next."

"This is not the way to start a funeral," said Cherie, tapping off the call. She swallowed hard to stop the tears.

Brenda reached out for her hand. "I'm really sorry to be the reason you can't go." She turned her face and blocked her cough with the arm of her sweatshirt. Worried, Cherie watched her hack away with the characteristic dry cough of the coronavirus. Brenda's test, like her own, had come back positive, but Cherie hadn't needed confirmation of the obvious.

Cherie squeezed Brenda's thigh. "I gave it to you. I'm the reason I can't go. I gave it to Daddy too, and that's why he's gone." The sobs erupted before Cherie could stop them.

Brenda gently rubbed her back. "It's okay, sweetie. You didn't know. No one knew. You thought you were doing everything right. There is no way you could have stopped it."

That made Cherie completely dissolve. She buried her face in Brenda's shoulder and sobbed harder. Brenda stroked her hair and made soothing cooing sounds. Who would have guessed that a tall, muscular cop, carrying a gun, could be so sensitive?

The phone ringing made them jump. Cherie picked it up. "It's Liz. They must be ready to begin." She wiped away her tears with the back of her hand.

"I guess she settled up with whoever wasn't wearing their masks."

Liz was requesting video, so Cherie tapped the pulsing red icon. "I'm here," said Cherie.

Liz's expression instantly changed when she perceived that Cherie had been crying. Her brows came together in a sad frown of sympathy. "I'm so sorry, Cherie. I wish I could give you a big hug. We're all here for you."

"Thanks, Liz."

"Mute your phone." Liz's face disappeared, and Cherie was looking into the interior of St. Margaret's Church. Liz's voice came through the phone speaker. "My wife is going to sing the entrance hymn accompanied by Lucy's daughter, Emily."

The video cut to a young, red-haired woman playing the piano. Cherie noticed for the first time that Lucy's daughter was growing up to be the very image of her mother. A soprano voice began to sing "On Eagle's Wings." The video feed switched to Maggie Fitzgerald singing. The camera angle changed to show the casket being brought into the church. The funeral staff was wearing masks. Evidently, Liz had won that argument.

The camera trained on Lucy, wearing a priest's choir robes and a white stole. She waited patiently for the casket to approach the front of the church. The funeral staff moved away. Lucy looked right into the camera, which zoomed in on her face.

"Cherie, as you requested, we are here to honor your father and see him to his rest. All of us care for you and we are here to help you bear your burden. Although you cannot be here with us, you can join your prayers to ours."

Cherie began to sob. Instantly, Brenda's arm was around her, pulling her close.

Lucy continued to look into the camera as she began the service. "The Lord be with you!"

The little congregation responded: "And with thy spirit." Cherie could hear Liz's voice near the microphone. Liz was praying? That was unexpected.

Maggie sang Psalm 23 to Emily's accompaniment. Each of those present read one of the scripture readings. While someone held the phone for Liz, she read too.

It was an abbreviated service. Finally, Lucy blessed the casket. As it was wheeled out, the camera tracked its progress. Lucy walked solemnly behind the casket, followed by Maggie Fitzgerald singing the exit hymn, "Amazing Grace," behind her was Emily, Lucy's daughter. The camera caught up with the casket being loaded into the hearse. Cherie realized that this was her last sight of her father's mortal remains, and her eyes began to fill. The hearse door slammed shut, but the camera angle shifted to Lucy's face.

"Thank you, Cherie for the privilege of seeing your father to his rest. We can't accompany him to the cemetery, but our hearts go with him."

Cherie unmuted her phone. "Thank you so much, Lucy. That was the most beautiful funeral I have ever seen."

"Stay strong. We'll see one another soon." Lucy made the sign of the cross in blessing. "May God bless you, Father, Son and Holy Spirit." Then she put her fingers to her lips and blew a kiss. "We all love you. You too, Brenda! Feel better soon!"

"We love you too, Lucy!"

The video feed ended, and Liz's voice came on the line. "That's it,

Cherie. Hugs from all of us. See you soon. Call me if you need anything."

Cherie turned into Brenda's arms and cried. Brenda pulled her up to her shoulder and held her tight. "It's okay, baby. It's okay. It hurts like hell to lose a parent. I know all about it." She rocked her back and forth. "It's okay," she soothed.

"I couldn't even say goodbye," said Cherie, weeping. "I can't even go to his grave."

"You will. Soon."

Cherie sat up and dried her face with the back of her hand. "You must think I'm a big baby."

Brenda reached for her face and kissed both tear-stained cheeks and her mouth. "I don't think anything except that you're hurting, and I understand." She pulled Cherie back into the crook of her arm. "After my father died, my mother and I were at odds. I hadn't spoken to her for years. And then she died. You had a good relationship with your father. You loved him and took care of him. He knew you loved him. That's all that matters, and that's why it hurts so much."

That only made Cherie cry more. Brenda held her tighter, as if that could stop the pain.

36

Liz made a cup of coffee for herself. She chose the extra-dark blend because she needed something bracing to help her shake off sleep. She'd stayed up with the others to watch Tom Simmons celebrate the Easter vigil service in Lucy's church. Tom had a boyfriend now, a former television broadcaster, who had some knowledge of camera work. He wasn't as skilled as Alina, but he had a good eye.

Although it meant a late night and not very much sleep, Liz was glad she had watched the service. Maggie's a cappella group, singing together virtually from their homes, had performed beautifully. Tom and Jeff had arranged candles on tall staffs around the darkened church to represent the absent parishioners. It was a dramatic and moving ceremony.

When Tom had kindled the Easter Fire, Liz had been close enough to Lucy to hear her murmur a little prayer, "Please don't let them burn down my church!" The little irreverence made Liz smile.

Liz took her coffee to the enclosed porch to escape the noise of the children squealing over colorful Easter baskets full of sugary treats that would only make them more wired. This year all the goodies had come from the drug store instead of the craft candy shop in Scarborough that made their own chocolate bunnies, jellybeans and peeps. The kids didn't know the difference, of course, and were no less delighted by the drugstore candy. Alina finally took the children upstairs to dress them. Ordinarily, they'd have new outfits for church this morning, but they only had what they'd brought from their condo. This year, everything about Easter was different.

Maggie found Liz hiding on the porch and came out to give her a kiss. "Good morning, sweetheart. Happy Easter."

Liz muttered something that sounded like "Happy Easter."

Maggie brushed Liz's gray hair back from her face. "You need to let me give you that haircut. How can you stand it?"

"I can't. I'm just afraid of what you might do to me."

Maggie laughed. "Don't you trust me by now?"

"I'm not sure."

"You're not sure?" asked Maggie, with mock indignation, hands on hips.

"Take it easy, Mag. I'll let you do it tomorrow when there's not so much going on."

"Come out and be sociable," urged Maggie. "It's a holiday."

Liz grunted. "Okay." She looked in her cup. Her coffee was gone, so she followed Maggie into the kitchen.

There was the usual traffic around the island where continental breakfast had been set out. Liz grabbed a brightly colored hard-boiled egg. She peeled the egg and ate it standing at the counter. As she chewed, she watched the activity around her and wondered how they hadn't already killed one another by now. Ordinarily, Liz's house guests came and went as they pleased. No one except close family ever stayed more than a week. Yet, after almost a month of living in the same house, people seemed to have adapted.

Liz grabbed an orange and headed to the media room where the preparations for the Easter Eucharist were underway. The alb and white chasuble Lucy had brought from the church after the funeral hung from a peg on one side of the stage. Liz had managed to find Easter lilies at the supermarket to decorate the makeshift altar. As she surveyed the scene from a seat near the back of the home theater, she decided it looked rather festive.

Erika flopped down in the seat beside her. Liz handed her half of the orange.

"Thank you," said Erika. "It's not easy having a wife in the religion business." Liz followed Erika's line of vision to Lucy's animated gestures as she conferred with Alina.

"I imagine not," said Liz, munching on the orange. She wrapped up the napkin full of peelings and stuffed it in her pocket.

"I see you spiffed up a bit," said Erika giving Liz the once over.

"It is a holiday. Just in case I accidently get caught on camera, I don't want my patients to see my usual Sunday morning attire."

Erika chuckled. "No, the ratty workout suit won't do."

Lucy saw them sitting together and approached. "Happy Easter to my favorite heathens."

"Technically, a heathen is a believer," said Erika, "but not in your faith. Lucy, I don't know why you haven't given up on Liz. She's quite stubborn. Perhaps more than I."

Liz turned to Erika. "I'm not reasonable like you, Professor. I resist out of conviction. I can't be swayed by a compelling argument or a pretty face."

"Oh, I don't know," said Erika. "I think in the end, Maggie will be the one to convert you."

"Never happen," said Liz and finished her coffee in one gulp. "Are you sure you want the kids here for this service? They are crazed on sugar this morning."

"They'll be fine," said Lucy. "Besides, it will be good for the parish to see children on Easter morning. Children are a sign of new life. I've asked Katrina to be the acolyte bringing up our stand-in for the Paschal candle."

"Oh God," groaned Liz. "She's got my entire family wrapped up in her religion business." Liz glanced at her watch. "Shouldn't you be getting started soon?"

"Yes," said Lucy. "Can you find Maggie for me?"

Liz found Maggie in the kitchen, putting away the breakfast food. "Lucy is ready for you."

Finally, everything was in place. Lucy had on her splendid white vestments. Alina was behind the camera, and Maggie was poised in front of her laptop to join the virtual choir. Erika and Liz were in charge of the children. Nicki climbed into Liz's lap. Katrina eyed Erika for similar possibilities but Erika's stern expression warned her away. "You're too big for that now, love," said Erika in a gentle voice to soften the message. "Aren't you?"

Liz could watch the entire service on the TV overhead. In one of the Zoom windows, the real paschal candle was burning at the empty church along with the candles representing the missing parishioners. The virtual choir sang "Jesus Christ is Risen Today." In the room, Lucy's beautiful soprano could be heard singing along, which inspired Liz to join in too. Despite her atheism, she considered herself a cultural Christian and liked the sturdy familiarity of church hymns.

The camera switched to the livestream of Lucy. "Alleluia! Christ has Risen!"

Nicki began to suck her thumb and made a pillow of Liz's breast. When the girl's eyelids began to droop, Liz knew sleep wasn't far away.

The service proceeded to the readings. Even Stefan, atheist without peer, had been recruited and read very well. Lucy had an amazing ability to enlist people in her projects.

Finally, the time came for Lucy's sermon. She'd been locked away for hours the day before, so Liz was curious to hear what she had to say.

As always, Lucy beamed a smile to everyone. "Good morning and happy Easter!"

"Happy Easter," murmured the gathering.

"This is the day the Lord has made! A magnificent day to celebrate life restored from death. The stone has been rolled away and the tomb is empty, but do we believe? Today's Gospel says, 'While they were talking and discussing, Jesus himself came near and went with them, but their eyes were kept from recognizing Him.'"

Lucy paused for effect. *She's so good at this*, thought Liz.

"The resurrection, which we commemorate today, is one of the most difficult doctrines of our faith. It requires that we set aside all that we know about the finality of death and believe that a man could rise from the dead. Have you ever seen anyone rise from the dead?" She looked around. "Neither have I. No wonder the disciples couldn't believe their eyes. Finally, Jesus broke bread and shared it with them, and they recognized Him. But when He appeared again, they had to feed Him some broiled fish to make certain He was real. That specific mention of broiled fish always gives me pause. I wonder if it was good as our Maine haddock."

There was a little murmur of laughter in the room.

"We can criticize the disciples for their disbelief, but aren't we just as blind? In the Gospel of Matthew, we are told that Christ appeared to Mary Magdalene in the garden. And in John's Gospel which I read today, the women told the disciples how they'd come to the tomb and found it empty. Of course, the disciples were skeptical. And after all, it was a group of women who'd brought them the amazing news. We women are used to being disbelieved. Ever take your car for service and talk about a mysterious ping? The mechanic tries not to roll his eyes, but we know what he's thinking."

Lucy stopped a moment for the joke to sink in.

"We see the world through the prism of our prejudices," she continued. "We live in silos of belief. Stubbornly, we cling to our beliefs rather than trust what we hear with our ears or see with our eyes. Despite the most reasonable arguments, the advice from doctors and scientists, or the evidence right in front of us, we hear what we want to hear. We see what we want to see.

"In the era of 'fake news' we hear all kinds of things that may be helpful or dangerous as we face a deadly threat to human life. Some people say the virus is a hoax. Let's think about that. Does a hoax cause the deaths of thousands of people?

"What to believe? Do we believe the evidence of our own eyes? Or do we doubt like the disciples? I'll tell you what I believe. I believe it's my duty to protect my life, the blessing of my God-given life, and the lives of the people I love. Because we are our brother's keeper, we must pay attention to the needs of others. Some of our neighbors have conditions that make them more vulnerable—the elderly, the handicapped, the poor. We must protect them because Christ instructed us to love our neighbor.

"But let's return to the empty tomb and the garden where Christ appeared to Mary Magdalene. Like her, I want to reach out and touch Him. But He says, 'Do not hold on to me, for I have not yet ascended to the Father.' How much do we want to reach out and touch our friends and family? Children and parents are separated. How do you explain to a small child that he can't have a hug from his grandparent? But he can't now, and neither can we. We must wait until it is safe to reach out and touch again.

"Even without touching Him, I believe that Christ has risen because I have seen Him with my own eyes in people who live right here in Hobbs. I have seen so many people reflect Christ by sacrificing themselves for others—so many front-line workers: police, firefighters, nurses, doctors and paramedics. Not only first responders and medical personnel, but ordinary people, the people who stock our supermarket shelves and man our gas stations. They have put themselves in danger for the sake of others.

"They prove you don't have to be a hero to reflect Christ. Jesus asks that you love one another as you love yourself. You love yourself enough to stay alive, right? Here's the good news. You can protect your own life and love your neighbor by following the rules, staying home and not spreading a deadly illness. You can love your neighbor by not giving in to your anger and being kind. God's love is in every act of kindness, no matter how small. In this difficult time, I have seen acts of kindness that bring tears to my eyes. You know what that tells me? Christ walks among us. He is risen, and he is right here with us." Lucy crossed herself and returned to the altar.

As the service went on, Nicki, who'd fallen sound asleep in Liz's lap, began to snore softly. Liz dozed, but she woke up when Maggie began to sing the communion hymn. The feed on the TV cut to the virtual choir singing.

Everyone approached to receive communion, even avowed atheist, Stefan Bultmann. After everyone returned to their seats, Lucy looked at Liz, who gestured to the sleeping child in her arms. She expected Lucy to give up her quest and get on with the service, but she approached. Her eyes were filled with such an ineffable look of love that Liz couldn't stop herself from reaching out to accept the bread.

"The body of Christ," said Lucy. She gave Liz a warm smile and returned to the altar.

"Damn that woman!" Liz muttered. "She seduces everyone."

Erika, sitting beside her, chuckled. "Yes, she does. She's like the Borg Queen. Resistance is futile."

After the service, everyone gathered in the dining room for Easter dinner. As much as Liz complained about religious holidays, she enjoyed the excuse for relaxed family dinners. While the adults cleaned up after the meal, the children watched Easter movies. They began with *Peter Rabbit* and went on to *Hop*.

Liz was reading *The New York Times* on her iPad, when a call from her service came through. She climbed over Erika's legs and headed to her office to take the call.

"Dr. Stolz?"

"Speaking."

"Dorothy Bergeron called for you. She thinks she may have the novel coronavirus. She sounds really distressed. She was so upset she couldn't remember her own phone number."

"Thank you. I can look it up in my files. Happy Easter."

"Happy Easter to you too, Doctor."

Liz opened the secure portal to access the patient files. She found Mrs. Bergeron's telephone number right away and entered it into her phone. As it rang on the other end, Liz reviewed the patient's details in the file. Mrs. Bergeron was eighty-six. She had no family nearby and no emergency contact listed. A year ago, she had been hospitalized for a case of pneumonia.

"Dr. Stolz. Thank God! I can't breathe."

"Mrs. Bergeron, if you can't breathe, you should call 911. Do you want me to call for you?"

"No! I don't want to go to the hospital and get the virus. It's not safe!"

"But if you can't breathe, you need to be in the hospital."

"Please, Doctor. I know you don't make house calls anymore, but I really need you to come." Liz debated what to do. She knew she should call an ambulance, but she felt sorry for the old woman, who was all alone and sounded absolutely terrified.

"All right, Mrs. Bergeron. I'll be there shortly."

After she hung up the call, Liz pulled her medical bag out of the cabinet in the credenza. She left it in the hallway while she went into the media room to tell her wife where she was going. "I need to see a patient who's old and very frightened. I'll be back soon," she whispered into Maggie's ear.

Maggie slid her hand down Liz's arm and grasped her wrist. "Honey, be careful."

"Always."

She looked up to see looks of concern in Erika's and Lucy's faces. "Don't worry. I'll be back soon."

Liz climbed in her truck and started the engine. She was glad it started up right away. It had been sitting for weeks. She had to back up carefully because there were so many vehicles in the driveway. As she drove to Mrs. Bergeron's, she decided to ask the ambulance crew to stand by.

"You sure you don't want me to call them in?" asked the dispatcher.

"Not yet. It's a holiday and they're with their families. I'll let you know if I need them when I get there."

When Liz arrived at Mrs. Bergeron's house, she noticed that the old Cape really needed a paint job. It was down to the bare wood. House painting was so expensive nowadays that many elderly people simply couldn't afford it.

Before Liz went into the house, she looked in her bag for a mask. Unfortunately, she found only the flimsy paper surgical masks with the elastic stapled to the sides. *Better than nothing*, Liz thought as she put the lower strap over her head. She put on nitrile gloves before she tried the door handle. Fortunately, the door was open. Many people in that part of town never locked their doors.

"Hello?" called Liz as she found her way inside. Somewhere, a cat litter box desperately needed to be emptied. Liz wrinkled up her nose. She hated that odor. She could smell piss, vomit, open bowels and a host of other vile human smells, but the stench of cat piss was something she couldn't stand. Otherwise, the house looked tidy except for the pile of newspapers on the kitchen floor and some bottles on the counter. "Mrs. Bergeron? It's Dr. Stolz," called Liz. Despite her insistence on informality, she still used her title with older patients because they seemed to prefer it.

"In here!" called a raspy voice. Liz had only to follow the sound of the coughing to arrive at her destination.

Liz's eyes took in the situation in a glance. Mrs. Bergeron was nearly blue from lack of oxygen. Liz took out her phone and called the ambulance dispatcher. "Send them over."

"Oh, Dr. Stolz!" cried Mrs. Bergeron between coughs, "Thanks so much for coming."

Liz took her temperature with a temporal thermometer. Up three degrees. The woman's skin felt clammy to the touch. Through her stethoscope, Liz could hear the distinctive crackling sound of congestion.

"Your lungs are really congested," said Liz. "I know you don't want to go to the hospital, but you really have no choice."

"Can't you…just give…me…medicine?" asked the old woman, the words coming out staccato between her breaths.

"There is no medicine," said Liz. "I called the ambulance. They'll be here soon."

"But my cat!"

"Don't worry. We'll make sure someone takes care of your cat."

"Okay. Okay." The woman closed her eyes. They were sunken from dehydration. She panted shallow breaths.

"You might breathe better if you sat up," Liz said and reached into the woman's armpits to help her up. The woman's eyes shot open, wide with fear. She grabbed at Liz's face, catching the strap of the mask, which broke.

The mask dangled uselessly as the woman coughed directly into Liz's face.

37

From the kitchen window, Maggie could see the light go on in the loft over Liz's woodworking shop. She could see movement, but it was too far away to make out anything but shadows. She guessed that Liz was getting ready for bed. She had everything she needed in her design studio. She'd built a Murphy bed into the wall. There was a shower and toilet, a refrigerator and a microwave, even a coffee pot. Sometimes they put extra guests in that little studio, but mostly it was Liz's place to hide from everyone when she needed time to herself.

It had been five days since Liz had self-quarantined. They were still waiting to see if the old woman would test positive for Covid-19. Liz had gone directly from Mrs. Bergeron's house to her workshop and locked the door. She wouldn't let Maggie near her when she'd come home that night. She'd texted a list of the things she needed and asked Maggie to leave them outside the door.

Is there anything else you need? Maggie had texted to Liz before she brought down the items she'd requested.

Beer and salty snacks.

Okay. Is that it?

You. I lust for you.

LOL!

I'm not kidding. I'm going to miss you.

Liz had talked about her own risks if she contracted the virus. She had smoked for years. Like so many surgeons, she was a daredevil who thought she could defy the odds. Maggie knew that Liz exposed herself to disease as a doctor, but there had never been anything like this pandemic before. On the news, they saw footage of the horrors in the New York hospitals where people by the thousands had the virus. The emergency rooms and ICUs were overwhelmed. It was like something out of a disaster movie.

How lucky they were to be in Maine where there were fewer than a thousand cases. Their new governor seemed like a sharp, level-headed woman, who made reasoned, smart choices. She'd shut down the state before the first case appeared. Every day she held a news conference with the state CDC director, a calm man, who explained things in language everyone could understand.

They'd had a few nice days after Easter. Maggie had taken the sling chair she used at the beach and sat outside the window of the workshop. She could see the big machines inside, the duct work and tubing to collect the wood dust when Liz built furniture. Liz's workbench was near the window for natural light. When they talked by phone, Liz sat on the bench top with her long legs dangling. Before they parted, they always mirrored their hands on the glass that separated them and gazed at one another wordlessly.

After she finished washing the dessert dishes, Maggie turned off the water and folded the dish towel over the faucet. An arm came around her waist and gave her a half hug.

"Oh Maggie, I know how you must miss her," said Lucy, leaning her head against Maggie's shoulder.

"I'm scared."

"I know. I'm scared too. But Liz is healthy and strong. She's young for her age. And she's a doctor. She knows how to take care of herself."

"You'd be surprised."

Lucy chuckled. "No, I wouldn't. Sometimes she's too stubborn for her own good."

Maggie didn't know why that perfect assessment of Liz suddenly brought tears to her eyes, but she turned into Lucy's arms and cried. Her friend soothingly patted her back until Maggie stood straight and dried her face with her fingertips.

"Will you pray for her?"

Lucy's sympathetic eyes gazed into hers. "I always pray for her...and you. I love you both. But my prayers aren't magic or more powerful than yours. You should pray too."

Maggie nodded. She knew that.

"Now come out and watch the chess masters face each other down. It's kind of like watching paint dry, but the facial expressions are fascinating. How many ways are there to deadpan?"

Lucy always knew how to cheer her. Maggie followed her into the living room where Emily and Stefan were locked in a death stare with the chessmen.

As they sat down on the sofa to watch, Lucy whispered to Maggie, "This is worse than baseball."

"Nothing is worse than baseball," Maggie whispered back.

The staring match with the chessmen continued. Finally, Emily moved her bishop.

Erika's phone rang. "It's Liz. She wants to know who's winning." Erika's fingers worked to compose a reply.

"What are you writing?" asked Maggie.

Erika looked up. "I am writing that *she* would be winning if she hadn't thrown the match to me. She has no patience."

"Tell her I'm winning," said Emily.

"Yes, you are, my dear," said Erika. "My poor father has no idea what he's up against."

"Oh, I do," Stefan said, wagging a finger. "I always study the skills of my opponent. It is essential to good strategy."

Erika's phone pinged again. "It's Liz. She'd like to Skype with us. She says she's lonely." Erika raised her blond brows. "Oh my. That is a big admission for the mighty Liz."

"Why don't we go into the media room?" suggested Lucy. "We can see better on the big TV."

"I think that's a good idea," said Stefan. "I wouldn't mind delaying the inevitable. I am about to be defeated by a mere girl." He gave Emily a threatening look.

They went into the media room. Alina used her laptop to open a Skype call on the big screen.

"Oh, it's so good to see you guys!" Liz said, looking at each of them one by one. Her lips flattened into a thin line. Maggie realized she was trying to hold back tears.

"Liz, old girl, how are you doing out there?" asked Erika in a hearty voice.

"It's not what I'm used to, but I'm managing." She picked up a guitar. "Hey, Mag. Bet you didn't know I have my Martin out here. How about a song?"

She began to strum an old Judy Collin's song: "Who knows where the time goes." She stopped in mid-phrase and adjusted the pegs to bring the guitar into tune. "Sorry but it's hot out here during the summer." She began the song again. Maggie joined in and then Lucy. Liz smiled. "Lucy, you're too good for this."

"No, I'm not," protested Lucy. Soon the three of them were singing the song, splitting amazing harmonies from the melody as Liz repeated the coda. There was enthusiastic applause after the song ended.

Emily headed to the piano and began to play "Both Sides Now."

"Where did you learn that?" Lucy asked. "It's decades before your time."

"My adoptive mother really liked it. Sing, Maggie."

Maggie began to sing, and she saw how Liz's face changed. Her eyes, looking directly into Maggie's, became misty.

"That was wonderful," said Lucy, patting Maggie on the shoulder and nodding in her daughter's direction.

"That's sweet of you to say, Lucy, but none of us can hold a candle to you," Maggie said.

"No disrespect to my beautiful wife and her many talents, but your voice keeps me going, even here in jail," said Liz. "I've been listening to your recordings on YouTube."

"I'm glad my voice comforts you, Liz. Would you like me to sing something for you?"

Liz's smile of delight was instant and almost childlike. "'Marietta's Lied' from *Die Tote Stadt*?"

Lucy took out her phone and scanned her playlist to find the accompaniment. When Lucy began to sing, Maggie saw Liz's eyes close in ecstasy. She knew she could never compete with the talent of this woman. Lucy had a sublime, once in a generation soprano. It was just criminal she had given up the operatic stage.

"*Je t'adore*," said Liz, touching her fingers to her lips when Lucy had finished the aria.

"*Je t'adore aussi*," replied Lucy. "One last song for my lonely friend in her garret. What's your pleasure?"

"Brahms' '*Geistliches Wiegenlied*,' *bitte*."

Lucy scanned for the accompaniment on her phone. "I'm not a mezzo, you know."

"I know. I'm letting you off easy tonight," said Liz.

As Lucy sang, Maggie knew it was ridiculous to be jealous of such a phenomenal gift. She sat back and enjoyed Lucy's effortless rendition of the classic song. She looked down the row of seats and saw that everyone was as moved by the performance as she was.

"Thank you for letting me invade your evening," said Liz, with her lopsided grin. "As you were."

"Good night, Liz," said Maggie, waving. Everyone was waving. The screen reverted to the desktop view.

Alina got up to switch off the computer. "It was nice to see her. She looks good."

Staring at the blank screen, Maggie desperately wished that Liz was still there. She missed her so much. Her eyes filled. Later, when she had privacy, she would put on her sexiest nightgown and Facetime Liz. That would give her plenty of incentive to stay healthy and come home quickly.

Maggie took a shower and put on the sheer nightgown. She looked out her bedroom window and saw the light in the workshop studio go off. She pulled out her phone to call and, in that split second, decided Facetime wasn't enough. What if something happened to Liz? What if she could never touch her or kiss her or make love to her again?

Maggie knew that Liz would be furious, but she took a canvas bag out of the closet and began to pack. She threw in the essentials: underwear, her makeup kit, toiletries, comfortable clothes for a week. Alina could bring her anything else she might need.

Maggie listened from the landing on the second floor. It was all dark below. Everyone had gone to bed. She crept downstairs, put on her coat and shoes and took the key marked "workshop" off the hook in the hall closet. She pressed it tightly in her hand as she considered whether this was a good idea. Of course, it wasn't, but Maggie decided she didn't care. She needed to be with Liz.

The wind was blowing as she headed down the path to the workshop. It was a clear night, and the moon shone brightly overhead. Maggie could see her breath in its light.

It took a few tries to get the lock open. Maggie had almost given up when the pins turned in the barrel and the door opened. She went into the dark shop. Chilled from her walk, she had hoped to find warmth inside, but it was cold. She guessed Liz was trying to conserve energy by running the heat pump in the studio instead of the gas furnace.

After fumbling, Maggie's hand finally found the light switch and flipped it on. She saw that Liz had been busy while she'd been quarantined. There was a table leg in the lathe and three matching legs on a rolling stand nearby.

Maggie hung her coat on a peg near the door. She didn't want to walk through the shop with bare feet, but neither did she want to alert Liz to her presence. She put her bag out of the way under the stairs, then took off her shoes before she ascended. Her feet could feel the dust on the steps. Liz might be a stickler for hygiene as a doctor, but she wasn't the world's best housekeeper.

Maggie breathed a sigh of relief when she got to the landing without any of the treads squeaking. She turned the knob slowly and the door opened without a sound. She could hear Liz breathing in the darkened room. The rhythm of her breaths told her that Liz was already asleep. Maggie raised the covers and slipped in beside her.

Liz twisted around and sat up. "What the fuck!"

"It's just me," said Maggie.

Liz breathed a sigh of relief. "You're lucky I didn't pull my gun on you! And what the fuck do you think you're doing here?"

"Shhh." Maggie laid a finger across Liz's lips to silence her. She took Liz's hand and slipped it in the low-cut nightgown.

"You're not really mad, are you?" asked Maggie as Liz appreciatively squeezed her breast. Maggie leaned forward and kissed her, pleased to feel the lips part and welcome her in. She probed Liz's warm mouth with her tongue.

Liz pulled away. "Yes, I'm really mad. I could give you the virus. I'd never forgive myself if anything happened to you."

Maggie nudged Liz down on the pillow. "I can't be without you anymore. I need you." She resumed kissing her as she moved over her body. Maggie knew from long experience how easy it was to seduce Liz. In a moment, she'd completely forget her anger.

Maggie wanted to savor the sweetness of their reunion with long, slow lovemaking, but Liz was too excited and came quickly. Satisfied, Liz was patient enough to make love to Maggie more leisurely. By then, Maggie was aroused enough to come on the inside. After the orgasm, Liz allowed her fingers to remain. Maggie squeezed them gently to tell her wife how happy she was to feel her there.

Liz sat up and pulled off her T-shirt. "It's warm enough in here to sleep naked. I want to feel your skin against mine."

"Oh yes," said Maggie with a sigh as she settled into the crook of Liz's arm. "Are you still angry?"

"Yes," Liz said. "But the damage is done now. You're stuck here until the test results come back."

Maggie laughed softly. "I know. Isn't it wonderful?"

"What about our guests?"

Maggie shrugged. "They can look after themselves. We've been taking care of them for over a month. Let them take care of us now."

"Hmmm. Hadn't thought of that, but this little studio is pretty cramped."

"I like that. It's cozy. Reminds me of camping in Acadia. It will be like a little getaway. A second honeymoon." Maggie snuggled against Liz's breast. "Go back to sleep. I'm here now."

38

"When we go over to the house, remind me that I want to drop off the rent check to my landlord," said Cherie.

Brenda gave her long, thoughtful look. "I want you to move in with me."

"What? Isn't that a little sudden?"

"We've been quarantined together for a month. You've seen me at my worst—sweating like a pig and hacking my brains out, but you still love me."

"I do love you." Cherie forced down her skeptical brow. What Brenda said made perfect sense, of course. Not many couples endured such tests of loyalty and devotion before they moved in together. "Are you sure?" asked Cherie.

Brenda nodded. "Absolutely sure."

"I still need to pay the landlord. We need time to move the stuff out of the house. Who knows if we can even get a mover. We might have to wait."

"We don't need a mover," said Brenda. "Our friends will help. You'll see." She pulled her service belt around her waist. Cherie noticed she cinched it past the worn mark. Her shirt and pants were looser too.

"You've lost some weight," Cherie observed.

"Yes, and I didn't even try."

"All that coughing takes energy." Cherie watched Brenda put on her uniform jacket and campaign hat. "I never realized how sharp you look in your uniform."

"Well, at least it doesn't scare you anymore."

"I didn't say that. But I am getting better with it."

Brenda put her arm at Cherie's back to guide her out to the porch. They agreed to take separate cars because Brenda had to report at two. They were still down a few officers with the virus, so Brenda had agreed to take a shift.

"See you there," said Brenda. She touched her fingers to the brim of her hat before she got into her truck.

As Cherie drove to the cemetery, she wondered how it would feel to stand at her father's grave. Before now, his death had seemed like something in a movie. Her last words to him being transmitted through a Facetime call only emphasized the idea that it was something remote, like a bad television show.

Her worry that she wouldn't find the grave vanished when she saw a familiar redhead moving along the row of headstones. Lucy was wearing her collar and black suit. The white stole around her neck fluttered delicately in the breeze. Cherie parked behind Lucy's SUV and got out of her car.

"Good morning, Cherie," said Lucy. She was wearing a black mask embroidered with a little white cross.

"I like your mask. Is that what the well-dressed priest is wearing in the age of Covid-19?"

"Mrs. Reardon made half a dozen of them. She sent some to Father Tom too. Pretty cool, huh?"

"Very cool," Cherie agreed, carefully measuring the distance between them with her eyes. "Thank you for doing this today."

"I promised I would. I like to keep my word." Lucy glanced around. "Is Brenda coming?"

"She should be here in a minute." As she said it, Cherie saw the familiar truck drive through the cemetery gates. Brenda put on her hat as she got out and walked to where Cherie stood.

Finally, Cherie allowed her eyes to take in the mound of fresh soil piled on the grave. She felt sad that her father was buried so far away from her mother, but they had considered that possibility when they'd discussed moving to Maine. Her father had planned to move her mother's remains, so they could spend eternity together. Now, Cherie would have to make the arrangements.

Lucy greeted Brenda and then began with the sign of the cross. While Lucy prayed, Brenda held Cherie's hand with gentle, reassuring pressure.

The prayers Lucy recited were only words, but Cherie found them comforting. After they said the Lord's Prayer, Lucy recited Psalm 121. "I will lift up my eyes to the hills from whence comes my help..." She ended the service with a blessing.

"Thank you, Lucy," said Cherie.

"I wish I could give you a hug." Lucy's eyes were so full of sympathy that Cherie could almost feel the hug they couldn't share.

"I know. Me too. Hopefully, soon."

"Mother Lucy, Cherie and I are going to get some chowder and lobster rolls," said Brenda. "Shelly's just reopened. Would you like to join us?"

"Oh, my word! Shelly's clam chowder. I've missed it soooo much. Yes, I'd love to join you."

They met at Shelly's Clam Shack on Route 1. The indoor restaurant was closed, of course, but they could order food at the window. A plexiglass partition had been put up with a little door to slide out the orders.

"Everything's different now," observed Cherie with a sigh. "How are we going to eat with masks on?"

"I can sit over there at the far table," offered Lucy.

"I have an idea," said Brenda with obvious enthusiasm. "Why don't we bring chowder and lobster rolls to Liz's house? I bet they'd love some. I'm buying."

Cherie gave her a worried look. "That's very expensive. I'll go half with you."

"It's all right. I haven't been anywhere to spend money for almost a month. And Liz wouldn't take any money for groceries. I owe her at least that much."

They ordered a dozen lobster rolls and what amounted to over a gallon of chowder, which the cook put in quart-sized, paper containers. Brenda handed three fifty-dollar bills to the girl who'd taken their order, but the owner came to the window. "That's too much, Chief," he said, handing her back a fifty.

"That's nowhere near enough for all that food," Brenda protested.

"Yes, it is. Thanks for keeping us safe. All of your people have done such a great job. Thank you."

Brenda tried to give back the bill he'd returned, but he closed the window and walked away.

"I wonder if he knows I've been laid up the whole time."

"It doesn't matter," said Lucy. "It's symbolic. Be grateful and let's go before the chowder gets cold."

Cherie called Liz on the way to warn her that they were bringing lunch.

"Good timing," said Liz. "I was just wondering what I was going to feed my little army. Tomorrow they'll be on their own because I'm going back to the office. You can be sure I won't mind leaving lunchtime to Maggie."

Cherie saw that parking in the driveway was tight and backed into a space between two pine trees. Lucy's SUV drove in with Brenda's truck right behind it.

Brenda had planned to drop off the food and then take theirs to Cherie's house to eat, but Liz came out on the porch.

"It's a nice day, come around and meet us on the deck. I moved a table for you to sit down."

Brenda put down the bags of food on the porch and backed away. Liz carried the bags into the house.

"I'll meet you on the deck," called Lucy, going in through the garage door.

They walked around the side of the house to the back deck and went up the stairs. Liz was weighing down a plastic tablecloth with colorful rocks. "Maggie's heating up the chowder," Liz explained as she set out forks and spoons. "It will be just a minute."

"How are you, Liz?" asked Cherie. "You look great."

"I feel great and really happy I tested negative. I was so relieved that Mrs. Bergeron only had the flu."

"That's good, I guess," said Cherie.

Liz stood straight and looked thoughtful. "Amazing to be grateful that an old woman has pneumonia from the good, old flu."

Maggie came out on the porch with mugs of chowder. "I'll leave it on this table. You and Cherie can pick them up." She brought over two spoons and set them beside the mugs.

Erika came out of the house, followed by her father.

"Hello, Brenda, how nice to see you looking so well," said Erika. "We were quite worried about you."

"Oh, I was quite worried about myself. I've never had any bug that bad. It was nasty." Brenda made a face for emphasis. "There were times I thought I was going to die."

"We're very glad that's over and you look great." Maggie brought a bag of lobster rolls to the small table for them to pick up.

"This is so crazy," said Brenda, taking off her mask so she could eat her chowder. "Liz, how long will we have to do this?"

Liz sat down with a mug of chowder. "Your guess is as good as mine. Probably until there's a vaccine."

"And when will that be?"

"Soon, I hope. Maybe by the end of the year, but that's optimistic."

Emily came out with a mug of chowder and sat next to her mother. She pushed the paper tray of fries closer so Nicki could reach them too. Cherie marveled that a girl with high-functioning autism could be so good with children, but Emily was always full of surprises.

"Cherie's moving in with me," Brenda suddenly said.

Cherie turned to her in surprise. "Did you need to make an announcement?"

"Of course. Everyone's here. Why not?"

"Congratulations," said Lucy, wiping ketchup off Nicki's nose. "I'm happy for you both."

Erika put down her lobster roll. "Liz, I forgot to tell you. Our refrigerator will be delivered next week. Then we can leave you and your family in peace."

Liz looked up and down the picnic table. "It was kind of nice having such a big gang in the house. Amazingly, we're all still friends. I'll miss you when you're gone."

"We're not gone yet," said Erika. "You must still put up with us for a while. But there's light at the end of the tunnel. I'd wager that you'll throw a party when we leave."

"I bet you're right," said Liz with a quick grin. "But I'll miss hearing Lucy sing me to sleep with lullabies." She turned to Stefan sitting next to her. "Professor, I think you should stay with us a while longer. There have been quite a few cases in that senior residence of yours."

"If it's not too much trouble," said Stefan. "The food is very good here."

Liz chuckled. "I always knew I missed my calling. I should have opened a B&B."

"Don't get any ideas," said Maggie. "You still haven't retired, and already you're thinking of your next job."

"Good thing she hasn't retired," said Cherie. "Can you imagine getting through this without her?"

"No, not me," said Brenda. A chorus echoed her words.

Liz raised her glass of seltzer. "Here's to the end of the pandemic and to getting through it together."

"Hear, hear," said Brenda and raised her glass.

Also by Elena Graf

Hobbs Series

HIGH OCTOBER

Liz Stolz and Maggie Fitzgerald were college roommates until Maggie confessed their affair to her parents. When Maggie breaks her leg in a summer stock stage accident, she lands in Dr. Stolz's office. Is forty years too long to wait for the one you love?

THE MORE THE MERRIER

Maggie and Liz's plans of sitting by the fire, drinking mulled wine, and watching old Christmas movies get scuttled by surprise visits from friends and family.

THIS IS MY BODY

Professor Erika Bultmann, a confirmed agnostic, is fascinated by Mother Lucy, the new rector of the Episcopal Church, especially when she discovers Lucille Bartlett was a rising opera star before mysteriously disappearing from the stage.

LOVE IN THE TIME OF CORONA

Police Chief Brenda Harrison shows an interest in Liz's biracial PA, but first Cherie needs to get past her loathing for all law enforcement since a state trooper shot and killed her sister.

THIRSTY THURSDAYS

Liz Stolz initiates Thirsty Thursdays, a weekly cocktail party on her deck, so her friends can socialize safely during the pandemic. Pretentious, overbearing Olivia Enright pursues Liz's friend, architect Sam McKinnon, and tries to push her way into the tight-knit group.

THE DARK WINTER

Erika hires Sam to build a sound-proof practice room for Lucy. Fortunately, the early Christmas gift is ready before tragedy strikes. As the women of Hobbs pull together to help a beloved friend deal with her loss, the dark winter brings tension and realignment in their small community.

SUMMER PEOPLE

Melissa Morgenstern, a high-profile lawyer from Boston, is spending the summer with her widowed mother. She's doing some trust work for Liz who introduces her to the attractive Courtney Barnes, Hobbs Elementary's new assistant principal. The arrival of Susan, Lucy's ex, complicates her deepening relationship with Liz.

STRANDS

Cherie hears her biological clock ticking and would like to start a family. When a shocking tragedy creates an opportunity for her and Brenda to become parents, their friends need to step up to make it happen.

THE RECTOR'S WEDDING

The sudden opportunity for Lucy to return to her singing career throws everything in her life into doubt—her vocation as a priest, her settled life in Hobbs, even her upcoming marriage to the woman she loves.

THE VANISHING BRIDGE

Susan is trying to find her place in Hobbs after leaving in disgrace. Bobbie always needs to rush away to take care of a mysterious older woman. Can they trust each other enough to tell the truth?

EXTENDED CAPACITY

A small town in Maine wakes up thinking it's just another winter day, but a tragedy has been set in motion by dark secrets from the past and an unfortunate series of recent events. The horror that every town fears is about to come to Hobbs.

PASSING RITES SERIES

THE IMPERATIVE OF DESIRE

A coming-of-age story that takes a brilliant aristocratic woman from La Belle Époque through a world war, a revolution that outlawed the German nobility, and the roaring twenties to the decadent demimonde of Weimar Berlin.

OCCASIONS OF SIN

For seven centuries, the German convent of Obberoth has been hiding the nuns' secrets—forbidden passions, scandalous manuscripts locked away, a ruined medical career, and perhaps even a murder.

LIES OF OMISSION

In 1938, the Nazis are imposing their doctrine of "racial hygiene" on hospitals and universities. Margarethe von Stahle has always avoided politics, but now she must decide whether to remain on the sidelines or act on her convictions.

ACTS OF CONTRITION

After the fall of Berlin, Margarethe is brutally assaulted by occupying Russian soldiers. Her former protégée, Sarah Weber, returns to Berlin with the American Army and tries to heal her mentor's physical and psychological wounds.

About the Author

Elena Graf has published four historical novels set in twentieth-century Europe. Two of the titles in the Passing Rites series have won Golden Crown Literary Society and Rainbow awards for best historical fiction. In addition to her historical series, the author has written a series of contemporary novels set in Maine. She pursued a Ph.D. in philosophy but ended up in the "accidental profession" of publishing, where she worked for almost four decades. She lives in coastal Maine.

Find out about events and new books at her website, elenagraf.com. You can write to Elena at elena.m.graf@gmail.com. Or find her on Facebook.

Elena is a member of iReadIndies, a collective of self-published independent authors of Sapphic literature. Please visit our website at iReadIndies.com for more information and to find links to the books published by our authors.

www.ingramcontent.com/pod-product-compliance
Lightning Source LLC
Chambersburg PA
CBHW071457110726
47908CB00003B/647